DISCARD

OPERATION
CALPURNIA

A
Guy Silvestri Mystery
by Maggie Rennert

OPERATION CALPURNIA

PRENTICE-HALL, INC., ENGLEWOOD CLIFFS, N. J.

Printed in the United States of America
Prentice-Hall International, Inc., London
Prentice-Hall of Australia, Pty. Ltd., Sydney
Prentice-Hall of Canada, Ltd., Toronto
Prentice-Hall of India Private Ltd., New Delhi
Prentice-Hall of Japan, Inc., Tokyo

10 9 8 7 6 5 4 3 2 1

Library of Congress Cataloging in Publication Data

Rennert, Maggie.
     Operation Calpurnia.

     I. Title.
PZ4.R4150pc [PS3568.E6]   813'.5'4   76-7540
ISBN 0-13-637835-8

For Betty, who fell in love with a nice boy named Bob Page. Which is how I got first Debbie and then Maggie—two perfect proofs that Time is no enemy and luck happens.

AUTHOR'S NOTE

Like most writers of fiction, I usually help myself to whatever information I find lying around in my landscape. But this time, I think the brainpicking was blatant enough to warrant acknowledgments. So I'd like to thank Philip Rennert (and some of his fellow-students at Yale); Betty Page; Baruch Schmidt, M.D.; and Lloyd Wisdom for answering questions about chess, law, medicine, and handguns, respectively. Doctor Schmidt's advice was probably the least tampered with, as I was afraid to take liberties with physiology; but all these obliging folk are innocent of responsibility for what I did with what they said.

OPERATION
CALPURNIA

PROLOGUE
The Roots of War

Whether the domino theory was in or out of fashion in foreign affairs, it was always operating in the domestic affairs of Claud Dozier, whose days were full of leaning dominoes. For example, his intention to start for work early that November morning—so he could leave his car off to be greased at the garage near his office—was easily toppled by Emilie Dozier, four years old and no fan of orderly planning. Though the timing was not entirely within her control, she may very well have chosen breakfasttime for launching her power struggle: she had had plenty of opportunity to observe that when the little hand neared the 8 and the big hand stuck almost straight up, Papa took off, leaving Mommy to represent the Establishment alone. But Emilie wasn't the first rebel to leave economic and psychological realities out of her calculations or to put her trust in the wrong clock. Her uprising failed that morning because the kitchen clock was fast and Papa could afford to be late to work anyway, and finally because Claud Dozier was not a man to be intimidated by falling dominoes. He recognized the little clunk-clunk of his collapsing plans, but he also knew what was only a game and what really mattered.

So Claud and Vera Dozier closed ranks promptly, and the

ructions ended with Emilie, now literally a smartipants, upstairs in her room sniffling and planning revenge. Meanwhile Vera wet a corner of one of the odd diapers that always seemed to be around and restored the morning neatness of Claud's haberdashery, which had suffered light damage from an overturned bowl of Rice Krispies. Vera herself had been closer to ground zero; but a casual swipe with the diaper was enough for her flannel bathrobe, a well-spotted veteran of encounters with Emilie. All young-executive splendor again, Papa kissed his wife and surviving children (the baby had been observing the proceedings from the high chair and was now looking thoughtful, but the two-year-old had opted for being an island entire of itself and was chewing toast with extra jam and an air of abstraction). Then Claud Dozier left his warm and busy home for the chill still outside world.

But because he felt hurried, he skimped on the ritual warming-up of his car engine. Like most rituals, it had developed from a need to contend with the forces of Nature, and on a frost-glittering November morning in western Massachusetts, the need still held. So another domino tottered when Dozier's motor stalled before he'd traveled the half-mile or so from his house to the Kings'; thus, as he rounded the bend in the dirt road, he was coasting down the gentle slope. Which meant, finally, that Julius and Callie King didn't hear a car approaching —and so Dozier, coming without warning on the scene in their front yard, saw the Kings as someone far back in a large theater might see a tableau on the stage. Suddenly they were actors, people he knew something about but didn't know, and Claud was an audience.

What he saw was innately dramatic, not to say melodramatic: dark-coated, immovable, Julius King hulked beside his car while the woman implored, one white hand on his arm and the other gesturing. In a long, full-skirted blue-green housecoat, silky and brocaded—and with the reddish-blonde hair she always wore in a sleek chignon now swirling down over one shoulder rather like the Botticelli Aphrodite—Callie King certainly looked theatrical, especially for 8:05 in the morning. She also looked very pretty. In fact, Claud Dozier found himself noticing, with some surprise, what a very damn good-looking woman Callie was. You could even say beautiful.

Claud didn't say "beautiful" when he told about it later, and he didn't mention the grace of her body in the silken robe, though he had certainly taken that in, too. But in a man with no taste for even innocent voyeurism, embarrassment pre-empted all other responses. For unquestionably he'd blundered on a domestic quarrel. And one, judging by Callie's attitude and gestures, of unmistakable intensity: even while Claud was some distance away, he couldn't doubt that she was pleading with her husband, and desperately. Julius King threw off her restraining hand and said something, his voice reaching Dozier as a short, heavy rumble. But Callie's voice was high and frantic, and a brisk little breeze picked it up, too. So Claud heard exactly what she said, while—rolling helplessly downhill toward her—he saw ever more clearly the anguish in her face.

Inspired, he announced his presence by noisily trying to restart his motor. Julius King turned toward the whir, but Callie looked away quickly. Dozier got the engine going and rolled up to his neighbors' yard with everything restored to seemliness— good-mornings were exchanged, and Julius produced a smoothly joshing remark about saving a dime by coasting down-hill. Claud remembered that later, because he'd noticed that the Kings certainly weren't saving many dimes: their front door stood half-open, presumably pouring precious heat out into the crisp November air.

But Dozier didn't mention the open door. Asked what else they'd talked about, he remembered saying "Where's Susan?" Perhaps inspired by the same sort of semisuperstition that moves people to get conscientious about their health when an acquaintance falls ill, he'd been suddenly struck with an impulse to take Vera out to dinner tonight—if Susan King, who was one of the few babysitters Vera would trust, was still available. It was Callie who answered quietly, her face composed if not quite to as-always. Maybe it was her pale lips that made her eyes look so big, and Claud had never noticed before how very green they were. But she said in her normal-Callie voice that Susan had had a sore throat and slight fever last night. She wasn't going to school today, and in fact, she was still asleep.

That was about all there was to that contretemps: good-byes were said or gestured, and Claud Dozier fed some gas to his now smoothly idling motor and rolled on his way. He glanced into his rear-view mirror once, locking into his memory the impression that would trouble him until the next spring. But all he thought then was that Callie must be feeling the cold, standing out there in her bathrobe. Come to think of it, Vera would certainly get a kick out of hearing that the prim-and-proper Mrs. King had been out in the front yard in her nightie, practically.

The tricky turn where you could easily go off the road and plunge a couple of hundred feet—even when there wasn't any ice on the road—came up then, and Claud Dozier turned his attention to his driving. And to dark thoughts about the odds against ever getting anything done about that curve, short of a march on the State House in Boston.

Lenny Pritchard, who worked at the gas station where that dinky little dirt track came out on the main road, saw Mr. Dozier's car go by as usual, and watched it until it turned right, heading for the expressway. Lenny had to open up early, especially in the winter months. But anybody whose car was going to refuse to start would already have found that out by 8 A.M., so Lenny was now probably free to hit the books for an hour or so, until the boss came in.

Because the society had decreed that Lenny Pritchard was entitled to higher education practically free, a part-time job at the gas station during the school year and full-time construction work during the summers would probably get him through college. But it wasn't easy, so sometimes Lenny used Claud Dozier to reassure himself: a college degree was what had got Dozier, who was nothing but the son of a Vermont farmer, a fine house and a pleasant wife to share it with. Mr. Dozier punched no timeclock at C. Dozier and Associates, Engineering Consultants, with offices in Springfield and Boston: if he went to work every morning at the same time, it was because he chose to. The kids could smart-talk all they wanted, but the true fact was, any time you ran under your own orders and nobody else's, what you were in wasn't a rat race.

Lenny watched Mr. Dozier's convertible slow to turn into the main road, moving smoothly under the sure hand of an educated man who knew how to use a machine. Then, his ambition recharged, Lenny picked up the expensive textbook with all the difficult diagrams and opened it to the first page of the stuff he was betting would be on the exam. But it was a struggle to give it his full attention. Because if Dozier had just gone by, King could not be far behind; and—this week, anyway —riding with Julius King, Ph.D., was his pretty daughter Susan. For whom Lenny, in secret and in no real confidence, some-times planned a fate rather like Vera Dozier's.

Another of society's decrees was that Lenny Pritchard and Susan King were equals; but the way the theory worked out in practice, Lenny's opportunities for meeting the petite blonde Susan were a little limited. Normally, she rode the school bus to Long Valley High and home again, and when she wasn't in school—well, Lenny didn't have the time or the money to run with the smart-ass set she hung out with sometimes. He was sure Susan's heart wasn't really in it, though that didn't help too much when he saw her, like at school basketball games and around, with Twirl and his satellites, who were loud in their uniform scorn for Lenny Pritchard and all other squares.

But Susan didn't come on like that with Lenny, she never had. And it surely meant something when she took the trouble to mention, about a week ago, that her dad, who was superintendent of schools, would be observing at Long Valley High for a while—and so Susan would be riding over with him in the mornings. When they stopped for gas that first morning, Dr. King sat there staring straight ahead, his big head too full of profound thought to waste time with the masses, it seemed. But Susan leaned out of the car window, smiling and chattering sweetly while Lenny filled the tank. Unless the Kings went off jaunting somewhere, that put enough gas in the Volvo to mean no more early-morning stops when Lenny could warm himself with the sight of Susan's hair gleaming softly in the watery winter sunlight. But at least he glimpsed her at the window every morning, and she waved as the Volvo rolled by at Dr. King's sedate thirty miles an hour. It wasn't much, but it was better than nothing.

That November morning, though, what Lenny got was nothing: he came out of the gas station's freezing, smelly little toilet just in time to see the King car about to disappear around the curve. It was a plain and simple case of getting one in the chops from Fate, because there *should* have been enough time. Mr. Dozier must've left later than usual, or Dr. King earlier—though the way he was driving, it looked more like he must be late. But Lenny knew how blind he was at that distance without his glasses, so maybe what looked like the Volvo lurching erratically was just tree shadows. Maybe that wasn't even the Volvo? He scrambled for his glasses.

He'd known it would be too late; even when he tried the side window, which looked out on the main road, the car was out of sight. And of course it had to have been the Volvo—why try to con himself? Nobody lived up that dirt road but the Kings and the Doziers, beyond whose house the road simply ended. Presumably the "new road"—which was all the name it had ever had, so far as Lenny knew—once looked like becoming a real extension of town. If it didn't, what fool would've put a gas station at the foot of it, just before it joined the main road?

But then something happened, or didn't happen, and that was that: the gas station was visible from the main road, and so got enough business to survive on—at the level of employing part-time Lenny, anyway. And the "new road" continued to be unpaved and less than two miles long, going nowhere except to the two houses.

Lenny glanced at the clock and confirmed his bad luck— 8:15 now, which meant that Dr. King had probably left on time after all; 8:10 was when he usually passed the station. So, anyway you sliced it, that was the end of sighting Susan for today. Disheartened, Lenny put on some water for instant coffee and began to study Fig. 3, which would surely be on the exam.

Exactly at 8:15, Josh Roberts, the custodian at the Mercer School, checked out a basketball to three boys who wanted to practice lay-ups before the school bell rang. The boys were all from the ninth- and tenth-grade classes parked at the Mercer, which was supposed to go only up to eighth grade, while the high-school building was being added to. To make room for these kids—their arrival at high-school age being a big surprise to the town council, Mr. Roberts would add drily whenever the subject came up.

The boys were Terry Cooke—the one actually charged with borrowing the ball—and Andy Drissel, both born in Long Valley, and Billy King, whose family had moved to town when he was ready for fourth grade. Josh had no trouble remembering that, because he'd had to get all togged out in his good suit to get his hand shook by the new superintendent of schools: *Doctor King, this is Josh Roberts, our custodian. . . .* Yuk. But even if their old man was kind of stuffy, the King kids—Billy and his big sister, whose name Josh couldn't call to mind at the moment—were real nice. And the point was, they'd all been around long enough, easy, so Long Valley could reasonably put together a high school big enough to hold them when they grew into it. Instead of cramming these boys in with the little kids till the walls were like to bust. To say nothing of giving three big boys like that—and this Andy was really good, too: look at that shot, now!—nothing but a sleazy postage-stamp playground to practice on. And they could only get that to themselves by coming early, before the little children arrived. Watching Billy leap successfully for a too-high pass that looked likely to end up in the brook a few yards behind the backboard, Josh Roberts thought it was unfair, just plain unfair to these kids.

At 8:35, Mrs. Price, school secretary at Long Valley High, took a phone call from Susan King's mother, who wanted to notify them Susan was ill and wouldn't be in today. Mrs. Price was certain about the time—she arrived at work at 8:30, and she was just hanging up her coat when the call came in. Callie King wasn't known to be a chatty type, and she was after all Mrs. Superintendent of Schools; but Mrs. Price liked Susan, so she took the liberty of prying a little. Mrs. King said it was nothing serious, just a sore throat that started last night. Mrs. Price thanked her nicely and hung up.

The next recorded time that morning—9:20—was *very* positive because it was a phone call to the King home by Mrs. Marietta Wilder, principal of the high school. The call was put in by Mrs. Wilder's office girl (Mrs. Price having departed on her daily jaunt to the Mercer, one of the chores necessary to keep records for a divided school) and it was the result of considerable thought and some consultation. For Marietta Wilder had a delicate problem: Julius King had made an appointment with her for 8:30, but he'd neither come nor called. She was more than a little annoyed, but if you're a high-school principal, you don't just call up the superintendent of schools and ask *Where the hell are you, bud?* Maybe especially you don't if you also happen to be the first Negro principal Long Valley High ever had—and you're trying to slide between the horns labeled Uncle Tom and Black Militant without scraping off too much of your tender tan middle-class skin.

Thus Mrs. Wilder waited half an hour without complaint. Then she wrestled with herself a while, juggling considerations of insult and overreaction and (off the record) consulting with Miss Crabtree, the doyenne of the teacher corps and one of Long Valley's noisiest old-fashioned liberals. As a result, Mrs. Wilder set 9:15 as the deadline after which This would be Too Much. When 9:15 came and Dr. King didn't, she waffled for another few minutes before she ordered the phone call to his home. So, what with one thing and another, there's no doubt that Mrs. Wilder knew what time she called.

There is some doubt about exactly what time Vera Dozier phoned Callie King, but it was about 9:30. The laundryman should have come by then, and Vera had some dry-cleaning for him to pick up—but she'd forgotten whether she'd told him to stop by that morning. The King phone didn't answer. Vera was listening to the radio at the time, and she thought the beep for 9:30 had come just after she tried to call Callie.

According to Harry Moody, the Eagle Laundry routeman who served the two houses on the "new road," he got to the King house at 9:45. The bag of outgoing laundry wasn't set out for him—that's what Mrs. King did if she wasn't going to be home—so he rang the doorbell. He heard it ring inside the house. When it wasn't answered, he rang again and then even knocked on the front door. The family must be sleeping in, he decided: the drapes were drawn across the front windows and the house looked still locked up for the night, sort of. Though of course there were no cars or bikes around, come to think of it.

But Harry Moody didn't think of that then. He just laid the laundry package on the doorstep and got back in his truck and left, turning around in the driveway. He wasn't supposed to go on up the road but he might have anyway, on the off-chance, except that he had had extra stops this morning and he knew he was already running late.

At 9:50 Mrs. Wilder, the high-school principal, tried the King number again and got no answer. She considered calling the Board of Education office in the Town Hall—maybe Dr. King had simply forgotten the appointment?—but she decided against it because it might give the impression Marietta Wilder thought Dr. King forgot appointments.

At 10:20, State Trooper Morris Coakley spotted the King car on the shoulder of the main road, about three-quarters of a mile beyond the gas station. Coakley was headed in the other direction—he was surveying frost damage to the road out beyond that point (out where a prominent town councillor lived, actually)—and the sun was in his eyes, so he couldn't see whether the parked Volvo was occupied. But there must have been something odd about the way it looked, because Coakley got out of his car and crossed the road to investigate, which is rather a lot of trouble to take. Maybe it was because the car seemed more abandoned than parked: the way the bumper was nudging a roadside tree was not only bad for the tree, it also gave an impression of extreme haste.

The Volvo proved to be empty, so the trooper did a fast survey of the surrounding underbrush to see whether somebody was "in distress"—as his report put it—or, more likely, sneakily dumping trash. But there was nobody around, and no sign of disturbance. So he concluded the driver had run out of gas—what other reason could there be for leaving a car at that spot, with no houses or stores anywhere around? Coakley shook his head sadly at the threatened tree: wouldn't you think people would take a little *care*? Then he crossed to his own car and drove on out the main road to continue his survey.

At 10:30, Marietta Wilder telephoned Vera Dozier to ask whether she had seen her next-door neighbors that morning. There was no answer, which was something of a relief: now that Mrs. Wilder had a chance to think it over, she wasn't sure whether that was such a good idea.

It was about 10:50 when Trooper Coakley, coming back

along the main road, saw the Volvo still there and pulled up behind it. This time, he looked it over with a more coldly professional eye. He tried the doors warily and found they were all locked except the front one on the driver's side. Coakley poked his head in and examined the car, taking note but keeping strictly hands-off. The keys were gone, the ashtray was overfull of filter-cigarette stubs of a common brand, the radio had been on when the motor was turned off, and the ledge behind the back seat held only a very road-dusty Kleenex box. Coakley got down and peered under the front seats, but all there was to see was a woman's silk scarf that looked as if it had been there for a very long time.

In the end, it was probably the very normality of the Volvo's daily-life contents that disturbed the trooper—enough, anyhow, so that he drove back to the gas station he had just passed. Lenny Pritchard was alone again, his boss having come and gone. He was also interested, but positive: nobody had come in for a gallon of gas; nobody had even called a cab and left his out-of-gas car to be picked up later. In fact, almost nothing at all had happened. Lenny had mostly had a dull-virtuous morning, split between his books and the underside of a Chevy; he was ready for some talk and, if possible, some excitement. He got rather more of the latter than he really expected, when he asked the trooper what it was all about and heard about the Volvo.

Because if Lenny was sure about anything, it was that Dr. Julius King was not the type to just abandon his car by the side of a road and walk off. Like, maybe the trooper didn't know it, but the owner of that Volvo happened to be the big chief of the Long Valley schools.

The trooper, who hadn't known, smiled and asked Lenny how he could be so sure—was the school superintendent a buddy of his, maybe? Well, no, Lenny admitted. But it just so happened that he did know Dr. King's daughter. He stopped short then and added in a different, scared voice that the school superintendent's daughter, who was seventeen, rode with him every morning. Her name was Susan, Lenny said. And she was pretty, real pretty.

Trooper Coakley, a kind man and an experienced police officer, began by assuring the kid it was nothing to get excited about. But he'd better make sure of his facts; he knew: a missing school superintendent is something you may or may not have to do something about, but a teen-age daughter also missing makes it certain that you haven't just stumbled on some accidental evidence—which it might be judicious to ignore—that school superintendents can also get up to some hanky-panky with somebody else's housewife.

Since, as a state trooper, he lacked intimate knowledge of the local scene, Coakley played it cautious. He called in for a vehicle-tag ident, indicating no need for haste, and then had a cup of coffee with Lenny. Even after Coakley received the word that the Volvo did belong to Julius King, he sat on with Lenny, asking questions and trying to get a better picture of what he was getting into.

Around 11:00 (she hadn't been sitting there all morning with one eye on the clock, after all), Mrs. Wilder called the Dozier house again. Vera, her freshly shampooed head draped in a towel, said peacefully enough that nobody had come up the road all morning. Mrs. Wilder made the mistake of asking "Are you sure?"—her voice perhaps a little shrill with long-standing frustration—just as Vera's towel slipped back on her head enough to reveal unmistakable evidence that that dratted Emilie had made the most of her mother's leisurely shower. The cookie jar stood on the counter with its lid beside it, which was not where it had been when Emilie was told that she couldn't have a cookie for the same reason she couldn't go out, because it was too near lunchtime. There would have been just enough time to wash Emilie's hair before lunch. But not only had Emilie rearranged her mother's plans, she had also assaulted the family budget by leaving the back door wide open. To be stuck with a whopping fuel bill because Emilie had had both hands presumably full of cookies was just too much injury-plus-insult, nicely balanced.

Smoldering, Vera said sharply into the phone that no, she wasn't that sure—even though she always spent her mornings watching the neighbors through her spyglass, you couldn't actually see the King house from here because there was a sharp bend in the road. Mrs. Wilder apologized hastily, but Vera wasn't listening, she was busy contemplating the sinus headache she'd have as a result of going out with a wet head. She hung up as soon as she could and took it all out on the two-year-old, who had it coming anyway. Then she shoved him into a sweater and the baby into the playpen—at least she didn't have to drag *that* one along while she tromped through the woods hunting for Emilie. The baby protested. But the two-year-old, having located a crime to fit the punishment, went quietly. Storing away the information that though you weren't supposed to touch the telephone, you were probably supposed to bang on the bathroom door and tell Mommy it was ringing.

Thoroughly annoyed with herself, Marietta Wilder decided to use her own resources. She ordered a call put out on the school intercom summoning Susan King to the principal's office. That brought prompt if unexpected results: Mrs. Price, returned from her errand to the Mercer, heard the Big Brother box and popped in to say Susan King wasn't in school today and to tell why. Mrs. Wilder jumped at the handy explanation that immediately presented itself—obviously, right after Susan's mother had called the school this morning to report a minor illness, it had turned major. Thus, since the whole family had rushed off to the hospital, everything from Dr. King's strange failure to keep his appointment to the unanswered phone was now understandable.

But not, alas, to Mrs. Price, who was looking unhappy. She was civil service, so it wasn't a question of her job security; but still, there was nothing much to be said for getting the principal mad at her. So she didn't like to point out what Mrs. Wilder didn't seem to notice, that by the time Mrs. King telephoned this morning, Dr. King should have already been at Long Valley High. Mrs. Price solved her problem by suggesting that they ask the other King child about it. Billy, in tenth grade?

Mrs. Wilder promptly phoned over to the Mercer School. She was told, of course, that they'd get Billy King and call her back. So she hung up and tried to do some work. As an intelligent woman, she understood that the time before they called back would seem unnaturally long to her; she bit her lip and went on working, or trying to. But when she let herself look at her watch again, the delay turned out to be no illusion. The fourth period over there had already started, so they should certainly have been able to pull the King boy out of class by now. Furious, she called Mercer again.

The Mercer School office, having discovered that the very student the principal wanted to speak to was unaccountably not to be found, had frantically called the boy's home. They got no answer and made the mistake of reporting that to Mrs. Wilder, who was already fuming at their slow-motion performance. She blew up and some diplomacy was then required, causing further delay. So it was nearly 11:30 before Terry Cooke and Andy Drissel, pulled out of social studies, testified to the jittery Mercer authorities that none of the bikes in the rack outside was Billy King's. After that, the best information the shame-faced Mercer could give the increasingly testy Mrs. Wilder was that Billy King had been recorded Present in Mr. Poley's history class, which began right after recess at 10:30. But it appeared the student had somehow left—not only the classroom but the school itself—before the class ended at 11:10. (In the circumstances, the Mercer thought it best not to pass on the observation of a student named Cindy that Mr. Poley had not actually called the roll—and in fact, he often didn't, Cindy had added, explaining maternally that he was inclined to be absentminded.)

By that time, Trooper Coakley had driven over to the King house. In the poorly landscaped front yard, there was nothing to be seen except a bike, apparently carelessly discarded, for it was fallen on its side under one of the weary-looking yews. The gravel driveway was empty and untidy; the brown leaves strewing it had been there for some time, and a small damp-looking spot near one end of the semicircle indicated that the family car regularly stood out in the weather. The front step was bare of milk bottles or accumulated newspapers. If the people had gone away—and the drawn drapes over the bay window on a bright day in November, when sunlight was welcome, did give that impression—they had taken care of cutting off deliveries but forgotten a conspicuous bike.

If they were home, though, they couldn't hear their doorbell. Coakley could—it seemed unnervingly quiet around here. He glanced at the shrouded windows and reminded himself there was no law against not liking sunshine. Then he eyed the fallen bike and decided to have a look around back. There, a small concrete patio abruptly gave way to a thicket of untouched undergrowth: either the Kings owned very little land around their house, or they lacked all taste for gardening. It wasn't likely to be a matter of expense, though, for several large windows, with the curtains drawn back, afforded a wide, clear view of a kitchen from which no luxurious appliance had been omitted. Coakley climbed the steps and peered in through the glass in the back door at the handsome, well-tended sunlit kitchen. Somewhere near it, the phone began to ring. It rang twelve times before it stopped, then started again and rang another ten. After Coakley listened to the silence, he went out to his car and put in a call for the Long Valley police.

The time was officially recorded: *11:30—Trooper requests LVPD squad car.* The reason was not, because it was largely unofficial, having to do with the fact that the lights were on in the kitchen for no apparent reason and the butter was melting in an uncovered dish where the sun was striking the drainboard.

Most important, Trooper Coakley *felt* something wrong, something interrupted, about the early-morning look of the breakfast dishes still standing on the table and the closed draperies in front. It seemed like somebody must have started to put the butter away and didn't finish, and it didn't seem like the kind of kitchen the butter normally got left out in. That was the only specific reason he could really have given, and he wouldn't have said it to anybody but his wife.

When he finished on the car radio, he went around the house and tried the kitchen door. It was locked, so he waited. But he began sniffing for traces of gas around the door.

It was 11:40 when Mrs. Wilder telephoned Vera Dozier again, to explain—offering news by way of an opening to détente—her fears that Susan King's sore throat had turned out to be a hospital emergency. Vera was in a better frame of mind now because the woman who came to "oblige" had arrived and was already started on the ironing, and a chastened Emilie was obediently washing her hands for lunch. Vera felt a little sorry she'd been so snippy before, so she offered to go over to the Kings' as soon as she finished feeding her baby. With a commonalty of curiosity established, the two women hung up.

At 11:50, LVPD Car 4 requested a backup—urgent—at the King house on the new road.

And at 12:00 noon exactly, a call went out for Police Chief John Vesey, even more urgently requesting his presence on that call from the new road.

It was about 12:10 when Vera Dozier pushed the stroller around the bend in the road and saw that Mrs. Wilder's guess might be right: even from here, Vera could see the big revolving light from the ambulance in the Kings' front yard. She hurried now, which was relatively easy; the road was bumpy, but at least it was downhill from this point to the slight rise just before the Kings'.

Then Vera came over the rise and discovered the light

wasn't on an ambulance but on a police car, standing in the road with all its doors swinging open. Another, parked more tidily, was in the driveway, drawn up closely behind a State Police car. But there wasn't a soul in sight, and nothing could be seen of whatever might be going on in the house—because Callie King's beautiful antique-satin drapes were drawn over the bay window, Vera saw with surprise. That was when she also saw the front door standing ajar. So she bumped the stroller over the gravel of the drive, thinking that she could just go in and ask, that's all. After all, why not? It was no sin to be reasonably curious, and besides, you were *supposed* to care about your neighbor.

She'd just managed to get the stroller over a sticky spot in the driveway when all of a sudden a cop came running out of the open front door and began throwing up alongside the lilac bush. Vera screamed and yanked the stroller around, as if to spare the baby the sight. The baby, who'd been torpid with lunch and a ride in the sunshine, woke from his amiable drowse and bellowed.

All sorts of noise seemed to start up then, from everywhere. A car skidded to a stop across the road and John Vesey, the police chief, got out—leaving the door open and a radio inside blaring loud enough to practically drown out the baby. Vera couldn't hear any words, just a loud blat-blat-blatt*blatt*, fractured sound like pieces of broken glass. Vesey came charging up the front walk, half-running, and puffing as though he was really running. He looked at the back of the cop who was still bent over, heaving, and he said "Jesus H. Christ" and then went on without stopping. Which wasn't nice, not nice at all. Vera realized then who the sick cop was—the second Johnson boy, the one who used to play on the high-school basketball team. He was only a kid, maybe nineteen or so, and you'd think Vesey would pay some attention.

The police chief did pay attention at that point: he spotted Vera Dozier and barked—positively barked—at her, "You go on home, Vera, you hear me? Right *now*!"

Vera had never wanted anything harder, what with the baby starting to cry all-out again and that radio blat-blatting. She tried to tell Vesey she was really doing her best to go on home. But he was yelling now—some of it language clearly not intended for her—and that made her so nervous the stroller got stuck worse. For a minute, she thought she might cry herself. But then Vesey went into the house, and that made things a little better.

Finally a nice cop, the kind with the big shiny boots, came out of the house and saw Vera's struggles. He helped her get the stroller turned around, then he told her—but nicely, not yelling at her—to please go on home, there was nothing she could do. She looked at his hands shaking on the handle of the stroller and then at his white, white face and she asked, "Is anybody—dead?"

The nice cop said "Everybody is, lady. All four of them." He blinked at her. "Now, please!"

Vera went then, of course. With the stroller safely out on the road, she stopped to look back just once. The nice cop was talking to the Johnson boy, who had stopped throwing up. He just seemed to be crying now, leaning over with his hands on his knees while the other man sort of patted his back.

Wheeling home as fast as she could, Vera heard John Vesey's voice behind her—this time yelling so loud it made him seem practically gentlemanly before. She couldn't make out any words but "God damn"—and all of a sudden she wasn't curious about the rest, she just wanted to get home. She did, in record time: she was already lifting the baby out of the stroller when she heard the siren coming to the Kings'.

Vera went into the house and phoned her husband, but of course he was out to lunch. He never was around when you wanted him. Then she had the good luck to think of trying Marietta Wilder, who turned out to be eating lunch at her desk. So Vera got to tell somebody. And somebody who really cared, too.

NEGOTIATIONS

1

THE NEUTRALS
(January-February, New York City)

" 'Nervous'?" Will Simons scoffed. "That's ridiculous." Then, taking up his stand on the other side of the argument, he asked indignantly, "Why wouldn't I be nervous? I mean, to become a pen pal to a triple murderer—I mean, wouldn't that make *you* nervous?"

"I guess so," Herk lied. In Will's shoes, he wouldn't be nervous but fascinated. A chance to find out something about how it was to be a 15½-year-old boy who'd shot his mother, father, and sister—well, that was an opportunity any writer would grab gratefully. Any writer except Will Simons, that is: if Will ever wanted to write about a youthful murderer, he'd simply invent one. And since all Simons's characters lived on some far-off planet in some unimaginable time, what difference did it make if they were nothing like real life? Simons was about 90 percent imagination and 5 percent commonsense capacities; the remaining 5 percent was assorted trace elements —all of them probably useful only for writing science fiction and listening to Bach, which was just about 100 percent of what Will Simons did with his time.

Herk peered through the window of Simons's apartment, which got washed every leap year. How much of the gray look of things out there represented a probability of snow falling on Manhattan's East 68th Street, and how much was just accumulated window-grime? Herk abandoned guessing and asked brightly, "How about a drink, hey? You got a drink in the house, Will?"

"I don't know." Ash-blond lashes blinked rapidly over pale-blue eyes. "I think I had a bottle of something, but I don't remember when." The long, narrow face closed in on itself, devout to the problem: Will had the face of an ascetic anyhow, but when he was actually thinking, he looked alarmingly like a fasting saint. "I could go look," he offered, apparently after having considered several hundred possible moves.

"Yeah, good idea. You go look." Herk had no real hope, though: the last time Will, who didn't drink, had rousted out a stored bottle, it had turned out to contain half an inch of coagulated curaçao. Will was irresistible, Herkimer thought fondly; and considering that, to Simons, any confrontation with the outside world was an ordeal anyhow, this one really did entitle him to have his hand held by Herk, his friend and former neighbor. But if that psychiatrist from Massachusetts didn't get here pretty soon, he'd find himself paying a house call rather than enlisting Simons in his project. Will-between-books was always in something less than mental health, but right now . . . This Dr. Cannon, Herk concluded gloomily, couldn't be much of a shrink if he didn't know that even the brightest idea would perish if the timing was off.

Herkimer, a drama critic by trade, earnestly believed all the world was indeed a stage. But he also knew that real life could get away with gimmicks that would get thrown out in the theater—like the first act of this venture, which would've been scorned by any honest playwright because it depended too utterly on chance. For at Enright-Carr, publishers of God-knew-how-many of Will Simons's science fiction adventures—and especially of the apparently endless series featuring a mythical land and its hero-prince, Trad—they knew exactly how precariously Will coped with the real world. Because Enright-Carr therefore guarded him assiduously against disturbing winds of reality, fan letters normally never got past the publisher's office, where secretaries wrote nice notes thanking the reader on behalf of Mr. Simons, acknowledged the typographical error on page 109, and provided answers to questionnaires submitted by graduate students doing theses on the sociology of science fiction. Technical questions about Prince Trad's quark-spear, mindwarner, and other advanced equipment were answered by Simons's editor, a spoiled engineer who invented most of Trad's hardware anyway: Will's own technological expertise was at about the level of a bright sixth-grader.

But Will's editor, and most of the other authority figures around the Enright-Carr offices, vacationed in Puerto Vallarta and other restful spots during January. So when the amazing letter from a Meyer Cannon, M.D., of Long Valley State Hospital, Mass., arrived on the desk of a puzzled secretary, she was left to make her own decisions. Adding up the M.D. and the fact that the letter said time was an important factor, she concluded that you had to take *some* risks, sent it on to Mr. Simons, and just hoped she'd be out of the way of any resultant explosion.

She was safe, as it happened: Will Simons never exploded outward—not that far outward, anyway. And besides, Herkimer and his wife Wendy had come into New York from the suburbs the day Dr. Cannon's letter penetrated Will's usually impenetrable lair. Wendy had soothed Will while Herk read the letter—from which Simons, a precise and meticulous writer but apparently a very sloppy reader, had somehow arrived at an impression that some "they," probably at the publishers', were scheming to have his brain-wrinkles ironed out. "Not even a civilian shrink," Will was proclaiming bitterly. "They had to get one straight from the nut-house."

It was clear to Herkimer—and any other nonparanoid—that this Cannon was not out to acquire Simons as a patient. But

Herk did think the nut-house angle ought to be checked out: patients presumably *could* rip off some letterheads and award themselves M.D.s. And Herk happened to have an old friend who was in a position to find out whether a Meyer Cannon really was at the state hospital in Long Valley, Mass., and was a doctor, rather than a patient.

Detective Lieutenant Guy Silvestri of the Buxford, Mass. police was a specialist in "human relations"—which, since Buxford was the home of world-famous Lambert University, mostly amounted to turning off and smoothing away incipient town-gown confrontations. Since he was also a member of the Governor's Commission on Human Relations and had become* a kind of folk-hero to both the social scientists of Lambert and the citizenry they studied, Silvestri—Herk figured—should be amply supplied with resources for checking on Will Simons's out-of-the-blue correspondent.

But Lt. Silvestri didn't even have to tap his resources, it turned out. "Sure I've heard of Meyer Cannon," he said as soon as Herk mentioned the doctor's name. "What did you want to know?"

Herk glanced over his shoulder. Will, having been efficiently gentled, was now showing off his single piece of technological expertise: his thin face bright with the perfect pleasure of Adam naming the contents of Eden, he was teaching Wendy how to repair her (mythical, Herk happened to know) broken typewriter. Since Will characteristically did only one thing at a time, he would pay no attention to anything said into the telephone a couple of yards away. So Herkimer spoke briskly, outlining the situation he and Wendy had walked in on, on a perfectly innocent January day.

"Of course Cannon is for real," said the genial baritone from Massachusetts. "He's supposed to be brilliant, too. Got some kind of tie with Lambert University—I'm not sure how,

*See *Circle of Death* and *Operation Alcestis.*

but it's against their religion to let a bright boy anywhere in the country go unattached to Lambert in *some* way. Cannon's a psychiatrist, said to be a very conscientious one. I don't know whether he's at Long Valley right now, but I can find out. It certainly sounds likely, though."

"Thanks, Guy." Herk read off Will's phone number so Silvestri could call back. "The thing is, this letter he sent my friend is—rather odd." He paused to check. Will had the typewriter's roller off and a collection of tiny screws laid out on top of the outline for his next book. "It seems this shrink has a patient who—well, a kid who murdered his whole family."

"Wow." The single syllable was sad. Buxford's human relations expert apparently couldn't be objective about such a major failure of human relations.

"Yeah. Well, it says here he doesn't communicate. But the doc seems to know quite a bit about him."

"He's gone around the perimeter, I suppose. Since he can't get in. I told you, Cannon has a reputation for being conscientious. But where do you come in? I don't—"

"It's not me, it's my friend. He writes science fiction, and the kid is a big fan of his. And it seems like he suddenly up and wrote a letter to his favorite author, though he's still not talking to anybody. So the doctor would like to see about setting up something as a way of communicating with the kid. I gather. I'm not sure whether he means a regular correspondence, or what—he sounds rather cautious."

"He'd have to be," Silvestri said. "It's an interesting idea. But dangerous, too. He doesn't know whether he's writing to some publicity hound, after all."

"That, Simons is not." Oops. Everybody, however preoccupied, was supposed to be roused by the sound of his own name, so Herk had been to some trouble to avoid using Will's name, until that slip. But it didn't matter, he saw now: Will just wasn't everybody. "As a matter of fact, he's—unenthusiastic—about seeing this Doctor Cannon. I think I can talk him into it, but I wanted to be sure what I'd be getting him into."

As to that, nobody could say, Silvestri remarked. But he himself didn't see how anybody could resist at least talking it over. And Herk could forget his worries about Cannon's authenticity, anyway.

"I really should've figured that, I guess." Herk grinned. "I mean, who'd make up a name like Meyer Cannon, for God's sake." He told the detective he'd be at this number for another hour, and then he hung up.

Silvestri called back well before the hour ended. "Cannon is at the Long Valley hospital this year, all right. And Herk, here's something—he's a member of a Lambert-sponsored team studying mass murderers. So it figures that he'd be zeroing in on a juvenile charged with multiple homicide."

"Why study them? Does it make a difference whether you murder one person or half a dozen?"

"I guess that's one of the things they're trying to find out, right? Did you persuade Simons to go along with the idea?"

"He's writing a letter now, suggesting an appointment early next month—Cannon said he could get to New York then. I'll mail the letter myself, just to make sure."

"Well, let me know what happens, will you? I'm curious about— Oh, listen, I also got curious about Cannon's unlikely name, so I looked him up. He's a Palestinian. Well, I mean his ancestry—actually, he's American. But his grandfather came here from Palestine."

"With a name like Cannon?"

"Who knows what it actually was? The immigration officers were kind of high-handed in those days. My grandfather used to tell how he fought the good fight to hold onto his Italian 'i' when they tried to make him 'Sylvester.' He could speak English, but maybe Cannon's grandfather couldn't. Or he was a rabbi instead of a rowdy, like the first Guido Silvestri."

Startled, Herb said, "A rabbi? I thought he was a—" He broke off: Will might not be all that absorbed in his letter-writing and Herk was not minded to introduce the word "Palestinian," with its images of ambushed school buses, into the consciousness of the skittish Simons.

"Well, what of it?" Silvestri was asking impatiently. "There were Palestinian Jews, you know. Or maybe you didn't—they never had any oil money to buy publicity with. But they were there, all right. And I guess not all of them stayed around to become Israelis."

"I wonder what his name was. Canaan, maybe?"

"Ask him when you see him," Silvestri suggested blithely. "Meanwhile, do I get to say hello to Wendy now?"

Remembering that a month later, Herk decided that Dr. Cannon's ancestral name was the thing least likely to be discussed today. It would be nice if Silvestri were here, though, Herk thought wistfully, to lend a hand now that the "interesting idea" was about to become reality. Because Wendy wasn't around this time, either, and it was a gray, cold day and Will was already strung so tight that if you tapped him you'd get a drum-roll.

A triumphant Will returned from his kitchen bearing a third of a bottle of Beaujolais. It looked as though it had spent some time in a very high-up cupboard. Herk pulled the cork out, with ominously little difficulty, and sniffed. He put the cork back in.

"Don't you want it?" Will looked around vaguely, then located the problem. "A glass. I've got lots of glasses in there."

"Yeah, well, don't bother. This is—um—well, it's for cooking rather than drinking, really." A sudden vision of Will dousing his frozen TV dinners with ex-Beaujolais vinegar made it momentarily difficult for Herkimer to go on, but he managed. Until, that is, Will generously suggested that Herk take it home for Wendy, who liked to cook. Struggling with a new image, Herk was saved by the doorbell.

New York in February is cold, and New Yorkers dress

accordingly. But Meyer Cannon's sweaters and lumber jacket and mittens were probably countrified even for Long Valley, Massachusetts: he made Herkimer seem startlingly urbane by contrast, and Will positively wispy. Then, listening to Cannon after all the outer garments and the introductions had been got out of the way, Herk saw that Meyer Cannon made everybody appear at least somewhat wispy. Nothing had been scanted in the making of Meyer, it seemed: his eyes were larger and darker-brown and brighter than most people's and his lips fuller; his black hair, silky and curling like a cocker spaniel's, looked as if vigorous cutting had only made it more thick and plentiful. His strong, square body, which would have been chunky except that he was also tall, seemed to be bursting with energy and vital juices. His face was lined not by age—he was certainly under thirty-five—but by mobility: he used it lavishly, along with his hands, to aid his urgent speech. Cannon talked very fast, not nervously but like a man who never has enough time; willy-nilly, you found yourself trying to help him by quickening your own understanding.

Herkimer had once opined, in a review, that no actor could deliver successfully the classic line "Follow me, men!" But he'd been wrong, he thought ruefully now: he was almost certain that if Meyer Cannon shouted that line or any variant of it, Herkimer—and probably lots of others—would get up and follow him. The name of Meyer's magic was easy to discern. It was ardor, always attractive and currently in short supply. But it was intelligent ardor, without self-delusion: Dr. Cannon, Herk noted, did not actually produce his patient's letter to Will Simons until he had apparently satisfied himself about the reliability of Simons and Herkimer. It was only then that he stated the cause in which he had by that time effectively enlisted them—the salvation of Billy King, now aged almost sixteen, who on an ordinary morning last November had shot to death his mother, his father, and his sister, and then had tried to kill himself.

He'd failed in that last—the bullet did no more than crease his skull, causing immediate loss of consciousness and a later need for surgery to relieve pressure. But without going into details (and Meyer Cannon was one of the few people who, when they said "without going into details," then didn't go into details), nothing that had happened to Billy King as a result of a gunshot wound in the head offered any physical explanation of an inability to speak. So the conclusion had been that Billy was psychiatry's baby, and he'd been ordered to the Long Valley State Hospital for observation.

"What will happen to him if he keeps on refusing to talk?" Will asked. With real concern, Herk saw, amazed: Will too, it appeared, had an urge to enlist.

"I don't know for sure." The doctor shook his curly head. "I guess a lot depends on what the Juvenile Court decides—he's theirs right now, of course. But if nothing's changed when he outgrows their jurisdiction—" He shrugged.

Nothing had changed, it seemed, in the intervening time: Billy King was responsive to the hospital rules and orders—"in fact, he's remarkably obedient," Cannon said. "I guess you could say he knows where he is and he wants to get along there, stay out of trouble. Except if it means he has to speak."

That included writing, too. Billy had been given a notebook some time ago, but he'd never used it. And then one day an attendant flipping through the notebook to make sure there was nothing hidden in it ("the patient is officially suicidal, you see," Cannon explained, perhaps a shade dryly) found the letter to Will Simons written on the last few pages. Billy had made no attempt to send it, and it was not really addressed.

"I recognized who it was meant for because I'd seen his collection of Mr. Simons's books in his room at home." Cannon smiled. "Anyway, I've read a few myself. Enough to know who Prince Trad is, at least." He took a photocopy from his pocket and held it out to Will. "Read it for yourself."

Will reached for the letter like a boy who'd just been

assured, by a particularly charismatic nature counselor, that this kind of snake really-truly isn't poisonous. Eyeing the faint parallel lines, ghosts of the notebook page, Herk wondered about the original. Had the cautious Dr. Cannon put it back, leaving it to be mailed only if he found that safe for his patient? To do that had meant slogging around New York in icy weather, and maybe in vain: "conscientious" seemed a rather mild word for Meyer Cannon, when you thought about it.

Will said, pointing, "He calls me 'doctor.' "

Herk read the salutation: "Dear Dr. Simons," Billy King had written in a scrawling but quite legible hand. Well, but he was in a hospital, a place where the people in charge are doctors. So it didn't sound nutty; in fact, you might even say it showed the kid had got it together. But then Herk read on. "Oh. He thinks Trad is a real person, doesn't he." What Billy wanted, it appeared, was for "Dr. Simons"—whom he seemed to see as a kind of prime minister—to tell Prince Trad about this bad mistake he'd made in one of his recent adventures.

"Well, but he knows I'm responsible for Trad," Will pointed out.

The boy did have a grip on reality, Herk conceded, even if it seemed a little slippery. He listened to Cannon outlining the rules of the game, so to speak: the answer to Billy's letter would have to insist on reality, on the fact that Will was real and had invented Trad, who wasn't real. But there was no reason why the letters couldn't go on from there, to encourage fantasizing by way of plot-spinning . . . With effort, Herk fought off the doctor's contagious ardor. Because if Will was going to be expected to write little homilies, disguised pep-talks maybe, Cannon could forget it.

"He hasn't seen the new book," Will said thoughtfully. "That episode actually turns out all right. Anyway, I think so. I think he's overestimating Fentry and underestimating Trad, but maybe I'm wrong." He looked around vaguely. "I had a copy of it somewhere."

"It's on the windowsill in the bedroom," Herk said. Will went to get it, leaving Herkimer to contemplate such incredibly humble readiness to consider reader feedback. He wasn't sure who Fentry was—presumably the villain?—but if *he* had invented Fentry . . .

He turned back to Cannon, who was looking at a copy of an earlier adventure of Prince Trad. "Excuse me, Doctor," he said. "I know Will seems to be really hooked on this idea, but—"

"Why not? He's a problem-solver, and this is a problem." Cannon's smile faded, leaving worry alone in his eyes. "It's something more to Billy, of course. If this works, it could be—a life preserver."

Herk felt like the second man struck by a bullet: the pity had spent much of its force in the big frame of Meyer Cannon, but there was enough still left to pierce Herkimer. Suddenly he could feel the suffering of the boy, locked up alone in his head with the terror and pain of that November day and unable to unlock his head. If this idea worked, though—if Billy King, unable to talk about himself, could talk about Prince Trad instead—then maybe the conscientious Cannon could get in to help him.

". . . I respect your fears for your friend," Meyer Cannon was saying. "But it may be that you're overestimating Will's fragility." The dark eyes regarded the book in his lap, then came up to look squarely at Herk. "I honestly don't think he'll regret the experience."

Well, maybe Cannon really had seen Will better in half an hour than Herk had in all this time. And Cannon had read some of Will's books, which was more than Herk had ever done, so it was possible. But there were practicalities nobody seemed to be noticing. "Okay, but—well, I mean—" Herk struggled, trying to think of a way to avoid saying what he meant. Which was that Billy King was, no matter how you sliced it, in a nut-house. And so maybe it wasn't so safe for him to know where Simons lived.

"I just thought—well, I suppose we could rent a Post Office box, couldn't we?"

"Oh, I see. I wouldn't worry about that. We could use a phony return address if you like, since I'll actually mail Billy's letters back. But he's far from being able to use that kind of information. And anyway, Billy isn't really—frightening."

Will came in then, crossing to the typewriter without a word to anyone: Old Singleminded had already gone to work on the problem, apparently. Herk began to go to work too, then—at wondering why a kid who'd killed three people wasn't really "frightening." And why Meyer Cannon, whose speech had coursed like spring floods up to that point, had required a noticeable pause before he came up with the word. Could it be that what the doctor wanted to say, but was afraid to or was not empowered to, was that Billy was "not really" something else? Like, maybe, a murderer?

Curious, Herk began to ply his interviewing skills. "If Billy does get to talking, do you know what he'll say? I mean, can he remember what happened, or is it like those amnesia cases in the soap operas, with the whole past a blank?"

"No, of course it isn't like that. If he can write, he obviously remembers something he was taught, doesn't he? But we can be close to certain he'll never recall the moment of his own head injury, and the time immediately before it. *That* memory is probably not retrievable."

"You mean it's locked up in his head for good? Or did it never get filed in his memory bank at all?"

"Something closer to the latter, I think." Cannon smiled. "But what went on before then is 'filed in his memory bank,' all right. And he shows good memory function in all other ways, so there's no reason why his whole past should be a blank."

But of course there were no guarantees, Cannon went on to say. Herk regarded him as attentively as any earnest student—and meanwhile listened to the small voice of his own divination function, you might say. Because *what went on before then* was supposed to be already known, even if not to the patient: what had led up to the moment Billy creased his skull with a gunshot was the killing of his parents and sister, right? Or didn't Doctor Cannon think so?

Will turned from his typing then and presented his results, waiting impatiently while Meyer Cannon read the x-ed-over, pencil-marked lines. The draft seemed to Herk to pretty well lick the technical problems created by the parameters Cannon had set for Will. *What Fentry can imagine, Trad can figure out, right?* was not exactly pep-talk, but it did make the point for young Billy that the bad guys don't necessarily have all the muscle and the good guys might be worth betting on. Will had even provided an old-fashioned "hook" to keep Billy writing: Prince Trad had made a mistake, but he'd turned it to good advantage—as Billy could see in the next book, which Simons was sending along. And he hoped to hear whether Billy agreed.

Cannon had a mild objection. He leaned forward, showing Will, who had lost all his vagueness; in fact, he looked as alert as a prizefighter at Round 1.

"I get it. Too close to your-pal-Will, right? Okay, wait a minute." Will whisked back to the typewriter, x-ed out a sentence and typed in another, and handed over the revised version. "That's nearer the 'Dr. Simons' feeling, isn't it?"

It was. They didn't want that doctor-notion encouraged any longer than necessary, of course. And Cannon *wished* there were some way this whole thing could be made less slow and cumbersome. Pain was visible, briefly, in the doctor's mobile face when he said that; then he went on explaining calmly that they had to take their cue from Billy. By moving out ahead, but never too fast or too far. And by remembering, always, to read every word for the way it would seem to Billy . . .

Herk sat there watching the solitary Simons learning to look intimately out of another person's eyes and knew this wasn't going to hurt Will at all, no way. That Time was hurting Meyer Cannon was clear: he knew some need for haste that he wasn't telling, possibly because he didn't know he could just shout "Follow me, men!" Well, maybe his loyal troops could find a way to help him anyway.

The healer and the problem-solver went on conferring. Meanwhile Herkimer, whose trade was noticing, made some promises to himself—like, to look further into some of the things he'd noticed.

2
THE CAUSE
(March-April, Long Valley, Mass.)

March 6

Dear Mr. Simons,

I don't know if this would work, but why cant Trad use Quillior for a messenger? That way he wont have to make a deal with the Pletian ambasador to get the shelter-ship. In "4-seas Land" it said Quillior was originely a Earth-man, then he had his body changed so he could live in Trad's galaxy. So he could just be put back the way he was, maybe. Then he wont need the shelter-ship. Of course maybe theres some reason why not. But youd think if the doctors could change him once, they could change him back too.

Billy

P.S. I have a friend, Doctor Cannon, that I could ask about it if you want.

March 18

Dear Mr. Simons,

I asked Cannon like you said. He wants to read "4-seas Land" first and see exsactly what they did when they operated on Quillior. Right now he *thinks* they could do the job, only theres a catch—they have to have Earthman organs to transplant in Quillior's body. Cannon says he wants to think about it some more and let us know for sure after he reads the book.

I cant wait for the new Pletian campaign to start. I made a map and put it up on the wall. Useing the last chapter you sent, it worked out great—you dont have to worry about page 134, I didnt have any trouble following it. Its' easy to see with the map how Trad will have them boxed once they beam on to the island. But I cant figure how he gets them to do it. I guess Im not so good on stratagy anymore. Please send the next chapter as soon as you can.

Billy

March 18

Dear Will—

If you can, would you try to keep up a mild pressure on Billy to get hold of *Four-Seas Land*? Maybe some need to confirm a small point, too small for him to remember without looking it up? Though I admit that may be a problem, as his memory of the past books seems enormous and almost infinitely detailed. Is that typical of your readers, do you know?

What I want to see is whether Billy can be made to mention that he has the book at home—which I'm pretty sure he remembers—and maybe even offer to lend it to me. But at least to ask about it. (That's the long-term aim, though. So let's not push it—easy does it, a centimeter at a time . . .) Thanks.

Meyer Cannon

March 28

Oh wow I see what you mean, it sure would look funny if Quillior was willing to be marooned on Earth after he went to so much trouble to get off Earth in the first place. I guess I just forgot because its' a long time since I read "4-Seas Land" over again. I wanted to look it up but I couldnt because the book ~~is h~~ isnt here. And I just didnt think about Trad not wanting his buddy light-years away instead of at his side, like you say. It seemed like such a good idea I forgot about everything else. Nuts.

Too bad your still hung up on that fleet maneuver for Chapter 11. What about if Trad used the same trick he pulled on Fentry in "Return of Prince Trad" when he got ~~h~~ back from the Acadamy and found Fentry had siezed the throne. The Pletians probly never heard of it because it happend *inside* the Kingdom. And it makes sense that Trad knows something works so he tries it again, right?

Good news—Cannon fixed it for me to learn typwriting, starting next week. Pretty soon you wont have to strugle with my chicken scratches anymore.

Your friend, Billy

From Meyer Cannon's notes

Feb. 26: Miss May Crabtree (68, white, English teacher L.V. High, good previous relation with B.) volunteered to play chess by mail.

Feb. 28: First mention to B.; Mar. 1: Second mention; Mar. 4: B. initiated discussion; Mar. 5: MC interview with Miss C; Mar. 6: Game approved.

Progress of game by Mar. 28: 1. P-K4, P-K4; 2. N-KB3, N-KB3; 3. B-B4, NxP; next move Miss C. According to Miss C., these standard moves. So B.'s ref. to impaired strategic ability (lttr. to S. 3/18) is probably only anticipatory anxiety, related to chess game but generalized.

Mar. 28 lttr.: "the book is ~~h~~"—almost certainly "home." Also note change in spelling of book title (see B. to S. Mar. 6), coming closer to the way it appears on title page. Increased visualization?? (S. instructed to avoid use of title, but if can't, to copy B.'s most recent usage.)

Note salutation and closing. Let's try taking his hint.

Mar. 29

Dear Will—

Would you please sign your next letter "Will," as you did last time, but without "Will Simons" typed underneath? And don't put any return address on the envelope, please. But it's important to use that same yellow paper—if you can't, phone me, because I'll have to alter the above instructions. Thanks.

Hastily, Meyer Cannon

P.S. As you'll see in Billy's March 28 letter, you don't need to worry about putting down his suggestions. Don't hesitate to call again any time such questions occur to you, of course. But that sort of thing won't hurt him, honest. MC

April 1

Dear Dr. Cannon—

Got your note, and can do: have yellow paper, will sign as instructed.
But it may take a while to dream up a reply to Billy's suggestion (Mar. 28, para 2), because it presents a problem. The truth is, I can't have Trad pull that trick again just *because* I used it in RETURN OF P.T., you see. Billy's right—in real life, people do try something that worked before; but in fiction, particularly s-f, you have to come up with a new gimmick. It's just a convention, like never having characters with the same names—e.g., everybody knows more than one Bob or a couple of Joes, but did you ever see that in a novel?
I assume this is more reality than you want Billy to meet right now? I'm sure I can manage to construct some other reason why Trad can't do it. But if my assumption is wrong

and I *don't* have to, will you telephone me? I don't want to
do all that exercising in vain.

Y'rs, Will

P.S. I hope you don't get the wrong impression from that
last sentence: I don't really mind the work if it helps Billy.
P.P.S. Herk just called and I told him about it. He says my
assumption is right. Okay, I'm thinking, I'm thinking . . .

April 4

Dear Herk—

Yes, thanks, I noticed the lack of salutation in Billy's
last letter to Simons. Also Cannon without the "Dr."

Tuesday would be the best day for me in the week of
the 16th—I'll be in Buxford to report to the Project committee, which meets at Lambert on the 18th. Dinner
sounds fine if you can make it early, as I'm not staying
over; I don't want to get home too late because I have early
rounds on Wednesdays. You go ahead and pick a place to
eat, though—I always eat at the University when I'm in
Buxford, so I have no idea where to go in town.

See you on the 18th. I'll be at Lambert (108 Merritt
Hall) till about 5, if you want to come there. Otherwise, let
me know where to meet you, okay?

Meyer

April 8

Dear Will,

I got Chapter 11 yesterday. The plan looked great and
it checks out on my map allright. Exsept theres a little
problem when they cross the Straits—wouldnt the current
be against them there? Of course they could use the Moses-
beam, it would work I guess if you had one on the lead
dartship and one on the flagship.

One thing Im not sure about, tho. The plan is really
great, but it bothers me that everything depends on *100*

percent surprise, so if the Pletians even pick up a very small clue its' all over. Shouldnt there be some way to change the plan at the last minute? I know their are no traiters among Trad's men and their all picked men tops at their job so he can count on no foulups, even in the tricky part where Zak's squad has to get the DNA gun across the courtyard between sweeps of the reassembler. But like right there—if the sentry gets a f̶e̶e̶ a beep from his mindwarner and turns around, their goes the ball game.

Thanks for explaining why Trad couldnt use that trick again in Chapter 11. I forgot about the Pletian computer histories of the Kingdom's royal family—of course that Fentry episode would be stored with the data on Trad. If I only had my books here maybe I wouldnt make so many dumb suggestions.

Your friend, Billy

From Meyer Cannon's notes

Apr. 8 lttr., B. to S.: (a) Hunch about no-salutation hint (Mar. 28) checked out—"Will" was what he wanted to say, all right. Fits with pattern in neurosurgery ward and here: no unease with authority-figs. until affection enters. Thus, MC identified as "friend" (Mar. 6) loses "Dr." in next letter (Mar. 18). And increasingly personal tone of letters (see Mar. 28, e.g.) goes along with unwillingness to call S. "Mr." plus "Your friend" signature . . . Conclusion: Look up father-Trad relation (think it was distant-respectful). Also, might check out Trad's other family relations (doesn't he have a sister?).

(b) "f̶e̶e̶"—that's got to be "feeling"! At minimum, it's first time B. preferred human to mechanistic (though briefly) in describing behavior. But we may be close to jackpot—will check, but I think one of his pals, either Terry or Andy, said B. told him he "had a funny feeling" during school recess that day. (Later assumed to be illness, but I think that's what the kid said in first interrogation.) FIND OUT . . . Conclusion: Come back to it, but better leave it lay for now.

(c) "There goes the ball game"—looked hopeful as possible father quote, but turned out probably recent when I questioned staff. One aide (Williams, 33, black, high-school grad) remembers corridor dialogue about chance of pay raise getting through legislature—thinks he said "if they don't get to it this week, there goes the ball game." No corroboration—W. doesn't remember who he was talking to. (Doubt that. Must be somebody who shouldn't have been in that corridor.) But says Billy certainly could've heard it . . . Conclusion: Source more likely W. than father.

(d) "I forgot about the Pletian computer"—response to Simons letter (Apr 5) turning down Billy's suggestion. S. wrote: "The trouble is, that episode is part of Trad's biography. And the Pletian computer stores profiles and biogs of Trad and Princess Trila because they're members of the royal family." (Solution to problem discussed in lttr. S to MC Apr. 1)

Cannon hesitated, frowning at his notes because he was really not quite sure enough of the rest to put it in. Billy's "I forgot" might be as casual an admission as it sounded, but it could also be a brief recognition of his loss of memory. The problem arose, Cannon saw ruefully, because he'd underestimated Will Simons's skill. The writer, accustomed to slipping information dextrously into readers' minds, had managed to make it seem that that information had been around all the time, presumably in some earlier book. He had thus maybe stirred up in Billy a self-consciousness about memory that Cannon would have preferred to avoid for a while. So now he had the results of an uncontrolled experiment, and he'd just have to guess what they meant.

There *was* some tension, he decided, scanning Billy's letter again. But they'd lucked out. Because even if you assumed Billy did think he'd failed to remember something and was a little shaken about it, his response had been to inch closer to asking for his books from home—and that was good. Cannon reminded himself to zero in on *Four-Seas Land* again, which would help to tip that situation a little further. He didn't need to remind himself to be more alert in the future: they definitely didn't need the risks incurred if Billy started worrying about his memory, impairing his frail self-confidence.

Cannon's gaze fell on the quoted example of Will's ingenuity, and he noticed that one question had been answered anyway. "NB—"he scribbled—"There is a sister, it seems. Ask S. about Trad's relations with Princess Trila."

3
THE ALLIES
(April 18, Buxford, Mass.)

The first time Herkimer had entered the elegantly furnished and appointed private room in the rear of Buxford's Napoli Restaurant, he'd been visited by a horrified suspicion that Lieutenant Guy Silvestri, whom Herk and all the rest of Buxford had believed to be Mr. Integrity, might be on the take after all. But the truth, though it did involve some illegalities, turned out to be simpler and less dismaying. It was only that, a very long time ago, Silvestri's grandfather and the father of the present owner of the Napoli were partners in a profitable if somewhat risky enterprise designed to obtain for a thirsty public the alcoholic beverages denied it by the Eighteenth Amendment. Their operation was a small but happy one: Guido Silvestri journeyed regularly to Canada and returned with what was served in teacups at the Napoli—a division of labor between the two men reflecting what they'd learned in the old country, where Silvestri had been the son of a smuggler and his partner the son of a chef. The two had the good sense to abandon their first American enterprise before they could be absorbed into the gangland bureaucracy that saw a good thing and took it over. Both proceeded to learn more legitimate ways of breadwinning; then they fathered families and lived out respectable lives.

But Silvestri's son, the father of Guy, was killed in an auto accident in his early thirties—so only one of the partners' sons lived to carry on the legitimate enterprise at the Napoli. Thus, whenever old Guido's grandson found occasion to repair to the Napoli, the proprietor's honor demanded that the lieutenant dine in the maximum splendor the establishment could provide. Nothing less was owed, in the name of tradition, to the only male descendant of the Silvestri line of distinguished smugglers —even if he happened to be a cop.

Herkimer not only knew this history but also, as is characteristic of newspaper types, he took it especially seriously because it hadn't been easy to find out. Thus he tended to see his friend as the product of opposites held in delicate balance, which might tip—or be tipped—at a given moment toward either the romantic extravagance of old Guido or the self-mocking cool of modern Guy.

"I'm a police officer, Herk," Silvestri said, gently but firmly.

Herkimer had been thinking romantic extravagance—like what a great set this little hideaway would make for Diamond Jim Brady drinking champagne out of Lillian Russell's slipper!— so he was stung into irony: "Yeah, I know. You're just a simple, red-blooded Buxford cop." Then he remembered he'd come here to make a sales pitch, and that kind of crack wouldn't help. For irony, which depends on the implied threat *I see what you don't mean me to,* would never move Silvestri, who didn't care if you did see through him. There again he was a divided man—on the one hand so reserved that "Guy's privacy hangup" was a frequent subject for ridicule among his intimates; on the other, he was so open and sympathetic that people found themselves telling him, on brief acquaintance, things they'd never thought they could say aloud. Herk had given this contradiction the benefit of his analytic skills as a critic and believed he knew how the mechanism worked (almost certainly without Guy's awareness). It was basically a physical accident: the tall, lean, bony-faced Silvestri looked such a very model of the strong-silent-loner that when the guarded dark eyes turned on you, unexpectedly revealing unmistakably friendly and generous interest, there was an immediate impression that you and you alone had been chosen as the beneficiary of all that intelligence and desire to understand. Thus Silvestri's encounters with his fellowmen tended to acquire, right from the start, an intensely I-and-Thou aura—with the Thou instantly warmed and flattered.

"What's the trouble, Herk? How come we're dueling?"

He had a second chance, Herk saw. This time, though, he'd better shake off the private-dining-room ambience, which didn't exactly lend itself to straightforward talk: Guy might be used to living with dualities, but it came harder to other people. "You come on with that simple-cop routine, what do you expect?" Herk's irritation with himself sharpened his voice. "I mean, I was here when you got appointed to the Governor's Commission, you know. And I even remember you as a grad student at Lambert, don't I? So when I bring you"—he nodded at the swollen folder spilling papers out onto the banquette between them—"a case of somebody getting chewed up in the machinery, and your only response is to rattle your badge at me—"

"All right, I'm sorry. But what I'm really rattling is the law of averages."

"*Averages!* What's averages got to do with it, for God's sake? Cannon isn't an average shrink. I'm not an average drama critic. I don't think you're an average detective-lieutenant, and" —righteous wrath had suddenly succumbed to subversive laughter—"I'm willing to bet you're a good three inches taller than the average Italian, besides."

Thus reminded of the cramped quarters, Guy shifted his long legs carefully. But he wasn't comfortable in the role of defender of statistics either, he thought, irritated: it was like getting shot in the wrong uniform. The sense of grievance stirred him to fight back. "Okay. But, although I know official wrongs are dear to the hearts of drama-lovers—"

"Oof. Pow. Help, I'm bleeding."

"Okay, sorry." Guy actually looked sorry. "But the fact is, very few people are wrongly charged with major crimes. Even if you insist on assuming policemen and prosecutors are all villains, surely you'll grant that they're not interested in wasting their own time. Nobody rolls the machinery if a defense attorney could blow away the whole case with one puff."

"Guy, that's just what— Did you read the summary I sent you?" Herk grabbed the folder and began hunting through it. "I've got a copy here."

Silvestri sighed, because building timetables was not his forte. He'd had to lead homicide investigations just twice, and both times he'd first figured whodunit and only then resorted to checking his intuition against a list of alibis. Which was what Herk's summary, a long list of times and unanswered phone calls, amounted to. Recognizing the sheet of paper Herk was now plunking down amid the splendors of the Napoli's china and napery, Guy reacted like a citizen handed a copy of the Defense Department budget: *anything* was better than having to read it word for word . . .

"Well, I certainly know the basic facts of the case," he said quickly. "The deaths occurred sometime between about eight ayem—when two of the victims were seen by a neighbor—and eleven thirty, when a trooper and a Long Valley patrolman entered the house. Apparently the medical evidence couldn't narrow the time. What did, if I remember correctly, was the delivery of the family laundry, somewhere between those two times."

"At nine forty-five." Herk pointed at it on the list.

"Okay, at nine forty-five nobody answered the doorbell, so the laundry package was left on the doorstep. But the package was inside the house when the officers broke in later and found—well, you know what they found, three dead and the boy an attempted suicide." Silvestri paused. Then he went on, his voice matter-of-fact, "All right. Since nobody but the members of the family had keys to the house, the reasoning was that only Billy King could have brought that package of laundry inside. At whatever time he left school and went home. I know the time wasn't established, but," he added hastily, lest the Defense budget be thrust at him again, "the consensus was that whenever it was, it was easily in time to commit the homicides before the officer got there."

"That's when they were killed, then, right?"

"Apparently not, or you wouldn't be so quick to pin me down. But I had a feeling the other end of the morning was out, for some reason." Silvestri sighed, and reached for the summary. "I suppose I have to—"

"I'll spare you the agony. Billy was seen at school, playing basketball, by the school custodian at eight fifteen. The Latin teacher says he was in Latin class all right during the first period. He not only was in his math class next, but he also took a test that wasn't even handed out till nine forty-five. He got an A on it." Herk smiled, not pleasantly. "Pretty good if he was about to rush off and commit three murders, wasn't it?"

Guy shook his head, denying the gambit. When it came to human behavior, he knew, it was impossible to construct an irony that would hold up as irony: anything, anything at all, was likely to topple over into incredible-but-true.

"All right, no editorializing," Herk promised. "Let's get on. You're right about the time he left school being up for grabs, but he was seen there during recess, which runs from ten after ten to ten thirty. So if he went home at—" Silvestri was shaking his head. "What's wrong?"

"It's not when, it's why. Why did he go home from school at all?"

"Well, he told one of his buddies during recess that he didn't feel good. But of course that was taken to mean he was overcome with guilt for what he'd done earlier. And he got feeling so un-good that he went home and shot himself." Triumphant, Herk saw that Silvestri had picked up the summary and was now actually reading it. "You don't buy that theory?"

"Half of it, maybe." Preferring intuition didn't mean flouting logic, and logic blocked that theory with the laundry package. Because if it pointed to Billy, as the only one who could have taken it into the house, it also said he must have done the killings before his tight school alibi began. Any other way, they should have been alive when the package was delivered at 9:45. "But half is no good," Guy said, thinking aloud. "If you can't make him for the homicides early in the morning, the suicide attempt later doesn't prove a thing. It's got to be double-or-nothing."

"Well, I give you credit for candor. However, your colleagues in Long Valley went in for what we might call a double-barreled theory, too. Except in theirs, the time of the murders sort of slides, to fit with when Billy was available."

"I'm afraid I don't follow you."

Herk noted the stiff tone. But it was too late now for winning ways, anyhow: it would have to be logic or nothing. "Okay, hang on, here we go. You accept the school custodian's statement that he saw Billy at eight fifteen?"

You could tinker with all those morning times, Guy supposed. But not by enough, because a lot of shots had been fired in that house—so even if the neighbor didn't come by exactly when he said, he still would've had to hear something. And then there was the family car, found—he glanced at the summary—over a mile away, but seen in the driveway at around 8:00 . . . "Some of the times may be a little doubtful," he said, scanning the page. Mrs. King's phone call to the high school, for one: if true, it meant nothing had happened until after 8:35; but it was only a voice on the telephone. The school custodian, though, could be corroborated—other boys had been playing ball with Billy King. "No, there's no reason not to believe Mr.—er—Roberts," Guy conceded.

"Right. That's why the cops needed both barrels, you see. If Billy didn't go home at eleven because he was guilt-ridden about what he'd done at eight, why, then, he went home to shoot them at eleven. And when the flaw in that jumps out at you, as I assume it has—"

"It has."

"—then you talk up those unanswered phone calls and the laundry package that was left on the doorstep because they were all already dead. In short, Billy King shot them *either* before he left for school *or* after he came home—whichever isn't countered by something else at the moment." Herk allowed himself a well-timed pause. "An either-or solution of a crime is a right handy device, isn't it?"

Feeling a little sick, Guy said, "Nobody could bring a charge if that's all they had."

"Well, they didn't have to. Everybody was free to speculate, and nobody had to substantiate. Like you said, they roll the machinery."

"Are you suggesting—"

"I guess I am, Guy. I'm suggesting that the machinery rolled even though a defense attorney *could* blow away the whole case with one puff." Herkimer hesitated, this time not for dramatic effect. Then he plunged: "Shocking as it may sound, I'm suggesting that because it was a juvenile case, everybody—maybe even with the fanciest motives—railroaded this kid. The nicest judge and the most honorable cops in fact screwed Billy King out of his simplest rights."

The silence in the small room was as heavy as its crimson velvet draperies. Nervously, Herk turned to rearranging the "public-relations kit" he'd carried up here from New York. To make a case, but it was possible he'd just blown it for good: that Billy had been dealt with unjustly seemed to him inescapable, but Silvestri was not the kind of audience for a round and ringing declamation. So maybe all that had been accomplished was to inspire Guy to defend his fellow cops from Herkimer's oratory . . .

Then he saw what was happening, and he relaxed. Because

Guy was up to the unconscious sort-of-handwringing that Herk had learned was not the finger exercises he'd once taken it for. Lieutenant Silvestri, most of Buxford knew, was an enthusiastic member of a local chamber-music group; maybe this limbering up the fingers of one hand by bending them with the other had once been an aid to playing the viola. But it was also, by now, a reliable sign of unconscious distress. When Guy had something hard but necessary to do, the long agile fingers exercised themselves.

Herk looked at the dark bony face, closed and silent, and refilled the wineglasses: it might be a long wait. But light danced on the facets of the cut-glass decanter when he moved it, and Silvestri stirred like a sleeper awakened. "Thanks. I'm sorry, I—"

"I know."

Guy smiled, doubting it. Long acquaintance had taught him that Herk thought of things as occurring in a kind of theatrical sequence featuring a single focal event, whether watched or participated in. But there was in fact almost never only one event going on: it was much more like a three-ring circus. And police officers learned early that they'd better keep an eye on the other rings. Belatedly, Silvestri began to do that now. "Where did you get all this stuff, Herk?" He poked at the bulging folder.

"Oh, partly from Cannon—he'd talked to the teachers about how Billy seemed in school that morning, and so forth. The rest is mostly from the papers."

"Your own paper?" Guy didn't think the *New York Gazette* would give a tenth of this lineage to anything, even a triple murder, in Long Valley, Massachusetts.

"No, the local papers, in White County."

"You've done a lot of work." It was apparently a comment, actually a kind of groan. Because if Herkimer had only sent for the back issues of the local newspaper—which he'd certainly have to do, where else would he get the *White County*

Democrat, formerly *White County Republican?*—he'd probably already stirred up gossip in Long Valley. Herk, innocent and ardent, rode out to right wrongs without seeing what Lt. Silvestri, obliged to consider the action in all three rings, had to see—that you couldn't stop with suggesting that Billy King hadn't killed his family. Or with the assumption, axiomatic among the New York literati, that venal or appallingly stupid behavior by authorities was a natural phenomenon. But if you knew that it wasn't, you had to ask why, in this case—

"I suppose you're thinking it isn't evidence," Herk said. "Okay, and I admit it can hardly be a picnic to start unscrambling stuff that's half a year old, almost."

"It doesn't sound inviting." That was putting it minimally. If Herk had already managed to alert somebody who didn't want evidence unscrambled, it could also be dangerous.

"Look, Guy, this isn't evidence either, but—well, you get to know something about somebody when you've been reading his letters for a couple of months."

"Like what?" Silvestri was inclined to doubt that Billy King's letters would be all that forthcoming.

"Well, like a couple of weeks ago, Will wrote the kid that some idea he'd been all enthusiastic about was just a no-go. And you know Billy's reaction to that? All he said was 'Nuts.' And then he went right on to offer Will another idea." Herk waved his hand in a wide oratorical gesture. "I ask you, does that sound like a kid who was down enough five months ago to try to put a bullet in his head?" The gesturing hand came up, the thumb cocked and the forefinger boring dramatically into Herkimer's right temple.

The example didn't seem to thrill Silvestri; he admitted that the boy didn't seem to be given to easy despair, but he spoke rather absently when he added, "Or anyway he isn't now, let's say. But Cannon's been doctoring him, and he's a very good shrink."

"Sure. So good he can cure a suicidal patient in a couple of months, without the patient even talking to him."

"The boy doesn't talk at all then?"

"Only to Meyer—and that's since the letters to Will began. But still only casual chat, I gather. The letters he writes to Will talk a bit more freely, but they're pretty short and to the point. I mean, they don't give away much—they just sound like any pen-pal-type letters from a kid. Full of ideas, casual about spelling, a little cocky."

"I don't really know what fifteen-and-a-half-year-old boys are like," Silvestri said, thinking aloud. His own first and thus far only son had recently learned what a birthday was, celebrating the occasion by rubbing birthday cake into his hair. Tony's father glanced thoughtfully at Herk, who probably knew better what boys of Billy King's age were like—Herk had once been a resident advisor for Lambert University freshmen, who weren't much older than Billy.

"Actually, math-type kids are not usually as social as Billy apparently was. I mean, you'd expect him to belong to the chess club, but he was also a heavy contender for the school basketball team." Herk nodded at the folder by his side. "Everything gets into the local weekly. And in a town where the hottest news in November normally is who slipped on whose icy sidewalk, you can imagine they weren't stingy with space when a local boy knocked off his whole family. So we heard that before the crime, Billy and two other boys had irritated a few people by daredevil bike-riding, with accompanying noise—oh, one of them, by the way"—Herk interrupted himself—"was Vera Dozier, the wife of the neighbor who saw the Kings that morning. She'd complained to the cops, last September, because the boys were waking her baby from its nap. And *after* the crime, the school librarian—answering one of those what-kind-of-monster-was-this-boy questions—solemnly told the press Billy King once returned a library book that looked like it had been left out in the rain. Thus revealing the kid's true iniquity. Let's see, what else?" Herk riffled the clippings. "Oh, yeah, he was on the technical staff for the school production of *Pinafore*. He ran the lighting board, presumably competently enough so nothing happened that made the White County weekly. And— What? I'm sorry, I didn't hear—"

"Nothing. It was nothing." Sternly, Guy rooted out the jouncy Sullivan tune that had apparently escaped the confines of his head. Then he went back to his memories of Buxford High and Latin, which had had at least one Silvestri in its school orchestra ever since the first of his squad of sisters reached high-school age. Thus it was by a kind of dynastic right that Guy, the youngest, got to play for the annual Gilbert and Sullivan operetta while—was it Angie, or Maria?—sang sharp on stage and Mama in the audience, surrounded by a school of aunts, managed to look equally proud and anxious.

"His sister sang the role of Buttercup," Herk said.

Angie, of course. Maria was in *Iolanthe,* the next year.

"Actually, it could be Billy's sister who made the difference, you know? They weren't far apart in age, and if she was the gregarious type, she'd be a likely socializing influence."

"Very likely," agreed the man who knew all about the socializing influence of sisters.

"On the whole, Billy sounds a bit young for his age. Sheltered."

You bet, Guy managed not to say aloud. Sheltering little brothers was one thing all sisters seemed to go in for.

"Why don't I leave the clips with you, Guy? It won't take long to read them, and I guarantee you things will jump out at you right away. About that morning, particularly, there were some really weird doings that—"

"Let's wait to hear what Doctor Cannon has to say, okay?" Silvestri knew Herk had sensed a softening and was trying to press his advantage. It would be useful, though, if

Herk didn't know he'd probably already won his point. Guy would have to make a quick private inquiry first, to see whether those "weird doings" had some rationale hidden from the news media. But he doubted that anything would turn up, because many of the details in the news clips could only have come from the Long Valley authorities—who had not, apparently, added any hedges, no-comments, or I-was-misquoteds. "Cannon may know something we don't," he explained. But if Billy's psychiatrist, whose sources certainly wouldn't be limited to official statements, didn't refute the picture Herk had drawn, then Silvestri would probably have to do something about all this. "I gather he wasn't exactly jumping at the chance to come tell me about it, though?"

"Not really. But it's not an anti-fuzz thing, if that's what you think."

"Never crossed my mind," Silvestri said demurely.

"It's more like a Hippocrates hangup, I suspect." Herk grinned. "Meyer agreed to come to meeting, but with the air of a recently deflowered virgin figuring what the hell, she might as well learn to play poker now, too. If you know what I mean."

"Oh, I do. I don't see how it could have been put more vividly."

"Okay, funny-funny. But it's true, isn't it—that if you do one unorthodox thing, then you're more inclined to try another?"

Guy nodded, sternly banishing personal rue, and suggested mildly that Dr. Cannon had probably known that for some time. "Does his willingness—however reluctant—to come here mean he agrees with you about Billy King?"

"Well, I'd say Cannon has—let's call it an intuition—about Billy. But if he had anything more, he'd have gone to the Long Valley authorities, I guess. Unless you mean he's trying to protect his mass-murderers study? Like, not wanting it messed up with inconvenient truth?"

"My God, no. I told you, I know something about Meyer Cannon."

"Then you know he's likely to have a very high-class intuition."

Guy agreed. And, playing it safe in view of that high-class intuition, he changed the subject. So that when Meyer Cannon was shown in, what was being discussed was wine. A controversial subject, but not one that even Herk could work up Machiavellian theories about, so there was nothing alarming in the air for the new arrival to intuit.

He was glad to have met Meyer Cannon, Silvestri knew by the time they'd finished dinner. The psychiatrist was forthcoming and friendly, a man very easy to like. But a little puzzling, because Herk had implied that Cannon's doubts of his patient's guilt would have to be wrung out of him. Maybe Herk was just losing his old-reporter knack, becoming less accurate as he got more colorful? Or else Cannon must have changed. Because he not only admitted to a conjecture of Billy King's innocence, he seemed to Guy very eager to get something done about it.

Cannon also treated Herk's notion that Billy didn't sound like a would-be suicide with surprising seriousness. But then, it seemed Herk hadn't been the only one who wondered: "The neurosurgeon knocked himself out trying to find something they'd overlooked, because the patient just didn't strike him as likely to be a psychiatric problem." Cannon shrugged. "He had to give up, of course—there simply wasn't anything there to damage the speech center. The bullet creased the skull, lacerating the galea and abrading the periosteum. The wound extended from just below the hairline in the mid-frontal region"—he showed them on his own head, drawing a finger from the widow's peak in the center of his forehead straight back through his curly hair—"to a point four centimeters anterior to the coronal suture in the midline. The exact language is a little daunting, I know. But you can see where it was."

"Yes, but I'm not sure *what* it was," Guy said. "Billy was unconscious when they found him, right?"

"Oh, sure. He was in shock from all the bleeding. He must've looked closer to dead than just unconscious. The hematoma—there was some intracranial bleeding as a result of the impact—apparently depressed respiration. So the doctor on the ambulance inserted an endotracheal tube and assisted respiration on the way to the hospital. He—"

"You mean it's really true?" Herk interrupted. "Young Doctor Kildare riding the ambulance, performing instant surgery? I always thought that was hoked up by the scriptwriter."

Cannon smiled. "Well, that much could be true—you do start resuscitation immediately, and there are times when that might even include minor surgery. But neurosurgery on the kitchen table would have to be the scriptwriter's own contribution—I don't think even the handsomest young doctor riding the ambulance would really be up to it. There *was* a dramatic coincidence, though." He offered it to Herk like a piece of chocolate to a child. "Billy was lucky—a Lambert University neurosurgeon—probably the best man in the East—was in Strawbridge at the time: he comes from there and was visiting his parents, so it had been in the local paper that he was in town. I'm told the cops got him to Long Valley in ten minutes flat. That sounds a bit exaggerated, but anyway, the report to the court says the subdural hematoma was drained within one hour."

Silvestri said, "The boy would be unconscious for some time after the operation, of course. So nobody would know about his speech until—when?"

"Well, the Babinski would be positive, at first, and then revert to normal. Then, with deep-tendon reflexes symmetrical and responses to pain normal, they'd start testing to make sure the cranial nerves were intact." The doctor stopped, apparently recalling who his hearers were. "Look, suppose, to test the patient's voluntary motor function, you tell him to touch his finger to his nose. If he does it, you also know he can hear and understand, right? So when you tell him to count backwards from a hundred and he doesn't, but you've already seen that he can carry out complex mental functions like reading and arithmetic, how smart do you have to be to figure he can't speak—and discover you're right when you hand him a pencil and paper and he can do it quickly and accurately? So, since you know that when you opened the skull things were remarkably clean and that the patient healed up beautifully afterward, you start playing around trying to find out what kind of aphasia you have on your hands. And finally you have to admit that there's an 'isolated motor aphasia with absolutely no deficit in any cognitive function.' Which means, 'It's there but I can't see why, so let's buck it to the shrinks.' " Cannon smiled wryly. "And then, because you're a decent man and you don't like having to write an empty report like that—and maybe because everybody on the ward thought it was a shame to send such a sweet, gentle kid to the booby hatch—you keep haunting the psychiatrist, wringing your hands and pressuring him to get off his butt and do something for Billy."

Guy nodded, knowing the feeling well. "What was Billy like when they handed him over to you, Doctor?"

"Well, his silence wasn't complete enough to be hysterical negativism, and it had gone on too long for that anyway. And pretty soon he seemed glad to see me when I came into his room. But the first sign—well, I imagine you've been told about his letter to Will Simons."

"But Billy does talk—to you, anyway—by now. Was that a result of the correspondence with Simons?"

"In the sense that it got him over the hump, I guess. World-making seems to hold a certain attraction for disturbed youngsters. As you probably observed for yourself"—the doctor grinned broadly—"if you were a policeman in Buxford around the time of the campus confrontations at Lambert."

"I did notice a certain correlation. So dreaming up science fiction worked like that with Billy?"

"Maybe. Anyway, eventually he got to a question he needed a doctor to answer, and there I was, a pleasant fellow who showed up every day. That's the minimal explanation. A more hopeful one is that it was an excuse. That he wanted to begin to talk because he wanted to recover." Cannon's face broke into a smile again, this time of pure happiness. "As of today, though, we have another step. I phoned before I came over here, and it seems that this afternoon"—he was actually beaming now—"Billy spoke to one of the attendants." Later, he would record conscientiously that it was Williams who'd been timidly accosted as he was going off duty at three o'clock. (*It was like he was scaring himself, Doc. He talked so quiet I couldn't hardly hear him at first.*) But right now, Meyer wanted only to rejoice. "He asked whether the mail had come—he's expecting a letter from Simons. I suppose he was afraid he might have missed the mail orderly, and he just couldn't stand not knowing. It was simply too important to him."

"What does this mean—in terms of Billy's treatment now?"

Maybe nothing right away, Cannon admitted. Maybe he'd get back to the hospital and discover that Billy had so scared himself that— Well, never mind; with any luck, they were on their way. Though it was still hard to say exactly where. Or how long it would be before . . .

Lieutenant Silvestri looked at the sudden shadow in the eyes that had been bright with pleasure a moment ago, and he knew why the actual Meyer Cannon was different from the reluctant participant Herk had been describing. "Now you really do have to know what happened, don't you?" Guy asked with something like pity. Because if the barrier Billy had erected was coming down, it would make an important difference what was on the other side. In restoring the boy's memory, would Cannon be leading him into confronting grief— which would be hard, but manageable—or into somehow coping with an all-but-unimaginable guilt?

"I don't *have* to know, I guess." Cannon hesitated, then let himself respond to the sympathy he saw. "But if I did, I could ... go faster. Maybe take more risks. This thing is—well, it's like a moon shot, in a way." His look held them, inviting them to share the hope and the hazards. "All sorts of trade-offs have to be tried so maybe you can have everything together for the moment when an opening comes. Only, with a human mind—particularly a young one—an opening you miss may never come around again: some of the process of growing up is cyclical, but a lot isn't. So there may be just one 'window.' And anyway, if too much time goes by—" He spread his hands. "Well, the longer the absence from normal life, the smaller the chance of its ever being normal again. So the price of proceeding too cautiously can be—unbearable." He stopped, admitting failure: he'd started off trying not to seem desperate, but then his every word had revealed how urgently he did need to know. And Lieutenant Silvestri, at least, had seen that. "The price is so high," Cannon finished, openly begging for help now, "that anything that'll reduce the need to feel my way around in the dark could be—life-saving."

In the silence, Silvestri cleared his throat. "I'm going to look into the case, Doctor. But you understand that whatever I find, I'll still have to go through channels?" He felt like a congressman ponderously debating whether to send help to a little country already under attack. It was unavoidable, but to Meyer Cannon, besieged by Time, it must seem insupportable. And if this did become an alliance between Cannon and Silvestri, that difference wasn't the only kind that would trouble it. There would be also, of course, the hazards that haunt all alliances in war—duplicated effort, information slipping down cracks, reinforcements not showing up when they were needed ... It was just as well he was being drafted, Silvestri decided. Because he would surely have had better sense than to volunteer for an operation like this one.

"It's all right, Guy." Cannon smiled. "I realize you're not a private eye who decides to take the case and then I whip out my checkbook. But when you get through wrestling with the bureaucracy, let me know who won, okay?"

"Bureaucracy?" Herk said. "For—"

"Would you really prefer it," Cannon interrupted, "if policemen could do anything that struck them as a good idea, without pausing to ask permission?" When Herk said he had a point, he only nodded pleasantly and went on writing "Meyer" and a number on the back of a card so Silvestri wouldn't have to fight the hospital switchboard. Then he said if they didn't need him, he'd like to get started back to Long Valley early. He wanted to look in on Billy, who might not be sleeping well tonight.

Guy pocketed the card and rose to see his guest out. Watching them, Herk suddenly saw that there was a kind of resemblance between the two men. It couldn't be purely physical, because though they both had dark eyes and hair, Cannon was a little younger and a lot heavier and hairier. Then he knew what it was: Cannon looked like the catcher on a team the rangy Silvestri would be pitching for.

And the game was about to start, it seemed, when Silvestri returned and picked up Herkimer's "kit," without a word. But the delighted Herk couldn't resist: "Oh, wow. Great. That's really great, Guy."

Silvestri eyed his friend's face, full of happiness for the injured innocent Billy King, Cannon the valiant doctor, Silvestri the nonconformist bureaucrat—knowing Herk, it could be any combination of dramatic roles. The trouble was, they were all cause for alarm. Herk was loyal and enthusiastic, and that had made him the prime mover here: without him, maybe the timid Simons wouldn't have let Cannon into his walled castle, Cannon would have let himself be trussed by a "Hippocrates hangup," Silvestri could have forgotten that he didn't really believe in averages. But now the prime mover would somehow have to be made to stand still . . . "There's one condition," Silvestri said. "You'll have to stay out of this."

"What? I gather you're serious, but why, for God's sake?"

Because one thing that was already clear about those three deaths in Long Valley was that they were unlikely to have been caused by some wandering nut case. Whatever actually happened that November morning must have been a result of something somebody in the King family had done or been—which meant that there were darknesses to be explored. And two men blundering around in darkness ran a risk of taking each other for the enemy, especially if one of them was impulsive . . . Guy couldn't think of any way to turn that into a short answer, much less a tactful one, so he only said, "Believe it, that's all." There could be a whole spectrum of reasons, ranging from the protection of Billy to the protection of parties still unknown, for somebody in Long Valley to feel very strongly that the facts should remain buried with the Kings. Fear for impulsive Herk, out of his league in a dangerous game, lent weight to Silvestri's voice: "I mean it. If you make one move in this business, Herk, I'll drop it. Instantly."

"All right, I believe it. But *why*?"

It was fear for himself that got Guy's tongue this time. In the kind of battle this would be, everything depended on intelligence work—expert reconnaissance and a detailed advance knowledge of the terrain—by disciplined troops with sophisticated skills. One rash up-and-at-'em man on your own side could do you more damage than the enemy. "It's a matter of insurance," he said, suddenly inspired.

"Oh, wow. How silly can bureaucracy get?"

"Very silly. But you see I can't help it, don't you?"

"I guess so. But can't I even know what's going on?"

Oh wow, indeed. Herk was clearly entitled. But it would be bad enough as it was, with the clock ticking away Billy King's chances for reentry into the world—while Meyer Cannon tried not to say *Hurry, please hurry* because he knew what that was like. If you then added Herk, hanging around demanding progress reports . . . Guy relieved the pressure by suggesting a compromise: when Herkimer came to Buxford again, which would be in about a month, he would get a complete briefing and have all his questions answered by Lieutenant Silvestri. That was a promise. But there would have to be a promise in return . . .

"Okay. Okay, I promise to mix out. It's a deal."

They had a final brandy, to seal the deal. And then they parted, because it was Silvestri's chamber-music night and Herk had come to cover an adventurous production by Lambert's experimental theater.

Herk walked slowly toward the "gown" end of Buxford, thinking of Billy King, a small figure caught in quicksand. With Guy joining Meyer Cannon on the rope, there was now a good chance they'd haul Billy out before it swallowed him. Guy had taken a little time deciding— But it was funny, Herk thought then, that it wasn't the decision, but a bureaucratic idiocy turning up afterward that had started Guy's finger exercises going again. Even during all that gruesome medical talk, his hands had been doing nothing more remarkable than pouring more of the Napoli's excellent wine. And then, all of a sudden at the end, there they were wringing themselves again, over nothing that mattered.

Oh, well, Guy would be a whiz on his viola tonight, after all that exercising. And tomorrow, probably, he'd descend on Long Valley and start knocking heads together, bringing order out of chaos in the clickety-click way only Lieutenant Silvestri could. It would've been nice, Herk thought, to have been invited in instead of out, to watch the show instead of just hearing about it when it was all over. But if that's what was needed to get the action started, okay. If it meant a long run for Billy King, Herk was willing to miss opening night.

The mirror was sort of wavy, probably because it wasn't glass—nothing in this place seemed to be made of glass. Maybe that was because Cannon, who was the boss here, just didn't like glass? But anyway he could see himself well enough to miss his white helmet. It was such a surprise when he first saw it, after they took the kill module out of his head—in that other hospital, the one where they did have glass. By now it was a surprise whenever he saw the helmet wasn't there anymore and all his hair was back.

He'd probably get used to it if he just waited. Just waiting had turned out to be the right thing to do all along—he told himself, nodding carefully at his helmetless image—because it took an expert to be sure the module was really gone, all of it. If it wasn't, there was no way to know what combination of words or numbers (especially chanted backwards) the module was programmed to respond to. That was why Cannon, who was the top expert, had stayed away until it was for sure that no more dangerous rays could be set off. Even then, Cannon didn't have him brought over here, to the headquarters, right away.

At least, he was pretty sure a lot of time had gone by after that day when they didn't think he was awake yet and the doctor said to somebody, *We're in the clear now.* The doctor was brave, all right—he'd had support troops and all the equipment you could see in the OR, back at the other hospital, and he'd probably worn one of those special green protective suits and all that, but still he was the one who'd had to get close enough to the module to cut it out. And that was no safe thing to do, no way. Because even though they put him to sleep first that didn't mean the module wouldn't start sending out the killer rays. Like it did that time he was in school and he didn't even know it was turned on and still it—

"We're in the clear, now," Billy whispered urgently. "We're-in-the-clear-now, we'reintheclearnow." Three times always worked. It did now, by making him remember Cannon, who'd sent his lieutenant in against the module and then stayed away himself even after the lieutenant-doctor reported that we're in the clear. Because Cannon was the commander, and commanders can't afford front-line risks. So when Cannon thought it was okay to come around every day, that was absolute *proof* it was finally safe.

Besides, Billy had done his own testing, too. First he'd proved it couldn't operate through a shield: Miss Crabtree was perfectly safe behind the chess game (she kept rashly trying to come closer, but he had better sense than to let her), and he could really relax with Will, who always seemed to know how to keep Trad between them even if he himself sometimes slipped. In fact, it was because he'd seen that no harm came to Will that he'd decided to let Cannon in. That was scary, because Cannon was his good friend and it was the people he liked best who were in the greatest danger from the rays if they were still— But they weren't: it was okay, nothing had happened to Cannon. And the odds were, it would stay okay as long as he was careful. Think before every step. And go slow, very slow . . .

Williams didn't count as a new step, since he was Cannon's henchman. There was no way to be sure till tomorrow, because Williams had finished his shift and gone. But logically, there was no reason to think he could come to any harm . . .

Still, until he *knew,* maybe he'd better stay on guard. Billy glanced through the open bathroom door at his bed—it could get real chilly late at night, and the bed was warm. But if he went back to it, he was likely to fall asleep. And once asleep, he'd have no control . . .

He knew he didn't dare take that much of a risk. So finally he sat down on the bathroom floor just inside the door, where if he started falling asleep he'd bump into the door jamb. He made himself sit up straight with his back against the wall so he couldn't get too comfortable, but after a while he thought it would be all right to wrap his arms around his knees against the chill. Then he just concentrated on not letting his eyes close until morning, when Williams would come back and that would prove it was safe to go to sleep.

The aide named Hughes had a narrow escape: after getting the scare of his life when his light flashed on that empty bed, he spotted the small pajamaed figure on the bathroom floor. *Fast asleep, but bolt upright, mind you!* He picked the boy up and carried him to the bed—*out cold. Like, he never even stirred.* And then, just as he'd got the patient tucked in, who should show but Doc Cannon himself. *At that time of night, can you believe it?* He fussed around awhile, but there was nothing to see except the boy sleeping like a baby, so he finally split. And what Cannon didn't know wouldn't hurt Hughes—*even if the kid catches a cold, who would guess how?*

So it was close, but Hughes made it. Only, he could hardly wait to get off night shift next week. *It was just too weird, man.* Williams could have it, with Hughes's blessing.

PREPARING FOR WAR

4

THE TERRAIN
(April 22-24, Long Valley)

From Dr. Cannon's notes

Extract, letter from Miss C., Apr. 20: . . . that silly knight move; but it was already on its way.

When Billy's move arrived today and I discovered that he had failed to see his opportunity to "clobber" me, I admit to a moment's selfish glee. However, I did also discern that the matter might have moment and should be reported to you. I am reasonably certain that you may take Billy's action to be genuine inadvertence; but of course a possibility exists that he is devising some strategy in which this move is a "gimmick."

I emphasize that I was not attempting to "rig" the game when I provided him with that—happily, missed—opportunity. I simply "goofed." Indeed, it was an error not uncharacteristic of my game; Billy has in the past occasionally profited because of similar "booboos."

As you are perhaps aware, Doctor Cannon, I add brief comments to the postcards bearing my moves, although Billy's still contain only his move and his signature. Unless you instruct me to the contrary, I shall continue on my course. I remain eager to perform any service you consider helpful to Billy's recovery.

Meyer Cannon eyed the swirling capitals of Miss Crabtree's

elegant Spencerian hand and considered the aesthetic satisfactions of the circle. It was the only satisfaction around. Billy had apparently failed to remember something from his past—something useful and not containing any dangerous memories. The doctor prepared glumly to file Miss Crabtree, said to be cordially his. But then the groves of quotation marks on the page caught his eye, and he couldn't help grinning. For Miss C. might keep careful typographical distance between herself and colloquialisms, but look at the way she'd forged ahead bravely, willing to use even the very latest slang if that's what it took to communicate with young Meyer Cannon . . .

He dialed her number, thinking *Miss C., you're*—he had to fish for it, but he finally got it—*the cat's pajamas, that's what you are.* Waiting for her to answer, he had time to sober appropriately. She lived alone in a big house and she walked slowly, so it would take her a while to put down her morocco-bound volume of—what? *Pendennis,* maybe—and get to her front hall. Where the telephone stood all by itself on a marble-topped Victorian table, managing to seem a marvelous modern invention too new to become just a part of the furniture.

Miss C. was at home. And discursive, but that was her natural style: as old ladies go, she was comparatively laconic. So it didn't take very long for Meyer to learn that the move Billy should have made was R-K1, but he'd moved his knight instead of the rook. Which piece has another name: *B. blew move involving Castle,* Dr. Cannon scrawled, just in case it proved significant when he had time to think about it.

Miss Crabtree returned to her parlor just as Trixie came through the swing door from the kitchen, carrying a tray. The teacher helped herself to the single glass of dark-gold sherry, ignoring the two tall tumblers of diet-free soda for the others.

Trixie said urgently, "We could do it without Twirl, couldn't we? All it would take is some organizing. They'd crumble in a minute, you know they would."

Miss Crabtree rolled the almond taste of the sherry on her tongue, because in trying times it was necessary to enjoy anything enjoyable. And she could afford to keep the girl waiting: oracles have privileges. But they also must deliver pronouncements. So Miss Crabtree put the delicate glass down and told Trixie flatly, "Any such action would be utter folly."

"But, Miss C.—" The small, breathless voice had to rest, it seemed, before it could produce more words. Then it came up with fighting words: "I didn't expect that from you, Miss C. I'm beginning to think Twirl doesn't really give a f— doesn't care about Billy at all. But you—"

The unattractive youth sprawled unattractively in the far corner of the sofa emitted a string of syllables signifying that Trixie had better be careful about putting down You-know-who. May Crabtree sat with her spine against the back of her chair, as she had been taught more than half a century ago, and faced the depressing fact that Trixie was not actually "beginning to think" anything at all. For she not only hadn't asked for Miss Crabtree's reasons, she hadn't even looked at the content of the statement. She examined neither Why nor What, only Who: it was still, for her, only alliances and confrontations, and behind those, bad magic and good magic. What disturbed her about finding Miss C. in apparent coalition with Twirl was that it required her to make decisions of degree—did Miss C. raise Twirl's credibility or did he lower hers, and in either case, how much? Waiting for the girl to finish dealing with the interruption, Miss Crabtree decided that if her magic was still more powerful than the regrettable Twirl's, the uneasy coalition might serve as a teaching tool. Unless, of course, Trixie decided to depose the oracle instead of, as the young said, "getting the message."

The oaf in the corner had been given his quietus now, and Trixie was awaiting more words of wisdom. Miss Crabtree nodded—carefully, because the doughnut-shaped hairpiece pinned to the top of her head was easily dislodged by sudden moves—and proceeded with the verbal sleight of hand necessary to maintain her oracle status while offering arguments, which is what oracles don't do. "I shall say just this: only Billy's enemy would have an interest in his removal from the hospital."

The shock tactics shocked, but not into thought. "From the nut-house, you mean. The fuzz—the police—shoved him in there for their own good, and you know it. Because he was in their way. Like in—"

"Please. If you are about to point out that confining inconvenient folk to mental hospitals is a device of tyrants"— the old faded-blue long-sighted eyes took in the signs that the oracle's status had been shored up: she had guessed rightly, it seemed, what the girl had been about to say—"you may spare yourself the effort. Information may be harmful when it is applied irrelevantly."

The sound from the sofa came again, and the girl seated on the hassock turned her head to deliver a brief, ugly imperative. Then she turned back, her long hair swinging in a lovely ripple. Miss Crabtree thought of the lines about wind in a wheatfield— *as if a thousand girls with golden hair/ would rise from where they slept and go away*—that she'd been reciting to youngsters for so long. And, too unquestioningly, she reproved herself now: actually, the color was like this, more tawny than the simple "golden" led you to believe. She took a moment to celebrate silently the holy duty to look for yourself, and look again. Then she went to work at teaching the girl to look even once. "In short," she said briskly, "to demand the freeing of a dissident in the Soviet Union makes sense. To shout 'Free Billy King' does not."

Trixie's eyes, artfully made up to look even larger than they were, fastened on the teacher reproachfully. "Billy's in there because they wanted him out of the way, so he couldn't talk. And that's like in Russia."

"The Soviet Union. Or the U.S.S.R., if you will. As for your observation, it may be correct so far as it applies to the intent of certain people—"

"Like Voorhees. Billy's so-called lawyer."

Miss Crabtree suppressed, with the ease and speed of experience, her rising impatience. Mr. Voorhees was in fact Billy's lawyer, no "so-called" about it: what the girl meant, doubtless, was that he didn't seem to be Billy's advocate. Miss Crabtree agreed with that observation: indeed she thought Voorhees would probably be delighted with any attempt to dislodge Billy from his present status. But she didn't see any point in conjectures about Derek Voorhees. The primary goal was to coax Trixie into thinking—instead of pointing to villains. "It is a mistake to stop with observation," Miss Crabtree said firmly. "The fact is, is it not, that those who assigned Billy to the state hospital are not necessarily participants in all the consequences of that act?" Too difficult, even though she'd stressed the word "assigned." There was no sign that the student was thinking, so Miss Crabtree boosted her up the next step by hand. "Now, what can be said of the person responsible for Billy's fate at this moment?"

"If you mean like Meyer Cannon—"

"I mean precisely Doctor Cannon. Have you any reason to believe he is in league with anyone who wishes to keep Billy silent?"

The girl bent her head. "No. I guess Cannon's straight."

"Very well. He is also treating Billy for an illness. What, then, may we conclude from that?"

"That Billy's really sick?"

"And?"

"And that he—belongs there?" The words proved too much for Trixie. "But he wasn't," she said hoarsely, "you know he wasn't. Before they—" The tears came, and she buried her face in slim, grimy hands.

Miss Crabtree's hands were very clean. They tightened on the arms of her chair as much as arthritic knuckles would allow. "But now he is." Her voice was unsteady. "Now Billy needs what he is receiving, where he is. I suggest to you that this is central, and all other aspects—including whose aims are also incidentally served—are nonessential. Susan understood that. She'd gone beyond praising heroes and berating villains. And her achievements must not be wasted, all her labors of—" Miss Crabtree stopped suddenly and then said in quite another voice, "Child, child. Come here." The girl came, kneeling beside the seated woman, hiding herself away in the voluminous skirt of Miss Crabtree's dress.

The knotty hand stroked the long, smooth hair. " 'I am not resigned to the shutting away of loving hearts in the hard ground,' " Miss Crabtree quoted. It was not a suitable poem for her classes—too prosy, too likely to encourage the young to ignore the strictures of rhyme and meter—but it spoke for her now, performing the highest duty of poetry. *Into the darkness they go, the wise and the lovely* sounded in her head, and she wept with the weeping child. " 'I know,' " she said aloud. " 'But I do not approve. And I am not resigned.' " Then, with difficulty, she got the embroidered handkerchief out of the pocket of her skirt and wiped the girl's flushed wet face.

Several Toll House cookies and another diet cola later, Trixie left—along with the rogue and peasant slave who had been permitted to provide transport for her. Miss Crabtree let the curtain fall back over her parlor window, preferring not to see the ungainly truck that served—illicitly, too—as Beauty's chariot. She carried the tray into the kitchen and left it there, excusing herself from dealing with the glasses right now. She was terribly, terribly tired—maybe because she really was too old and frail to serve as the lone defender of a society under siege. But at least the day's effort, if hard and painful, had been effective: Billy King's slim lifeline, threatened at once by the yearning folly of those who wished him well and by the machinations of those who didn't, would hold for now. And perhaps that poor anguished girl had begun to learn that evil men may do the right thing though for the wrong reason—a difficult lesson. Trixie was too young to be confronted with the limitations of simple ardor; but then, she was also too young to have been confronted with the loss of Susan—who had herself been much too young for what she had had to learn.

Never mind; what mattered was, Billy could still be saved. *That* much of Susan's work could still be carried on. To let a lust for revenge impair the attaining of that objective would be . . .

Shaken with rage anyhow, Miss Crabtree held to the smooth cold edge of the kitchen sink and wept for the living children and the dead one. And finally for the knowledge that rage was exhausting but produced nothing nourishing. What sense did it make, this railing against the adults whose follies had brought death to Susan and darkness of the mind to Billy? The perpetrators were also victims; dead, they were beyond guilt or anger. The advice to refrain from speaking ill of the dead was designed for the living, who had better things to do than waste themselves in helpless fury.

She swiped at her eyes with her swollen knuckles and told herself that though she couldn't seem to manage charity very well, pragmatism should be easier. And even the horrid alliance pragmatism currently demanded could be borne, if not with ease. She turned to climb slowly to her bedroom to rest for the next battle in the long defense of reason against mindlessness—like dangerous games of follow-the-leader, and stylized questions that produced easy answers.

"Miss Crabtree, to begin with," Meyer Cannon said into the telephone. "She certainly knows Billy well. And she's a sharp old lady, observant and articulate."

Silvestri raised his eyebrows. Clearly, Cannon's list of people Guy should talk to out in Long Valley was not going to be the same as the one he had already compiled from news stories and the demands of protocol. "Miss May Crabtree?" He found the name on another list, of Long Valley High School teachers. "Billy's English teacher, right?"

"His sister's too, I think."

And probably guaranteed pro-Billy, Silvestri suspected dourly. "Why not his math teacher? I'd have thought—"

"I know. But he doesn't seem to have had anything to do with Miss Dyer outside of class, and she hasn't written to him since he's been here." The doctor paused. "She's quite young. And this is only her second year in town."

"I see." Guy did, at that: new teachers usually got two-year contracts. And if young Miss Dyer was interested in having hers renewed, she might well be shy about showing interest in the boy Long Valley considered a monster. "Okay, Miss Crabtree, then." But Billy had had no English class on his last day at school, Guy remembered. "You talked to the teachers who saw Billy that morning, didn't you, Meyer?"

"Sure. If you can hang on, I'll get my notes."

Guy said he could hang on. While he waited, he added Miss Crabtree to the list of people he would be seeing—if he got this venture cleared at the State House, and after he'd done all he could at this end. Protocol demanded that John Vesey, Long Valley's police chief, be contacted by the lieutenant himself: Vesey might not feel terribly cooperative to begin with, so Silvestri couldn't afford to send an underling. Also on his own list for formal reasons were Derek Voorhees, Billy's attorney of record, and Claud Dozier, the neighbor who was the last person known to have seen Mr. and Mrs. King alive. But the people at the school were another matter: Josh Roberts, the custodian, could probably be skipped altogether; and if Billy had behaved normally in his first class, which was Latin . . .

Billy had, according to the returned Dr. Cannon. Scratch Mrs. Armour, Latin, 8:40 to 9:20. The second class was math, 9:30 to 10:10—that was Miss Dyer, and Billy had been there, all right: Herk had mentioned a math quiz. But there was a twenty-minute recess after that. Guy thought it was hardly enough, but he asked about it conscientiously—and then dismissed it when he learned that Billy had had a heavy basketball date during that day's recess. The third period began at 10:30. "History, with Mr. Poley," Guy read. "You talked to him, too?" That was the class Billy had walked out on. And it was sometime before that class that he'd told one of his friends he didn't feel good.

"Sure, he's my neighbor." Cannon's voice held a smile. "Just about everybody talked to him, including the school principal. It turned out Poley was kind of sloppy about calling the roll. My guess is, he was hung over."

"Oh. Would Mr. Poley be a useful source for—"

"I'd doubt it, Guy. He's a nice enough fellow, young and good-looking and apparently quite popular with the kids. My wife thinks he's an inspired teacher, too—I don't know whether I mentioned it, but she's still relatively new in the United States, and she's been studying for her citizenship exam. So she's kind of a connoisseur of American-history teachers, and according to her, Jim Poley can really light the subject up."

"But he didn't for Billy?"

"Well, Poley is more the older kids' idol. Especially the girls. And his kind of teaching generally appeals more to the kids who need to have their interest stirred up. Whereas kids like Billy eat up curriculum: they don't need frills, they could learn history just as well if it was still a string of dates and battles."

"Yes," Guy said, to stem the flow of information he didn't need. (Except as a novice parent—which kind of schoolboy would Anthony G. Silvestri turn out to be, he wondered.) He abandoned Mr. Poley, and Billy's school life in general, to turn to a question that stood all by itself on his list: did Meyer happen to know whether, when Billy was brought to the local hospital's emergency room, his right hand and arm were okay?

"I do know," Cannon said—while his unspoken *Why?* transmitted itself just as clearly. "I reviewed all the reports for that meeting at Lambert the other day. The answer is, there were no injuries to his hand or arm—unless you want to count a couple of mostly healed abrasions, the sort of thing you'd expect to find on a physically active youngster. It's all in the record in detail, because the police asked about it, too."

"Did they. Do you know why?"

"Well, I gather it had something to do with a test to see whether he'd fired a gun—I guess you'd know that test?"

"Yes."

"There was a minor hassle, because of the head injury—the medical people objected to any extra handling of the patient. But Derek Voorhees apparently negotiated a compromise, and the cops did their test. On both hands, actually. But only the right hand proved positive."

"Yes," Silvestri said again. Absently, because it was not the test results but the surrounding circumstances that provided food for thought. "If Billy was unconscious, he couldn't have asked for Voorhees." He drew a box around that name on his list. "So how did he happen to be there?"

"Oh well, this is a small town, Guy—the cops know who knows who, and so forth. The Kings had no relatives, and they knew Voorhees was Julius King's best friend."

"I understand." It wasn't hard: even in Buxford, the police knew who knew who and so forth, though maybe not to the same extent. "Do you know why the test was done on both the boy's hands?"

"Seems funny, doesn't it? Maybe they just didn't know he was right-handed. Though you'd think—But I guess things were pretty frantic right then."

What was it you would think, Guy wondered. Meyer could be suppressing a professional criticism: *you'd think* the medicos should've been able to tell, maybe by the muscle development or something? Or had he been about to say that *you'd think* Billy's father's friend would know the boy well enough to supply that information? Guy underscored the name "John Vesey" and added a question mark. Because it was Long Valley's police chief who'd ordered the test done on both hands—maybe because he too had concluded that that unlikely shot, back across the *center* of the head, made sense only if a right-handed Billy had had to use his left hand. Otherwise a right-handed person who wanted to shoot himself in the head would put the gun to his right temple, just as Herk had done when he'd acted it out in the Napoli Restaurant—where Meyer Cannon, demonstrating the location of Billy's head wound a little later, had been forced into an obviously awkward position of his right arm. But if Chief Vesey had also reasoned that way, why had he stopped. Guy dropped his speculations—out of respect for Meyer Cannon, who'd waited quietly, forbearing to satisfy his own curiosity (which Herk never could have managed!)—and asked his final question: he had the names of Billy's friends, Terry and Andy. But didn't Billy's sister have a best friend, too?

"Yes, Laura Bradlock. They call her Trixie." Cannon hesitated. "Look, Terry and Andy were pretty shaken by all this. They're just kids, remember. I don't know this Trixie, but she's only seventeen and—"

"It's all right, Meyer. I have a kind of—specialist—on my staff. He'll know how to talk to the girl. If it turns out we have to."

Cannon said apologetically that he hadn't meant— Then he acknowledged that maybe he *had* meant, but he was reassured. The two men exchanged promises and thanks and hung up.

Guy added "Laura Bradlock—Trixie" to his list of interviews to be assigned to Sergeant Alonso—assuming, that is, that Lieutenant Silvestri did actually march up to the Governor's Commission appointment to cover what amounted to a closed case in Long Valley. That was the only way he could do it. But whether he wanted to depended on how convincing was what had "jumped out" at him, as Herk had predicted, from his investigations thus far.

Guy leaned back in his chair and let himself "think

Herk" on a simple problem: given a few basic facts, construct a reasonably credible scenario, and never mind worrying about proof. Actually only one fact was really needed, and it was probably solid—Claud Dozier had seen and spoken to Mr. and Mrs. King at 8:05 that November morning. Dozier was either telling the truth or lying, but he couldn't be seriously mistaken. So, until some reason emerged for the neighbor to have concocted the story, it could be assumed to be true.

Taking that as the starting point and adding Herk-type liberties like the assumption that Billy King had gone off to school leaving his parents and sister alive, Guy found that with no holds barred on the play of imagination, quite a lively scenario could be constructed. The laundry package, which had been featured heavily in the script starring Billy King as a multiple murderer, also played a part here. But this time the central figure was Harry Moody, routeman for the Eagle Laundry.

Moody, it seemed, had been granted a presumption of innocence denied to Billy. The uncorroborated statement that he'd arrived late at the King house was accepted without question, and nobody, apparently, had even asked Harry Moody why he was late. Or how late 9:45 was. Considering that nobody expected a laundryman to keep an exact schedule, Mrs. Dozier's inquiring for him at 9:30 could mean he was already quite late then . . .

So in a brand-new scenario, Harry Moody was not late but rang the Kings' doorbell at, say, 9:00, and was admitted, bringing in the laundry package later found in the front hall. After that, you could have your choice of Herk-type dramas, depending on how well Harry Moody knew Callie King. Or since "double-barreled" theories were apparently acceptable in Long Valley, it didn't really matter whether Moody was an illicit lover or a sex nut. Thus you could have Susan, who wasn't normally at home when the laundryman came to the house, precipitating a crisis by interrupting a passionate scene between her mother and Moody. And/or an innocent and virtuous Mrs. King discoursing politely with the laundryman until the unexpected appearance of her pretty daughter—who'd been dressed only in pajamas when she died—suddenly unhinged Moody's unstable mind.

Either way, if Julius King returned home at just that moment and rushed to the defense of his wife and/or daughter, that explained the gun. Because one of the things that had jumped out at Lieutenant Silvestri, if not also at Herk, was the lack of evidence that Billy King ever had any acquaintance with the murder weapon. So certainly King, or even Mrs. King, taking the .38 revolver from its hiding place was a more logical assumption than anything yet offered. This wild and woolly soap opera, Silvestri conceded, would win no Critics' Circle awards. But it fit the framework better than the story swiftly concocted last November around an unconscious boy who'd tried to kill himself (though it did seem somebody on the Long Valley force—presumably its chief—had had some doubts). And finally, this scenario disposed of the 9:20 phone call from Mrs. Wilder, inexplicably unanswered if the killings happened only after Billy came home from school more than an hour later, for Harry Moody, standing in a welter of blood and death, would hardly answer the phone. What he would have done is beat it out of there and resume his delivery rounds—which he must have done, or even the Long Valley police presumably would've noticed . . .

Silvestri hauled back his hostility, which was apparently raring to go. His own foolish scenario wasn't exactly a replacement for what they'd come up with in Long Valley, he reminded himself. For one thing, it left unanswered some questions that had remained unanswered then. Like, why didn't Julius King keep his 8:30 appointment? And why would Mrs. King phone the high school (assuming she really did), when she should have supposed her husband was already there and could report Susan's illness? But it did demonstrate, almost effortlessly, a reasonable doubt about Billy King's guilt.

And that the Long Valley police must have known that. Maybe Herk's charge of "railroading" was too strong, but what about his scornful observation that the time of the deaths had been established as, in effect, whenever Billy was available? And what about—Guy gave up sawing on the reins and let himself think what he hoped he would never have to say aloud—the whole overly casual assumption of attempted suicide, in the interests of which all reasonable and simple explanations had been swept aside for monstrous and elaborate ones? So that you ignore a commonsense reason for Billy King's feeling ill at school—like he was coming down with the same bug his sister had—and thus surround his decision to go home with an air of psychic disturbance. Which you'd need because, even though the exact times involved were still a little uncertain, what was obvious was that there really hadn't been much time for an innocent normal boy to work his way up to suicide.

True, Billy had walked in on a sight that would unnerve a veteran infantryman. But why not assume he'd behave in any of the usual ways people did in shocking situations—like throwing up, or crying? Or, perhaps the most likely one, running? Maybe a hysterical young boy was not likely to think of picking up the phone and calling the cops. But wasn't he especially likely to do something physical, like run—whether to escape or to get help— either up the road to the Dozier house or down the road to the gas station?

All right, Billy had not run; he'd picked up the gun. And he'd fired it. But attempted suicide wasn't really the only explanation of that, particularly not when the doctors doubted it and the physical evidence was dubious enough to have set Chief Vesey wondering. Meyer Cannon had been handed a patient officially tagged as suicidal, but that was because when the court disposed of Billy, nobody, including Billy's lawyer, had offered any information to the contrary. The police presumably hadn't developed any, despite their chief's early doubts.

That couldn't be because they were too busy, Guy decided

sourly, since they seemed to him to have done little except talk to the press. For example, about the laundry package—which didn't actually mean anything except that Billy had gone into the house, which was obvious. The inflation of that into The Big Clue was almost certainly the media's doing, but Lieutenant Silvestri had an uncharitable impression that it had been welcomed by the police, doubtless because it offered an image of brisk detecting. Somehow he found that particularly galling—maybe because it made Herk's rhetoric about "honorable cops" seem not so overblown . . .

Okay. Even if he got his own anger out of the way and got objective instead of building a defense for Billy King or agonizing about ideals of justice, what Guy came up with looked like—at a minimum—enough bungling and/or ego trips so that the taxpayers were entitled to have the whole mess investigated. But, considering the nature of the problem—he concluded, looking grim—it would be better if his data came through unofficial as well as official channels. So, before he departed for the governor's office, he put in two calls—one to tell Sergeant Alonso to stand by, the other to a TV producer who might be able to come up with a fast survey of how things had looked from outside officialdom in Long Valley last November.

5
INTELLIGENCE
(April 26, Long Valley and Boston)

"Pay dirt!" Herk proclaimed. "Admit it, Meyer. We finally struck pay dirt. You might even say"—laughter did nothing to mute his excitement—"the mother lode."

Cannon held the phone at arm's length, but the vibrancy, not the volume, of the voice was what was making things on the desk seem to jump and wiggle. "I don't know, Herk." His heart wasn't in the role of killjoy, so he added, "I'm sorry. But I'm just not sure what it means yet."

"Oh, wow, how objective can you *get*? Here the kid deliberately tosses the mother out of the picture—and you say you're not sure what it means? Don't you fellows even acknowledge Freud anymore?"

"Sure. But I don't have to be limited by him, any more than you have to write like Shakespeare. And . . . well, it's not as simple as you make it sound." For Billy had not "tossed out" Prince Trad's mother, he had substituted somebody else. "Put Will on, okay? I want to get a clearer idea of how much change was involved." Cannon waited, rereading the underscored sentence in his copy of Billy's last letter to Simons. The "pay dirt" Herk was insisting on occurred in a dependent clause in a sentence making quite another point: . . . *because when Trad and*

*Trila set up a new kingdom on Jocalia they didnt have any
cell-starter kits with them either . . .*

"Doc? Herk said it was too important to wait, we have to
call you." The note of apology made Will Simons's voice wispier
than ever.

Meyer set about reassuring him, while taking note of his
distress: something would have to be done about restraining
Herk. "It was quite all right to call," Dr. Cannon said. And yes,
he had a copy of the letter. But he didn't have *Four-Seas Land*
handy, so if Will could give him a kind of rundown on what
actually happened in the episode Billy was now—er—revising?
"Has he changed anything besides the character? And how
important was it that it was Queen—uh—"

"Cybilla. It was after Fentry seized the throne. Killing the
king, Trad's father. Trad was away, and by the time he got
home, Fentry had captured Princess Trila, Trad's sister, and was
holding her as a hostage."

"But not Queen Cybilla?"

"Well, not exactly, Doc—he was trying to get the queen to
marry him, you see. To legitimize him as king." Simons
stopped, because of a choking sound from Long Valley,
Massachusetts.

"Excuse me," Cannon said hastily. He should have better
control—but he'd simply been overcome at discovering how
right his Shakespeare-Freud analogy had been. Apparently the
heirs of both browsed among their legacies, using whatever
seemed handy at the moment. "Please, go on."

If Will was aware that some aspects of his plot might sound
familiar to *Hamlet* audiences, his voice didn't reveal it. "Well,
Queen Cybilla was Fentry's captive but he was wooing her, so
she wasn't in the tower with Princess Trila. That's how come
the queen got loose when Trad attacked the castle."

"But his sister didn't get loose, I take it."

"No, Fentry put everything he had into the defense of the
tower, and Trad got clobbered—lost several of his best men,

tons of equipment, and so on. But meanwhile Queen Cybilla got hold of a 'ship, so she and Trad fled to this uninhabited planet, Jocalia, to set up a new kingdom." Will added, on a clearly defensive note, "They got Princess Trila back, you know. In *Land of Trad*."

"I see. What Billy's done is make a simple substitution—of Trad's sister for his mother—is that it? But the main point is about survival without elaborate technology."

"That's right, Doctor. The chapter we've been discussing has Zak and his squad marooned on a strange planet. That's what Billy's talking about."

"Then it doesn't make any difference to his point in the letter, does it? That it was actually Prince Trad's mother who was with him on the planet Jocalia."

"No, his mother isn't ailing or aged, if that's what you mean. But Herk says—"

"Yes. I'm interested in what *you* thought, Will. Before Herk dropped in. You read Billy's letter and—what? Did you notice what he'd done?"

"Well, yes, I noticed it, but"—the thin voice sounded suddenly defiant—"like you'd notice a typo or a misspelled word. I just didn't think it was any big thing. I mean," Will added hastily, "I would've called it to your attention, sure. But—"

"But not because you yourself thought it was significant, is that it?"

"That's right."

Cannon heard the sigh behind those words and smiled: Simons was standing up to the fiercely positive Herkimer, but it wasn't easy for him. "When you wrote *Four-Seas Land*, Will, do you remember why you made it Queen Cybilla and not the princess who fled with Trad to Jocalia?"

"Sure. It was a plot necessity."

"I don't think I understand," said Cannon, who rather thought he did. But this would let Will argue with Herk, which he didn't seem able to do on his own.

"Well, to begin a new civilization, Trad needed things the queen had—like experience and knowledge and all. I mean, Trad isn't very old, you know. And Princess Trila's even younger. So if I set them on Jocalia to start from scratch, it'd be just babes in the wood, sort of." Will talked easily now, words coming at his command like obedient pets. "That would send the thing off in all sorts of other directions—like, they'd have to be rescued, since they don't have Queen Cybilla's special powers. And a pretty young girl in Fentry's hands is more dramatic. Anyhow, look at the mess I'd be in if it was Princess Trila on Jocalia. I'd've had to come up with *two* love interests instead of just the Jocalian girl Trad meets, and—oh," Will said wearily, "a million complications I don't need."

Meyer, sunk under the flow of complications he didn't need, said, "Yes, I see."

"But look, Doctor, it really isn't like—I mean, all these reasons—well, I'm just sort of making them up, in a way. Because you asked me. But I didn't really think like that then, you know. I didn't sit there saying, should I make it his mother or his sister, and why. And all that."

"I know," Cannon soothed. Doubtless analytical pieces had been written about Simons's Prince Trad series—nothing that sold so many copies could go wholly unremarked in the review journals—but Will had presumably never read them. And Herkimer had probably not bothered to turn his critical talents on his friend's books before. So this must be Will's first experience with the gap between the storyteller and the literature professor . . .

"Look, I'm not Shakespeare. I don't write about universal human symbols and all that. Everybody's getting too *fancy* here." Will spoke like a man at bay, attacking the numerous and powerful enemies closing in on him—violently, but without much hope. "The people in my books— Well, it's not what they are that matters, it's what they do." Behind him, Herk's voice rumbled in the room. "Ah, you just don't understand," Will said, to nobody in particular.

But not to everybody, Cannon thought. "Does Billy understand?" he asked.

"Sure." Simons's relief was obvious. "I know he argues with me a lot, but he—he knows—" He stopped, uncertain or unwilling to define what Billy knew.

Meyer Cannon didn't need to. "That's all that really matters, Will. I want you to remember that," he said, putting the weight of his authority behind the effort to restore innocence. Feeling like a boy who had wantonly disturbed a bird's nest, he set everything back in place as best he could. Only when he thought Simons—who was, fortunately, more adaptable than a bird—was likely to be able to sing again did Meyer ask to speak to Herkimer.

"Hello, Meyer. I get six strokes of the cane, I suppose."

Cannon sighed. "It's not that you're not right—there *are* more universalities in his characters than he knows."

"There have to be. One success without it, okay. But not over and over again, not unless—"

"All right, Herk. But not now and not here, you understand me?"

"By golly, I get invited out more often than a debutante." Without explanation, Herkimer burst out laughing.

Too exasperated to wonder what was so funny, Meyer warned, "Look, I don't want you jiggling my instruments. They're delicate."

"I'm sorry." Herk added "I really am," but his rueful voice was enough. "I won't do it again. And I hope I haven't—well, messed up your readings."

Cannon said earnestly, "As a matter of fact, it's been useful." He left it at that, and the chastened Herkimer didn't probe. So by the time Meyer hung up, he still had, safely tucked away in his head, the useful clue a Will Simons unexpectedly stirred to literary analysis had provided Dr. Cannon.

Silvestri was not kept waiting long in the impressive offices in Boston, but he fretted anyhow. Restless, he helped himself to a copy of the list of State House doings scheduled for this week and studied it with all the desperate attention of a waiting diner reading the label on a catsup bottle.

Except that this was immediately rewarding: Derek Voorhees, Guy learned, was one of the witnesses scheduled to testify (translation: to lobby) at a hearing today on a proposed land-use law. So if Guy lucked out, he could begin as soon as he finished here—assuming, of course, that there were no problems. His tension somewhat eased, he read on peacefully, even discovering, with some interest, that the Massachusetts League for Secondary Schools would be having a get-together in Room 410 next week. Then the door of the sanctum opened for him.

There were no problems, but it was a slowish business. It could have been quick, if only everything had been up to the quiet, bright-eyed, mild-as-milk man known as Mike to nearly everybody, although nobody alive could really be said to know him well. Not even the governor, whose career Mike tended the way a professional gardener tends a garden. To Mike, Guy Silvestri was an exotic plant growing in a corner of the governor's garden like a camellia in Massachusetts—not the usual thing for that climate, and thus requiring sheltering and careful attention, but what a triumph for the garden show! So Mike was interested in coddling the local hero and symbol of integrity who meant pure-white sweet-smelling flowers to show off at election time; Mike was inclined to say yes whenever possible, genially and promptly, to whatever Lieutenant Silvestri had in mind.

The genial Mike saw no real difficulties now: if Silvestri had a hankering to ride to the rescue of some kid in the nuthouse, you could count on him to do it quietly—and in fact, he was popular enough with the local press so he could even refuse them information without their lynching him for it. Suppose it did get noticed, though. With the public now muttering about how much juvenile hoodlums got away with, how could it hurt the governor if word got out that he'd sent a man to look into the operation of the juvenile laws? It would be better to keep it quiet, because what Silvestri was asking permission to do wasn't exactly that and he might well get difficult if a lot of puffery happened. But the lieutenant knew the difference between an enemy and a windmill. So, though he'd be unhappy, he'd probably concede that calling a coat a garment lacked specificity, but as long as Mike didn't call the coat a pair of pants, he wasn't lying.

Thus, even if the worst came to the worst—which Mike always allowed for—and the whole bit got into the media and had to be turned into what it wasn't meant to be, Silvestri probably wouldn't get sore enough to quit. That was an outcome Mike couldn't afford. But the odds were that Silvestri could in fact operate in the quiet he wanted. And that if the lieutenant, who had no shortage of smart-cells, thought this Billy King had been handed a raw deal, the kid really had. In which case, wrong would be righted, and by an emissary of the governor whose bold eye and protective arm encompassed even a far corner of the Commonwealth. And if that happened, Silvestri couldn't object to Mike's taking the lid off for the media—the kid would be entitled to have his innocence proclaimed far and wide, wouldn't he?

What took time was waiting while the governor caught up with what his right-hand man had seen at once. Guy rather liked the governor: once he'd recognized that the silver-haired, velvet-voiced man who turned oratorical passions on and off with the ease of a con man was indeed for real—that the tilt of the head once acquired in order to hide a double chin was now as natural as anyone else's natural posture—it was not hard to like the governor. And even to respect him in the same way support troops respect those who sooner or later have to get out there under the guns. Many things Guy thought desirable were able to happen because the governor was in office. And, though desirable ends didn't justify *any* means, neither did those ends have to be arrived at by means Guy Silvestri found personally attractive. So he smiled and chatted and waited patiently, and then at last got to shake hands and accept the governor's regards to Silvestri's good lady.

Silvestri's wife's name was Kate, and the governor wouldn't have been allowed to forget it—it would have been slipped into the conversation for him to pick up, long before they got to good-lady time—if his right-hand man didn't know Guy didn't mind the governor's forgetting. Mike worked twelve hours a day, six days a week, even when there wasn't any crisis; so he wasn't any more of a mind to waste time than Guy was. Thus, when the governor had made his gracious exit, what was left to do was disposed of briskly: what did the lieutenant need? Predictably, Silvestri's needs were few and practical— time, his own and a few of his staff people's, and a little smoothing of the ways so records would be readily available and the Long Valley police would prove cooperative. The genial Mike urged the lieutenant to call if he turned out to need something else and wrote down the names of Sergeant Alonso and detectives Rubin and Merchant, who must find doors open when they came on the lieutenant's missions. Then the two men parted, without shaking hands, and each went off to do what he was good at.

The timing hadn't worked out exactly, so it took a little more patience before Silvestri managed to encounter Derek Voorhees leaving the committee hearing. The Long Valley lawyer was certainly one of those with whom ways could be smoothed by Mike, but there wouldn't be any need, not if Silvestri refrained from surface-breaking questions. He introduced himself and explained his "little assignment" to survey recent juvenile cases. He'd noticed, he said, that Mr. Voorhees had been stuck with a rather messy one—that multiple homicide in Long Valley about six months ago?—and the lieutenant wondered whether Mr. Voorhees could find some time to talk to him about it.

" 'Stuck' is the right word, you can believe it. I'm more than willing to help, Lieutenant." Voorhees's smile was like his handshake, big and vigorous, sending messages of earnest palship. "But I don't know how much good I can do you, because actually that was my one and only venture into juvenile proceedings."

"I gathered you were more or less drafted," Guy said, wondering whether this heartiness with its undercurrent of pleading was the man's natural manner.

"In a manner of speaking, I was. But Julius King—the boy's father—was my very good friend." The handsome face clouded with an oversized sorrow that reminded Guy of the governor's staginess. Except that he had to remind himself now of what he'd remembered without effort about the governor, that artificiality didn't necessarily mean insincerity. "Maybe the closest friend I had in the world," the voice went on, its timbre suitably altered.

"I'm very sorry."

"Thank you. But—well, loss is part of life, isn't it." A gesture indicated that no reply was required. "So naturally I had to do what I could for Julius's son. Even though . . ."

"Of course." The pause had been an invitation to interrupt. Only, it was like being invited to contribute to a political campaign, and it produced the same kind of reaction in Silvestri. "Are you still acting for Billy King, Mr. Voorhees?"

"Oh, call me Dick. Everybody does."

Immediately, Guy knew everybody didn't—and that everybody was told to. He said nothing, freed of the necessity to reply because they had to go through the door single-file.

"Yes, you could say I am," Voorhees went on, when they were side by side again, on the wide, steep State House steps. "But there isn't actually much activity in the case anymore." His smiling gaze turned upward to acknowledge the sun with approval. "Mmm, feel that. I'm a native son, so I know better than to trust it, this early. Better use it while we can, though, don't you think so?"

Silvestri was also a native son of Massachusetts, where people wait through long winters and snatch at spring, but warily. So far as he knew, he completely shared the other man's stated attitude toward sunlight in April. And yet something in Silvestri was busily rejecting even that tiny alliance: the bald, quite unfair truth seemed to be that there was just something about candid, hearty call-me-Dick that Guy wanted to be no buddy of. Disliking himself, he stood there, a hypocrite under the eye of the sun, agreeing and understanding, while friendly Dick explained that he was waiting for a ride back to Long Valley. He had to stand out here because to ask anybody to park in the State House area would be just too much. But he could talk to the lieutenant right now, right here, if that was okay? If Silvestri cared to join him on this bench—

"Why not?" Silvestri said. "We've both paid for it." At which not-that-witty sally Voorhees exploded into huge laughter, all but slapping his thigh—and thus freed Guy from qualms about hypocrisy. Which in turn enabled him to produce a convincingly friendly-chat voice to ask about Julius King in.

"We hit it off right from the start, Julius and I did, from the day he came to Long Valley. It's not that big a town, so two fellows whose golf games kind of fit are likely to spend time together pretty regularly. And then, since Julius was new in town and he had a good bit of settling-in to do, I knew I could be helpful—and I was glad to be. He was," Voorhees said solemnly, "a man you could really admire." He sighed, waited an appropriate three seconds, and then returned to his narrative voice. "Just to give you an example, he bought that property out on the new road in exactly fifteen minutes. We went out and looked at the house, then stopped for a cup of coffee while we talked money. Julius knew precisely what he wanted—told me how much to offer, how much he'd go up, and so forth, all to the dollar. Then we drove on back to the fellow's office, and they were shaking hands on the deal in no time."

"A man of decision," Guy said, riskily skirting the edge of

irony. And thinking about Julius King's curiously unilateral decision-making. Not only had he presumably left his wife in Pennsylvania, though the children were old enough six years ago so it should've been possible for their mother to join their father for a few days. But even if King was doing the house-shopping on his own, you'd expect him to call his wife and at least describe the house before he bought it.

"... very characteristic," Julius King's friend was saying. "No shilly-shallying, a no-nonsense kind of chap. He had a good mind, and he used it." A sigh followed that, and Guy tensed for a we-shall-not-see-his-like-again speech. What came, though, was less lofty: "You can't know how distressing it is now. Seeing a valuable property slowly decaying, while the taxes mount, because the house has to stay as-is until the estate can be settled. Nobody's fault, of course." He smiled painfully at Guy. "I wouldn't want you to think I'm complaining, though. Because the police have been just wonderful all through the whole mess."

"They certainly seem to have done their best to be helpful." They also seemed to have changed, at some point, from bloodhounds alerted by Billy's curiously located head wound to lapdogs content to be patted by Voorhees. . . . Silvestri turned his head as if to dodge the sun. "Do you have any idea how much longer—"

"Well, I'm trying to move the machinery, but you know how that is. The best deal is to file for commitment while the boy is still a juvenile. We all want to avoid the ordeal of a trial, of course—I must emphasize, Lieutenant, that all personnel involved have been remarkably understanding. Sensitive and cooperative." The lawyer sighed. "But at the moment every-thing's being held up while some idiot psychiatrist at the state hospital drags his feet."

"Oh? What's the difficulty?"

"Well, I'm being unfair, I suppose. The doctor probably thinks he's just trying to do his job. But I may have to light a fire under the good doctor pretty soon. I don't like to make speeches, but—well, I do have a moral obligation. Julius wouldn't have liked to"—the break in the voice was, this time, somehow more genuine—"to leave a mess."

It was the wrong moment for it, in a way, but Guy sensed vulnerability, so he took a chance. "He loved his son, I suppose."

"Oh my, yes. He had such plans—not only university, but grad school—all of it taken care of. He always—"

A light-colored convertible halted at the bottom of the steps and honked. "That's my ride." Voorhees rose. "I'll be glad to arrange an appointment if you need any more information, Lieutenant."

Guy took an envelope from his breast pocket and studied scribbled notes on its back. "I think that'll hold me for right now, thanks. I'll have to talk to a few people out in Long Valley, too."

"John Vesey, of course?"

"Of course."

"A grand fellow, the greatest. The kind you can really rely on in time of trouble."

Rely on for what? To stop asking questions? Guy glanced at the waiting convertible and decided to gamble. "Is that another of the late Mr. King's friends?"

"Oh. It's Claud Dozier. He and Julius were neighbors. Come and meet him, do."

It was awfully hard to tell, but it was at least possible that there had been an unwilling note in the smooth voice. But even if it was there—Guy reminded himself as he followed Voorhees down the steps—it could mean nothing more than that Voorhees didn't like being drafted either.

Leaning in the car window, the lawyer made the introductions. "The Lieutenant is going over a batch of juvenile cases, and one of them is our local tragedy last year."

Guy registered that, once again, actual mention of Billy

King had been avoided. But he was concentrating on Claud Dozier, an attractive man whose frosty coloring—pale hair, almost white in the sunlight, and pale blue eyes—was curiously at odds with his warm smile. Dozier told Lieutenant Silvestri he was in Boston every Wednesday and offered the number of his Boston office. He'd be available, he said diffidently, if he could be of any help.

Guy wrote the number down on the back of his envelope and, by way of confirming a hunch, remarked that he probably wouldn't be spending much more time on Billy King's case. Then he thanked both men—meanwhile watching Dozier's face close on its disappointment—and wished them a pleasant ride home. They all agreed on what a lovely day this was, and nobody took exception to the hope that there would be more like it soon. Finally Voorhees went around to get into the car.

But the traffic was heavy, and he had to wait on the curb. Dozier leaned out of the car window to ask "Will you be seeing Billy, Lieutenant?" He seemed to have a very soft voice.

"I don't think so," Guy said, wanting to add *I'm sorry.* Dozier nodded, Voorhees climbed in and said something that was lost in the slam of the passenger door, and the car moved off.

Leaving Guy to .meditate on what one sunny day had handed him. Like, to begin with, Derek Voorhees's clear indifference to the reality of Billy King, combined with inexplicable behavior about it. Because if he didn't care any more about his friend's son than it seemed, he should be eager to get out of the way and let other people take over—and surely it would be socially and professionally acceptable to hand over Billy's case to an attorney who specialized in that kind of practice? Yet it was Voorhees himself who was hurrying to file papers. Portrait of a heartless man yearning for legal tidiness in settling Julius King's estate, maybe. In view of his own acknowledged dislike of Voorhees, Guy ordered himself to keep that portrait firmly in mind. It was certainly just as valid an explanation as, say, a desire to see that Billy King never got to a real day in court.

Dozier, though, was another matter entirely. At least, there had been indications that Claud Dozier wanted to talk to Lieutenant Silvestri about Billy King. Only, it seemed, not in the presence of Dick Voorhees.

Guy started to put his envelope away and then paused to study the notes on its back. "Oatmeal (baby)" presented no problem except for the built-in one of Kate's handwriting: she would never have got out of a Massachusetts second grade till she'd learned to write better than that. "Cfee" was coffee—he happened to know they needed it anyway. Squinting in the sunlight, he decided whatever that was before "white cake mix"—"Annie"? "Emory"?—was probably a brand name and would be revealed by a survey of the supermarket shelf. But the last item remained hopeless. And then, suddenly, it wasn't: with the exhilaration of a child's first experience at reading, Guy knew—just knew, absolutely and all at once—what "frfrfrpot" was. *Frozen French-fried potatoes* danced in his head as he got into his car.

It really was a lovely day, and doubtless a harbinger. Because as he was parking at the shopping center, before he got anywhere near the cake-mix shelves, the gods were good to Silvestri again: it came to him that "*any* white cake mix" was what his good lady, who didn't want to put him to any trouble, had written.

6

RECONNAISSANCE
(April 27, Long Valley)

"Cannon, did you ever read *Four-Seas Land*?"

"No, not yet. I haven't been able to lay my hands on a copy." Sitting on the neatly made bed, Dr. Cannon looked across the room at the skinny boy in new jeans and a polo shirt that was not new—it came from his bureau drawer at home and the observant Miss Crabtree remembered that he'd worn it often, so there was a chance he might be especially fond of it. But so far, he'd shown no sign of recognizing it. "Why do you want to know?" Cannon asked. He didn't try to make it sound like an idle question.

"Well, you said you wanted to. So I was wondering if I should—" Suddenly, moving jerkily, Billy turned back to the map on the wall. "If I should make a new map. That's what I was wondering." His laugh had a creaky sound. "This map's about had it. But if I make a new one, the way Will's going, he's liable to run right off it." He turned all the way around then, so there was no possibility of his looking at the doctor. "I don't know what to do." The big brown eyes, guarded but seeking, studied the conventional pattern of the institutionally cheerful curtain at the window. "I mean, should I wait or take a chance?"

As they settled themselves in the artificial hush of Channel 10's screening room, Sergeant Alonso asked, "We looking for anything in particular, Lieutenant?"

Yes, for whoever's hiding. Somebody in Long Valley had killed three people that November morning. And then, either accidentally or by design, had been swept out of sight in the course of what looked very like a cover-up. Because Guy didn't want to say that, not yet, he answered with a brusque question: "Didn't you read the material I gave you?" He recognized his assistant's snappy "yessir" as a reproof, and deserved. "Did anything strike you about it?" he asked, more mildly.

Ed Alonso was Silvestri's sergeant precisely because he was bright, and he'd never been required to dissemble. "Come on, Lieutenant, if something wasn't supposed to strike me, the question wouldn't be on the exam. Okay, obviously the answer is in the way the case was handled." Alonso shook back his too-long hair and sank his bony body deeper into the plush seat not made for slouching. "If your point is that the Long Valley troops messed up, I agree. But when they come on a feller standing in a mess of corpses with a smoking .38 in his hand, you can't—"

"They didn't come on a feller, they came on a boy—and that's what makes the difference. Billy King has a solid alibi for a key time. If he'd been an adult, that couldn't have been brushed aside."

"All right, granted they were sloppy. It's a small force, and look at the kind of case. I mean, any homicide would probably cause some flap out there in the sticks. But one that 'hath the primal eldest curse upon it,' as somebody said—well, have a heart, Lieutenant."

"I do. I also have a dim view of our educational system," Guy added dryly. "Because the somebody who wrote that was Shakespeare, for Hamlet's uncle to say. And it goes on, 'a brother's murder'—which, as it happens, is the only kind not involved here."

"Technically speaking," Alonso amended. "So okay, I cheated. But not really."

"No, not really." *Hamlet* raised possibilities to be considered, at that. For it had seemed to the student Guy Silvestri, reading the numbered lines in English class, that Hamlet spent an awful lot of time working himself up about his mother's sex life. Though Hamlet was older than Billy King, a nonabstract view of Mrs. King might be useful. For, if Guy remembered correctly, fifteen and a half was quite old enough . . .

Right now, though, there was the education of Ed Alonso to take care of. "But you're on a big sophisticated force, and you were booby-trapped too, weren't you. Just like the troops in Long Valley." His eyes on the blank screen in the front of the room, Guy asked, "Does your quotation fit if, say, the laundryman did the shooting?" Or, for that matter, if Claud Dozier had coveted his neighbor's wife? Shakespeare wasn't the only handy source, after all, for observations on human relations.

"Oh." Alonso grinned. "To quote an anonymous observer, 'Silvestri is hell on brash young men.' Okay, the laundryman. Unless he's a metaphor?"

"No, he's Harry Moody, address in Long Valley. It would be interesting to see what he looks like. I'm pretty sure I'll have to talk to him."

"Right. Anything else?"

"The town. The whole scene, really—who seems to matter, the general shape of things."

"It's a small town, Lieutenant. And all small towns have learned from television to be afraid of being small-townish. So the bankers wear sideburns. And if your unmarried daughter gets knocked up, your friends will feel sympathetic as well as superior. Ick. But," Alonso added seriously, "I think it's an improvement anyhow."

"Yes. It has its costs, though." Without that learned aura of sophistication, that supermarket-psychologizing, would Long

Valley's inhabitants have been as ready to desert simplicities like logic and justice, in the name of what they accepted as up-to-date penology? Guy frowned, because he didn't like chiefs who gave vague instructions but he couldn't see how to avoid being one right now. "What we'll be seeing here is a hodgepodge of videotapes, some that were used and some rejected for one reason or another. They're mostly from the news coverage out in Long Valley last November, but Julius King probably made a speech sometime anyway—he was school superintendent, after all. I don't know how much use this will actually be, but at least we can get a look at some of the people."

"Well, that's just about what happens when you come on any case, isn't it? You interview a bunch of people without knowing who's really going to matter. So this is just sort of an electronic shortcut, it sounds like."

Put that way, it sounded even more distrust-worthy, Guy decided. But he didn't get to point out the hazards of "interviewing" people who could neither hear your questions nor ask their own, because a miniature cataclysm seemed to be about to hit the little room. The metallic voice of the TV producer was preceded by a booming sound that enhanced its air of heavenly pronouncement: "Ready, Lieutenant. Remember, if you want a blowup of any shot, just push the button. Got it?" The voice ended in an appropriate thunderous *clap*, and darkness descended.

And then, abruptly, they were in Long Valley, on a November day of bare trees and patches of snow lying on the brown earth like whipped cream on a chocolate cake. A young man in a fur-lined jacket accosted people, holding up a microphone before each one as if offering a lollipop. A white-jacketed resident from the small local hospital said he had nothing to say to the press, and didn't get the lollipop—the reporter had to tell the microphone himself that a famous Lambert University surgeon was on his way here right now.

Without transition, the overcolorful voice disappeared and so did the November day. Guy pushed his button as Julius King—a tall, imposing figure—was introduced, somewhere indoors and in evening clothes, by a balding man who talked about capital-*E* Education. In the background, a woman with chiseled features under smooth pale hair looked very like a newspaper photo Guy had seen of Mrs. King.

Then it was outdoors and November again. A hairy face—nothing but eyes peering bright and wicked from a thicket of long hair, moustache, and beard—swam into view. The camera moved slowly downward, checking jewelry, embroidered denim jacket and the rest of the counterculture chic.

"Yours," Guy told the Silvestri team's specialist in the local coffeehouse scene. "You want a blowup?"

"What for?" Alonso sounded like a Lambert neurosurgeon being offered a chance to do a tonsillectomy. "I've seen him around, anyway. He goes by the name of Swirl, I think."

"Twirl," Guy corrected. The *Ur*-hippie had just told it to a proferred lollipop. As if he had thus incurred somebody's wrath, the film jumped and he was whisked away. Guy decided the effect was interesting, at least when you got used to it. The trick was to go along, without fighting it or trying to make order out of it—as he had tried to tell Kate, that bigot, about the Bartók he loved and she couldn't stand. In the long run, what came out that way really reached you better . . .

Long Valley Police Chief John Vesey had flicked on and off several times before he was interviewed at length in a standard nonjumping film segment interchangeable with a hundred others showing police chiefs at scenes of tragedies. But Vesey's long-squint eyes and sober horse-face were familiar by that time: a relation existed between the viewers and the man saying, "It seems Doctor King kept his gun in the bottom drawer of his desk. We know that from the oil stains in the drawer."

"When *is* this?" Ed Alonso whispered.

Behind Vesey, an ambulance with its back doors swinging open stood in what looked like a hospital driveway. "That afternoon, I guess. Or as soon as a TV mobile unit could get there, anyway."

"That would make it the fastest damn lab work *I* ever saw." The sergeant subsided promptly then, because on the screen the police chief was now presiding over the meeting of the newsman and Derek Voorhees, who'd just been "upstairs" checking on Billy's condition.

Now that he had seen Voorhees in person, Guy could recognize the effect of shock revealed in the pictured face. But the lawyer's voice was the same: it lived by explaining intricacies, and apparently it had gone on working smoothly, like a machine that keeps running though its operator has been taken ill. "All I can tell you is, we may never know. There were no warning signals of any kind—and Doctor King was particularly qualified, you realize, to spot them if they'd been there. But what we all saw was a normal, apparently happy boy." Voorhees's gloved hands spread in a helpless gesture. "Why he should suddenly take his father's gun and—do this terrible, terrible thing to his family—well, that's beyond us. All we have is facts."

Guy was aware of a stir at his side and Alonso said something undistinguishable but probably rude. Then the film jumped and a young woman with short dark hair tossed by the wind was saying impatiently, "Well, if you just *look*, you can see it's quite a trudge between our houses. And anyway"—she paused to shift a snowsuit-muffled child, jutting out her hip to make a sort of ledge for it—"I'm not the kaffeeklatsch type, and Callie wasn't, either." A larger child, hooded and jacketed, too, pedaled a toy car across the background from left to right, drawing the viewer's gaze to the house—big and modern, but lonely-looking against a background of wilderness. She looked like a pioneer woman—she even stood like one, sturdy and self-sufficient on her cleared spot of land in front of the modern equivalent of a settler's sod house in Nebraska. It was easy to think of her as seeing other women only at the odd hoedown or quilting bee . . .

She made an attractive vignette, but Guy rather thought it hadn't been used. Because Vera Dozier was an unsatisfying interviewee, asking more questions than she answered. Was Billy still unconscious? Did the reporter know whether they'd operated on him yet? She'd tried to get into the house because maybe he'd need pajamas and stuff, but it was all locked up and the cops were chasing everybody away. She'd listened to the radio news, but all they said was—

In the background, the toy car overturned, and small booted legs waved in the air. Then abruptly a baby face, eyes and mouth round and of nearly equal size, zoomed toward the viewer, filling the screen, a drop of drool on the lower lip magnified as if for the cover of *Scientific American*. The sound track became a kind of braided yowl, and the picture swung like a small boat in a heavy sea. It righted itself briefly, showing the woman kneeling to tend the fallen motorist. Then it flicked off, and Alonso's laughter rang out in the stuffy little room. Guy translated what he'd seen—she'd thrust the baby at the reporter, who promptly handed it on to the cameraman, who nearly dropped his camera while trying to hand the baby back—and decided that talking to Mrs. Dozier would not be an unpleasant chore. But he'd better count on plenty of time for it.

What followed—Twirl holding forth on "the family in Amerika" in a voice that instructed you to spell the name with a "k"—seemed almost a figure of order by contrast with Vera Dozier. And if you peeled away the "yeah-man"'s and ignored the provocative tone and gestures, what was left were shrewd observations and the fluency of a very good salesman. But this was Alonso's territory, so Guy listened chiefly for evidence of pro- or anti-Billy sentiment. On the whole, he concluded—after Long Valley's hippie had appeared again and again, in both smooth and jagged bits—what was visible was more ritual needling than sympathy for Billy. Apparently everybody was a They to Twirl, and all Theys were garbage.

The laundryman, turning up between consultations with the oracle Twirl, was a real shock. "He's just a kid," Alonso said, surprised and faintly accusing.

"I didn't know." Recognizing some need to apologize, Guy looked at Harry Moody telling a lollipop his name. "I was even wondering whether he had something going with Mrs. King, maybe."

"Well, why not? Mature ladies have been known to take up with young lads."

"Not *that* young," Silvestri said flatly, watching Harry Moody show the public just where he'd placed the package of returned laundry. The smooth-coiffed demure-looking Mrs. King might loosen her stays, but not for the benefit of this uncertain youth with the reedy voice and nervous hands. He looked too young—and, more important, too immature and incompetent—even for Susan King. Guy listened while Harry Moody described, more and more rapidly, how hard he'd tried to get an answer at the King house that morning. The detective's instincts told him the youth was lying; but the detective's experience also told him that it didn't have to be about anything important, or even relevant. Moody was still protesting virtuously when the camera left him for Lenny Pritchard, who looked just as young and a good deal less nervous.

Lenny was photographed at work on his part-time job, so Guy examined the gas station, which could have been a desert outpost if only that had been sand instead of underbrush around it, while Lenny told about seeing the two cars just after eight o'clock that morning. He was lavish with information about the cars, and about the exam he'd been studying for, but he had to be asked before he recalled seeing the green Eagle Laundry truck. The camera surveyed the frozen-dirt track called "the new road" and then went back to Lenny. Who said—with no ease or loquacity, and with what looked like real pain—that Susan King had been a sweet, beautiful girl and it was impossible to believe she was dead. The camera angle had shifted: behind his head as he talked, the main road to town was now visible through the side window. Several cars went by, but of course the traffic by that time, what with TV vans outside the gas station to be gawked at, would be at least double the average figure.

"Do I take him?" Alonso asked.

"No. Leave him for now. I may talk to him myself." If nobody had asked Lenny Pritchard how many times he'd seen the laundry truck go by, or when, then Silvestri would have to.

A couple of you-could-have-knocked-me-over-with-a-feather interviews followed, adding up to nothing more than an impression that the average local citizen felt cold, was excited, and didn't know much. Then Miss May Crabtree appeared—briefly, but long enough for Silvestri to see what Meyer Cannon had meant by "articulate." For she didn't answer a single question, but she did deliver a concise lecture on the mapping of the brain, which she'd looked up because you couldn't get any information out of those hospital people about Billy's chances of recovery. When she finished, Miss Crabtree simply turned and walked away. The wintry sunlight glinted on her silver hair, yanked severely into a sort of doughnut on top of her head. Guy had a feeling the camera followed her stately progress up her front walk because the man operating it was fascinated: probably nobody in his experience had ever just stopped talking while still receiving the full attention of the media.

Certainly somebody was fascinated by Twirl, who appeared again then, this time embracing the war-memorial cannon in front of the Town Hall. After which the screen first went blank and then filled with a series of static photos garnered for the lieutenant's benefit. He had seen some of them before, in the newspaper clips. Susan King wore a small sedate smile for the Long Valley High School yearbook, and then a big happy grin at somebody's birthday party—a lively, spirited girl who probably looked very like the other girls in her class, but prettier than most. Billy King squinted into the sun from the front row of another yearbook photo—the chess club, gathered around the awesome bulk of their faculty adviser, Miss Crabtree, in a flowered dress that flowed over the adjacent club members. Then one Guy hadn't seen; a snapshot of Billy, on hands and knees, making a face at a baby (the Doziers', maybe?) who was crawling toward him across a field of carpet.

A studio portrait of a little girl with tied-back long curls sitting on an upholstered bench beside an even littler boy with slicked-down hair and short pants and his feet nowhere near reaching the floor: that would have to be Susan and Billy, aged, at a guess, four and two-and-a-half. Then Mr. and Mrs. Julius King in evening dress, smiling in a sharp, professional-looking flash photo, maybe (by the evidence of clothes and hair styles) half a dozen years ago. They looked somehow professional themselves—the Big Man on Campus who'd naturally married the Homecoming Queen, and here they were, back for the tenth reunion . . . No, not the Homecoming Queen, Guy decided. The college president's daughter, maybe: there was something about even a younger Callie King that didn't look as though it ever ran for election. She was too cool. A fair lady, all right, but not in a democracy.

That showed up too in the last picture, recent and obviously for a newspaper—a ladylike portrait of the ladylike wife of the superintendent of schools featured serene brow and neatly molded nose and lips, the eyes intelligent and polite, the pale hair drawn into a sleek knot on a slender neck encircled by a single strand of pearls. Alongside her, Julius King, gone a bit jowly since the college-reunion photo, looked too dark and heavy, almost gross. Except for the steel-colored eyes, which apparently had never looked anything but austere, at any age.

The Kings were still on the screen when a padded door opened behind the watchers and the program director stuck his head in. Guy rose to thank him, but he held up a staving-off hand. "I got one more thing, Lieutenant. But I wanted to warn you, it's for a documentary so it's a little hokey."

Silvestri's lips twitched, but he proved master of his face. "What kind of documentary, Wally?"

"A network thing on American Family Tragedy, or something like that—these kind of cases from all over, now and in the past, with like a narrator talking about Lizzie Borden, you know? It's not released yet, but they sent this promo they figure is local for us." The small harried-looking man raised his shoulders in a shrug. "That's the way they think."

"I know." To the network people in New York, Massachusetts was Massachusetts. But in fact, except for legal necessities like vehicle licenses and divorces and the occasional election of a governor, Long Valley had no "local angle" for Wally's audience; people in Boston and Buxford were more likely to have common interests with California, or even Europe or Africa or Asia, than with western Massachusetts.

"It could pay you to take a look, though," Wally said. "The network people have different pix. Stuff the folks out there didn't know they had when *we* asked them, or else they held out till they were offered real money. If you'd like to—" He looked pleased at Guy's nod. "Okay, fine. I'll open the mike here, so if you want to freeze it anywheres, just say so." He vanished, and the door seemed to, too, its padded edge disappearing in the padded wall.

Ed Alonso settled back in his seat without a word. Guy grinned sympathetically, guessing that the knowledge of the open mike was silencing the sergeant. And then the grin froze, and Alonso's aversion to public speech gave way before the need to express dismay, as the easily recognizable voice of the network's Famous Man filled the room. Guy avoided looking at the picture—the fat, smug voice was enough without the matching face, too—and watched Alonso instead. Ed was still young enough so it was hard for him to accept the possibility of wisdom coming from the unwise or unlovable, but Silvestri knew it could. So it would be too bad if Alonso was too busy hating the narrator to pay attention.

Norman Ayling was strictly a phenomenon of television, where the daily sight of a man telling the news from all over brings with it automatically the tacit belief that he speaks what he knows, and therefore that he must know a lot. The bland humorless face, the speech without regional accent or flavor, stirred no prejudices and created no factions: Ayling had risen to his current eminence by the same rule of human social behavior that produces the "dark horse" in politics. Since, unlike his competitors, Ayling had started with no background in newspaper journalism—or anything else, for that matter— nothing he was given to read ever conflicted with his own knowledge or experience; from the beginning, he'd pronounced all scripts with total belief, and he encountered no occasion for ethical or philosophical objection at any time on his way up.

By now, though, he was full of certainties. A few years before, the middle-aged Norman Ayling had become a fervent disciple of the greening-of-America cult (after, naturally, it had lost whatever verdancy it owned). The result showed up in a turtleneck sweater, sideburns, and a tendency to be a patsy for any dogma he believed "progressive." Which meant, most of the time, that he served the interests of people who'd spotted a trend and made a buck out of it. Because by then, the real progressives had of course moved on—they had never been admirers of Ayling and generally ignored him, although the younger and less disciplined among them greeted any mention of him with retching noises—and many of the stances once taken in the name of "the people" had since become the property of such markedly unpopulistic types as oil sheikhs.

But Norman Ayling, rolling on, was now himself so much a factor in any news event that whatever he warned, guessed, or predicted was almost certain to be correct. (And if he should ever be wrong, the captains and the kings involved—aware of the price of offending Ayling—maneuvered busily to save his face.)

Therefore the public now believed, probably unassailably, that Norman Ayling was one of the country's best minds. And there was a widespread impression that if only he wasn't so busy, he'd take time to be President of the United States.

"This is where it happened," said the faintly oily baritone with its implied promise to bring order out of chaos. Guy turned from reproving Alonso, who'd been demonstrating his youth and lack of discipline by making retching noises. On the screen Derek Voorhees, lounging in an armchair, was saying chummily, "I wish I could say there'd been a single hint, Norman, but there just wasn't. Whatever hit Billy, whatever caused him to pick up that gun—well, it came out of the blue."

"And these are the people it happened to." The King house—clearly expensive, but with the landscaping equally clearly limited to what went with the builders' contract—appeared on the screen with the faces of Julius, Callie, and Susan King tilted above it. The voice went on to describe how Julius King, Ph.D., had come to Long Valley to be school superintendent, wooed from a similar post in Pennsylvania six years before. Since Guy had nothing to learn from that, he concentrated on the dreary-looking front yard, all tired yews—except for a single lilac bush that seemed out of place—and stubbly crabgrass surrounding a semicircle of messy-looking gravel driveway. Silvestri studied it absently, committing the scene to memory without intending it.

Then he was learning that Callie King had not been a college president's daughter, though something not far from that. Her parents were dead, however, and so were her husband's: "Susan and Billy," the voice said over that studio portrait of two solemn tots, "had neither grandfathers nor grandmothers." There was a single surviving relative, an aging spinster who lived in Ohio and was a second cousin of Callie King. And who clearly lacked drama. Norman Ayling abandoned her, once she'd served to show the thoroughness of his research staff, and went on to announce gravely, sadly, "And this is the boy who made it happen." Billy King stared, startled by a flashbulb, from between two men leading him up the shallow steps of a large building. Peering, Guy thought it was Meyer Cannon who was leaning over in an apparent attempt to fend off the photographer. That would be when Billy was transferred to the state hospital, because Cannon hadn't come on the scene till then.

"Oh for God's sake," Alonso said loudly.

"Don't listen to him, just look at the pictures." A good many of them were new: Susan King danced, and swam, and smiled with the rest of the cast of *Pinafore*; Julius King was one of a foursome, which included Voorhees, the day somebody made a hole-in-one; and the always-smooth Callie King and the always-ruffled Vera Dozier apparently belonged to the same League of Women Voters branch and had once sat together, looking really as different as day and night, at a luncheon featuring a newsworthy speaker.

Altogether missing, Guy noted, was the endearing snapshot of Billy and the baby, which had been available to Wally's crew and therefore to the network. A narrow-eyed Billy appeared, alone and unsmiling, and after a minute Guy realized the face had been extracted from the chess-club photo—leaving behind Miss Crabtree's flowered voile and the sunshine that explained Billy's squint. Then, as if by contrast with her dour little brother, came Susan, a fun-loving American girl on an outing with her class at the lakeside summer home of Long Valley's celebrity, Itzhak Malevanchik. The famed conductor, it seemed, traditionally invited Long Valley High School's seniors to disport themselves on his acres, although—equally traditionally, Silvestri suspected—Malevanchik himself was appearing with Cleveland's or somebody else's symphony that weekend.

The high-school students had been chaperoned—Ayling assured his public, while the cameras lingered on the beautiful long-legged girls in their bikinis—by teachers and volunteers from among the parents. He showed some of each: Mrs.

Armour, who taught Latin; Mr. Poley, who taught American history—"his students call him Roley," the voice-over explained, exulting in discovered wit; Mrs. Bradlock, the mother of Laura . . . Guy leaned forward, hoping for a glimpse of Trixie, Susan King's best friend. But there was only her haggardly attractive mother, in a conservative one-piece bathing suit, talking to the Latin teacher. "*And*," said Ayling, heavy with portent, "Mrs. King, the mother of Susan." The picture flashed, held—and Silvestri, his voice sounding odd, called out "Freeze that!"

Callie King stayed there then, caught forever and unbelievably lovely, standing barefoot in grass and fluffing out her long red-gold hair to dry while she smiled at somebody lying on a blanket nearby. In the upper left-hand corner of the picture, a scantily clad boy and girl leaped almost simultaneously for a ball, their slim taut bodies outlined against the sky. But Callie King, in a long striped robe that must have been loose before the wind that had caught the ball also caught it, wrapping it around her—Callie was a sight to stir men's blood.

"The lady was built," said Alonso. He cleared his throat. "Really built."

"Yes. So it seems." Silvestri eyed the outlined breast and thigh, and then his gaze traveled to the oddly girlish face. It was the first time he'd seen a picture of her smiling, he thought. She looked incredibly different.

"What do you mean 'it seems'? With all those bikinis in sight, she's the sexiest thing around." Alonso sat up, peering. "Who's the man over there?"

"The history teacher, I guess." The man was lying on his stomach, his face turned toward Mrs. King but half-hidden in the angle of his arms. He seemed to be grinning. But what was mostly visible was the body of a youngish man in conservative bathing trunks—a reasonably shapely body but no beach boy— and seal-dark hair that was probably not so sleek when it wasn't wet. "We can get a closer look later," Silvestri said, and raised his voice to tell Wally he was ready to move on.

But Guy's mind refused to move on: it stayed with Callie King, the mother of a seventeen-year-old girl, looking like a virgin goddess. That was only an accident, he told himself—her air of secret, special dignity came of the fact that she was standing on a hilltop, and she was dressed when nobody else was. A moment before, she would have been another bathing-suited figure like Mrs. Bradlock, probably; a moment later, she would have been herding the teen-agers, or maybe unpacking a picnic lunch.

But what the eye takes in cannot be entirely rejected. So the impression that Callie King, whatever else she had been, had been a woman to inspire passions was what Guy—and Alonso—took away from Wally's viewing room.

Ed Alonso had not only impressions, but also a particularly interesting question: what had happened to the outgoing laundry at the King house that November morning? "There should've been some, right? It was the regular laundry day—it must've been, or the neighbor lady wouldn't have been expecting Moody. So why didn't Mrs. King put out the bundle of laundry to go?"

"Why should she? She expected to answer the doorbell when Moody came."

"I'm not so sure, Lieutenant. Maybe she was going out."

"Well, what if she was? Her daughter was home anyway."

"Yeah, but sick, remember? Why would she want her daughter hopping out of bed to answer the doorbell when she could just put the bundle on the front step instead?" Alonso frowned. "It's not important, I guess. But it just seems *wrong.* Like, if she was going out, where was she going? Nobody seems to have been expecting her anywhere."

"Maybe she was just going shopping? But you have a point," Guy conceded. The really interesting question, though, was not *where* Callie King was going but *how,* since she had no car. It was possible she meant to call a cab, of course—but maybe somebody was coming to pick her up. Somebody who then should have appeared at the door before the state trooper did. Or, among all those interviews, somebody saying Callie King had phoned to cancel an appointment that very morning . . .

Guy left those implications for later and turned to a question easier to research: *why* didn't Mrs. King have a car? Sixteen was driving-license age in Massachusetts and the Kings had a daughter a year older and a son coming up on it, and they lived way out where the only transportation was the school bus—and yet they apparently owned only one car. But Julius King's salary should have stretched to two cars, even if inexpensive ones.

Back at his office, Guy dictated for Alonso's notebook, "Any car registration for Mrs. King? Or more than one for King?" He consulted his own list of questions. "Oh, yes—this Twirl. He's probably not as central a figure in Long Valley as he seemed. But see what you can pick up." If there had indeed been a cover-up, the counterculture types might well know it—though they apparently hadn't cared to challenge it. "Who is he, really? How long has he been in Long Valley?" He left it at that: Alonso didn't need priming questions. "You can put Rubin on the record-digging. And, if he can get it without making waves, I'd appreciate a firsthand account from somebody who rode on that call from the trooper at the King house."

Alonso pursed his lips for a whistle, but then he only asked, "Anything else for Rubin?"

"Yes, Derek Voorhees. Is he married, or has he ever been?" Guy decided to wait on Dozier—he'd know better what he needed, if anything, after he talked to the man. "And find out whether Mrs. Wilder—the high school principal—will be in Boston next week for a professional powwow at the State House. Room 410." Somewhat guiltily, Guy noted the awe in his assistant's usually skeptical look. This was how reputations for genius got started, and it wasn't really fair. "If she is, send Merchant—No, wait." Detective Merchant was black. "That could strike her as blatant wooing, couldn't it? Better take her yourself."

"Yessir," Alonso said, not mocking this time. "What do you want from her, impressions of Doctor King?"

"Yes, and anybody else. But mainly, her phone calls that morning. The one to the King house at nine twenty is important, so let's be sure it stands up before we hang too much on it. And then, the two King children."

"You mean were their grades slipping, that sort of thing?"

"Yes. Mainly Susan." Cannon would know about Billy's grades, or other signs of strain that might have shown up at school. "What the teachers thought of her, and so forth. But gently, Ed—I don't want any talk stirred up in the town yet."

"I could run out there and interview Miss Crabtree," Alonso suggested eagerly. "*She'd* keep her mouth shut, all right."

"Nobody's to set foot in Long Valley; that's an order," the lieutenant said. Then he grinned. "And I'm taking Miss Crabtree myself. Rank has its privileges." He departed then, leaving a mutter of discontent behind him. But it was not likely to reach the proportions of revolt, not yet.

7
PERSONNEL
(May 14, Long Valley)

Detective Lieutenant Silvestri's special staff, whose members had been discovered one by one during the course of his career as the Buxford force's golden boy, had been acquired by techniques ranging from intramural diplomacy to bureaucratic theft. So far, it was composed of one noncom, Sergeant Alonso—a younger, cooler version of Mike, the governor's right-hand man—and three "other ranks" with useful specialties. Occasionally, extra hands had to be called in to aid with particular problems. But most problems yielded to the skills of Jack Rubin, who always saw the underside of everything and could melt perfectly into any human scene; Lou Merchant, who, if he'd not been born the wrong color and a quarter-century late, could have made millions in Wall Street in the wide-open days before all those dreary regulatory agencies; and Roosevelt Jones, whose expertise with black militants and *soi-disant* revolutionaries may have begun because other people assumed nobody with such a name could possibly be an ex-Tennessee hillbilly.

The four were known to the Buxford force as "Silvestri's whiz kids," but they had other names for themselves. Rubin and Alonso had been, originally, Silvestri's "henchmen"—until

Alonso, in a rare rank-pulling moment, announced, "*You're* his henchman, I'm his myrmidon." Merchant, who sometimes practiced a black-militant sneer (not with any noticeable success) around the office, tried to refer to the four as Silvestri's "darkies," but it didn't catch on even with him. And Jones, the last to be chosen and thus afforded an overall view of the mix of race, creed, and color ("You look like a Brotherhood Week poster," Silvestri once told them disgustedly), called them "the American legion." But whatever their concepts of themselves and the group's role, all four members of the team had these characteristics in common: they felt lucky to be with Silvestri, to whom they were devoted (though never uncritically), and not one of them had ever exhibited either reverence or any lack of self-esteem.

"Charisma" was the way Silvestri's colleagues tried to explain his staff's admiration for the lieutenant, but in fact it was much simpler than that. The "whiz kids" served Silvestri well because he served them well. Since he didn't feel threatened by cleverness or imagination in the ranks, he indulged individualism, and even quirkiness, to an extent that would have whitened his superiors' hair if they'd known. They didn't, because one of the things the lieutenant did for his team was front for them in the bureaucracy. Their reports, wildly informal and full of confident judgments and loose assertions, entered the files of the Buxford Police as models of paper work—wooden-worded and filled with exact dates, times, and reference numbers supplied by Silvestri (and, when things backed up too much, by Merchant, who could do it if bullied). The lucky four who enjoyed this service gave service in return: secure in the knowledge that the price of initiative would not be hours of typing reports in triplicate—and that bad hunches and honest follies would never get past the lieutenant, who took a tolerant view of both—they interpreted their assignments broadly and scorned overtime slips as just one more bureaucratic hangup. They worked until the job was finished, consulting their own resources and each other, and following up in whatever direction seemed to make sense; but if an assignment didn't make sense, they said so promptly, thus saving man-hours that would have demonstrated nothing except respect for rank and an eye on the someday pension. As a result, they produced the biggest bang for a buck, bureaucratically speaking, and thus won the lieutenant the power to indulge them some more—for the commissioner, who knew it wasn't just charisma, also knew it worked.

But for the system to work, the lieutenant had to wade through reports and bring order into their chaos by psyching out his team. By mid-May, nearly a month after Silvestri's first casual order to Alonso on behalf of the then-potential Long Valley investigation, a considerable amount of written chaos was waiting for the lieutenant to do his thing with. Very individualistic chaos, -for the team's reporting styles echoed the differences in character. For example, Rubin wrote down as little as his conscience allowed, to spare both himself and the lieutenant the pain of his typing; whereas Alonso, who had to do things well before he could feel free to scorn them properly, was an exquisitely skillful typist and composed flowing essays shaped by the demands of euphony and of a length dictated by the requirements of elegance.

What that meant—as Silvestri had learned by experience, sometimes bitter—was that almost anything could be buried anywhere. So he went on reading Alonso's report carefully even after he'd extricated the fact that Mrs. Marietta Wilder had indeed been in Boston (for what Alonso described ingeniously as "a shriek of high-school principals" at the State House) and that the sergeant had interviewed her and verified the times of the phone calls from her office that November morning. But then, it seemed, Mrs. Wilder had taken to the engaging Alonso and chatted on at length. So Silvestri, who'd already supplied a date and invented a location—both omitted by Alonso—for this interview and stated its purpose as "Corroboration of 9:20 A.M.

phone call," read on and on about the high-school principal's views of Authority (frail, frail), especially when it came to Authority's way of dealing with the public.

If he'd been less conscientious (or less scared), Lieutenant Silvestri might have missed the plum embedded in this second-hand pie. But he stuck his thumb into Sergeant Alonso's paragraph exploring the byways Mrs. Wilder's opinion of the Establishment had led to and came up with this: ". . . example of how utterly untrustworthy is the L.V. fuzz, their first report—was that Billy King was dead, too. That they never even explained or apologized for the error, argues haughty Marietta, proves their contempt for the public. Maybe. But it did seem this could use some looking into, as *we* never heard of such report (did we?), not even as a They-say rumor. So I sneered delicately, suggesting that that's all it was, right? Not right, insisted Mrs. W.: she didn't get it from any They, she got it from Vera Dozier, right after that gentlewoman came home from an outing with her baby to the homicide scene. (Is there anything, anywhere, to match the incredible American public?)"

Yes, said Silvestri to himself, there is. Like, for example, the incredible bumptiousness of clever young sergeants. He shook his head and went on reading: Alonso's limitations could wait.

". . . couldn't push it farther back than one step: Vera Dozier got it from a cop at the King house. Not Chief Vesey and not a rookie named Johnson, both of whom Mrs. D. knows and saw at the scene. A strange cop. But he told her 'all four of them' were dead in the house. My suggestion that Mrs. Dozier, understandably excited, might have confused things a mite only got me clobbered more than a mite. Oddly enough in view of certain edged remarks made earlier, it seems Mrs. Wilder has a very high opinion of Vera Dozier—who may look and sound scatterbrained but is highly intelligent, though currently exploited as a mere housewife and baby-breeder, and so whatever she said the cop said, you can count on it that's what the cop really said. So there. . . .I covered my retreat by pointing out, in tones of dignified reproach, that we really prefer the term police officer.' Score, Love all."

Silvestri shuffled through the reports in his In basket and found what he was looking for. There must have been some trading of assignments, because he was pretty sure he'd suggested Rubin. But it was Jones who'd filed the graceless but thankfully brief report Guy had scanned and put aside, registering only that it was negative. He found the place easily: Jones was big on Roman numbers.

II. Long Valley Police at Homicide Scene: Theres a lid on this, Lt., did you know that? I got a wiggle in with some troopers I know, but all I get so far is ~~mysterious~~ misterious hints and looks. My guess is its a long story, with some hard feelings involved somewheres. So it looks like it will take time.

Also money—I had to sit on a card game with the troopers, and those boys play high. Sgt. Alonso says I cant collect my $8.50 because nobody told me to lose. But when I play poker *not* in the line of duty, I don't lose. So its not fair. If the Regulations are against me I'm ready to go right on up to the U.S. Supreme Court. Please advise, yours truly, R. Jones.

Sternly not grinning, Lieutenant Silvestri poked around in his desk drawer until he found a pad of petty cash slips. He dialed Alonso's extension, and filled out the order to pay Jones his $8.50 while he waited. Then he said "Ed? I want to see Jones this afternoon at— He's where? All right, then Rubin—one of them, anyway. Here, when I get back." He hung up, tossed the signed voucher into his Out basket, and took off for his appointment across the river in Boston.

Claud Dozier was not as tall as he'd looked sitting in his car—he was maybe five-ten, but wide shoulders and a sturdy build made him seem more massive. His white hair was obviously premature; even the second time around, it still startled, springing thick and wavy about a quite young, squarish face with the weathered tan of a man who spent much time outdoors. He looked healthy and happy, as though he knew he was indeed well fed and well cared for. Well dressed, too: the tweed of his jacket included a lilac thread that gave the whole a misty color particularly suited to Dozier. The fit of the jacket implied custom tailoring, but Silvestri thought that unlikely. Probably the exploited Vera made or remade her husband's clothes— which left Guy, on the lookout for clues to Claud Dozier, out of luck.

Silvestri was engaged in that search because from the moment he'd entered the Boston office of C. Dozier and Associates—the decor was Austere Modern and quite obviously had little connection with C. Dozier himself—it had been clear that Dozier was a citizen looking for a cop. But figuring out why he'd flagged down the passing Silvestri instead of calling the cops at home promised to be a long business; Dozier seemed to have something he wanted to tell, but also seemed to feel he shouldn't come right out and say it. Surely this wasn't the "antifuzz hangup" Herk so blithely assumed to be general in the populace? Guy suspected a pro-truth hangup: maybe what Dozier knew was unfair to someone, or less than completely rational, thus tongue-tying a responsible citizen and a man who liked right angles. But whatever the obstacle was, there was something he wanted to unload. And the way to help him do it was to find the question it would be the answer to.

Silvestri was looking for that question while he steered the conversation gently and listened to the results. It was going to be worth the time, he concluded. Because Claud Dozier was that handiest source for learning about a society: the observer who belonged within it but had a commitment to objectivity. Ideally, he could have been more perceptive; but that was compensated for, from Silvestri's point of view, by liberal quoting from his Vera—who did really seem to have quite an eye.

The Claud-plus-Vera combination seemed to be particularly

useful when Dozier was describing the relation between the two households on Long Valley's "new road." Reasonably cordial but not close, was what it added up to—except for the children, who seemed to be around frequently: Susan was not only Vera's but also the Dozier children's favorite babysitter, and Billy and his friends had made forts and hunted tigers in the woods behind the Dozier house—where they were alternately hollered at and fed homemade cookies—since they were around ten years old.

Why not behind the King house, Guy wondered. There should be woods there, too. No cookies? But he left that, and its implications about Callie King, for later, because an impression had been building from the accounts of cookouts and calls and the occasional planned evening with the Kings. Guy had a feeling he was on the trail of the question that needed asking, and maybe now he was even far enough along to risk nudging things a little. So he said quietly, "You didn't like Julius King, did you, Mr. Dozier?"

"No." Dozier frowned. Which figured: clearly he was the kind of man who liked to know why things were the way they were. And he didn't like having to say—though he did say, conscientiously—that he'd had little reason for his feeling. Not till after that day in November, anyway: "It's not a nice thing to admit, Lieutenant, but I have to say it was a relief, in a way, when it came out what a hypocrite Julius was." Even ex-post-facto reason was better than none, it seemed. "It really would get to me," Dozier confided, more at ease now, "when he'd spout all that gun-law talk. I thought he honestly believed it, so I kept on trying to be tolerant and all. But maybe my subconscious mind knew better all the time? Because I don't usually have a fit when somebody disagrees with me, but he'd get me good and sore every time."

"King was agitating for a gun-control law?" Guy was in favor of one too, but it seemed a good idea to keep it to himself right now. So he just observed mildly that nobody else had mentioned that about Julius King.

"Oh, well, he didn't run around buttonholing people, I didn't mean that. But they weren't *friends* of ours—when we got together, we'd just talk about whatever was on the six o'clock news. Nothing personal, if you know what I mean."

It would have been hard not to know what he meant. But it also seemed that the choice of that particular topic for conversation had resulted less in political disagreement than in a culture clash between the urban King, to whom guns were an abstract monstrosity to be legislated away from clods by the intelligent, and the rural Dozier, who obeyed laws but balked at being penalized for refusing to see a gun as a symbol. "You wouldn't catch *me* keeping a handgun in the house," Dozier said. "So it was really something, wasn't it, Julius having a .38 laying around all the time he was raving about how sick-sick-sick you were if you went hunting."

The lieutenant nodded, noting silently how very unlikely it was that Billy could have known of his father's gun at all, much less where it was kept. Finally he asked aloud, "Did anything else that came out afterward about the Kings surprise you?"

"If you mean did I see something bubbling around in Billy all the time, I did not. And he wasn't secretly getting ready to blow up, or any of that crap." The Breton-blue eyes sparked angrily. "I never did believe Billy shot them, Lieutenant, and I don't now."

The shape of the right question to ask was beginning to appear. "Well, whatever actually happened, it doesn't sound like the Kings were the happy family everybody claimed."

"*I* never claimed that. I told the cops I saw Callie and Julius having an argument that very morning, when Billy wasn't even around. But they just took no notice, it looks like."

"Maybe they didn't think it sounded like much of an argument." Guy surveyed the man behind the desk. His eyes had lost that anger, but his hands, which had been idly flexing a metal ruler, were now gripping it tightly instead, and the square face had paled under its tan. Portrait of a man waiting to be hit with the hard question, Guy decided, and moved in with a soft one instead. "But it was a real serious quarrel, wasn't it?" Then he suggested gently, "Something about what you saw that morning is still bothering you."

"Yes, it is. But I don't know why, in case you're going to ask me." The square, competent hands began to bend the ruler again. "Yes, I do know," Dozier said abruptly, watching the silvery arc between his hands. "It was Callie. She looked—well, different. But she wasn't quarreling, she was begging."

For what? It wasn't safe to ask that yet: Dozier would have to wrangle with what official indifference last November had let him shelve instead, the need to be extra-fair because he knew he didn't like Julius King. Suddenly inspired, Guy said, "You know, it isn't fair to her, is it? The way all the information is about him, what he thought, what he was like. And hardly anybody seems to remember anything about her." It worked—as Dozier thought that over, his tension visibly lessened.

"Well, *I* remember Callie, all right." His look turned inward. "She'd run out the door, I think," he said slowly. "It was open behind her, and she was standing there in the driveway like she didn't feel cold at all. But all she had on was this long green silk kind of housecoat—no coat or anything—and high-heeled fancy slippers with her bare toes showing. All that long hair was sort of swooping down over one shoulder— It was kind of red, her hair." He brought his gaze back from memory. "Funny. Before that morning, I always thought she had blonde hair."

And before this minute, Guy had assumed Mrs. King was dressed when Dozier saw her that morning. She had been when she died: the official reports duly listed the blood-soaked garments—the usual underwear and pantyhose, sweater and skirt, and green satin "mules." Her hair had not been done up in its customary chignon, but her face was expertly made up . . . "In the photographs, she seems a nice-looking woman," Guy said with a blandness he didn't feel. Because if Billy was at the Mercer School at 8:15, and the school was far enough away to ride a bike to, could he have been still at home when his mother got dressed?

"Well, she was certainly nothing you'd be ashamed to walk down the street with. Normally, you wouldn't go to any trouble to do it, though."

"But that morning—?"

"Oh well, that wasn't in the same ballpark. Not with Long Valley, even. If you could've seen it—"

Guy was trying to, summoning up the early-morning winter quiet and the suburban householder Claud Dozier setting off for work—and then finding himself abruptly translated into a wholly other context, in which a beautiful lady *en negligée* came running out of the house to star in a scene of passionate pleading . . .

"She told him, 'I'm begging you,' " Dozier said suddenly. "She had her hand on his arm, like she was trying to hold him back."

"You heard her?"

"Just a few words. 'Don't go. I tell you, I just *know*. So *please* don't go." And then she said 'I'm *begging* you,' looking at him like—" Dozier set the ruler down on his desk and smiled, briefly and with what looked like self-mockery. "Well, would you believe Iseult? Or Guinevere?"

"I was thinking of grand opera," Guy admitted, smiling too. But he was remembering the photo of Callie King on a mountaintop, looking like the stuff of legend. Your ethnic culture might determine the legend you picked, but it came to the same thing. Some kind of tragic queen, beautiful and doomed.

"That's all I heard, Lieutenant. But afterwards—well, I just couldn't get it out of my mind."

Wondering how long it would haunt him too, Guy said, "I can see why."

"Well, I hope you can, frankly. Because it doesn't mean I

had any kind of yen for Callie. That was the only time I ever saw her like that, anyway—so I hardly would've had time to work one up." Lightened of his burden, Dozier was a very different man, relaxed and even amused. And friendly, perhaps because he felt grateful to his liberator. "Besides, there's a big difference, you know. Between gawking at Iseults and chasing them."

"Julius King chased one," Silvestri observed. "It makes you wonder, doesn't it—like, what did he have? He couldn't have been all that good-looking, in spite of his big blue eyes, and he was never a millionaire. But he went after the big-league beauty and got her. What with?"

"Maybe he had this sexual magnetism you read about."

"Without causing any twitters from the other women? There weren't any, were there?"

"No, there weren't," Dozier admitted. "Well, Julius was always smart, they say. Maybe that was it."

"Come on. I was no dope in school, were you? And there must've been thousands like us. But there was something special about Julius King."

"Just because he got the girl? Well, maybe the competition wasn't as heavy as you think," Dozier said shrewdly. He tilted back his chair and picked up the ruler. "I never wanted any virgin goddesses or tragic queens. Did you?"

"No, I don't think so. But I'm not sure why." Sour grapes was the obvious explanation, but it didn't fit: Guy Silvestri at, say, twenty-one, had been quite sure he could get himself any goddess around.

"It's just too *hard*, that's why," Claud Dozier said. "I know what I wanted, back then—all the good things my father had, and less of the tough times. It was that simple. But common sense said it couldn't be easy. So I guess I figured that the way I thought a man ought to live, he'd have to have help." His quick, sweet smile appeared again. "Well, nobody really gets married according to plan, though, do they?"

It was not a question, but Guy said no anyway.

"So all right, it wasn't just that Vera fitted my job description for a helpmate. But she did fit with what I had in mind—and that wasn't to build a palace and then install a queen in it."

"Julius King was the other kind, you think? One of the ones who don't want help?"

"Like I said, I didn't really know him that well. But he sure liked to be—well, the king—at home. And I heard it was the same in the schools." Dozier put the ruler back on the desk and squared it neatly with the edge. "Still, I've got to be fair, Lieutenant. It could've taken another ten years for a Negro to work up to high-school principal in Long Valley, even though it's a real liberal kind of town. But Julius just up and appointed Marietta Wilder, without discussing it, and after that there was nothing to discuss: she could do the job, and everybody could see her doing it. So—" He ran a hand through his frosty hair. "Hell, it isn't simple, is it?"

"To say what kind of a man any man was? Never. But whoever killed King"—Guy caught the swift objection in the other man's look and thought *So that's it*—"wasn't analyzing him but reacting to him. As a tyrant?"

"Well, he was that, I guess. But I don't think I can help you, Lieutenant." Dozier cleared his throat. "To tell the truth, I never did believe anybody murdered Julius. The way I read it, he was shot in the head, from up close. So he could've done it himself, couldn't he?"

The truthful answer was, in Guy's opinion, *No way.* Because he had seen the nauseating mess left when half a man's head was blown off, and he had known battle-hardened men to flinch from the sight, just barely managing not to take to their heels. So it was impossible to see a frightened boy running *toward* it—and yet Billy would've had to in order to pick up the gun because King, dead instantly, could not possibly have done more than just drop it. You had to argue, then, that the gun had not been beside King's body when Billy found it, and therefore that King couldn't have been the last user of it . . . But Silvestri wasn't here to participate in a debate. He asked Dozier a question instead: "Why would King kill himself?"

"Because he killed Callie, that's why." Dozier had to concentrate on his ruler to get that said. But then he lifted his blue gaze. "The car proves that, doesn't it? He started off to work, then stopped and went home because he'd made up his mind to kill Callie."

Interesting that the logical Dozier should leave unexplained the fact that Julius King had presumably walked home. Guy didn't ask about it, because he was not certain the reason for King's abandoning his car had ever been brought to Dozier's attention: the Long Valley police had been immensely talkative about Billy King and tight-lipped about everything else. Which raised some serious questions, but not for Dozier. There was a better one to ask him—one he might be best equipped to answer. "What about Susan? Did King kill Susan, too?"

Dozier's eyes retreated from the encounter. "I never saw him acting the least bit fond of her. Or vice versa, for that matter. But that doesn't mean— It's still hard to imagine . . ." His voice trailed off.

Guy waited quietly, noting that it wasn't hard to imagine Julius King killing his wife. Or maybe any man killing Callie King? There was something about tragic queens that—

"If Susan saw him, maybe," Dozier said, too loudly. "I'm—sorry. It's a terrible thing to say. But I guess I do think if Julius decided he needed to—to protect himself—he could've shot Susan." He looked at the detective almost beseechingly: Claud Dozier was too proud to ask for mercy, but he wanted out of this alien world of dark speculations. "That must be why he— I mean, I figure he could just about get himself to do that. But even Julius couldn't stand it, once he saw what he'd done. So he turned the gun on himself."

Guy gave him a chance to rest—that had been hard work. Then he led Dozier into an exploration of the King family and its interrelations, encouraging the use of anecdotes: they were helpful, once you knew where the narrator of them stood, because you could sometimes see what he wasn't intending to tell you. Dozier was no Herkimer, and anyway he wasn't that sure about making a pitch for Julius King as killer; but even in the accounts that ended up indecisive—often because of Dozier's tortuous attempts at fairness—the picture of King as a heavy-handed monarch, consulting no one, was consistent. And it matched Derek Voorhees's flatteringly intended portrait of a man not accustomed to consulting his wife, indifferent to his children as people . . . Except that the incident of the Doziers' car added something, a callousness, maybe even a viciousness, not directly visible before.

It started when Vera Dozier decided that with three babies on her hands, she wasn't able to get enough use out of her car to justify the taxes and insurance. It would be cheaper to take taxis when Claud wasn't around. Sell it, Vera ordered. Dozier set about that listlessly—it wasn't much of a car. But then it occurred to him that with the Kings' two big kids and Callie lacking daytime transportation, it might prove handy for them, so he figured he'd ask Julius before going to a dealer. When King turned him down, Dozier thought he might have over-priced it; but King said flatly that he didn't need another car, at any price.

"If anybody wanted to go anywhere, he'd take them. That's what he told me, word for word. Callie was sitting right there, but he didn't even put on a show of asking her." Dozier's face reflected remembered embarrassment. "Maybe I was just imagining it, but it seemed to me he was enjoying himself—the way he talked, like he was sort of tasting the words. And she was embarrassed, that's for sure. Nasty, the whole thing. I had a feeling I'd run into an old family argument, so I left. But when I got home, Vera chewed me out for asking him about the price. The way she saw it, King just didn't have the money, and I'd put him on the spot."

"What made her think that, do you know? Could Mrs. King have confided—"

"No, it wasn't that, it was Susan. She babysat for us every spare minute, and Vera thought that had to be for the money, because Susan just wasn't the kind of a girl who didn't get asked out, you know. But any night she wasn't at our place, she was sitting for somebody else. It certainly did look like the girl was hungry for money."

"Maybe her father gave her a small allowance as a matter of principle." Only after he'd said it did Guy recognize the presumption contained in his suggestion.

But Dozier too, it seemed, had no question about who'd made the King family's allowance policy. "Sounds like him, doesn't it? But if Susan had a complaint about her allowance, I know she would've told Vera. She spent a lot of time with the girl, helping her with her sewing—Susan was crazy for dressmaking, and Vera's kind of an expert." Dozier smiled. "Anyway, all the guesswork was wrong, wasn't it—I mean, I heard King turned out to be in good shape financially. I always thought Vera was all wet anyway. She wasn't there that afternoon and I was: King wasn't embarrassed, and he wasn't haggling either. I told you, he was enjoying it. I can't prove it, but I just had a feeling." The light-blue eyes begged for release: the responsible citizen Claud Dozier wanted to help if he could, but the man who soothed himself by handling a steel ruler had only limited tolerance for talking about things he couldn't prove.

Guy got him off the hook by letting him do what he was good at. So Lieutenant Silvestri acquired a rough but neatly drawn map of the "woods"—apparently just uncleared land, not really heavily wooded—behind the two houses. And he also got, incidentally, an answer to the question that had occurred to him earlier: Billy and his friends had played behind the Dozier house because there was simply more room there for hiding and chasing. The brook was much closer at the back of the King house—"the so-called beach," Dozier said, was just a cleared space down by the brook, almost directly behind the Kings' place. The kids had trodden out a fair path by now, going there in the summers. "But right after that the brook takes this bend— Look, I'll show you."

Dozier turned a piece of stationery sideways and drew the brook starting high up at the left. What was up there, he said in answer to Guy's query, was a few old farmhouses. They were probably not even inside the town line. "The woman that helps Vera out with the housework lives over there. She comes across the fields—if you drove, you'd have to go into town and out again, and it'd take you three times as long." At the rectangle that represented his own house, the brook was still a few inches above it; but the wavering line was almost halfway down the page by the time it reached the King house. Judging from Dozier's map—he was neat and respectful of his tools, and he used his ruler, so Guy was inclined to trust his drawing—the brook didn't begin to curve upward again until it was behind the gas station. A culvert carried the brook under the main road to town, and then there was a small natural gorge. "So you don't see it too much after that," Dozier said, penciling in the gorge, "till it comes out behind the grammar school over here." He drew a small square at the upper right, where it looked rather like a postage stamp, and printed "Mercer School" in neat square letters.

How long a bike ride was it from the Mercer School to the King house? Well, that depended on how hard you rode, and whether you took the short cut to the "beach" and then came up to the house from the back. But with all that stuff growing in there, you'd probably need a machete— Dozier's voice faded and his eyes shifted, looking for somewhere to look. It didn't matter: Guy had already noted silently that "all that stuff" wouldn't be growing in November. But Claud Dozier, who knew perfectly well who'd ridden a bike from the Mercer to the King House, couldn't even manage a halfhearted attempt to mislead without obvious suffering.

"Well, but how much time are we talking about?" Silvestri pressed him. "An hour? Five minutes?"

"Oh, less than ten minutes, I guess. Depending on whether you have to wait for traffic. Because whether you go the back way or the front way, you still have to cross the main road."

Countrymen's estimates were always on the low side, Guy thought, watching Dozier fill in neat curls of underbrush alongside the brook. For Billy King, who rode the course regularly, say ten minutes, then. Which was just exactly the length of time between Mrs. King's being seen in her housecoat, without stockings and makeup, and Billy's being seen on the school playground. So no district attorney in his right mind would attempt to argue that the boy could have killed his mother before he left for school. Guy thanked Dozier and tucked the map away.

"Go see Vera if you can," Vera's husband said suddenly. "She may not tell me everything she knows. I'm her first loyalty, but I'm not her only one, maybe."

"Callie King?"

"Well, I just wouldn't be too surprised. They weren't buddies, but Callie didn't get out much. Vera was the nearest woman, and she makes good coffee."

Guy shook hands—meaning it, this time—and said he would certainly try. He thanked Dozier and left.

He would have talked to Vera Dozier anyway: at some point, Lieutenant Silvestri would need to know why Mrs. Wilder got no answer when she tried to call Mrs. Dozier at 10:30 that November morning. The way the investigation had proceeded in Long Valley, it was unlikely that anybody had tried to reconcile Mrs. Wilder's list of her phone calls with Mrs. Dozier's statement that she'd been at home all morning. It mattered, though. Because although it was now virtually impossible to entertain any suspicions about Claud Dozier having an affair with his neighbor's wife, his own wife might not have come to the same conclusion. And the energetic Vera didn't sound likely to just fold her hands and weep, in that case . . . The possibility would have to be kept in mind. But nothing could be done to follow it up until Guy was ready to make his move into Long Valley—which even Alonso had now begun pressuring for, he remembered wryly. It just wasn't time, though. Not until he could at least defuse John Vesey.

Back at the office, he found both Rubin and Jones waiting for him. An inefficient use of manpower; but on the other hand, there were two streams to be navigated, so maybe it paid to double up. The lieutenant told Rubin and Jones the notion he wanted checked out, by way of both the state troopers and a Long Valley rookie named Johnson. He'd like to have both speed *and* discretion, he said, but if it came to a choice, what was more important was not even to ripple the waters: if this was what he thought it was, it would be useless unless how Silvestri found out about it was Top Secret. He asked if that was understood and, assured that it was, dismissed his troops.

Then he called Wally the TV producer and confessed error. It seemed the lieutenant had failed to push the button when he should have at one point during that session with the news clips, and now he was in trouble. Was it too late? He could describe the scene he needed a photo of—it showed the King house, with the front yard and the driveway in the foreground . . .

It wasn't too late. Wally would fix it for him right away, and yes, he'd save the lieutenant's face by making sure nobody knew who the photo was for.

8
COMMAND POSTS
(May 16, Long Valley)

"Hey, Billy, did I tell you? I finally got hold of a copy of *Four-Seas Land*." Cannon's smile expected approval, but his eyes were too wary to expect anything. The deserted courtyard was probably the best setting for this, and Billy's willingness to come out here with him was promising, but it was still going to be risky. Meyer glanced at the yellow-green leaf buds on the surrounding young trees and hoped they would do their thing: spring was one of the oldest medicines in the world, so at least it should help. "I haven't read very much of it yet," he went on, "but I like it." Will Simons was very good at what he did, sliding you so deftly into Prince Trad's world that it was easy to close it over you.

Billy paused to poke the toe of his sneaker at a clump of violets. But he was clearly taking time out from a war: his body hugged the chimney angle of the old brick wall and his eyes regularly checked the windows of the arts and crafts room across the way. It was supposed to be empty, and Can-An wouldn't lie. But he might not know all the enemy's tricks . . . "How far along are you?" Billy asked politely, as soon as he got a moment off from guard duty.

"Well, you have to realize I don't have much time to read after work."

"I know. But like, what's happening where you're up to?"

Quit stalling, Meyer told himself. "Nothing really, right now." From the corner of his eye he saw Billy abandon the violets to look at him, and he made a conscious effort not to stiffen for the plunge. "Well, let's see. Trad is at school, but he hasn't been there long." Meyer swallowed. "He's having a lesson on the ferret-ship, and—"

"Which lesson?"

"The third." It was getting harder. "Trad won't be able to solo on the ship till next time, but after that he'll—"

"I know." Quite evidently Billy did know. His face was like a small fist.

"Where I stopped, Trad was on his way back to the dorm to change out of his suit." But Meyer knew what was just ahead: Prince Trad would pick up the mindwarner signal that meant his kingdom had been attacked by Fentry and his mother and sister were—well, not killed, but it was close enough for severe discomfort. Close enough so Billy almost from the first had been trying to use it as a message to Cannon. The doctor had thought to wait till the desire for help became pressing enough to make Billy offer to lend him the book, but now there'd been enough other evidences so Cannon had decided to go without that. Mentally crossing his fingers, he continued blandly, "So nothing's really happening yet, but—"

"It's a silly book," Billy interrupted. Quickly, he looked over Cannon's head.

Meyer took the opportunity to check the windows, too: what if someone happened to go into the arts and crafts room right now and maybe decide to glance out of the window? He'd ordered that room locked, but he should've explained why—an aide could decide it wasn't important and let it wait . . .

Billy said harshly, "It's not my favorite book. It used to be, but it isn't anymore." Abruptly, he sat down on the ground.

It wasn't difficult to get that literal message, *I don't want to go on.* Meyer stopped, keeping his body between Billy and the windows—thus easing their separate anxieties—and said casually that hardly anybody had the same favorite book after they were grown that they'd had as kids.

"What was your favorite book, Cannon? When you were a kid?"

Surprised, Meyer said truthfully, "*The Black Arrow*. By Robert Louis Stevenson, the same guy who wrote *Treasure Island*. But I liked *Black Arrow* better." Readying for the next question, he decided the reason probably had been the hero's girlfriend—Joanna? At the time, Meyer had been interested in picking up information about girls. Not that there'd been much in the book, he remembered. Either because of Stevenson's own innocence or his censors, this Joanna wasn't—

"What's it about?" Billy asked.

So much for trying to prepare answers. "Let's see. The hero's name is Richard, and he's about sixteen, I think. It takes place during the War of the Roses, in England. I've forgotten most of the details," Cannon confessed, "but there was a lot of action, fighting in castles and so on. And I remember one big fight in deep snow—that one was a beaut."

Billy looked away, as he always did when he made overtures. "Do you still have the book?"

So they were going to go after all, but by a different route. And maybe faster? "Well, I haven't got it at my apartment." Cannon watched the devout study of a dandelion going on at his side. "But I'm pretty sure it's in my old house. Where I used to live when I was a boy." He let the resonances of that gather, meanwhile thinking that he'd have to reread the book before he could let Billy read it, and finding the time would be a problem. But if this was heading where it looked like, it would be worth it. "I'll see if I can find it for you if you want. It's really a great story." Locating the book would be no problem: his mother could produce, practically instantly, things like the second-prize certificate Meyer won in his sixth-grade spelling bee, so she could certainly come up with his favorite book.

Suddenly, helplessly, Cannon saw *The Black Arrow* before him, big and substantial, satisfying to hold—not like one of those flimsy paperbacks that fell apart in your hands. With illustrations by somebody named Wyeth, full-page paintings of men in jerkins drawing crossbows, and the appropriate line from the text always printed underneath. There was one called a "frontispiece" (*Did you ever see that word again, in all your life?* asked Nostalgia, swift and keen). It was listed with the others, in the front of the book. But you could find the pictures easily anyway, because they were on special shiny paper . . .

"Well, I guess"—Billy half-turned toward Cannon but couldn't quite make it—"I guess I wouldn't mind reading it."

"If you're in a hurry, we can try the library. But if you can wait, I'd really like to lend you mine."

"No, I'll—I can wait."

"Fine." Now that the moment was suddenly here, Meyer felt ready for it after all. "I'll call my mother and ask her to look for it," he said easily. "But it may take me a while to get over there and pick it up."

Billy scrambled to his feet, in such haste that he forgot to protect himself from spying eyes in the arts and crafts room. "Where is your—?" He couldn't make it. He simply stood there, a small boy trying to be smaller, his head down and tucked in, like a bird in wild weather.

The first thing he needed was rescue from the dangerous word. "My house?" Meyer said smoothly. "Oh, about a hundred, hundred and ten, miles from Long Valley." He began to talk about roads and distances, which was the closest Billy could approach right now to the big old house with Mama and *The Black Arrow* in it. The house Billy, now starting to walk beside him again, perhaps wanted to move into—a real-life childhood. Meyer thought gratefully that to grow up reading books and getting into trouble for either slamming doors or forgetting to close them was a piece of luck. But you could get along with a poorer, harsher childhood—as long as it stayed put till you were through with it. Dr. Cannon knew that Meyer-who-became-Dr.-Cannon was probably a better identity for Billy to borrow than Prince Trad, who was always the same age and always either at war or about to be. But inside that knowledge there was also, somewhere, a lucky Meyer saying to unlucky Billy, *Here, have some, I have plenty,* holding out the delicious and nourishing past . . . Well, that would have to be watched. Because it would sustain Billy, but it wasn't his own. Eventually, when his own was found again, he'd have to move into it. And Meyer would have to remember to get out of the way.

"Cannon." Billy leaned against a tree. A birch, too slim to hide behind; but it would do for support. "In your house— Did you have a sister?"

"No, only a brother." Meyer Cannon looked at the white, drained face and launched promptly into a funny story, carefully irrelevant, about Amos, who was three years older and had thought up a hair-raising escapade into which Meyer had trustingly followed him. It didn't matter to Billy, so Meyer didn't add that Amos, too, had now grown up. But thinking about Amos, now an oceanographer, Meyer wondered whether it was because of the comfortable, loving childhood in that house that both its sons had become explorers of dark and unknown worlds. But still real worlds, not like Prince Trad's . . .

When Billy's color looked better, Cannon took him back to his room and observed that there was time for a nap before lunch. He left a heavy-eyed Billy sitting on the side of his bed, fighting the idea but apt to lose, and went to make sure there would be a tray for Billy when he woke—which Cannon was sure would be well after lunchtime. They'd finally managed to get a little weight on him, and Meyer didn't want to lose ground.

Not losing ground was the problem preoccupying Cannon as he walked back to his office. The forward motion had to be kept, but at the same time the territory ahead was still uncharted. What he needed, he decided, was a holding action of some kind—real and at least somewhat connected with the past, but safe—to keep Billy working at till Silvestri came through.

Cannon called Buxford, but Lieutenant Silvestri was out. The polite voice of Sergeant Alonso came on then—apparently there were instructions for calls from Dr. Cannon. He offered to help and then, when that wouldn't do, to take a message. Meyer tried to think of something besides *For God's sake, hurry*—which would be cruel and, he hoped, unnecessary. But, while *We have to know more about Susan* was certainly more helpful, it was just as difficult to leave as a message. Finally, Dr. Cannon just thanked Alonso and said never mind, he'd call back later.

When Silvestri and Herkimer came in, their arms full of brown bags from the delicatessen, Alonso's note was on Guy's desk. He rescued it from the grand sweep with which Herk made room for their lunch. *Dr. C. called,* Guy read while the odor of just-unwrapped dill pickle teased his hunger. *No-thanks to canIhelpyou, no message. But he thought hard before he said he'd call back later. Strong aura of unhappiness.*

The old one-two, Guy thought—Meyer unhappy, Ed needling. Let's all give Silvestri another nudge in his already bruised ribs . . . Well, let them: better to be black and blue than be the fellow who ordered the charge of the Light Brigade. There was an enemy out there, which nobody seemed able to remember. So there would be no move into Long Valley until they were properly equipped, and that was that. Guy turned with a sense of relief to Herk, who just wanted to know what was happening but wasn't forever yelling *Go-go-go.* "Well? Do you feel adequately informed now?"

"I've digested the tidbits you handed me." Uniting literal and figurative digestion seemed to cause Herkimer no problem. "The stuff mostly cancels itself out, doesn't it? You find out Fact A, but then Fact B more or less makes it useless." He chewed, considering. Then he delivered the verdict. "Not at all like TV detectives."

"What is, after all?" Guy bit into a corned-beef special and managed to get his tongue to a drip of cole slaw before it reached his chin.

"Granted, I suppose—though I'm beginning to think reality is highly overrated. But don't you have anything *new*? As opposed to stuff being verified or not verified?"

"Why, sure." Using his elbow, Silvestri slid out Merchant's report, which had surfaced in the Herk-caused shuffle, and turned it so the photocopy clipped to the top page faced Herk. "Registry of Motor Vehicles," he said indistinctly. "Last October."

Herk read aloud, " 'Susan Caroline King.' Maybe it isn't the same one, though. Wasn't she too young for a driver's license?"

"Sixteen's the age in Massachusetts. And she's the one: she had to produce a birth certificate. Plus signed permission from her parents. In this case, from her mother—with Callie King's maiden name and the address in Long Valley. So it wasn't another Susan King."

"You don't miss a trick, do you?"

Guy smiled modestly—as indeed he should have, since this trick had been entirely Merchant's own initiative—and deftly reclaimed the learner's-permit application. Herk had had enough time if he was going to look: there was no obligation to thrust upon him such goodies as the fact that Susan King had given a Buxford address for herself. Presumably she'd wanted to apply in Buxford because the Registry office in White County was in the same building as the Board of Education, where Julius King's daughter couldn't afford to be seen if this venture was to be kept from him. Very likely it had been kept from Callie, too—that "parent's signature" hadn't been checked, but Silvestri would be less than astonished to learn that it was a forgery.

"I don't suppose anybody remembered her," Herk said. "Just another pretty little girl in a hurry to start driving."

"That's right." Nobody had taken a good look at Susan King—not even, Guy thought, eyeing the filled-in-form, to see whether her hair was really "Bl." and her eyes "Br." He said sadly, "She was only five feet tall." It was a form of mourning, certainly not important. What *was* important was that an "adult driver" had had to appear with Susan—which Herk didn't seem to know, but Merchant did, so he'd come up with a name, at least. A description of Thomas A. Mallinson would also be handy, but *The clerk remembered a boy with her* was all Merchant had been able to report. And since Mallinson's date of birth had been recorded, along with his Social Security number, on the "wheel slip" retained at the Registry, they already knew he was nineteen. But that was all they knew: the address the Social Security number tracked back to was 27 Morrison St., Buxford, the same one Susan had given. Apparently young Thomas wasn't worried about receiving Social Security checks, for the address was a phony, in Merchant's expert opinion: ". . . a commune, sort of. Nobody there ever heard of Susan—or anybody else I might ask about, maybe. I backed off, figured you'd put Alonso or Jones on it if you really care. But they looked like it's against their religion to bullshit a black, so I figure it's straight. And why not? Any well-connected type who needs an address is free to use that one, and Tommy obviously was a w-c type even if the girl probably wasn't."

Herk was reading the brisk items listed under the sardonic heading, "A Day in the Archives" (which he either hadn't noticed or believed usual in police reports). The Volvo had turned out to be registered in Julius King's name, as had a VW in Pennsylvania before that. King obtained a driver's permit in White County within thirty days of his move to Massachusetts, as per Registry rules, and duly renewed it thereafter; but Mrs. King, who'd had a valid Pennsylvania permit when they arrived, let it expire and never applied for a Massachusetts one. "One car," Herk noted. "And Susan about to get her license. Looks like Pop was going to have to walk. Or buy another car."

In view of Julius King's reported edict, *If anybody wants to go anywhere, I'll take them,* that seemed unlikely. But then who had taught Susan to drive? It wasn't the high-school driving course, according to her permit application. And Thomas Mallinson didn't own a car registered in Massachusetts, so whose car had she used? Who, besides the mysterious young Thomas, had helped her with what must have been a rather complicated secret project ending in the trip to Buxford last October? Mrs. Wilder had told Alonso that Susan's school attendance was "spotty" since September, so that probably explained where she got the time (and, since Mrs. W. didn't blame seniors for goofing off because the last year was such a waste of time, that also explained why Susan's parents weren't told she was playing hooky). But if Susan was up to all this without her parents' knowledge, more than just the time involved needed explaining.

"That reminds me—about Julius King's car, Guy." Herk abandoned Merchant's report. "I was wondering, what was the matter with it that morning?"

"What makes you think anything was?"

"Oh, come on—why would he walk a couple of miles if he could've turned around and driven home? I noticed the news clips were vague on the point, just talked about the car breaking down. But how?" Herk peered at Guy suspiciously. "Don't you know what the trouble was?"

"I could find out for you." The Long Valley police were uniquely able to answer that question, and they'd have to: thanks to good old Mike-the-right-hand-man, Lieutenant Silvestri had enough clout to pry the simple but oddly secret mechanical information out of Chief Vesey. But it would mean coming out into the open, which Silvestri wasn't ready to do. Nudged again, from still another quarter, he said recklessly, "What's the difference? There aren't that many reasons why a car would start up all right and then have to be abandoned— smack up against a tree—a couple of miles later." After two bad turns on a downhill road, one of them featuring a drop of several hundred feet for a car out of control . . . Fortunately for Julius King, he drove slowly. Or had he been just enough alerted by his wife's passionate pleas that morning, even though he apparently decided to ignore them, to make a saving difference in his reactions?

"Somebody frammised the Volvo, is that what you're telling me?"

Guy retreated. "That would have to be proved."

"Well, not to me, baby." Herk smacked the desk top lightly. "That's it, it answers both questions—King wouldn't want the car tended to at the gas station because that would mean local gossip. And if he'd just discovered somebody had been fooling with his steering, he'd be upset enough to forget to phone the lady he had an appointment with." He stopped, brought up short by a problem. "The kid in the gas station—what's his name?"

"Lenny Pritchard. If you're wondering why he didn't see King coming back, that's no problem." Guy remembered the boy's vaguely peering look, characteristic of the nearsighted when they take their glasses off. He probably couldn't have seen and wouldn't have heard: automobiles were what Lenny would be listening for while he was studying; irrelevant sounds like footsteps across the road would be filtered out. Besides, King could easily have ducked out of sight for that patch of road. "If King didn't want to be seen," Guy said, "he didn't have to be. He knew Lenny Pritchard was there, so—"

"Did he?" Herk smiled. "*Was* little Lenny there, right at his post?"

"What's this? A TV script?"

"A scenario. You should try it. Because you legal types offend dramatic values, you know that? Like, here's Julius King, a mean man, it seems. Nobody likes him and—"

"Well, that's a bit sweeping," Guy said, thinking of Voorhees.

Herk's gesture, dismissing the objection, was more than a

bit sweeping. "But then, given that, where do you go? Into the kind of logic like the neighbor you told me about—King was a bad guy, therefore he was a murderer. But what any good writer can plainly see," Herk said modestly, "is that what the meanie is likely to be is a victim. He hurts people, and they—"

"All right, don't beat it to death. So what?"

"So whose victim was King? I know the rule of thumb says the wife, but that's an average—with a lot of poor helpless little women added into it. But Mrs. King was—what? Thirty-eight? A college graduate, a nice-looking woman, and I bet she had some money of her own, too; after all, her parents were well-to-do, and she was their only child. So no, not the wife: she could walk out, get away from the meanie. If she didn't want a divorce, it was probably because she got her kicks out of being pushed around by Julius."

Guy found with surprise, and some alarm, that he was objecting to that picture of Callie King. "Well, who, then?" he asked.

"Who *couldn't* divorce King? Not if Mama wouldn't move, and she apparently wouldn't."

"Billy? Oh, great. Which side are you on, Herk?"

"Billy wasn't there, remember? He was in school, taking a math test. But Susan wasn't in school."

"You're kidding."

"Am I? She was seventeen, and pretty. And right down the road, every day, was this Lenny Pritchard, who was—what? Nineteen? Twenty? And who just happens to be the best-qualified person on the scene to do tricks with King's car, right?" Herk held up a hand in a traffic-cop gesture. "I don't want to be accused of writing your lines for you, Guy, but don't bother to give me the one about how this is too slim. The fact is, it's fatter now than when I first thought of it. Because Susan's driver's license points to a whole secret life, doesn't it? What do you bet it wasn't Mom or Pop who taught her to drive and took her for the test? Let's be *real* rash; let's say Susan had plans."

"And if we do?"

"Then suppose we say Lenny wasn't at the gas station that morning, he was at the King house, where something was supposed to come off. Something besides Pop running off the road, let's say. Because Susan stayed home from school for a reason. So Lenny goes up there—"

"Mrs. King was home," Guy said. "She was wearing house slippers."

"Does that mean she hadn't *been* out? She could've taken her shoes off after she came home. Maybe that's how come her daughter and Lenny didn't hear her. And then once she caught them—"

"Shooting her instead of saying 'Mama, we love each other' seems a bit extreme, but okay. That still doesn't explain Susan, though." All the scenarios, however ingenious, ran into the problem of Susan. But Herk was entitled, so Guy went on: "That was an aimed shot, Herk, I'm sure of it. Right through the carotid— It couldn't be the result of a revolver being waved around in a scuffle, no way."

"Okay, *An American Tragedy*, then: he aimed. Was the girl pregnant?"

"Hell, no," Silvestri said, and then wondered at his vehemence. Because in fact he didn't really know—but surely it would've leaped to his attention if it had been in the autopsy report? It occurred to him then that he didn't even know whether it said Susan King was a virgin.

"All right." Herk's expression said you couldn't have everything, and he was prepared to make do. "So the boy just felt squeezed anyhow. Maybe she was pressuring him to take her away from all this, and he's just starting college and has no bread, right? Come on, Guy, give an inch."

"Okay, it's possible." Even if she was a virgin, it was at least possible.

"Thank you, Lieutenant Hard-to-get. Any more objections? Don't tell me Mrs. King was hit with some kind of special shot, too."

"No, she wasn't." Both shots—the one in the femoral artery and the one in the spleen—could have been wild, even accidental. "She could've just got in the way," Guy conceded.

"Either way—trying to protect her daughter, or her husband. I don't suppose you have any question about why Lenny would shoot King. In the head, right? Well, that's not impossible, is it?"

"It was awfully short range."

"So? They were fighting for the gun. Or maybe Lenny heard him coming and hid, then jumped him." Wearily triumphant, Herk sat back in his chair. "Those details can be worked out." A remembered detail spoiled the pose then. "Whose gun was it, come to think of it?"

"Nobody's, apparently." Merchant's Item 1 had been brief enough to be easily remembered: *Gun permits—Zilch on J. King and his Mrs. both. Never in Mass., and Penna. says no, too.*

"You mean it wasn't registered? Great. Lenny'd have no problem getting hold of one."

Guy was tempted to observe that Lenny might have had a problem keeping his gun in Julius King's desk drawer. But Herkimer had apparently decided to ignore that oil stain (he had to know about it, it was in the news clips), and it would be mean-spirited to hold down his creative flight with leaden facts.

Silvestri had lost his chance anyway: Herk was soaring now. "The important thing is, you admit it's not physically impossible. And it fits the alibis, too, doesn't it?"

"It could." If the owner of the gas station came and went at just the right times. Lenny Pritchard wouldn't have had to be away from his post long, and he could've left the phone off the hook—nobody telephoning a gas station would be surprised if the line was busy. And he could easily have been back in time to see Harry Moody's laundry truck go by. "But I'm not so sure it really fits the characters," Guy said slowly. It could, though: Herk's scenario was like a badly printed color picture, with blue trees and a green lake. But if you straightened out the slipped plate, moved it just a little, you could have green trees and a blue lake. If the dramatist's character Herk was proposing didn't fit Susan King, it could—

Guy didn't get to think about that anymore because Meyer Cannon called back then, and a few minutes after he'd said "Hello," it was clear to Silvestri that he was running out of time to think. For Derek Voorhees had made his move, via a painful irony: on the basis of the fact that Billy King had now recovered his ability to speak, Voorhees was demanding a court hearing to determine the boy's status. And, according to Cannon—who sounded frantic—they could only lose by that. He couldn't possibly say Billy was cured; and the ordeal itself might destroy the progress he'd made so far.

"I was just beginning to gamble," Cannon said desperately. "I'm starting on a new move, too—I'm waiting now for the go-ahead from an education man I consulted." The new move involved some kind of mathematics lesson, Guy gathered. A kind of "package" based on the quiz Billy had taken on that November morning, his last day at school—which might topple him into memory, but if it did, it would be "more or less safely," as Cannon put it, because the landscape, though familiar, would be without people. And the quiz would be surrounded by exercises, old ones to give him enjoyment and self-confidence, and a new one to provide a challenge—bait to keep Billy wanting to move forward in case tweaked memory made him want to run back and hide again.

"It certainly sounds like a good idea," Guy said into the phone. But Cannon only answered glumly that they'd never know whether it was. Because Billy would surely be committed, and the effect on him would be completely destructive. Billy's desire, nursed along by Cannon, to come out of the silence he'd imposed on the past, would flicker out. And, conditions being what they were for the institutionalized patient—as opposed to Billy's present "observation" status—he would probably get little or no therapy of any kind. So he might never again get as close to reality as a math quiz, even . . .

What the doctor needed most right now, Guy decided, was first aid. He turned the job over to Herkimer, who could give a short course in public-relations techniques—which might possibly help to make the odds less discouraging. Meanwhile Lieutenant Silvestri got out Rubin's report on Derek Voorhees: it was know-your-enemy time.

Herk hung up. "Meyer will never be able to do it."

Guy knew "it" was, in effect, to act as Billy's lawyer. And it was true that Meyer probably couldn't do it. What Herk had been outlining on the phone, and what probably anybody except the honest Cannon would have seen at once, was that if Billy's progress was a weapon it was double-edged. If Voorhees could use it to get Billy into court, Cannon could use it to keep him out. Voorhees might produce contending shrinks, but none could have Cannon's credentials in the eyes of the court: as the doctor who'd brought Billy along to this point, his word had to count enough with any judge to get at least a delay ordered.

But the hopelessly conscientious Dr. Cannon couldn't make himself say anything that would sound like a promise of a cure, or even of progress within a given time. Instead, he would come across as mulish and obstructionist, or maybe just sentimental, while Voorhees would be only a reasonable man asking to have things made orderly—which was something courts were in favor of. "Meyer thinks of the court as Voorhees's turf," Guy said aloud. "He's afraid even to try playing on it."

"Well, whose turf did it turn out to be last November? All right, I know, it was a mistake. And this isn't supposed to be an adversary proceeding, but it will be, won't it? With Voorhees disguised as Billy's lawyer, but nobody except Cannon, who's lousy at it, actually representing Billy—" Herk looked down at the report on Guy's desk. "This about Voorhees? Is there anything in it that could get him taken off Billy's case?"

"I doubt it." Rubin had summed up succinctly: everything

about Voorhees's biography sounded like a handbook for how to raise a homosexual. So Rubin had gone hunting, but there was nothing to be found in the Boston hangouts or on the mailing lists that included even the shyer closet queens. *Film clubs and art magazines, the kind you'd expect—negative. He hangs out with sports types some, but mostly golf—no coaching little boys or taking them on overnight trips, etc. No visible love life, not with man, woman, or child. If you can believe it. I don't, so I say let's have a look at his bank accounts. That way, even if we don't find some kind of money-business with J. King, we might at least find a love nest or a blackmailer. But I'd have to do that in Long Valley . . .* "There could be something in his finances." Guy said. "Any kind of reason why he'd like a free hand with King's estate would do. But it would take time to find it, even if it's there."

"You've got about a week, I'd say. Even Meyer can probably stall that long. But I wouldn't count on any more."

"I can threaten Voorhees, maybe, in that time." If Rubin were sent to Long Valley and proceeded to research fairly conspicuously, word would get to Voorhees at once. And if he had something to hide, he might panic. But to count on that alone would be tactically inadvisable, so—"I think," Lieutenant Silvestri said slowly, "it would be better to go for broke."

"You mean like, tie up the whole case?"

Herk looked frightened, Guy saw with wry amusement. Apparently it was fun to spin murder plots, but when they threatened to become living theater . . . "If we can show Billy couldn't have committed a crime, then there's no charge to be made or dropped, no prosecutor waiting with machinery ready to roll. What's done with Billy then is likely to be entirely a matter of medical advice." Though Herk refused to realize it, it was a court's need to see that law violations were punished that gave Voorhees his real clout in urging action. If it was only a matter of bookkeeping, the court wouldn't hesitate to put the boy's welfare before the need to tidy up the estate.

"You're talking about wrapping it up—announcing whodunit, like in a detective story?"

"Yup."

"But you don't *know* whodunit."

This sort of opening, Guy thought, comes to a man only once. "Then I'll have to find out, won't I?" he asked urbanely.

"Oh, wow. In a week?"

"I can do it in a day," just-plain-Silvestri said seriously. "If I can get one thing I need first." He watched Herk look at the phone, expecting drama. But this was real life: neither Rubin nor Jones came through on cue, with the message-to-Garcia vital to Silvestri's war.

Herk left soon afterward, and Guy went back to work. Which meant, specifically, reading Alonso on Twirl—an essay absolutely untranslatable into Buxford Police daily-report forms:

Lieutenant—

As you thought, Twirl's prominence in the TV news was disproportionate. However, he's not without a niche in Long Valley's affairs, because he operates what amounts to a suburban outlet for the Buxford counterculture biz. Without looking into his income tax returns, no one can say with complete certainty that he seems to be doing well at his trade; but I do say, with fair certainty, that a smart boy who doesn't mind work apparently can make it on the other side of the looking-glass, too.

He is a smart boy, graduated—as Ronald Simpson—with above-average grades from Long Valley High School, though he comes on as a dropout. That was four years ago, so he may have sold people on his image by now. Of course, Miss Crabtree (for one) could set the record straight. One wonders why she hasn't.

Pursuing the obvious line from here, I met with no interest from our own drug squad or from the serious narcos. Twirl may be doing a little something in their line, but if so it's only light stuff and probably for personal use. They admit he's visited

---

regularly by the circuit rider who works out of Buxford every week ("Ah yes," I murmured knowingly: why let them think our little Div. isn't *au courant?*). But it seems that's only for banking and other necessary services to Twirl's outpost trade in headshop bric-a-brac and similar trendy merchandise. In short, they simply refuse to take him seriously back at headquarters—several varieties of headquarters—and I think their vast yawns are authentic. So I'd say Twirl is no part of any drug-squad undercover deal, either way. And, since he can't be big enough to have anybody serious protecting him, I don't think you'd be stepping on any toes, there or here.

But, to sum up, you're not likely to get anywhere. He adds up to just a businessman making a buck and staying out of jail while running what amounts to a Radical Mafia. His hippie artifacts may impress the Long Valley young, but he also wows the local business community—which just happens to know how much insurance he carries on his artfully shabby pad. And the town's elected leaders probably see him as something close to an unofficial ward heeler bringing in the youth vote, so to speak. So I have a feeling you'll find Twirl more interesting in terms of anthropology than law enforcement.

You know, I can't figure it out—does the general tolerance of this young monster make us a corrupt society, or only a sophisticated one?

Sergeant Alonso's final question was so interesting to the ex-anthropologist Silvestri that it wasn't until he was on his way home that he took up again the matter of Herk's scenario. Which would have to be adjusted to accommodate the one "detail" Silvestri thought was really central, the grand-opera scene in the Kings' driveway that November morning.

Guy spent the ride home tuning into a hunch, and by the time he was standing in his own driveway, he knew it was right: there was something wrong with the way he'd been seeing that scene. It did belong on a stage, but not as opera: the dialogue Claud Dozier had overheard just didn't translate into Italian, somehow. Well, if nobody broke into song, maybe what it was was a play? *That* was something he could have asked Herkimer about. But it was too late—Herk had left town, and it was hardly worth a long-distance phone call. Besides, he'd helped enough today: without even knowing it, he'd probably solved three killings and launched Voorhees onto the skids.

9

TWO MESSAGES TO GARCIA
(May 20-22, Long Valley)

Williams told himself to stop waffling: you had to take *some* chances. He was acting like Laverne when she was learning to drive—when she used to wait so long you could scream out loud, and even then after she finally poked that beat-up Chevy out of a side street, she'd get scared and just hang there, looking over her shoulder to see what was coming at her. What scared her husband was that if she stayed there long enough, looking back, something *would* come at her, all right·...

Well, she was over that stage now. Thinking about it had made Williams feel better, though, so he finished quickly. But still taking care to write neatly so the Doc would be able to read it, because it really must be important—Billy had never before held onto a letter to that Mr. Simons. This one wasn't finished, but he wasn't writing any more on it, just worrying it: he kept it under his chessboard, and every time Williams looked at it, the last three nights, he could see it had been taken out and put back. But that was all. And there was nothing in the log about Billy sending out any other letter to Mr. Simons, either.

Williams paused to consider whether he ought to add something sort of begging pardon for minding what maybe wasn't his business, just in case. Of course they *said* it was his business—it was something he'd observed, and Doc Cannon said to report anything you observed. But Laverne was right, the kind that did the most talking about how we're all on the same team and so on, they might could decide the fastest that you were out of line.

Dammit, there he was, doing it again, looking over his shoulder. He'd already decided, Williams told himself angrily. He'd studied the whole thing over and decided to take the chance because Cannon wouldn't have any other way to know. The Doc looked at the letters Billy wrote, but only when they were ready to be mailed. So if this really mattered and Cannon didn't find out because Williams was too chicken to tell him, that might could be a hell of a thing for Billy . . . Besides you have to trust your own feelings, when you come right down to it. So take a chance. Do it.

Williams signed his name with a flourish. Then he wrote "Aide" under it, telling himself it was because Williams was such a common name. He put that out of his way and picked up the other page, on which he'd copied out what Billy wrote—the only way he'd been able to think up to get the letter out and back while Billy was sleeping, because the only copying machine on this ward was in the office and that was locked up before the night shift came on. To go off the floor was impossible: what with one guy's wife having a baby and another off sick, it was practically just Williams and Hughes alone on the floor most of the night. So this would have to do. He read it anxiously once more, because if you weren't an M.D. you didn't know what counted. Even the spelling mistakes counted sometimes.

Like, it sure needed a shrink to figure what there was in these few sentences to get Billy uptight. It seemed like he was only telling Mr. Simons not to count on Zak—whoever *he* was—getting the message because sometimes even when somebody's mindwarner was working fine, he just didn't listen because he wanted to practice basketball— No, that part was crossed out.

Williams crossed his out, too, just like Billy had: everything mattered, so maybe that did, too. But he was thinking it couldn't be that mindwarner talk, *that* was nothing new. So now, when Billy was so much better that some days you could swear he was practically normal, why should he get so hung up about it?

All right—enough. If it wasn't important, Cannon would let uppity Williams know, one way or another. But right now, quit fadiddling . . . Williams folded the two sheets of paper and sealed them into one of the striped-edge envelopes used for mail within the hospital. He addressed it to Doc Cannon's office and then stuck it in his pocket and got back on the ward: there was still some time left on his coffee break, but the patients didn't seem to know it.

Changing out of his whites at the end of his shift, Williams found the letter. He carried it in his hand, upstairs to the lobby, where there was an inside-mail box on the reception desk. He'd started across toward it when Hughes stuck his head in the front door and hollered, "Come on, man, I already put in overtime just waitin' for you."

"Okay, okay." There weren't too many ways to get home at this hour: if you didn't ride with Hughes, you ended up doing a lot of walking. "Comin' right along," Williams called out cheerily. He pivoted, slipping a little on the freshly polished floor, and tossed the envelope as he wheeled. He heard the familiar light *thunk* when it hit the box, so he kept on going. It had been a hard shift and he was tired—this once, then, it was easy to remember not to waste time looking over his shoulder.

So he didn't discover that what the envelope had hit was the outside of the box. From where it slid silently down to the already cleaned floor, to lie in the farthest shadows under the receptionist's desk.

"All right," Silvestri said, "let's have the details."
Rubin glanced at Jones and saw him seeing the same thing

—from the minute they'd told the lieutenant they were ready with the story, he'd had an edge on him you could shave your beard with. Like, you could hear his carburetor racing, practically. It was go-go-go time for sure—you could put your money on it, they'd all be back on regular duty this time next week.

Jones said uneasily, "Well, sir, I only went through the troopers. So maybe Rubin better—"

"I have no time for Alphonse and Gaston minuets," the lieutenant snapped. "Now, this trooper—er—"

"Morris Coakley, sir."

"Thanks. Okay, Trooper Coakley called in to the Long Valley police and got a rookie named Johnson. Rubin, why a rookie?"

"Oh, well, it didn't sound like anything much, Lieutenant. This kid—Matthew Johnson—he just happened to be close by because he'd been driving people to their school-crossing posts for the lunch hour." Rubin felt worried: it wasn't like the lieutenant to act like an efficiency expert about what was just an ordinary human thing. "Nobody would've thought it was anything but a routine call," he added.

"Let's skip the editorializing," Silvestri said. He saw Rubin's astonishment. "All right, listen, I want it understood. I'm not out for scalps in Long Valley, but I'll make all the apologies necessary—or possible—for them." He smiled wryly. "And if perfect objectivity is beyond you, how about being partisan this way—over here, where I am. Okay?" Their grins said it was. "Good. Now—who entered the house first, Coakley or Johnson?"

The trooper, Rubin said. The front door had a good Yale lock and a bolt besides, but neither one was in use.

"Coakley said later he was surprised," Jones put in, "because the house looked locked up for the night. But he tried slipping the lock on the front door, so he wouldn't have to break the glass in the back door."

Rubin took it from there: "When they got in the house, they

just about had time to see the place was full of bodies—one of them was partly in the hall, too—and then they heard this noise from upstairs." He nodded, acknowledging the coming question. "A faint crackling sound, is the best description I could get."

"Coakley wanted to go upstairs right away, because he figured somebody might be hurt," Jones said. "But the kid told him the whole family was—uh—accounted for, in the living room. So then he decided to go easy, because after they listened some more it sounded like somebody might be tiptoeing around up there. That's when he sent Johnson to call for a backup. Meanwhile Coakley went outside and around back to look over the possible exits from the upstairs windows."

"The trooper did all the thinking, it sounds like," Silvestri noted.

"Well, sir, he's a ten-year veteran with his head on straight. And the rookie was in bad shape right from his first look. Coakley must've really thought so, too, you know? Because he stationed the kid in the front hall in case of an attempt to come straight down the stairs, but he took Johnson's car keys—that's how much confidence Coakley had that the kid wouldn't get jumped, right? It was the best he could do, though, because he had to cover the back—he'd found a likely-looking drop from a bathroom window upstairs, and just a step to some woods behind the house, right handy to get lost in."

There had been no argument afterward about the decision not to rush the upstairs: it had been Coakley's decision, but the local police agreed that if anybody had been up there, he'd have been trapped, so why be a hero? Where the trouble between the state and local police seemed to start, Guy decided, was with the trooper's assumption that Johnson had checked the victims while he himself was around back. True, Coakley hadn't told him to, but it was regulation procedure. And if the rookie didn't know that, he'd seen it demonstrated, because Coakley himself had made sure Susan King was dead before the noise from upstairs interrupted them.

After the backup came, the upstairs rooms were investigated by Coakley and Long Valley Patrolman Valeriani of the backup team. They found the source of the noise—a radio left on, very low, in the girl's bedroom. "That's what was making the crackling sound, they say. It must've been awful damn quiet in that house," Rubin finished skeptically.

"Yes," the lieutenant said soberly. "It would have been."

Rubin blinked, acknowledging correction, and took up the account again. Valeriani put in a call for Chief Vesey, and then he and his partner started a routine check of the kitchen and cellar. Matthew Johnson, presumably having held together as long as he could, then came apart. "So when the chief showed up, Johnson was outside upchucking into the shrubbery and Coakley was at his car reporting in to his own people. The two Long Valley boys were in the house, but still nobody had actually checked the victims."

"Then it was Vesey himself who found out about Billy."

"Right, Lieutenant. He noticed that the blood on the face was still fresh, was how it happened." From there, it was by the book, with Vesey seeing to that personally—and making sure that Billy, who obviously had a head wound, wasn't moved. "They didn't find the weapon, so they assumed it wasn't left on the scene, and I guess that started them thinking in terms of some wandering nut, you know. Until the ambulance got there. The doctor went to put a needle in Billy's arm, and that's when the .38 turned up. Recently fired, one round left."

"Where was it, under him?"

"No, beside him. But his jacket had flapped open, and it was covering the gun. The way I heard the story is," Rubin said with unseemly enjoyment, "that's when Chief Vesey really started tearing up the place and everybody in it. At top bellow. And including the state trooper, which caused a certain—um—subsequent coolness between Chief Vesey and the C.O. at the White County barracks."

"I heard Vesey apologized to Captain Zablocki later, sir," Jones said.

"And I heard he refused to. You can take your pick, Lieutenant. And your guess about the state of the détente now."

Silvestri nodded. "You said there was a lid on this, Jones. How did you get in?"

"Well, sir, Rubin did, really. I got a certain amount from the troopers, but only after they knew I knew. And on a no-name basis."

"I got in by way of Johnson," Rubin said. "He was very upset—on sick leave for quite a while after, and so on. It sounds to me like he got real gentle treatment: he's back on duty now, I hear, and nothing seems to be held against him. But what happened, while he was upset he told his troubles to his older brother. And Big Brother—he's in business in Boston, which is how I got to *him*—he got real shirty about the way the kid was treated and—"

"But why?" Jones interrupted.

"What do you mean, 'why'? That's Human Relations, baby —wait till you've been here a little longer. We had one come in once who—"

"Rubin."

"Okay, Lieutenant. Well, that's it, anyway—the brother went around spilling enough vows of vengeance, et cetera, to leave the trail I picked up. He didn't keep it up for long—maybe he got a message from Long Valley?—but the traces were still there. Only just, though: Jones was right about the lid on it, sir. The only way in was through somebody mad at Chief Vesey."

"The troopers weren't *very* mad at him, sir," Jones said.

Rubin agreed: "Nobody really is. If you hadn't come up with the steer to Johnson, Lieutenant, I'd still be looking for an opening. Because it had to be somebody from outside—the men have really closed ranks around Vesey. And I don't think it's pressure; it looks to me like it's spontaneous. Vesey's their own, and they do seem to think he's really okay."

"Even the troopers, in a way," Jones said. "Like, that fantastic trip to Strawbridge, to get the specialist for Billy's head? That was Vesey, you know—he just grabbed wheels and went. And they say the way he drove, he should be racing at Indianapolis."

"There's no question"—Guy looked from one to the other —"that the whole operation was Vesey's? His alone?"

Jones nodded eloquently, and Rubin said, "All the way, Lieutenant. As far as his boys know, anyway."

The silence lasted about half a minute. Then Silvestri smiled—a slow angelic smile. "Jones, get us some coffee, will you?" He reached for the phone and began to dial Alonso. "Rubin, you're it. Can you leave for Long Valley tonight?" He didn't wait for an answer, because Alonso had answered his phone. "We're moving out, Ed. Get in here and let's set it up."

Setting it up turned out to be a process where Alonso got to say, "That'd be the twenty-fourth, Lieutenant?" and then almost nothing else until "See ya, Lieutenant" a quarter of an hour later. The interim was filled with orders, the most detailed one involving Rubin. He was to take off tonight, establish himself in a Long Valley motel and report in its name and phone number by safe means, and then begin tomorrow morning— after first having checked with Merchant on what he'd dug up in the probate court in Pennsylvania—pursuing certain researches into the finances of Derek Voorhees. It was not exactly an undercover deal: Rubin would need to use his official status in his researches out there, but there was no reason why a J. Rubin of Buxford, so registered at a motel and driving a car that matched in case anybody checked out its plates, should discuss his job history with the proprietor. And if J. Rubin should happen to catch sight of the visiting Lieutenant Silvestri in Long Valley day after tomorrow, Rubin was to wait to be recognized and go away quietly if he wasn't.

The arrangements for the visiting lieutenant were to begin formally at noon on the 24th, but informal arrangements must be made for talks earlier that day with Lenny Pritchard and Mrs. Claud Dozier—the latter preferably before 11:00 A.M. Chief Vesey was to be told, clearly and emphatically, that Lieutenant Silvestri proposed to spend exactly one day in Long Valley, no more. That was important. Alonso nodded, understanding why: a man could put up with anything, just about, if he knew in advance it was going to last for only one day.

Somebody said "Yessir" and Guy paused to sip the brown fluid that was melting its paper cup. Then he went on to dispose of Merchant, who was to forget about tracing Mrs. King's money for now. He should take off instead for the community college attended by Lenny Pritchard and there find out everything there was to know about him. Including how he'd done on the exam he was supposed to be studying for on the morning of the homicides. And also including girl friends, if any, and the question of what access Lenny might have to types who could get him a .38 for a price. Merchant was to make no noise in his researches. Rubin, on the other hand, was to be so noticeably discreet as to cause a certain amount of comment.

Jones made the mistake of asking, "What about me, Lieutenant?" and was assigned—by a Silvestri who seemed visibly leaner and sharper than usual—to find a better source of coffee. Then the lieutenant asked what everybody was standing around for, and left without finding out.

Sergeant Alonso, also seeming to operate at a different metabolic rate now, told Rubin, "Haircut. Tie. Your FBI-man suit. Then report, ready to go, to get your briefing, ammo, and communications."

"Ammo?"

"You'll need your State House ticket, too—otherwise you'll have no authorization in White County." Alonso paused to take note of Detective Rubin's surprise. "Yeah, ammo. Did you think you were going to a tea party? It's homicide, and there'll be hostiles out there. If you'd kept that in mind," Alonso concluded icily, "maybe you wouldn't have been nagging the hell out of the Lieutenant, pushing him to roll, all the time he was trying to get you better odds for when the shooting starts."

"Me? *I* never—"

"Move it," Alonso said, and turned to the job of locating Merchant.

Rubin moved it, but he paused in the doorway to pass on the treatment to the freshman. "Don't feel bad, old buddy," he told the crestfallen Jones. "They also serve who only stand and wait." Then Rubin left, while he could still do it voluntarily.

10

THE CIVILIANS
(May 24, Long Valley High School)

Marcia Dyer's cherry-red silk jersey dress was at once a perfect equivocation and a demonstration of the futility of equivocation. Because the dress was longer than they'd had in mind at the Buxford boutique where she'd bought it and also shorter than the Long Valley school board would think appropriate, but this double failure at conformity had not resulted in any personal gain. For the clinging fabric made explicit the curve of bosom and the skirt stopped soon enough to reveal nicely turned ankles all the way up to well-shaped thighs—and yet somehow the whole sexy intent was demurely denied: in spite of the dress, maybe in spite of anything she could wear, Miss Dyer would still have been cast as a librarian in a 1940s movie. But a small-part librarian, not one who undergoes a glamorous change, because her brown hair already hung to her shoulders in soft waves, looking as pretty as it possibly could. And she didn't even wear glasses to take off and become a Desirable Woman.

It was typical of Marcia's effect on the male that her colleague James Poley showed no visible interest when she came into the teachers' room at Long Valley High. True, he looked hung over. But he was at least enough awake to be drinking coffee and grading papers, and for Poley, that should have meant he was up to at least a gleam in the eye when a short pleated red skirt flipped past. But there was no gleam. Only a weary "Hi" that seemed to be trying to sound fond but just couldn't manage the effort.

That could've been because Marcia's skirt didn't actually flip. It looked designed to, but there's a limit to what can be done with accordion pleats, and Marcia Dyer's walk was like her voice, muffled and sure of nothing except the need to be lady-like. Not that any of that was in her conscious thought: when she bent her knees to get down to her bottom-row mailbox, instead of simply bending over at the risk of offering the world an extra-length glimpse of pantyhose, that was because Marcia Dyer had long ago foreseen the problems of short skirts and had established policies designed to solve them. As a result, the idly watching young man not only glimpsed no glimpses, he didn't even notice the attractive litheness required for the maneuver. What Poley—at the moment uninterested, but never *that* uninterested—registered was only guardedness and competence, the two qualities that already constituted his image of Marcia anyway.

He returned his bored attention to a student's ingenious summary of the economic condition of the United States in 1861 and its effect on the outbreak of civil war. At twenty-eight, Poley's own high-school days were not lost to his memory, and besides, he was an easygoing, good-natured man. So he was doing his best to find something kind to write in the margin about an assertion that linen spun from the South's flax was needed for the sails of New England ships and that's why war didn't break out earlier. And then Marcia plunked down a typed note on the Formica table top and accompanied it with what, for her, amounted to an angry oath.

Poley saw the "Dear Marcia—" and went on to what was more relevant, the end. He recognized rather than read the clear, round signature and then didn't bother with what lay in between: Marcia would tell him anyway, so why wade through

Marietta Wilder's prose? She was a good-enough deal as principals went, but she was unfortunately not immune to the archness of her ilk. Which presented a problem, because James Poley wasn't quite color-blind enough to feel comfortable sneering at anyone of Mrs. Wilder's shade of tan—but what else could you do with orders cutely dressed up as friendly tips? Roley did what he often did with uncomfortable situations: he pushed back the Romantic-poets lock of dark hair straying over his forehead, dismissed his moody-and-tormented look in favor of centering an engaging smile in his big dark eyes, and turned sympathetic attention on a troubled lady.

Standing over him, Marcia successfully wrestled down an impulse to take his poor curly head between her hands and crush it to her bosom. Her voice was even more flat and muffled than usual as she described Meyer Cannon's request, duly submitted through Mrs. W., for a "math package" for Billy King. Marcia hesitated before she said Billy's name: Roley was sensitive and emotional, and she had no wish to make him unhappy.

But he seemed actually pleased. "Great. Does that mean Billy's going to have a visiting teacher?"

"I wouldn't think so." Marcia read out the description of *the ideal combination, Dr. Cannon says*: two or three days' review work, a copy of the quiz Miss Dyer gave on the last morning Billy was in class, and one unfamiliar and slightly more difficult problem. "He'd be working on this by himself, it looks like."

"I thought they already found out his brain wasn't damaged."

"I guess it isn't. He's been playing chess by mail—with May Crabtree—for some time."

"Well, then," Roley wondered, "what's the point?" But soothing, not inquiry, was his forte. So he added, "And why the flap? You keep copies of your quizzes, don't you?"

"Yes, but in my notebook. And they want the same kind of paper and ink and everything. *I realize that probably means wrestling with the hectograph monster,"* she read aloud, *"and I do commiserate. But it seemed the least we could do, so I'm afraid I said it would be no trouble. Try to forgive me."*

"Ugh," Roley obliged. "I guess the purple ink is important. Though I can't see why."

"Some kind of attempt to jiggle Billy's memory, I imagine."

"Oh, wow. Meyer really has some groovy ideas."

"You think it would be groovy? For Billy to remember?" Marcia's gaze lingered on her colleague's handsome face.

"Yes, of course I do." He flushed under her glance. "Billy's got to get well, whatever it takes." His voice was not as guarded and muffled as hers, but it held a note of defiance that Roley himself seemed to hear and then grab at like a tired swimmer reaching a boat. In the small silence, he could almost be heard gathering strength. And then he managed to swing aboard: "You're just peeved about having to hectograph the bloody thing, that's all." He smiled, engaging and now at rest. "Come on, Marcia, admit it."

She didn't do a very good job of that, but the bell rang for the next class, so she got away with it. Roley gathered his papers and looked helplessly at his coffee cup.

"Go on," she said. "I'll take care of it."

"Thanks." He was starting out of the room when he asked, "You're free this period, aren't you? You going to hang around?" He turned back, but not in time to see the small, involuntary hope that had flickered in Marcia's eyes. "Like, long enough, maybe, to give me a ride home?"

"All right. I'll be here at the end of the period."

He smiled with genuine pleasure. "Great. I'll buy you a soda, okay? On the way back to the Reservation."

Marcia started to answer, but of course he had not waited: he knew his power, Roley did. The only thing that saved her pride was that he knew it so *generally*—which fortunately seemed to keep him from being aware of his specific effect on

Marcia Dyer. Though he had plenty of chance to observe it, for it was now more than a year since they'd begun living under the same roof, technically anyhow, in the big old hotel that had been cut up into small apartments to house Long Valley's few nonhomeowners. The inhabitants of what they themselves had nicknamed "the Reservation" were mostly two-year transients—unmarried, like Miss Dyer and Mr. Poley, or childless couples like Dr. and Mrs. Cannon.

It was not that Long Valley society was closed against the Reservation, exactly (though of course nobody who hadn't lived in town for a generation could be considered a real citizen anyway). But in actuality, few tenants of the Reservation had any real interest in the crabgrass problem or the hazards of roof gutters choked with leaves; in the living rooms of Long Valley, they were polite foreigners, and entertaining them was an obligation but exhausting. So it was avoided, on both sides, as much as decency permitted.

Thus, nonabsorption by the local society had some part in creating the kind of cozy outsider-huddle that existed at the Reservation. But the chief cause was the weather: most "transients" arrived in September, with winter closing in soon after, and in Long Valley winters, anybody you could visit without going outdoors acquired automatically a certain extra attraction. Then, also, there was the phenomenon of Devora Cannon, who loved cooking and company and came of a culture that emphasized being part of a group. Given her own personality and the fact that she was the only one at the Reservation who didn't have a full-time job, it was inevitable that she would become, in effect, Mama. True, she was one of the younger members of a house population that didn't include anyone over thirty-five. But it was also true, and more persuasive in terms of human relations, that it was Devora who took your package to be mailed at the Post Office or waited at home for the man who was supposed to come to repair your TV; it was Devora who had a savory casserole ready on a winter evening or a tray of cold drinks on a warm one. And where there is a Mama, there is a family.

A "family" obligation at the Reservation was what Marcia had been about to remind Roley of when he took his confident departure. But it could wait till he returned from his class. So she dismissed it for now and went about the business of assembling the material requested for Billy King. Meanwhile, the long hubbub in the halls finally died down, so the pucker of irritation between Marcia's eyes began to smooth itself out. It was because she was practically allergic to noise that she didn't mind being the teacher assigned the largest amount of "commuting" between the high school and its annex at the Mercer. Unquestionably, being at the bottom of the faculty totem pole had something to do with Marcia's having been awarded that distinction. Commuting was thoroughly unpopular despite the staggered schedules of the two schools, designed to allow traveling teachers twenty minutes for a journey that needn't take more than five. That was supposed to "sell" the proposition, but its results—for example, having a second-period class that began at 9:20 on Mondays and 9:30 on Thursdays—only blew minds more easily daunted by numbers than Miss Dyer's. But for her, commuting was not only a breeze but a boon, substituting for the ordeal of student racket in the halls a quick, quiet ride across town to the Mercer School on its outskirts.

Once it was quiet outside the teachers' room, Marcia's chore gave her no trouble: she was nothing if not orderly, with all her lesson plans and quizzes available for easy reference. She copied several classwork problems and one meant for homework onto clean sheets of paper, noting conscientiously for Cannon's benefit that these would have been written on the board. Then she turned to her class quizzes and found the extra copies (she always hectographed extra copies) of the one she'd handed out that November morning. Her hands shaking, she clicked open the notebook rings and lifted out the purple-printed page. The next page, thus revealed, held a list of grades:

Billy King had scored 96 on that quiz. Marcia snapped the rings shut and closed the notebook. She got up and found the communal scissors in the drawer of the table, because the left-hand edge of the paper would have to be trimmed to remove the three holes she'd made to put it into the notebook. Otherwise, the resemblance would not be complete and the attempt to jiggle Billy's memory might fail . . .

It was almost as if, all of a sudden, that dreadful noise in the halls had started up again. Marcia leaned over the table and buried her face in her arms; she was all alone in the sunny room, but somebody might come in while she was sitting there helplessly remembering that awful day. And sorting out from the commotion in her head the clear voice that was telling her what she had to do now. Not that she didn't know, really: the logic was inexorable, leaving nowhere else to live unless she wanted to emigrate into irrationality. And she didn't—logic was her native land, she didn't know how to live anywhere else.

Once she had come to terms with it, she worked quickly. When the bell rang for the end of the period, she was back in the teachers' room, with the stains of "wrestling with the hectograph monster" already washed off her hands. Wincing at the clamor of the bell, she finished copying out a problem from one of the twelfth-grade units in her notebook. She labeled it neatly in parentheses—"(New Work)"—and added it to the old lesson plans. The quiz page, which did not need trimming because it had never been in the notebook, was already tucked into a large envelope. She had closed the clasp and was sealing the four sheets of paper into the envelope when Roley held the door of the teachers' room for Mrs. Armour and then followed her in.

Marcia sorted her papers and put some of them into her briefcase, along with her notebook, while the small exchange of small talk was going on in the room. Then Roley said "Ready?" and they left, with him carrying Marcia's briefcase as well as his own clump of textbooks and folder of ungraded papers. Over his shoulder, Marcia saw Eleanor Armour smiling at her the way you do at a pupil who's finally getting the hang of it.

Leaving school for the day seemed to evoke in Mr. Poley a kind of high spirits usually associated more with schoolboys than with their teachers. He fretted at the need to drop Marcia's envelope off at the school office. "It's the stuff for Billy, isn't it? So why can't you just take it home and give it to Meyer?"

"I'll only be a minute. You can wait in the car, if you like."

Oh, well, maybe she knew Cannon wasn't going to be home tonight. Roley followed her cheerfully, twinkling at Mrs. Price while Marcia was handing over her package. Yes, he agreed, it surely must mean that Billy King was recovering— Cannon hadn't asked for any schoolwork before.

They were already installed in the little red Volkswagen when Roley discovered that Cannon was indeed going to be home tonight. "No soda," Marcia said firmly as she started the motor. "We're summoned to help with out-of-town company at dinner, did you forget that? Devora would be crushed if we showed up without appetites."

"Oh, Lord, I did forget. Who's coming? I mean, are we invited as a treat, or to soothe Devora's insecurity about her English?"

"Probably the latter, since I don't think she knows the man. Meyer met him in Buxford, and he's in town on business or something. He's going back tonight—that's why we're eating early. She told me his name, but I can't remember." Marcia frowned because she didn't like vagueness. "Something Italianish."

"*Doctor* Italianish, I bet. It's probably not her English Devora's nervous about, it's having to talk to a strange shrink with probing eyes. Poor little girl." Roley gestured grandly. "Do you think it would be overdoing it if I soothed her with a few passionate embraces?" He rolled the window down and let the brisk spring breeze ruffle his Byronic curls while he whistled a sentimental tune.

Infuriated but helpless, Marcia found herself going through all the stages of recall necessary to identify the song. "Do you really need all that excuse for your passionate embraces?" she asked waspishly. *Come to me, my melancholy baby,* indeed. "I should think you'd got beyond that point anyway."

"Oh come on. You can't seriously think I've been— *Devora?*"

"Who knows?"

Roley glanced at her with both curiosity and amusement. "You're being silly."

"Am I?" Marcia rolled down her window and turned the car to the right, away from the center of town and their route home. "Devora's pretty. And Meyer leaves her alone a lot. So it's a logical possibility, isn't it?"

"Oh, come on. Why should a woman who has Meyer Cannon want to bother with me?"

The look of total seriousness on the handsome face was irresistible. It was precisely this kind of sudden dash into realism, Marcia thought, this evidence that Roley could delude himself but not all the time, that saved him from being—well, something she could have resisted. "You win," she said. Her smile was rueful, but genuine.

"Thanks. Well, I *think* so." He sat up, peering out as gravel scattered under the wheels. "Hey, what's this? Are we going boozing in the middle of the afternoon?" The only other car in the parking lot of this roadside bar and grill on the edge of town probably belonged to the bartender. They'd be the only customers . . . Engaged by the sense of not only naughtiness but nonconformist naughtiness, Roley said happily, "Nobody ever tried to corrupt my morals before. Oh, wow!" Eagerly he helped the lady out of the car.

"Well, I didn't see how a drink could hurt our appetite for dinner."

"Oh, man. Your line is, 'Let me take you away from all this.' Don't you know *anything*? I see I'd better run this show."

Marcia not only let him do that, she even managed to suppress the disturbing thoughts that arose when she noticed how very easily he ran this kind of show. But for once, just once and for an hour—she told herself, she pleaded with herself —let Roley's innocence prevail. Because, phony as it is, it's so much *lighter* . . .

She had shucked off the weight of her knowledge long before she finished the Tom Collins ordained by Roley—"a rite of spring. You cast off your winter martinis, but you get to keep the gin." That sounded terribly witty in the long room, empty except for a faraway anonymous figure polishing glasses, silent except for the low mutter of a broadcast voice. What difference did it make that another woman had succumbed last spring—and, for all Marcia knew, still another last month or last week? Her eyes sparkled in the dim light blued by the far-off TV set that kept the bartender uninterested in them. Her laugh was free, without caution. And, like Roley's, without memory.

By the time they emerged, her red dress seemed to fit her better somehow. True to their obligation to stand by Devora Cannon in her hour of trial, they'd been prudent: Roley had had only two drinks, and Marcia not even that much. But still, it was likely that her short skirt would at last have flipped jauntily—if only they had not encountered, in the parking lot, a Responsibility. Or at least that was the way Marcia, grown instantly dim and sober-faced, saw the town hippie and his two cohorts: Youth, for whom she had to set an example.

Roley seemed to see them quite differently. "Hi, Twirl. Guys." He opened the car door for Marcia and stowed her deferentially, meanwhile asking the boys how they were making it. Then the door was closed and she sat in the sealed silence of the VW while Roley sauntered across the gravel to exchange more talk with Twirl. He looked rather serious, but Roley was wearing an almost servile grin. Unnerved, Marcia leaned across to unlock the passenger door. But to roll down a window would have been an admission of something, so she folded her hands in her lap and waited, watching a TV play with the sound not working. It was funny how small things jumped out at you this way, she noted idly. Like Twirl's fantastically expensive Italian shoes. She'd seen them in Buxford only last week, in the window of one of those shops near the Lambert campus that nobody—except a Lambert student with a plush-lined daddy—could even afford to go into. But if she hadn't been sitting here in her fishbowl silence, the shoes would have passed as just a part of Twirl's bizarre and implicitly poverty-stricken image.

The sidekick standing beside Twirl, like one of those aides in photos of heads of state conferring, was just as hairy as his master but genuinely poor, it seemed: his rags looked authentic, and they hadn't been much before they became rags. The other boy, also standing by but at a respectful distance, was only a tall shadow at first. Then Twirl moved, drawing Roley aside for a word apparently too confidential even for his followers to hear, and Marcia saw the third boy clearly. He must be either a visitor or a very new convert: his extraordinarily fair hair, short and well-brushed, positively gleamed in the long afternoon light, and his neat, ordinary clothes had undoubtedly started the day not only clean but probably pressed too. But maybe tomorrow would be different, Marcia thought guiltily, now that the boy had seen Twirl being treated with elaborate respect by Mr. Poley. With Miss Dyer not noticeably objecting.

Thinking of herself and Roley that way stirred up a school context and Marcia suddenly recognized the fair-haired boy. Tommy Something—she'd never had him in her classes, because he was in his last year when she started teaching in Long Valley, and he'd finished all his required math. But he'd been pointed out to her by a science teacher proud of his pet student. Surely such a student had gone on to college, though? He *couldn't* have just drifted into that disgusting Twirl's horrid gang . . .

Miss Dyer saw Tommy's head turn in her direction and she looked away quickly, presenting a disdainful profile that might help belatedly to show him how things really were. Anyway, he probably went to Lambert now and was just home on vacation, she soothed her smarting guilt feelings. It was the end of May, after all ... Roley was finished and coming toward her, so Marcia hardened her air of ladylike aloofness. By the time he got in the car, she would have chipped as easily as porcelain.

He didn't seem to notice. "Okay, now you can take me away from all this."

"Certainly. If you're sure you've finished serving as a model for youth."

"What 'youth'?" Roley asked lazily. "That Twirl"—he nodded toward the three, just vanishing around the corner of the building—"is probably as old as you are. Or damn near."

"Well, the blond boy isn't—he's only a year or so out of high school. Tommy Something."

"Mallory? Something like that. He's Twirl's token straight. I never could remember his name, because it's only for record-keeping. His mother remarried, and he mostly goes by his step-father's name." Roley gave Marcia a tantalizing grin as she looked over her shoulder to back the car. "I don't have any trouble remembering *that* name, because you wouldn't believe Tommy's mommy. A very, very handsome lady. Definitely something to brighten a PTA meeting." Marcia clanged the gears unnecessarily. His eyes bright with laughter, Roley went on needling. "Her husband works for Itzhak Malevanchik, runs around the country booking concerts or something. So the pretty lady had lots of time for conferring about Tommy's school problems."

"There couldn't have been many, from what I heard. But doubtless you managed."

"Well, not for long. Her husband wised up and started taking her with him." Now that he'd wrung signs of overt anger from Marcia, the game was less interesting. "Nice for Tommy, of course—left alone with a big house and car and a slew of credit cards. But *my* life got duller," he finished, ready to wind up hostilities.

But Marcia wasn't ready to. She was fascinated to learn,

she said, biting off the words, that today's gossip would end up traveling coast to coast with the Maestro. Even if Twirl didn't embellish it, it couldn't fail to be interesting—Miss Dyer and Mr. Poley boozing it up in mid-afternoon. In what was obviously a dubious roadhouse.

"Oh, man, you're too much. Believe me, Twirl won't gossip about you and me, Marcia." Roley's tone was as light as ever, but his sidelong look at her was not. "It's true those kids know everything that goes in this town, but Twirl's better at picking out the real news than your favorite commentator.is."

"Are you saying he won't talk because there's really nothing to talk about?"

"I am. Mind-blowing, isn't it?"

"Well, I suppose you know." Marcia sat up straight, her red dress neat on her upright and unmolested body, and drove competently and courteously. Instead of flinging herself down and kicking and screaming until her face got purple.

"I do know. Even if there was something, it wouldn't get gossiped about in this case." Roley's voice acquired an edge of sadness. "A secret is safe with Twirl, you see, if it fits in his moral code."

"You must tell me about his moral code. Of course, we're almost home. But I imagine it won't take much time." There, take *that*: socko to softness. Pow, to prove Marcia Dyer didn't want any, anyway.

She hadn't laid a glove on James Poley, though. Having his own need to divert his thoughts, he proceeded to do so. "If you look at it, Twirl is no different from some of the classic historians. Except that he doesn't have any pretensions to objectivity."

"How reassuring," Marcia said brightly. "It's a great comfort, to be flattened under the bulldozer of history." Roley picked up his cue and improvised an amusing lecture on History as Squelch—leaving Miss Dyer to confront in silence the painful fact that it was herself she really needed to beat up on. Roley had been, as always, completely consistent. It was Marcia who wasn't, who'd decided Roley's fecklessness was shocking, that the way he managed to gambol about in borrowed innocence was wrong, *wrong*—and then turned around and helped him do it again. There'd been one minute there, only a split second really, when he'd sounded as if he just might be thinking about the past instead of shrugging it off. And what did Marcia-the-mess do? What she did every time, every damn time—run in and help divert him, so he wouldn't hurt himself . . .

When they drew up at the Reservation, Roley had just finished a story about the historian Josephus and Marcia was wearing the kind of smile worn by all Mr. Poley's colleagues when they listened to one of his inspired monologues. There was no need to lock the car here, but Roley waited while Marcia collected her stuff from it.

"Well, see you at dinner." She joined him on the flagstone walk leading to the front door.

"Yes." He didn't seem to notice that she was juggling her briefcase and a sweater while she hunted in her purse for the house key. He just stood there, looking up at the shuttered sunporch that was Meyer Cannon's study. "I'd be careful what I say to the guest of honor at dinner," he said suddenly.

"Oh? Will he be squinting into my unconscious?"

Belatedly, Roley seemed to come awake. He fished in his pocket for his own key. "It's not that." He came up with a handful of junk and held it on his palm. "The thing is, he's not a shrink."

Obviously, there was more to say. Marcia studied the objects in his hand—some coins, a door key, a pocket knife—and waited for whatever was coming. *Twirl*, guessed the temper-tantrum child in Marcia who wailed for sweets snatched away. It was all Twirl's fault, all the trouble had started with Twirl . . .

"Actually," Roley said, "who's coming to dinner is a cop." Absentmindedly, he put all the stuff back in his pocket without making any attempt to use the key.

So Marcia had to get hers out and let him in.

11

FIELD REPORTS
(Some Delayed)

Excerpt, memo from Miss Virginia Lamb, typing teacher:

. . . to achieve the level he's reached in this short time. The bright pupil has little advantage in learning typing (what difference it does make is in accuracy rather than speed), since there is no substitute for the physical act, performed over and over until it becomes automatic. Thus Billy must be practicing extensively, as well as turning in all his assignments. A model student all around.

But I hardly know how to deal with your questions about his classroom relations, Dr. Cannon, because the short answer would be, there aren't any. Billy knows the other students' names, I determined that, and he certainly knows mine. But his conversation with me consists of "Good afternoon, Miss Lamb" and I've never heard him speak to them at all. The only interest in them he shows is in their grades. I know it's not unusual for boys of his age to be highly competitive, but I've never seen it without any joking or kidding around, issuing challenges, groaning about errors, etc. Billy acts as if getting the best grade in the class was his job. He comes to work at it regularly and works till the whistle blows, then stops—so to speak. I can't describe his attitude as robotlike, though I thought of it, because there's clearly an act of will involved: he *intends* to be the best. Unless you can say he's his own robot?

I've tried complimenting him on his successes, but I get only a polite response. If he's trying to please somebody, it isn't me ... I also tried giving him an exercise I thought would interest him especially (it's all about the maximum weights for various classes of prizefighters, designed to mix numbers and text). He did it perfectly, but showed no more pleasure with it than any other exercise ...

Note by Dr. Cannon, May 23:

No comment on fellow students to MC or Williams, either. W. escorts Billy to and from class, remembers Billy did comment on prizefighter exercise (telling W. all the maximum weights under the Marquis of Queensberry rules) but didn't say anything about class—W. figured Billy just likes numbers, that's all. I agree. Recommend: Get name of likely fellow-student from Miss Lamb, try casual reference to him (her?) and see what happens. NB—Lay off top-of-class angle: J. King may have pressed for high grades, even though that was no problem for Billy.

Interim report, Detective Merchant to Lieutenant Silvestri:

Lieutenant—

Alonso says you have to have it before you leave for Long Valley in the morning, so half-assed is okay.

Your buddy's guess was right: Mrs. King did get a big chunk of bread from her parents. Amount cleared after probate costs, inheritance taxes, and other dreck (her dad was a fool—he could've saved plenty by perfectly legit estate-management methods) was in neighborhood of 60 grand. Time—shortly before they moved from Penna., thus most details provided by fellow in Penna. bank whose hair is still standing on end (as is mine) because Mrs. King just handed the whole boodle over to her hubby, who just put it in the bank. Despite earnest chat from bankers about their dandy high-interest bonds, etc.

Most interesting from our point of view is two withdrawals by King, soon after, in checks to cash amounting to 35G's. (Penna. accounts now closed, but other amounts went more conventionally: e.g., 20G's to savings account in Mass., where it still is, according to statement filed by Executor Voorhees.) What did King do with all that cash? Doesn't seem to have plunged in stock market, gambled, taken trips abroad, bought consumer goodies beyond reason or even paid off the mortgage—financial picture of deceased man fits man living on salary, not in trouble or in debt but not accumulating more than any man would who expects to be paying two college tuitions soon. Maybe he hid it in his mattress or buried it under rosebush. But, wild guess (partly me, partly obliging fellow in Penna.) is a con of some kind. Probably more sophisticated than a magic moneymaking machine, but same sort of thing. Bank man sez (off record) King seemed exactly the type, a classic mark for a con man. Alonso sez King shapes up from reports as arrogant know-it-all given to acting quickly and asking no advice. That sure fits—it sounds like I could've sold him some gold-mine stock myself.

Penna. bank feller also sez King had no financial-type pals there. So if somebody conned him about 35 G's worth, it was likely to be his new pal Voorhees, who he was lucky enough to meet when he moved to L.V., right? And Voorhees is now in a position to write it off for the estate.

I suppose you want to know can we get him (an unreasonable question considering that you're yanking me off in the middle of the job). My guess is, probably. You have to give gold-mine buyers fancy stock certificates, at least—so King must have got some form of receipt. An honest executor would find it, and could probably collect: they can't hang you for giving a friend bad advice, but Voorhees wouldn't be dumb enough to leave himself open to fraud charges.

I'm told you want Rubin's inquiries in L.V. to stir up some dust, so I gave Alonso five questions for R. Just having them asked should raise eyebrows in town and get V. uptight. And the answers will tell me where to look next.

I suppose somebody will tell me why I have to stop in the middle of a promising inquiry to go chase Lenny Pritchard. Ed says it's because you have to come up with a result *today,* so you can't afford logic. Okay, I'm trusting you. This once. Y'rs truly, Louis "Patsy" Merchant.

8:15 A.M. May 24, Anderson Building, Long Valley State Hospital:

Henrietta "Nettie" Desjardins, fifty-two, receptionist, arrived at work, carrying today's posy for her desk vase. She always left her desk absolutely clean at night, so she was annoyed to find an envelope sitting in the middle of her blotter. It was inside mail, addressed to Dr. Meyer Cannon at his office in the admin building, and it looked like somebody had mopped the floor with it. But where it clearly belonged was in the inside-mail box, which was not more than six inches away. People are so *lazy.*

It occurred to Nettie that she could just give it to Dr. Cannon, who passed by her desk at least once every day and usually a lot more often. On his way to see his pet, that rotten kid who'd killed his whole damn family and so of course got all the attention in the world. Treated like a little prince, with his own room and people waiting on him hand and foot—while other people, putting up every day of their lives with mothers who got lousier as they got older, didn't get so much as a thank-you from anybody alive.

Nettie decided she had better things to do than hand-deliver Cannon's mail. Let him wait, like everybody else. She dropped the letter into the box, where it would be collected with all the other striped-edge envelopes at the noon pickup.

Noon, May 24, Buxford:

Roosevelt Jones, manning the phone in case a call came from Long Valley while Alonso was out grabbing a bite, took a message from Merchant reporting his arrival at the community college in Massachusetts. Then Jones went back to reading the transcript he'd found lying on Alonso's desk. It was the briefing given yesterday for those privileged characters, Alonso and Rubin, to fill them in on Long Valley. Jones had begun reading it just to get in on what was going on, but by the time he got to page 2, it started to get interesting: the lieutenant was supposed to be some kind of expert in that sort of thing, and he certainly sounded like he knew what he was talking about. Jones found his place and read on, in the middle of a paragraph tagged "Lt. S.:"

... to keep in mind that Long Valley is artificial in the sense that the pattern of development for these small, enclosed towns was molested. You know what it's been in the ones here in eastern Mass., and in New Hampshire and Vermont too. The shoe factory or the textile mill closes down, and then people in town manage to get along by taking in each other's washing, with maybe a few jars of jelly sold to the tourists in the summers. Then the kids who've grown up and gone off to college decide it's a nice place to visit Mom and Dad but not to live. So you get a sort of equilibrium of decline, with just enough of an economy to support the present working force. But it won't support an apprentice group, and no apprentices are applying, anyway.

Sgt. A.: A perfect circle, right? The young don't stay because there's no future, and there's no future because the young don't stay.

Lt. S.: I don't know about that neat cause-and-effect balance, but yes, Ed, that's the general idea. However, western Massachusetts has a different culture to begin with, so they were spared some of the elements of that pattern of decline— just as they had not enjoyed some of the advantages of the opening-up in the New England culture. The towns suffered, but in the sense that all farming-associated communities were suffering: they hadn't yet developed polarizations, patterns of distrust, and so forth. To put it briefly, if simplistically, they hadn't arrived at the point where a hell of a lot has to be *un*done before anything constructive can be done.

And then, Long Valley had this special bit of luck. Some time back, Itzhak Malevanchik, the symphony conductor, bought himself a summer place in Long Valley because it was close to the summer music festival but also far enough away so he could get a little peace even when the annual do was on. As it turned out, he liked the place so much that he started staying there more and more of the year. And what inevitably followed —Malevanchik being who he is—was a kind of enclave of other quiet-rich types, mostly people successful in the arts, who wanted privacy and could afford to pay for it. Unlike the Social-Register-type rich, though, they took some responsibility for their hideaway: they wanted Long Valley to stay the way it was, but they recognized that something would have to be done to make that happen. So they made things happen—just the right things, at just the right time, as it turned out.

Det. R.: With money, Lieutenant? I don't know, even if they put half of the town on their payroll—

Lt. S.: No, Rubin, these were new-style lords of the manor, democratic variety. And they really did plan, with expert help, rather than just dispense largesse. To start with, they'd added a dash of tourist business—from the music festival —just by being there. Not enough to make the townspeople summer slaves, but it did ease the money pinch. Then, the town needed a supply of young blood. Okay, a national forestry experiment appeared nearby in White County, funded by Washington and guaranteeing a steady flow of young scientists who'd spend a year or so in or around Long Valley. Enough time for them to make their economic mark by supporting a few theaters and restaurants and generally livening the place up, but they were still transient enough so the political power remained where it was, and the shape of the town didn't alter.

Sgt. A.: Your lords of the manor must've had Massachusetts clout besides—the state hospital provides a handy influx too, doesn't it?

Lt. S.: That's right. The doctors are older than the forestry researchers. Usually married, maybe with small children. They come on special deals of one sort or another, nearly all time-limited—a residency, a foundation-subsidized study, and so forth. But there's work for them on the permanent hospital staff, and maybe for their wives—they're often in the same or associated fields. So a few couples may settle in town—*if* they like it, and if they don't need more city life than the occasional weekend off in New York can offer, then it can work out nicely. Sometimes. Or for a while. But whether it finally does or not, it alters that equilibrium of decline, and—along with some other results of planning—what you get is a kind of big-city small town. Small enough to feel at home in, but still with something going on in the evenings besides church socials. A provincial life, but by choice—and that can be cozy rather than confining . . .

3:30 PM, May 24, Long Valley—Taped interview with certain personnel, requested by Lieutenant Silvestri of Buxford.

Chief Vesey: Let the record show that the following are present—Captain Stan Zablocki and Trooper Morris Coakley of the state police, and Chief John Vesey and Private Matthew Johnson of the Long Valley force. Chief Vesey presiding. Oh, and I'm asked to say that Lieutenant Silvestri apologizes for not being able to be here.

Capt. Zablocki: Where is he?

Chief V.: Over at the high school. I couldn't say what he's doing there, but I'm sure it must be very, very important. [Indistinguishable noise] Okay, now, let's get at it. Coakley, Johnson—I show you an eight-by-ten glossy photo and ask you if you recognize the scene in the picture.

Johnson: Yes, sir.

Coakley: Yessir, it's the King house. The front yard.

Chief V.: That is correct, Coakley. For the record, the photo was made by a TV cameraman on the day of the triple homicide. Now, I show you the circled spot on the left-hand side of the driveway. Did you see that dark spot on the driveway when you went to the house that morning?

C.: Well, yes, sir, I noticed it.

Chief V.: Johnson, was it still there when you arrived?

J.: I'm sorry, Chief, I don't remember noticing it.

Chief V.: Dandy.

C.: If I can say something, Chief—I didn't think anything of that spot, even though I did see it. I mean, there wasn't any garage, so if they kept the car in the driveway, it was natural there'd be an oil stain there. I didn't really notice it either, sir—it was just part of figuring the car was gone, that's all.

Chief V.: Very clear. Good thinking, too.

Capt. Zablocki: If I can put in a word, Chief—I just want to point out that Private Johnson not being the first on the scene, like the trooper was, he had no reason to survey the area carefully. He would presume that had already been done.

Chief V.: Thank you, Captain. Now, Coakley, you assumed—very reasonably, of course—the stain was oil. Did you examine it at all?

C.: No, sir.

Chief V.: Well, can you tell us now what you might have noticed about it? Anything specific.

C.: Well, it was roughly circular, but with spiking around the edges. Like—well, like a notary seal, I guess. Only not so even.

Chief V.: I show you an enlargement of the spot. As you can see, it does look something like a notary's seal. Good work, Coakley. Now, can you remember how large it was?

C.: Not too clearly, sir. I'd say about six inches across. At a guess.

Chief V.: Well, that— Yes, Johnson, what is it?

J.: Nothing, sir. I just remembered I did see the spot. Later, after—

Chief V.: Yes. Well, can you give us an idea what size it was?

J.: No, sir, I didn't mean that. I didn't really look at it.

Chief V.: Dandy. Thank *you*, Private Johnson. Now, Trooper, I want to tell you your estimate is good, very good indeed. For the record, I have here a report obtained from the

Army Map Service people by Lieutenant Silvestri. They took the dimensions of the doorstep and front door of the house from the plans on file with the County and—

Capt. Z.: My G— I mean, they were busy—er—thorough, weren't they?

Chief V.: He's got a team of whiz kids, Stan. Take all the time in the world, and all the manpower too.

Capt. Z.: And no expense spared, I guess.

Chief V.: Yup. Well, the Army experts estimated the diameter of the stain—when the picture was taken, that would be about two hours after Coakley saw it—as twelve and a half centimeters. I'd say that was pretty good observing you did, Trooper.

C.: Thank you, sir.

Chief V.: Johnson, I hope you're paying attention. Take a lesson on how much a good officer can see when he's not even really looking.

J.: Yes, sir.

Chief V.: Now, one more question, Coakley. Did you notice anything about the color of the spot? It looks like there's sun on it, in the picture.

C.: Well, but it was November, Chief. There was sun in the yard, but just that pale winter sun, you know.

Capt. Z.: Where the sun hit it, Coakley, was the spot iridescent?

C.: Oh, you mean those colors, like oil?

Capt. Z.: Yes, yes.

C.: Gee, I'm sorry to let you down, sir, but all I remember is just a black blob.

J.: Not black. Brown, more like.

Chief V.: What was that, Johnson?

J.: The oil stain, Chief. I didn't see any colors in it, but I did notice it later. When I—When Vera got her baby buggy stuck in it.

Chief V.: That would be Mrs. Dozier, the neighbor lady.

Capt Z.: I see. Thank you.

J.: It was sticky. Sort of like maple syrup. She was trying

to turn the buggy around, and the stuff was sticking to the wheel.

Capt. Z.: Good work, Private Johnson. I congratulate you, Chief.

Chief V.: Well, it looks like we can get together a little talent out here, too, can't we?

Capt. Z.: Right. Even without the benefit of the Army and a million-dollar budget.

Chief V.: Christ, Johnson, didn't you turn that thing off? You knuckle—

THE LONGEST DAY

12

INVASION OF LONG VALLEY

People were starting to leave home for work in Buxford when Guy Silvestri, who'd left home for work several hours before, finished at his office and took off in his battered Dodge. He stayed on the throughway until one exit past Long Valley and then backtracked via small roads unlikely to be under the constant purview of Chief Vesey. So that, with any luck, when he arrived at the gas station only Lenny Pritchard was yet aware that Lieutenant Silvestri was in town.

The subsequent interview was brief, but it was enough to knock out Herkimer's version of *An American Tragedy*. Clearly, if it had been up to Lenny, there would indeed have been a drama starring Susan King and Lenny Pritchard. But *Seventh Heaven*, maybe, or some other old-fashioned tale ending in a cottage small by a waterfall . . . Guy told himself the boy was young and would recover, found that thought about as much consolation as people usually find it, and drove on up the new road. He got to the Dozier house before eleven o'clock.

Nothing happened there except justification of Dozier's boast about the quality of his wife's coffee, and some conversation about how much easier Vera's life was now that her eldest went off to play-school four mornings a week—the latter complete with explanatory anecdotes, some of them reaching back to last November, about the exploits of that dratted Emilie. Vera had just washed her hair: she was toweling it dry, quite unselfconsciously, while she talked with the policeman Clotie had said was "all right." So it was possible that today's shampoo was providing inspiration for a convenient lie about having washed her hair and then chased out after Emilie that November morning—thus satisfying Lieutenant Silvestri's curiosity about the unanswered phone call from Mrs. Wilder to Mrs. Dozier. But it was also possible that Vera Dozier had always washed her hair on Wednesday mornings and still did. After he'd listened to her talk about Clotie and the kids and the neighbors, Guy chose the second possibility on the basis of his own conviction that Mrs. Dozier was not a victim of jealous passions or much else except, probably, the built-in frustrations of the housewife. He also concluded that Marietta Wilder was right about Vera's acumen, and that Claud Dozier, who hadn't got married according to a plan, had clearly lucked out. And finally, Guy judged that what Vera Dozier told him in answer to a question about Callie King was just what Vera said it was, entirely speculation.

After that, Lieutenant Silvestri had just about enough time before noon to make the roundabout trip over the town line and back again—the one the lady who came to help Mrs. Dozier avoided by walking across the fields—and thus enter Long Valley as if he'd just driven from Buxford. He parked in the lot that served the small huddle of town buildings, watched over by a patrolman who peered at the Buxford vehicle tags on the Dodge. To give him time, Silvestri strolled briefly in the immediate neighborhood. He paused in front of the Long Valley Public Library to wonder why the building should be round, like a lighthouse. He would have liked to go in and see whether the bookshelves curved to match, but it was advisable to stay in sight. So he crossed the street to peer at the Long Valley High School and superintend, with his fellow citizens, the construction work that had closed off half the building to add an extension. After a few minutes of that, he looked at his watch and went into police headquarters. Where, it seemed, he was expected.

But where he also would have been given a quick brushoff, he concluded after a while, if it weren't for his State House imprimatur. Silvestri had hardly imagined glad cries of welcome from John Vesey—who likes an outsider coming around to poke his nose in? But there should have been some trade-off: Vesey was no fonder than any other police officer of the juvenile laws, which could make handling the simplest case turn into something like a forced march through a field of cooked spaghetti, so, all other things being equal, even a busybody from Buxford should have been at least a little welcome if he was supposed to be doing something about *that* mess. But all other things weren't equal, and Chief Vesey wasn't free to weigh long-term benefits. By the time Guy was conducted to a ceremonial luncheon, he had concluded—reluctantly, because he rather liked Vesey—that the chief's need to cover up his troops' goof at the homicide scene had led him into an obligation to protect something or somebody else.

Since it wasn't possible to brush off the well-connected Lieutenant Silvestri, he had been surrounded instead. Guided on an inspection tour, introduced around, and taken to lunch, Guy was guarded like a basketball opponent's star forward: whatever way he might turn to go, Chief Vesey or one of his team blocked not only the path but even the view of the basket, with a degree of energy reflecting the degree of perceived danger. That last offered certain advantages to Silvestri—by feinting passes, it was relatively easy to see where Vesey thought the most defense was needed.

The correlation had to be rough because some people in town seemed to be outside the reach of the defense. Silvestri's announced intent to visit Miss Crabtree, for example, apparently couldn't be prevented even if it gave Silvestri a clear shot at the basket. (The fact that Guy was to dine at Meyer Cannon's before leaving this evening was like that, only more so—two free throws from the foul line, with Vesey's team lining up helplessly to watch.) But the laundry routeman Harry Moody was at the other end of the spectrum: the Long Valley police just couldn't have been more helpful in arranging for Lieutenant Silvestri to see Moody after he got off work. Silvestri promptly concluded that their failure to ask Harry Moody the right questions had been mere inefficiency, and not even recognized as such . . . Mrs. Wilder, and the high-school staff, seemed to be in about the middle—nobody tried to keep Guy from going, but Vesey's assistant went along, presumably so the visitor wouldn't get lost crossing the street.

Late afternoon found Silvestri briefly alone in Chief Vesey's office, waiting to be conducted to the scene of the homicides. And summing up the possibilities. For if it hadn't been difficult to come up with an inference that Vesey was in some kind of alliance with Derek Voorhees—*Mr. Voorhees would know about that* was obviously believed to be the safest parry to any Silvestri thrust—listening to overtones had also revealed a lack of enthusiasm and maybe even some disdain for the formula, or its subject. Which could mean the chief just didn't believe Voorhees could really keep Silvestri off his neck, but it could also stem from a reluctance to deal with Voorhees at all. If it was that, maybe the chief could be persuaded to change sides?

Diplomacy is wearying work, and besides, Guy would have been ripe for a late-afternoon droop by now anyway. So he was having to force himself to use his moment alone for checking his "shopping list" of things to be looked into at the King house. Fatigue didn't help, either, in deciphering the brief scrawls that had been adequate once. Guy remembered what he wanted to know about "Laundry pkg." and "desk drawer," but "amb. JK?" puzzled him.

John Vesey was a big man whose current corpulence was an addition, not a change. He had a tread to match, and it set up palpable vibrations in the old wooden floor of the old building. Thus, when the chief entered, he found his visitor, who'd benefited by the floor's early-warning system, studying the map of Long Valley on the wall with his empty hands clasped behind his back.

"Ready, Lieutenant?" Vesey's booming voice couldn't manage to be soft, but he was at least trying to speak gently. And he apologized, with a big smile, for having kept the visitor waiting.

Guy returned the smile, wondering whether Vesey, too, had got up very early this morning and was getting tired of diplomatic games. "No problem, Chief. But you know, it seems wrong to steal your time for such a simple chore. I mean, one of your men could let me into the King house just as well."

Vesey wasn't about to let Silvestri go there unaccompanied, and Vesey knew the lieutenant knew it. "Well, now, you know," the chief said genially, ushering the visitor out, "you got me so interested in this case, I reckoned I just had to make time. So I've got it fixed up here to let me take you on out there myself."

"Sorry, Chief." Silvestri looked at him, poker-faced. "I have this staggering power of persuasion, I know." He turned away quickly then, because the rules of the game called for avoiding an open embarrassment that would have to be revenged, and let himself be led out of the building. In the parking lot, he stood blinking at the sunshine for a moment before he said he was parked "over there," nodding in the direction of his dusty Dodge. "I'll follow you, Chief."

"Well, now, you might get lost, Lieutenant." Politely, Vesey opened the passenger door of the police car for his guest.

"I know the way," Guy said.

"I know you do, Lieutenant." Vesey smiled. "That's right dusty, out there on the new road, ain't it?"

Vesey was waiting, courteous but insistent, beside the car that was not covered with the dust of the road to the Dozier house. Technically, Guy thought, he could insist right back, and win. But it would blow all chances of winning Vesey over, and it was certainly too soon for that. Thus it seemed Silvestri was not only going to have company, he was also not going to control how long he got to stay at the King house.

But he didn't have to go quietly. So he said, "I didn't learn anything you didn't know all the time, Chief. Right?" He got in the car and Vesey started the motor. And proved that he, too, knew the rules of the game, by observing that this was really more convenient—or didn't the lieutenant remember he'd be coming back here to see the Moody boy?

Guy said, "Oh, yes, that's right," and turned to watch Long Valley unrolling beyond the window. In the process, he managed to check his watch. He wouldn't get an exact figure because the police chief was tooling along idly, instead of racing desperately, and because the starting point hadn't been quite the same. Still, it was interesting to discover how really brief a journey it could be, in other circumstances, from hereabouts to the new road.

Vesey stopped the police car in the gravel driveway of the King house and explained that everything inside would be exactly the way it was last November; the lab boys had been made to clean up after theirselves, and they'd put everything back except the food standing out in the kitchen. And—oh yeah, except Billy King's schoolbooks: Dr. Cannon had taken them, but there should be a chalk mark in the front hall to show where they were found. As for the outside, the boy's bike had been taken away (they could hardly have left it out all these months) but another chalk mark, on the left as you went in, would show where the bike had been sort of leaning on the shrubs.

Guy listened to that. But he also listened to the indications of unease as Vesey spoke of that November morning, and decided that the rookie Vera Dozier remembered seeing vomiting in the King front yard had not been unique in his reaction.

The chief had handled nausea better, but if Guy's guess was right, Vesey was troubled by a great reluctance to go into that house. So Silvestri, who much preferred to see it on his own, might be able to arrange that if he could think up a way to get Vesey off the hook.

Fishing in his head, Guy got a bite: the Rubin-Jones verbal report had included some mention of a contretemps between Vesey and Trooper Coakley's commanding officer . . . "I suppose it's a minor point," Lieutenant Silvestri observed as they closed the car doors—quietly, out of unspoken deference to a scene of so many deaths, "but was the state trooper ever checked out? I mean," he went on, carefully not seeing Vesey's stunned look, "somebody *did* verify that this—er—Coakley actually had an assignment, the one he said he had, out in this direction that morning?"

Vesey took a tagged key from his pocket and bent to unlock the front door of the house. With his face thus hidden from the visitor's gaze, he said that offhand he couldn't remember all the details, naturally, but he could look it up and see what they got when they checked into that before.

Silvestri doubted that; Alonso, verifying the trooper's story, had discovered he was the first person who'd asked. But Guy said nothing until the house door was unlocked. Then he nodded at the car and wondered aloud whether the matter couldn't be checked by radio. Apparently following, he actually led a somewhat dazed Vesey back to the car.

"Well, now, it's got to take awhile, Lieutenant . . ."

"Sure, that's okay. Silvestri leaned into the car and extracted the long flashlight from its bracket: the electricity in the house would be cut off and no house was *that* bright, even though it was a sunny day. "Take your time," he said genially. "I'll need a good while to look around anyway." With more confidence than he really felt—because Vesey might be less reluctant to enter the house than Guy thought, or conscientious enough to overcome it—he strolled up the overgrown path to the front door. By the time he got there he knew it had worked: the chance to one-up the enemy at the State Police barracks, plus the need to protect his own record, had provided enough weight to topple Vesey off the tightrope of virtue.

Guy went in and closed the door. He stood with his back against it, letting his eyes adjust to the closed-up gloom before he turned on the flash, aiming it at the floor. He could remember the general layout from the Long Valley police reports, but he wished now he'd paid more attention to the dimensions, so he'd know how much room there was before— Chalk marks on the floor sprang into the slowly advancing arc of light, and Guy stopped and played the flashlight to left and right until he found the laundry package. It was at his right, lying on a wooden settee that would be behind the door when it was opened. The package was sizable and probably quite heavy— even if Mrs. King thriftily changed only one sheet per bed per week, it would have to be weighty—and the brown paper was the flimsy kind, not designed to permit much handling without tearing and stuck together with paper tape that read *ry Eagle Laundry Eagle Lau.* Under a thick layer of filtered dust, the paper seemed intact and, so far as Guy could see, free of bloodstains.

But what made him stand there, keeping the light on it and frowning, was not that fact, puzzling in view of how much blood had been so close by. It was a deep crease running the whole width of the package—as if it had been stood on end, and then sagged until it nearly doubled over. Which certainly didn't fit with the way it was now laid out, neat and perfectly flat, on the wooden seat. If that was indeed where it had been all along, then where could it have acquired such a crease? Not in the Eagle Laundry truck, surely, where packages were stacked in a way designed to keep them uncreased. And the routeman would certainly have acquired a habit of keeping it that way: even if Harry Moody was in a hurry, he would probably have laid the package down the way it was now.

But Billy King, who was fifteen and a half and careless, could have just dumped it. Not on the settee but on the floor at the left, just inside the door. If he opened the door with his right hand—holding his schoolbooks under his arm, or in his left hand?—and then, with the door still only partway open, bent to pick up the laundry package from the doorstep, that would make sense. The door itself would interfere with his view of what waited for him: from where he stood, there would be nothing to see except the carpeted stairs just ahead. So why wouldn't he just drop the package, or even shove it along with his foot, without picking it up, until it leaned against the wall at the left of the door? That seemed more likely than his juggling both books and package while he closed the door. His books had not been dropped there, Guy discovered, swinging the light over: the promised chalk mark was absent. But then, Billy probably would have a place where he always put his books down. They were his property, whereas the laundry package was only a nuisance, so there was no reason why he wouldn't treat the two burdens differently.

Guy took the light back to the settee on the right of the door, and saw that that was where Billy's books had been. On the floor, half under the wooden seat—where he'd dropped them when he saw what the open door had hidden from his view? But in that case, even if he'd also carried the laundry package over there, which seemed unlikely, would he drop his books and yet lay the package down neatly? Who *would* do that, anyway? Anybody, not only Billy, catching sight of the fallen girl, lying in her own blood in the archway leading to the living room—Guy stopped, shaking his head because he had seen that sort of thing before and ought to remember: a shocked adult, especially one given to orderly habits, would do just that—finish the act by laying the laundry package down neatly. Somebody, not Billy, picking up the doubled-up laundry package Billy had left on the way in (perhaps it was even in the way of the opening door?), and then coming upon—Guy moved the light to trace the outline of Susan King's body, and thought of yet another possibility. Suppose it was an *unshocked* adult, someone prepared for what would be seen in that house?

But that kind of speculation didn't need to be done in this place and in the limited time he had here. He forced himself to consider, instead, as coolly as he could, the shot that had knocked Susan King backward as she stood in the entrance to the living room. From the angle the single bullet had struck her in the neck, she must have been turned slightly sideways, looking to her left. With the carotid artery, windpipe, and cervical spine all hit, she would have been unconscious from the first: she didn't die instantly, but she couldn't possibly have moved or made a sound. *That one was about as fatal as a shot can get,* the Buxford doctor to whom Lieutenant Silvestri showed the report had remarked. And it was also—Silvestri knew even more certainly, now that he had seen the way it was—in no real sense an accident. Maybe the aim had been untrue, but that one-in-a-million shot had not been random.

Skirting the chalked outline, Guy went into the living room. He'd known it had to be a large room, if only because the nature of the victims' wounds implied a certain distance. But if Susan had been coming into it, there was only one corner, at the far end of the room, from which anyone squeezing off that shot had an uninterrupted line of sight . . . Guy went to the other corner first, the one near the kitchen—where Susan presumably had been looking.

It was much brighter there, even this late in the day, he didn't need the flashlight. He turned it off and stood wishing he could turn off, too, the way he felt when he saw the chalked outline of Callie King's body and the dashed line extending from it that was known as "traveling blood." Her clothing would have soaked up a good deal of the profuse bleeding from the first, nonfatal shot. But still, she had clearly done a lot of moving about, either purposefully or not, in the half hour or less she could have lived. According to the medical examiner, she had been conscious. And, Guy thought, looking at the stains on the rug—and even on the polished floor beyond it, where the blood had soaked into the wood itself—she had suffered great pain. He couldn't remember now whether he'd read that or just known it because tragic queens don't get off easy . . .

He blinked until the dashed chalk line was visible again, and then grimly followed it back from the edge of the rug. It led to a miniature vestibule where the telephone stood on a small table between the dark opening of a windowless pantry on the left and the bright opening into the kitchen on the right. But of course the trail could have gone the other way, Guy reminded himself: it was a mistake to read physical evidence only from where you yourself stood. In fact, Callie King could either have been near the telephone and trying to get into the living room (perhaps to the front door? or the upstairs?), or in the corner of the living room and trying to get to the telephone.

Or maybe there was some other possibility? Guy went to stand in the pantry and look from that direction. He turned on his flashlight so he wouldn't stumble over anything in there, and that was when he saw, looming pearly in the permanent dusk of the pantry, the plump white bag with "Eagle Laundry" stenciled on it. Trying not to disturb the dust, he probed into the bag. Towels, washcloths, a fluffy bathmat, and sheets—the expensive wash-and-wear kind, he noted. Surely it was extravagant of Mrs. King, who owned a washer and a dryer, to send these to the laundry? Aware of his sudden absurd sense of disapproval (*You've lost a fan, Callie King . . .*), he shone his light into the bag, peering closely. Maybe there was some special problem requiring professional laundering?

He didn't find any, but he did unearth the printed list the Eagle Laundry provided for its customers. The numbers of each article were neatly filled in the blanks, and the date of that November morning had been properly written at the top. So the outgoing laundry had been quite ready to be collected, he was thinking as he put the list back into the bag—and suddenly felt his finger nipped. Silvestri reacted with the speed of good physical condition and long training. Both of which proved embarrassingly surplus when, ready to trap whatever had bitten him, his cautious light found what looked like a political campaign button—except that it was a particularly poisonous green with "PLEASE" printed across its equator in big black letters and "me, baby" in tiny letters directly underneath.

Sucking his wounded finger, Guy eyed the long pin descending from the button. The pin was sharp, but the button was too top-heavy; it had probably always fallen easily out of any lapel—before it had finally fallen into the laundry bag. From whose lapel, though? Clearly, it was an artifact of the younger set. But its cheerful vulgarity was too advanced for Billy, who seemed to have been still too preoccupied with simpler contests like chess and basketball to go in for this blatant opening gun in another form of combat. Susan, home from school, might well have helped to collect the laundry. But, while wearing this button on her pajamas?

Well, it was too late to do anything but speculate now. You could forget about fingerprints; and not even Vera Dozier, who seemed to notice everything, had mentioned anyone's having a taste for this sort of costume jewelry . . . Silvestri jiggled the pin back into the center of the mass of laundry. Then he closed the bag and left the pantry—and the evidence that surely wouldn't have been lying around, undiscovered and unexamined, if anybody in charge had proceeded with any responsibility. *Then* maybe somebody would have discovered the jaunty self-advertisement that had never been meant to go out with the laundry; now, it didn't seem possible even to know when it had been accidentally added. Before or after, say, whatever time it was that morning when Callie King's body was hammered by two shots from a .38 revolver?

Which was said to belong to her husband . . . Squinting along the edge of the living-room rug, Guy saw the chalk outline of Julius King's body in the opposite corner of the room, clear in the light from behind it. The detective crossed, dodging around that chalk line too, and peered into King's study, which could be entered only from the living room. Once it had been meant as a dining room; he could see where a door from the kitchen had been plastered over. A table and chairs were probably supposed to stand in the big picture window looking out on what should have been a garden at the side of the house.

But Julius King's desk had been placed so that he sat with his back to the window. Guy had to walk around the desk before he could see the open drawer at the bottom left. The drawer had been found open, either because it was yanked in haste or because whoever opened it knew that the revolver was kept all the way in the back, behind an upright panel of plywood that in effect amounted to a false back for the drawer. The contents of the drawer had probably been determined by the fact that it was deep enough to take things too bulky or otherwise not suited for filing in desk drawers. Like a huge box of Christmas cards—Guy lifted it out and looked in and found, right on top, a typed list several pages long, of names and addresses in alphabetical order. He flipped to the W's to look for Marietta Wilder, and then checked the names of two teachers he remembered offhand—Miss Dyer and Mrs. Armour. They were all there: it was an official list, all right. And Mrs. School Superintendent, he discovered when he turned back to the first page, had been crossing the names off as she finished with them. Poking farther into the drawer, he found the addressed envelopes in another, smaller box. They were all written in the same feminine hand, which looked a little like Susan's (but not enough to clear that parental-permission signature Susan had produced for the Registry of Motor Vehicles). No one had helped Callie with the chore, it seemed—though, since it had been well into November and she was only up to the C's, she could have needed help.

But there was no sign of Julius King's hand, helping or otherwise, in that drawer. He certainly didn't own the file of recipe cards annotated and amended in the Christmas-card handwriting. And the photo album at the very bottom of the drawer also carried notes in that hand only—though Mrs. King seemed to have lost interest in dating and commenting on the photos after a while. Her one-word eloquence, below the first snapshot in the book, gave Guy pause, though: there was Julius King, younger and smiling a smile that even reached into his clear blue eyes, standing in front of a small brick house with tall purple iris beside its front door. With one hand, he was holding the hand of an adorable little girl in a pale-blue coat; with the other, he was steadying a stroller from which a lively-looking Billy was trying to climb—presumably to get to Mama, who was taking the picture. "Daddy!" she'd written underneath, and a date about fourteen years ago. In the light of the impressions Guy had been receiving about Julius King, it was a bit startling. But not really, he reminded himself: there must have been a time, however brief, when Julius and Callie King had been happy together . . .

One thing any police officer learns, in self-defense, is to keep the daily round of strangers encountered—the crooks and the victims, and those who are often both—away from his own doorstep. So Lieutenant Silvestri very carefully did not think about a photograph, so recent that it was still lying about in his own living room, of himself standing behind a stroller with an equally ebullient occupant, in front of a house in Buxford. But he did pile the contents of the drawer back into it briskly and leave it—half-open, as he'd found it—and then the room itself, without delay.

He stood in the doorway of the study for a moment, though, looking from the chalked outline of Julius King's body, a few feet inside the living room, to where Callie King had died in the little vestibule bright with sun streaming in from the kitchen. "Amb. JK?" wouldn't take any time at all: the answer was, no ambush of Julius King had been possible. There was nothing to hide behind or leap down from—in fact, there was nothing at all, except bookshelves lining the wall between the study and the opening from the kitchen. Even the lamp needed to light the bookshelves was mounted on the wall, presumably so there'd be nothing on the floor to trip over in what was obviously a traffic lane.

At the other side of the body, an armchair was drawn up to the hearth that was just in reach of the mark of King's outflung hand. But the chair was not the kind you could hide in, and anyway it was too far away. Since there was no chandelier for a Lenny Pritchard to swing from, according to the requirements of Herkimer's scenario, what was left as a jumping-off place for an assailant of King was either the top shelf of the bookcase on the one side or the mantelpiece on the other. Perhaps, given Sherlock Holmes's edict about the improbable being the solution if it was all that was left, one should conclude that Julius King was shot by a cat.

The attempt to be funny didn't succeed, though, in heading off Guy's slow anger. He couldn't make himself forget that nobody who'd stood here last November and seen this had questioned for a moment, apparently, the idiotic assumption that Julius King, who was six-feet-one and husky besides, stood still in the corner between the bookshelves and the fireplace and allowed his five-foot-eight, skinny son to somehow blow the right side of Daddy's face off. But once everybody "knew" that what they had here was a teen-aged matricide/patricide, common sense gave way wholly and at once to amateur psychologizing: the news media speculated on American family tragedies, and the police obliged Derek Voorhees, who didn't want a mess, by not doing anything to interfere with the image of Julius King as victim. Even if it required ignoring the laws of physics . . .

Anger was out of place, Silvestri reminded himself. Making himself move on even if he couldn't make himself be un-angry, he went to the fireplace and eyed the mantel ornaments and the firetending tools. Nothing of interest. His foot slipped as he turned away. He glanced down, saw the trouble—the bricks of the hearth were shiny with wax—and then righted himself and went on trying to control his thoughts. Which were now sliding over into self-accusation, because he could see that his fury was no better than Long Valley's had been: they had reacted not like a society but like a tribe, and he was doing the same thing—only substituting his law-enforcing tribe of public servants for the lawmaking society he also belonged to . . . He took a long breath and charged himself to remember that he had no writ to be here as either an avenger or a shocked tribesman.

His hands were wringing themselves in an unconscious gesture Herkimer would have recognized, as Guy headed for the heavily shadowed front of the room, where Billy had been found. It must normally be sunlit by that large bay window—a wrought-iron plant stand with spread curly feet held half a dozen pots of now-dead house plants. But Guy needed his flashlight because the dark-green draperies were drawn closed, as they had been that morning.

Billy would have looked closer to dead than unconscious, Meyer Cannon had remarked on that April evening in the Napoli . . . Letting his rage seep away, Guy recognized how easy it must have been in this dim light, for the young rookie Johnson to assume that still another silent figure covered with blood was dead. Billy had been very much covered with blood, too: the awkward middle-of-the-head shot that turned out to do so little significant damage had nevertheless caused the copious bleeding that came with all scalp wounds. It was all very understandable, really—a mistake that Billy King could have died of; but since he hadn't, just a mistake. Everybody had been lucky, and everything had been done to repair the mistake. Guy thought suddenly of Chief Vesey like a racing driver (or like a man trying to outrun his conscience?) on his way to get the doctor for Billy.

In fact, you might even say the worst consequence of the mistake was just what was happening now, the enforced recruitment of John Vesey, who had that single mistake to cover up, into the larger cover-up designed by Derek Voorhees to sacrifice Billy. Vesey, if Silvestri succeeded in cutting him loose, could very probably supply a good deal of what would be needed to expose the cover-up. It should be possible to make him a suitable offer: after all, if you could promise crooks immunity in order to get their help, surely you could let a good man off the hook for the same purpose?

Guy saw the flaw in that the moment he thought of it—the difference was, good men have consciences. They have to let *themselves* off the hook first. Shaking his head, he turned and went upstairs, where there were facts to deal with. Which was much, much easier.

The upstairs had that candid-camera stopped-action look, too. But there it was less depressing because Guy knew what he was looking for. He went through the rooms like a shopper in a supermarket, seldom persuaded by impulse to stray. And without the chalk marks on the floors, it was easier to keep his cool.

He whisked past Billy's room after one quick look that took in Billy's own décor—the shelf of Will Simons's books over the desk, and a Mobius strip hanging from the ceiling light fixture. The room must have presented problems to Vesey's men, ordered to restore everything to the way it had been: the way this had been, with drawers hanging open and the closet door ajar, it looked as if it had been incompetently searched . . . He did too remember what fifteen-and-a-half-year-old boys were like, Guy thought. He left Billy King, who was after all in Cannon's sector—there was no point in having an ally and then trying to cover his sector too—after noting that Billy had made his bed before he left for school. Presumably it was Billy who'd restored it to its daytime status as a studio couch: nobody else, entering that wild disorder, would have stopped with just making the bed.

Billy had also left the top off the toothpaste in the bathroom he shared with the fourth bedroom, Guy discovered.

Looking in from the bathroom door, he surveyed that bedroom carefully—it was in use as a sewing room, he saw, and if he was right, there was a lot to be found here.

The sewing machine had been put away in that little blue desklike thing between the windows, he guessed. But an ironing board standing open in the middle of the room held several large pieces of a homemade paper pattern, with the cloth still pinned to them. Guy turned one over and eyed the brilliantly colored, summery fabric printed with huge tropical flowers. Then he crossed to the tidy wall cabinet full of neatly filed pattern envelopes and studied them for a minute before he took down a few. Some of the paper covers were yellowed at the edges, and the top ones were dusty; one envelope contained a photograph torn from a magazine and another a hand-drawn sketch in addition to the pattern pieces. But unless Callie King was given to dressing rather kittenishly for her age, all the patterns were Susan's—and it was she, presumably, who had done all the sewing too.

Guy put back the patterns he'd examined and started to turn away, and then a nearby pile caught his eye. He pulled out the top one and read the information on the envelope carefully; then he went through several stacks until he found others like it. Finally he put them back too. He stood there surveying the shelves, considering the order of their arrangement and making a rough estimate of the number of envelopes, before he left the room by the hall door.

Susan's bathroom was at the end of the hall, opposite the stairs. She seemed to have had a free hand in decorating it, and her hand had been light, humorous, and dexterous with arts-and-crafts. Guy recognized as an example of particularly skillful macramé work the intricate corded hanging that covered the window—the one, he saw when he peered out, that had worried Trooper Coakley. It should have: there was an easy drop to the overhang above the back steps, and then from there to the patio. Pulling his head back in, Guy caught sight of the fat blue

jar standing on the window ledge and he had to smile. He'd
grown up with five sisters and one bathroom: it wasn't until
several years after he'd left home that he felt entirely rid of the
smell of Noxzema.

In Susan's bedroom, he was stirred to more reminiscence.
A closet running the whole width of the room was so full of
clothes that many were doubled up on the hangers, in the
fashion the Silvestri girls (who all together had had less closet
space than this) had taken for granted. Guy worked his way
back into the corner and lifted out the last hanger. He scruti-
nized its contents and then put it back and riffled briskly
through the dozens of dresses, pant suits, short skirts and long
skirts, and some garments of a type he'd never seen worn by a
woman who wasn't on television. He glanced at but didn't
touch the shelf above, which held hatboxes and a large box of
sanitary napkins, and he ignored the shoe rack—which was tiny,
considering the quantity of the hanging clothes. Then he took a
last quick look at all that color and inventiveness and energy
and folly and started to slide the closet door shut. But he
stopped for a moment, to eye the snapshot of Billy and the
crawling baby, pushpinned to the inside of the door. Now that
he'd been to the Dozier house, Guy recognized the background,
if not the baby. So it must have been the Doziers who had lent
their copy of the photo to Wally's TV crew. Much good that
did, Guy thought sourly. He closed the closet door and crossed
the room to stand beside Susan's narrow bed.

Even Herk would see at once, Guy decided, that this was a
young girl's bed, never shared. Why was that so particularly
moving, he wondered, feeling the sadness like something palpable in his throat. He shook his head, denying himself tribal
passions, and concentrated on the small square table beside the
bed. An aspirin bottle and a glass that had once held water—but
since, he saw, had been dusted for fingerprints—reminded him
that Susan King had had a fever that November morning. She'd
been sitting up in bed like a patient, too: the triangular

propping pillow was behind her slipcovered sleeping pillow. Her portable radio, with the earpiece cord still plugged in, lay among the disturbed bedclothes as it had when Coakley and Valeriani, their weapons ready, cautiously investigated the crackling sound from upstairs. One of them had switched Susan's radio off.

Guy put the little radio down and turned back to the bedside table. The small box of pink tissues had been finger-printed, and so had the wildly decorated, heart-shaped writing pad and matching pencil. There'd been nothing about them in the report, but that only indicated nothing worth noting had been found: Susan's fingerprints on Susan's pad and pencil were not newsworthy. Neither were the jottings and doodles Guy discovered when he flipped through the pages. Except one sketch, which seemed to be a design for some costumes: four stick figures were arranged around a central vertical line—a microphone?—and elaborately ruffled shirts and pants, cleverly varied from one figure to the other, had been sketched in on three of the figures and shaded to show detail on one of them. A singing group, maybe? They looked like three boys and a girl, though it was hard to tell. Guy let the pages flip back almost all the way, and then he saw that the second page had something written on it in the looping impatient hand he recognized from the learner's-permit application. The writing was less legible here, but Guy figured it out, perhaps because he had just been thinking about popular music: "Fear Me Not, Baby" was not exactly a song to remember, but the music-loving Silvestri had found it less trying, during its mayfly lifetime, than some others that rent the air of Buxford. Under the title of the song, Susan had scrawled something that looked like "the prickles"—which you could assume was some group who'd recorded "Fear Me Not, Baby" except that such a name would be just too gross, wouldn't it? Guy decided it probably wouldn't but it probably wasn't "the prickles" either. And if it was a singing group its name could be almost any combination of words, probably

English but not necessarily. Wondering whether it consisted of three boys and a girl, he put the pad back on the table and turned to go.

But it was not that easy, he found. The life on view in this room struck him as so especially *preparatory*, somehow, that to turn away and walk out, thus baldly, officially, declaring it come-to-nothing, stirred up a heavy charge of tribal discomfort. He hovered in the doorway, seeking some kind of permission—from himself? from whom, then?—to close the short biography of Susan King. A life of wild colors and hopeful experiments and easy-come easy-go songs like "Fear Me Not, Baby" . . . All of a sudden it hit him then, a possible thing the song, taken together with the transistor, could mean.

He dashed back and snatched up the pad, tilting it into the light from the window, and there it was: "974-2-700," with the 7's crossed in the Continental manner currently fashionable with kids in Buxford. It was right under the unreadable word that was presumably the name of the "artists"—which is what the disk jockey would have called them. Or whoever had phrased a telephone number the way Susan had written it. With the result that someone dusting for fingerprints would take it for the catalog number of a record, if he noticed it at all.

But Silvestri could almost hear in his head the light, slangy voice repeating the phone number to call (*Got that, you guys? That's ninesevenfour, two, sevenhundred . . .*). And would the first to call get some kind of prize? Susan had seemed to the Doziers to be in need of money, Guy remembered. He found an envelope in his pocket and copied the song title and the number. He hesitated over the mysterious "prickles" and decided to leave that out unless it turned out to be needed: why convulse Alonso, whose risibilities were easily tickled by ignorance in his superiors? . . . Guy leaned over and copied the number the radio had been tuned to, which might not be relevant if the police officer who'd turned it off had had to fumble for the right dial. But it was a common type of portable, so maybe he'd known.

It wasn't much, Guy cautioned himself as he left Susan's room; but he felt better anyway. He turned toward the front of the house: the upstairs phone would be in the master bedroom, and that would be where Susan was heading when she got out of bed, barefoot and without a robe, in a hurry to be the first to call 974-2700. The phone was the first thing Guy saw from the doorway, but it wasn't between the two beds. It was placed to serve, primarily if not exclusively, the occupant of the bed nearer the window. That, it seemed, was Julius King, because a green silky robe that must be the one Claud Dozier saw was lying across the other bed. Both beds were unmade, and when Guy poked his head into the connecting bathroom, he found the door of the shower stall ajar and a huge primrose-colored towel crumpled on the floor beside the mat. Mrs. King, it appeared, was less tidy than her children.

Or maybe she had had less time than anybody thought. Say she came in immediately after Julius King drove off. Upset and chilled (she must be cold out there, Dozier had noted), she would leave the breakfast dishes and head for a hot, soothing shower. She could collect herself enough at least for a smile as she passed Susan's open door—or maybe it wasn't open, maybe Susan opened it only afterward? But even if Susan was awake, she was plugged into her radio. There would have been no need for conversation, so Callie had gone about her own business, dressing quickly after her shower and then starting to brush her hair—and then what? Did she notice it was past 8:30 and stop to call the Long Valley school from her bedroom? Or had she remembered in the meantime that she'd forgotten to put the butter away—and so she was phoning from downstairs, the little vestibule near the kitchen? But then why *didn't* she put the butter away? Certainly not because she was collecting the laundry: the laundryman couldn't have been due yet, so she would give either her hair or the breakfast dishes priority.

Since Callie King had apparently done nothing but bathe, dress, do her face, and make a phone call, it began to look as though 8:35 was not just one end of a time-span in which the deaths were assumed to occur. Maybe the twenty minutes or so before 8:35 was in fact all the time she'd had. Which would narrow things down by nearly an hour. And it would also mean, by the way, that the laundry must have been collected the night before—which implied a different set of lapels around for that button to have fallen from . . .

Suddenly irritated, Guy reminded himself again that it was a waste to speculate now when that could be done, maybe even better, somewhere else and at another time. The thing to do here was to stick to the sad, visible actualities. He went over to the dressing table and looked at the hairbrush and comb that had certainly been fingerprinted, and had doubtless yielded the expected long strands of reddish-blonde hair. The only other actuality he could see was an empty cardboard frame of the kind photographers provide, with a foldout on its back to make it stand upright. It had held that portrait of little Susan and Billy, he guessed—the one lent to the TV people by the remarkably cooperative police, or perhaps simply lifted by an enterprising media man. Who had probably not been daring enough to go as far as Silvestri did now, though gingerly: not liking it, he pulled open the drawers of the dressing table and made a quick survey. A small sewing kit seemed to verify that the sewing room was indeed Susan's territory. Nothing else looked interesting—hairpins, pins, a single earring with a stone missing from its setting.

But all actualities weren't positive. Guy tried the drawer in the bedside table, then the bathroom medicine cabinet and the closet shelf. Finally, he opened each drawer in Mrs. King's bureau, looked at what there was to see without searching, and ran his hand around the sides. Her purse was lying on top of the bureau; when he'd finished, he went through that, too. But it was all without result—which was after all a result, tending to confirm what had jumped out at him while, in the desk drawer downstairs, he was busy confirming a previous hunch. This one should be able to be checked out by asking the experts, though. He made a mental note and, hewing to his no-speculating rule, let it go at that.

But not-speculating on unhappiness didn't make it easier to ignore the fate of the sad woman who'd begun with so much: once, she'd been a beautiful and brainy daughter of wealth and privilege . . . Oppressed and unsatisfied, Guy surveyed the elegant untidy room. Callie King had had a liking for opulent satin draperies, it seemed. But up here, they were pulled back, letting in the sun that had been kept out of the living room below. Guy went over to the big front window, which at least should offer a nice view.

It did. The dreary-looking front yard had no trees to interrupt the view from the window—of John Vesey having a nap. Grinning like a naughty boy, Guy shifted his position to get a better look. It was true: presumably exhausted by playing games with the persistent nosybody from Buxford, Chief Vesey had retired to his car to wait. The passenger door was open, to make room for Vesey's booted feet. His wide-brimmed hat was pushed back on his head, and his sunburned face was tilted up to the bright sky. Which wasn't disturbing him because his eyes were closed against the glare—and, the watcher at the upstairs window was willing to bet, they had been for some time.

Guy stayed at the window only long enough to be sure of his luck. Then, all but running, he went down the stairs, turning to his left, and entered the kitchen. One glance around the even now brilliantly sunny room told him why Trooper Coakley had known there was something wrong when he saw the light on: with the melting butter and the breakfast dishes standing around, the effect of something interrupted—and not casually— must have been powerful.

The kitchen door was locked, but only with a skeleton key. Guy turned it and pocketed it. Real back-door security, it seemed, depended on the screen door's catch. He clicked that off and pushed the door outward—gingerly, because if anything was going to squeak, this would be it. But he was in luck again. Without making anything like enough noise to disturb the sleeper in the front yard, Silvestri was out and across the tiny patio and heading into what the countryman Claud Dozier had scorned as "the so-called woods." It would have taken endless scheming and maneuvering for Silvestri to pry himself loose from Vesey's determined escort for long enough to have a look at the woods and the brook on his own; free and congratulating himself, Guy found the break in the underbrush that constituted a path to the beach in summer and skimmed along it happily, keeping a wary eye out for poison ivy. Everything else seemed to be growing here, so why not that?

He hadn't gone more than a few yards when a whip-crack of sound abruptly ended the breeze-moved, insect-stirring semi-silence. Silvestri meant to stop in his tracks, but his trained muscles knew better: when the second shot came, he was already flat on his face in the leaf-moldy underbrush. In which just about everything seemed to be growing, so why not a few copperheads? Mere poison ivy would be a stroke of luck.

The first thought Guy thought he had was the absurd one, *Vesey couldn't be that sore!* But once again his conscious mind operated less smoothly than the mechanisms at the service of the unconscious, for he heard Vesey calling his name before he had fully registered the meaning of what he'd heard just before that. Guy shouted, "From the beach!" to warn Vesey that he, and not Silvestri, might be in the line of fire; only after that did he realize the car he'd heard starting must have been in the neighborhood of the beach, so it was very unlikely that there'd be any more bullets to dodge. Unless the Long Valley police chief now turned out to be a trigger-happy type— Anxious to leave his present location but unwilling to become a victim of a failure of communications, Guy crouched and listened. Then he decided it was safe; Vesey, apparently satisfied that Silvestri was alive and would keep, was crashing down the path in a straight line toward the brook; he wasn't going to sneak up on anyone that way, but he wasn't doing any careless shooting, either. Guy stood up and called out, "He's gone. I heard the car."

"Yup. You see it?"

"No." Guy's foot nudged something soft, and he recoiled instinctively. Then he bent to look.

"Silvestri? You okay?"

Vesey could see him, apparently—it must have looked as though he'd fallen, for the booming voice was suddenly sharpened with concern. Guy called out to Vesey that he was okay and would head for the brook. Then he picked up the soft object and included it in the rudimentary cleaning-off he was attempting with his hair and clothes.

When he got through, what he had was recognizable as a child's toy, a stuffed animal of unknown genus; it looked as if it might not have been in really good shape when it became part of the forest floor, and it had not improved since. Whatever it was, it was dressed in what had once been tweed shorts with matching suspenders, and a silk or nylon shirt that had probably been red. The shirt apparently hadn't proved too tasty to whatever lived under that leaf-mold, but the shorts had been sadly nibbled away. All the way through, too, Guy noted, brushing away shreds of the foam-rubber body leaking out of a tweed-trimmed hole.

Then he took another look at the lilac thread in the tweed, and stopped wondering: Vera Dozier wasted not. He tucked the nibbled creature under his arm and picked his way carefully back to the path and on down to the brook. The car certainly had not been here, he realized as he emerged onto what must be the beach: it was hardly big enough to spread a towel out on. He heard Vesey's heavy tread at his right and waited.

"Silvestri? It's me." A moment later the Chief emerged from a thicket, beating back a thorny branch with his Texas Ranger hat. "You don't scare easy, do you?" His red face showed frank admiration.

Not when I'm sure whoever's shooting at me is trying hard

not to hit me... "I did some instant foxhole-digging back there," Guy said instead. He dropped the stuffed toy down on a rock behind him and used both hands to examine the tear near the left knee of his trousers. A three-cornered tear was beyond Kate, he knew. Maybe even beyond his sister Angie, who was the real expert. "I thought the car was here," he said morosely.

"Uh-huh. It's a trick of the sound hereabouts." There was a clearing just the other side of this stuff, Vesey went on, gesturing at the thicket from which he'd emerged; it'd take one of them little foreign cars, or at most an American compact, but nothing bigger. "Something was there all right."

"Tire tracks?"

Vesey shook his head. There wasn't anything to make tire tracks *on*—it was just crushed weeds and dead leaves underfoot. But the long grass rimming the clearing was just springing back up; so it was clear there'd been something the size of a car there, and not more than a few minutes ago. He stopped, looking suddenly embarrassed. "I'd like to say, Lieutenant, we really don't have much of that kind of thing around here."

Guy stared, wondering whether he was being accused of lowering the tone of the neighborhood.

"I mean to say, Long Valley is a right nice town. When a feller comes to town, we like to think we can offer him—"

Guy finally realized he was being offered an apology. He smiled in relief, and then in pleasure. Because now, with Vesey feeling that he owed Silvestri, it might be possible to substitute a natural alliance for the unnatural fencing that had been going on all day. "Well, what I always say is," Lieutenant Silvestri said carefully, meaning to open doors, "when there's no harm done, it never makes sense to act as if there was." He paused. "If you see what I mean."

John Vesey's eyes looked small, possibly because they were in such a big face; but they were big enough to contain a sizable gleam of intelligence. "I guess so. If you figure what counts is, something got learned." The heavy rumble of his voice stopped;

that, it was clear, was as far as he was going to go toward asking favors.

Guy nodded, believing the message: not only young Matthew Johnson but every other man on the Long Valley force could be counted on, in future, never to ignore the rule about checking for signs of life . . . "I agree," he told Vesey. "When you know it won't happen again, you've got everything you need. And I don't see any point in going on and on about it." Silvestri's tone was casual, faintly bored, and certainly final.

Chief Vesey sighed. "Yeah, well. Say, listen, if somebody's going to be taking potshots, maybe you ought to have—"

If the interruption hadn't been so fast, the consequences might have been bad: Silvestri was not as iron-nerved as he seemed, and Vesey was faster on the draw than he seemed. But the child darted from the path so suddenly that the stuffed animal was gone from the rock behind Silvestri by the time he finished turning to look. And John Vesey's hand had only got as far as the flap of his holster when the small red-sweatered figure, clutching the toy, danced past the two slow-moving giants to stand still in front of them. Crooning to the filthy animal while she waited for the brains of the retarded to cope.

Guy stared down at a little girl with Breton-blue eyes, a squarish face, and dark, wavy, wind-tossed hair. He'd never seen her—she'd been at play-school at 11:00 this morning—but there are times when even the most cautious detective will risk a deduction. "Hello, Emilie," he said.

"It's the Dozier girl." Vesey had started the sentence, so he finished it. But his eyes were way ahead of it: they turned to Silvestri, remembering reasons for reproach.

Guy shrugged, and spread his hands. "Okay. But from now on, I won't have to free-lance, will I?" He held his breath, hoping the truce wouldn't come unstuck and thinking that either way, he could use a drink. Whether as celebration or consolation, he was entitled, by golly.

Emilie Dozier planted her fat legs apart, eyed Mr. Big and

Mr. Bigger, and said defiantly, "Mine. I losted Pongo and Mommy touldn't find him, but now I did."

Silvestri's brain sparked feebly. "I bet Santa Claus brought you a new one." For surely that toy had been lying in the woods since before Christmas? He felt like an idiot, though, talking about Santa Claus— How did you question a child this young, anyway? How could you tell whether she understood? Maybe she just didn't have the vocabulary to answer questions . . . Right now, he decided, what he needed was Jones, who could conduct a conversation with anything that owned a voice. A drink, and Jones—he was entitled to both.

There was no lack of vocabulary, it turned out. No, said Emilie, she had *not* got another Pongo from Santa Claus. Then she said it twice more, stamping her foot for the last one—she was not a good liar. But she was an ambitious one, because what she apparently had in mind was not only to deny the existence of another Pongo but also to get in a few jabs at the new baby. It was because of the baby there wasn't any room in Santa's pack, she said flatly. (*Come on,* thought Silvestri, a minor expert on infants, *that baby's more than six months old.* Then he realized he was sinking to Emilie's level, which you were definitely not supposed to do, according to the book.) And that was why, Emilie lied fluently, she didn't get any new Pongo. She didn't, she *didn't,* and if anybody said she did they were a stinking stinker— She stopped, overcome by her own temerity, but nobody said anything about the bad words. Which made her nervous, so she went on to say—even faster and with more w's standing in for r's and t's for c's (it would make a hell of a cryptography test, Guy concluded, just before he gave up)—that she was four years old and could have two or free or eleben Pongos. Because she was the oldest, and—"Mine!" She shrieked suddenly, abandoning reasoned discourse and starting up a frantic whir of nearby insect life. The sea-blue eyes were abruptly lakes, and Guy thought, specifically and positively, that what he really wished for was Kate. Forget those other two wishes . . .

"Say, are you allowed to have gum?" Chief Vesey asked. "Or don't your mommy let you have it because you're too little?" He peeled the paper off a stick of chewing gum, invitingly.

It was the challenge that had done it, Silvestri decided, watching a dirty paw whip out like a striking rattler. He had no sympathy for that evil old man Vesey, who deserved to have his gum ripped off by what must really be the fastest thing alive . . .

Vesey said, in the same mildly inquiring tone he'd just used with Emilie, "You a drinking man, Silvestri?"

Guy stirred to life. "I am now—yes, sir."

The small, gently curved flask Vesey held out would fit in a shirt pocket—and probably had, Guy realized. "Thanks. This is real handy."

"Snakebite," the Long Valley chief explained.

Guy looked at Emilie, who could have profited from this model of laconic exposition. But she was totally occupied with the wad of gum—which, Guy recognized belatedly, had been the idea. Vesey's first-aid kit had something for every emergency.

"Come on, Emilie," the chief said. "Time to take you home."

Emilie started to speak and discovered she'd been had. Then she thought of the device of taking the gum out of her mouth so she could tell Vesey she wasn't allowed to go anywhere with strangers except somebody's daddy or a policeman.

"Well, but I'm a policeman, don't you remember?"

Emilie had put the gum back in. She shook her head.

"Well, I am. And I got a police car to prove it." Vesey seemed to read her mind. "Yup, with a red light on top and all. Come see."

Emilie considered, then took the proffered hand and let Vesey—whom she obviously didn't remember—lead her into the woods. Silvestri, who was somebody's daddy, shuddered and followed.

13

CANNON'S SECTOR
(5 P.M.)

Will Simons's dislike of using the telephone showed itself in two opposite ways: either he stated his business brusquely enough to make a commissar wince, or else he wandered through verbal meadows like an English vicar on a walking tour, going nowhere much and being maddeningly high-minded about it. When Meyer Cannon heard who was calling, he was briefly uncharitable enough to hope he'd get Manifestation Number One, because he simply didn't have time to sweat out the vicar.

But Cannon was a doctor, not a literary critic. Almost at once he heard in the wispy voice the unmistakable sound of suffering, and his healer impulse arose and swatted him: forgetting haste, he began to probe gently for the matter embedded in the verbiage like a splinter in flesh. "I suppose I should have, but I didn't really notice," he said into the phone. Will was right, though—it *had* been rather a long time between Billy's letters.

"Well, it certainly hasn't been very long, not really long at all." Horror at being taken for an accuser had at least brought Will back from his wandering. "It's just that Billy usually— Oh, it's nothing, really. I don't know why I—" He stopped, and then Meyer could almost hear inspiration striking him. "I must have mixed up the dates, that's what it is. You know how unreliable I am."

Meyer sighed, wishing for some cosmic administration that would give you more time as you collected more responsibilities. "Billy almost always answers your letters the very same day," he said flatly. Because it wasn't good for Will to creep away into his *persona* to hide. "So it is unusual. But it could've been caused by things he can't help. Hospital routines. Delays in my own office, even." He listened to Will's well-of-course and other grown-up mutterings designed to hide his childish pleasure; meanwhile, Meyer tucked the phone into the crook of his shoulder so he could get his notebook out of the drawer. But he already knew what really mattered—something was happening to Billy that Cannon didn't know about. "I'm glad you called this to my attention," he said, his tone businesslike. "Because it should be looked into."

"Billy isn't—?"

"No, he's all right." Slowly, emphatically, so as to give maximum comfort, he added, "I see Billy every day, Will. And trained people are with him all the time."

"Yes." The sigh was audible. "Of course."

"What I meant was, it's necessary to find out the reason. It could be something as simple as running out of writing paper, and for some reason not wanting to ask for more. That's the sort of thing."

Will said eagerly, "Yes, I see."

It was invaluable, Meyer went on to say, to have inconsistencies in Billy's behavior pointed out to him. Meanwhile, he flicked silently past pages of jotted clues to the puzzle of Billy King. They looked like reconnaissance reports in a war, he thought. "But that doesn't mean every inconsistency is a symptom of illness. Like, not asking for something he needs could be a way of punishing somebody, himself or somebody else. Or it could be that he's been busy or careless, and *that* could be a sign of health." He paused, letting the implication sink in. It would hurt, but inflammations must be treated. "Just approaching normal living, I mean. After all, unless there's a medical reason, we don't usually answer letters that promptly, do we?"

"I see what you mean."

Meyer thought he probably did. "Fine. Well, let me see if I can find out what's happening here. You wouldn't have any ideas about it, would you, Will? I don't remember where things were, in your letters . . ." He let his voice trail off, knowing he would be rescued. Will might not be the perfect type for para-medical work, but his insecurity had its advantages: he didn't expect to be the center of your universe.

"It was nothing special, really. I don't think Billy cared for an idea I had, but that wouldn't—I mean, we've argued before."

Meyer said quickly that from what he'd seen, disagreeing with Will made Billy write more, not less. "It must be some-thing else. When I know, I'll call you, okay?"

"Okay." Simons hesitated. "That's an interesting notion, about the return to—um—normal living. Do you think maybe—"

"Probably not this soon," Cannon said gently. "Not yet, Will." He let the words lie there for what comfort they could bring to Will, who had been a long time finding a true com-panion to play with on his desert island. Now he didn't want to go back to being lonely, and who could blame him? Meyer knew how sick an adult with a childhood illness could feel, so he would help as much as he could. But it was love that would succeed, in the end, in persuading Will that life as Robinson Crusoe, even with a Friday around, wasn't really good enough for grown-ups.

"This your next move?" Cannon picked up the postcard, one of a supply addressed by Miss Crabtree to herself. He could read chess notation but not easily, so he eyed the board rather than bother with the gibberish that would be on the postcard. "How's it going?" Each side had captured three pieces, he saw. But that didn't necessarily mean the game was even.

"Well, I've just moved here." Billy pointed to his remaining bishop, sitting on a square in the rook's row, far into Miss Crabtree's territory. He shook his head at Cannon's look of congratulation. "No, I'll probably lose. But I *could* get a draw."

"Oh? Depending on what?"

"On whether she falls in my trap. Miss Crabtree's better than I am, but she doesn't take it seriously enough sometimes. Or maybe her head is just somewhere else." His voice held a businesslike patience with Cannon's ignorance.

"I get it—if she doesn't notice what you're doing, she's in trouble?"

The boy grinned. "It's better than that—she's already trapped. I think so, anyway. This move—" He caught sight of the postcard in the doctor's hand. "Could you mail that for me yourself, Cannon? It would be faster."

"Sure, on my way home." Meyer stuck the card in his jacket pocket, leaving the top of it showing so he wouldn't forget. "Pretty soon now, as a matter of fact. I just dropped in to congratulate you; then I'm through for the day."

"Congratulate me? What for?"

Billy was neither greatly puzzled nor greatly interested, Cannon noted. "The typing exam. Didn't anybody tell you what a whiz you turned out to be?"

"Oh, that."

Something felt out of key: when Billy wanted to be scornful, he did better than that. "Listen, don't knock it. I once tried to learn typing, so you have my respect."

"What happened, did you flunk out?" Meyer Cannon's life story had been of great interest to Billy lately. But not now, it seemed—his attention had returned to the cheap plastic chessmen the Commonwealth of Massachusetts supplied to the hospital's game room.

"No, I learned. But it took me ten times longer, because I just couldn't make myself do those boring exercises the way you did." Cannon smiled. "I have to hand it to you, the way you went at them."

"Well, typing is a useful tool."

Meyer had been about to say that Will Simons doubtless appreciated Billy's neatly typed letters. But he pulled up short, because it seemed somebody had changed the signposts; he might have to take a different route. "So they say," he said, and went over to sit down on the bed. The bland words, and staying out of the patient's direct sight, were a form of idling in neutral until he could read the directions better. *Useful tool,* for example, struck him as odd, foreign—an importation from somebody else's speech?

Billy picked up his rook. "It really is," he said mildly. He looked at the piece in his hand then and set it back on the board, where it had been castling the king. Meyer leaned back against the foot of the bed, availing himself of the chance to rest. But Billy seemed to perceive the silence as disbelief. "Honest," he argued. "All it takes is those two things."

The voice was Billy's, but the words somehow weren't. "What two things?" Cannon asked softly. All it took for what? To win the chess game, or— The postcard in his pocket creaked as he sat up. His weariness was still with him, but he waited now like an infantryman expecting an order to move out—knowing this was what he was here for, but unable to help a certain dread. In the corner of his mind there was even a tiny shameful wish that whatever was waiting out there would go away and come back when he wasn't so tired.

"If you're sixteen years old and you can type," Billy said, "you can be independent." His hand moved among the White captives at the rim of the chessboard, tidying them into a row— pawn, knight, bishop. "That's all it takes."

Who? Certainly Long Valley's superintendent of schools had expected his son to go on to college. Sixteen was the minimum age for working papers in Massachusetts—but who would have told Billy that, so precisely and emphatically? Surely not

Miss Crabtree, who believed everybody ought to spend at least four years studying English literature. Surely not anybody at school, for that matter: why would any teacher or counselor talk to a boy with good grades and a marked ability at math about going to work instead of to college?

"Legal and solvent," Billy said. "Two things. If you're legal"—his voice faltered—"and—"

Cannon moved slowly, as he had to. But it took effort, because Billy's hand was already raised to his head.

"Then *nobody* can make you—" The back of his hand was now rubbing across his forehead.

Cannon stood beside the table, looking down at the boy's grimace of pain. "Let's just take it easy a minute, Billy." Nothing in his voice revealed his fear. "Put your head down—just for a minute, okay?" It was not okay, and he would not be obeyed. With effort, Meyer did only what he could do without being noticed—without moving Billy's left arm, Cannon put two fingers on the inside of the frail wrist and began to count the pulse silently.

"Prince Trad," Billy said, "doesn't need—" He felt the touch at his wrist then. The secret sign of loyalty— He struggled to acknowledge it, but a dark-green curtain kept getting in his way. He couldn't see who had come, signaled by the prince's distress; but he guessed it was Can-An, who was loyal and devoted, and would understand that the idea of taking off for the planet Jocalia alone could scare even Prince Trad. Can-An was transmitting, but the interference was— He managed to order, "Wait." Then the icy realization came: it wasn't just jamming, they'd turned a nemmo-scrambler on him. He could hear the voices it summoned arriving in his receiver. Desperately, he rotated his past-finder: it had been damaged, but there was just a chance it could bring in what he needed now, the voice that had said, *If they want to be miserable, okay, let them. But we could have a good life* . . . But it was no good; he was adrift in the scrambler-swirl.

"Wait!" he called again, fighting the noise and the big heat in his head. He could feel his hair getting drenched with sweat as he strained and strained, trying to get her back. He *had* to: he couldn't start over on Jocalia alone, she couldn't expect that. "Trila," he cried, knowing it wasn't right, wouldn't do the trick. He saw her again for a milli-second, the image hardly distorted: she sat strapped in her couch with her audio plug in her ear. *Victory to Trad today!* she called, smiling as he went by in the companionway, on his way to the galley.

How could he know she meant to leave without him? She did it again now, the image disappearing, shoved aside by the green curtain. He tried to push it away, but it was hard to raise his hand against the pull—it wasn't like Earth, where things like that came easy. "Can-An," he ordered. "Help me find—" They jammed it, of course. Nobody could help him and he couldn't remember the Earth-word for her because of the scrambler. He said "Trila" again, knowing it wasn't the right name. He hung on against the sudden cold for just one more swing—only long enough to tell Can-An again to wait for orders. Then the cold stillness enveloped him, and he sank.

Cannon caught the boy and carried him over to the bed, moving with the extra urgency of a man who'd been denied action when he knew it to be needed. But there was nothing he could have done: if he'd got Billy's head down far enough and fast enough, he might have prevented the faint—but at too much cost to the therapy, because it would leave Billy with an instant and possibly irremovable impression of assault. It was obviously better to let him go ahead and lose consciousness, and deal with your own rage afterward ... Meyer pushed the call button to summon help and then began snatching pillows from the bed and the armchair and stacking them to raise the patient's feet.

The aide named Williams appeared and Dr. Cannon said "Fainted" and went on about the postponed business of doctoring.

Billy's pulse rate was already improving when Williams returned. Meyer broke open the small emergency container of spirits of ammonia. The sharp odor pricked at his own eyes while he held the vial under Billy's nose.

"He's coming now," Williams said. He laid a wet compress on the boy's forehead and then, from opposite sides of the narrow bed, both men watched Billy's eyelids open briefly.

Dr. Cannon handed over the vial to Williams and smiled down into the blank brown eyes. "It's all right, Billy. You're all right." He noted the promising arrival of some color in the small face.

Williams came in with a light blanket and spread it over the boy, tucking it loosely around his shoulders.

"The wave!" Billy was almost inaudible, but it was obvious that he thought he was shouting. "Look out, Can—" His body cringed away. His mouth stayed open, but in terror.

Cannon folded Billy's hand around his own and covered them with his other hand, wishing he knew whether it was Cannon or Can-An who'd been warned just now. Unless you were sure where Billy was at the moment, words could be dangerous and even touching him was something of a risk: right then, the Pletians could be attacking . . . Then Meyer knew it had been a risk worth taking—in the braid of their hands, Billy's fingers curled in a tight infant grip that certainly did not belong to Prince Trad. "Ride the wave, Billy," Cannon said quickly. "Just ride it, and it will bring you back."

Williams, his face full of concern, leaned over the bed to snug the blanket. Billy's eyes opened suddenly and discovered the black face. "Will—?" He said it clearly, and with obvious pleasure.

And surprise? Meyer wondered, as Billy slipped away again. Then he saw it, and felt almost like laughing: Billy had never seen Simons, so why couldn't Will be black? It might even make particularly good sense that Simons, who was different from Prince Trad and everybody in his kingdom, should also be a different color. So Williams was transferable—whether as himself or Will, he was somebody responsible for Billy/Trad.

Meyer felt it in their joined hands when Billy slipped all the way into sleep. It would be brief, he thought, and not deep. He knew better than to assume the sleeping boy was not receiving stimuli, so he got up and took the aide across the room to brief him. Cannon finished by stressing that Billy was to get no medication—and added, out of weary knowledge of the frailty of human institutions, "No matter what *anyone* says." It would be too bad if some well-meaning fool blocked off this useful turbulence— Maybe he should stay and watch, himself. But, aside from the fact that that would mean stranding Devora with a dinner guest she hadn't even met yet, he needed his conference with Silvestri very badly . . . "If he wakes enough, give him warm milk," he said aloud. "If he won't take it, don't push—try weak tea with sugar. But warm, not hot." Every bit of information was valuable now, the sooner the better, and Silvestri must have learned *something* today. "If he wakes up and complains of a headache, you can give him ten grains of aspirin. If you absolutely have to."

"Yes, Doctor." The aide hesitated. Then he said, "Don't you worry."

Williams would be on duty till midnight, and Cannon could get him sprung from other duties to stay with Billy all the time. But would even that be good enough? "If he wakes up, maybe you better have them call me at home, okay? But you stay with him while they call, you understand? And don't let anybody sedate him." It could get hairy for Williams, maybe. "I can be here in ten minutes," Cannon said, his eyes on the aide's face. "Whatever happens, you could hold out for ten minutes, couldn't you?"

Williams's smile was very white in his dark face. "I won't leave this room, Doc. And nobody'll get to give Billy nothing, I promise you. The other aide on duty is a friend of mine—I get in any trouble, Hughes will call you. I just won't leave Billy, no matter what."

He meant it, literally, Cannon saw. And promptly stopped worrying: they were in business, and it was only a matter now of getting the logistics arranged. They discussed the details briskly, and then Cannon stayed on duty while Williams went to call his wife because he always called her during his break and she would worry. It didn't occur to Cannon that Williams was being deprived of his break: he was dealing with a colleague, not an employee.

While he waited Cannon occupied his time by straightening up the disordered room. He thought vaguely about having a phone put in for the evening, but the experts had gone home and so far as he could see, there was nowhere to plug one in. He eyed the monitor high on the wall, wondering whether something could be rigged with it; but the only thing he knew about it was how to switch on the box on his office desk that was the other half of this thing. It was designed to let Dr. Cannon keep one ear on his patient while he worked at his desk, but if it had any other attributes, they were a mystery to Meyer.

Besides, what he needed wasn't technology but information—what the hell had Silvestri been doing all day? *His best,* a voice in Cannon's mind murmured. But the rest of it went on complaining, hugging its grievances, protesting that he had to know what had *happened,* dammit . . . He did know one thing that had happened, he remembered then, discarding his tantrum like a raincoat after a shower. The information had been there all the time, in his notes—where he'd just this afternoon seen the exact words. *It's not what they are that matters, it's what they do,* Will Simons had said of his characters, when Billy inadvertently substituted Trad's sister for his mother. Because, it seemed, his own sister was the one with whom Billy would be starting a new life. But how? And where was Billy and Susan's planet Jocalia?

Maybe Billy didn't know. Maybe, Cannon thought suddenly, Susan hadn't yet told him? It could be this memory was the last one within his grasp: something said and left there, huge and not yet completely understood, while Billy went off to school. In the lives of youngsters, important discussions often had to be postponed while they performed the chores their elders had set them. Only, Susan wasn't there after that morning to tell Billy the rest of it. So there the memory stood, like a boulder in the mouth of a cave, blocking all the light. And much too big for Billy, even when he made himself Prince Trad, to move by himself.

Maybe what Billy had called Can-An for, Meyer was thinking when Williams came back, was to help get the boulder out of the way. What would come after *Can-An, help me find,* then, was what only Billy, not Trad, could remember—*Susan.*

The voice from the bed, thin and taut, jerked Meyer like a caught fish. He leaped, but Williams was closer. The aide was holding Billy's hand, and Billy was still warning, in that pseudo-shout, that the wave was coming, when Meyer got to the bedside.

Billy's eyes flicked open. "Will—" He gasped out the syllable, then gulped air and closed his mouth, like a swimmer going underwater.

"Just you keep ahold of Williams," the aide said. "You can swim real good, Billy. Just you try." With his free hand, he lifted the compress from the boy's forehead and wiped the pale face.

Meyer took the cloth and went to wet it again. When he came back, Billy was asleep. "It'll be longer this time," Cannon said. He looked across the bed. "You did fine."

"Thanks. I'll be right here till you come, Doc."

"Okay. But catch some sleep." Meyer put the boy's thin arm back under the blanket. A marathon runner, he thought, would have a pulse like that. "You'll know it if he wakes up," he assured Williams. Unnecessarily, he knew—clearly, the aide felt the almost palpable weight of anguish in the room whenever Billy rose into consciousness. Satisfied, Meyer turned to leave.

The whisper followed him: "Doc?"

"Yes, Williams." He spoke in a low voice, showing Williams that there was no need to whisper: Billy was further under now.

"Doc, I just—I mean, what's this wave he's so scared of? Like, is it just bad dreams or does it mean something?"

"It means something, all right." Cannon passed the back of his hand across his forehead, much as Billy had done earlier. "The wave is—well, I guess you could say it's grief." Billy had to enter that sea sometime, but it should have been on a calm day and after he'd had some practice. "Something went wrong," Cannon said. "I didn't expect this, not yet. The timing got screwed up somehow. So he didn't get enough warning." Billy had been playing on the beach—which Cannon had coaxed him onto, from the safe shadow-land of Trad—when all of a sudden he looked up to see the great green curling wave, coming right at him . . . "Naturally, he panicked," Meyer finished.

"Pore little kid."

Meyer looked back over his shoulder and smiled: Williams was a Massachusetts product but apparently his mother was not, judging from the model he used when he needed to do some mothering. "He'll be all right, Williams. You'll see." It was too bad memory had been allowed to open directly into grief. But the fact was, Billy *had* been learning to swim and he did have something to hang onto, so he needn't be swept fatally far out to sea.

Passing by the little table, though, Meyer was reminded that it wasn't only natural perils Billy needed rescue from. He was a war victim, too. And doubtless he would to some extent continue to be the victim of his parents' war. But he didn't need to be also the victim of society, whether it had merely blundered—as Cannon was inclined to think—or served the interests of a malefactor, as Silvestri obviously thought.

Well, they would find out what happened, he and Silvestri. Or reason it out or maybe just manage enough lucky guesses. Cannon set the plastic knight down and looked around the small room so full of wars—Prince Trad's battle map on the wall, the kings and queens sending forth their pawns on the chessboard, and the hardest-fought one of all, the battle against the darkness threatening the boy in the bed. Meyer Cannon had no particular yen for battles, but if he had to fight, he fought to win. And on the side of life. And with comrades-in-arms—

He glanced back at the white-clad figure sitting by the bed, holding the frightened boy's hand. "You want anything before I go, Williams? I'll wait if you want to get a cup of coffee."

"No thanks, Doc. 1 don't want to leave him right now. Not while he's still hanging on like this."

With love as a comrade-in-arms, how could anybody lose? "I'll have a cot put in here," Meyer said. "When you think it's okay, grab some sleep. The first rule of the shrink trade is, any night is always going to be longer than you think."

Williams grinned. "I'm willing to learn the trade, Doc."

Meyer looked at him and nodded. "Okay. The second rule is, don't try to be a hero—call for help." He nodded again, said "I'll see you later," and went out to order the supplies Williams would need while he was holding the fort.

It wasn't until he was padding across the quadrangle, on his way from the wards to the tall administration building where his office was, that Meyer allowed himself a few moments for breast-beating. The image of Billy as a child playing on a beach wouldn't go away; it was a charge against Meyer. Because the turning of the tide should not have happened unnoticed. Cannon had not been such a fool as to trust the tide tables, somebody else's calculations: he'd been watching, his eye on the actual boy on the beach. He'd seen the slow advance of the water's edge up the sand, and known he'd have to hurry but reckoned there was still time—and yet he must have reckoned something wrong, because all of a sudden Billy was scooped up and flung into the whole sea of memory.

Well, if it was some riptide, okay, Meyer conceded as he unlocked the door of his office. He couldn't pretend to control the sea, or even to chart it with complete accuracy: there was always the risk in this work, which was neither quite science nor quite art, that some timing would be misjudged or the event prove, in the event, unpredictable. But what was inexcusable was the failure to notice that something not predicted was beginning to happen. At least *one* of Meyer's indicators should have picked up at least one of the signs—for surely there would have been several of them: nothing in human beings really happens out of the blue. To have misjudged was a hazard of the trade, and forgivable; but not to have noticed was unforgivable.

Cannon waded into the mess on his desk with furious energy, trying to do *something* right, at least; it was already past the time he'd said he would be at home, and he hadn't even opened his mail yet. He dialed his home number and waited, holding the phone with his hunched shoulder while he used both hands to open and dispatch to the trashbasket what turned out to be two copies of the same plea for funds. No wonder that organization always needed money . . . He smiled when Devora's voice sounded in his ear. Still sorting mail, he said "Hi, I'll be leaving in a minute. I'm sorry I got delayed, but you know."

"Not to worry, darling. We're still on the canapés, so no need to be frantic."

"Silvestri get there yet?" Meyer moved another striped-edge envelope to the pile at the corner of his desk. One thing he certainly had no time for was administrative twaddle from the hospital offices. Devora said Mr. Silvestri had arrived and was super. And why hadn't Meyer told them he was absolutely smashing-looking. Like Gary Cooper, actually.

"I haven't thought of Gary Cooper in years." Meyer had the pile winnowed down to a library notice and a letter from Prof. Macauley, who was spending this year in Palo Alto thinking about the future of the social sciences. He told his wife he'd have to take her to the movies more often, so she wouldn't be still living on reruns seen in Tel Aviv: Americans, he said firmly, had forgotten all about Gary Cooper. Then he said he'd be home right away, and let her hang up while he opened the big manila envelope somebody from the Mercer School must have delivered by hand, because it had not gone through the mail. He shook the contents out part of the way, enough to scan the three handwritten pages and the purple-inked one that must be the math quiz. He shoved them back in, unwrapped the phone from his neck, and hung it up. Then he crossed the room and pulled open the bottom drawer of the right-hand file cabinet.

Billy King had wrapped his schoolbooks in heavy paper covers—trimmed in green and gold, the Long Valley High School colors—and they must have looked neat as well as patriotic, back in September. But by November they had been tossed or kicked onto the verge of the basketball court too often: all the original labeling, and even the doodles, were worn off. Meyer finally recognized "MATH" in faded capitals on the spine of one book, pulled it out, and stuck the Mercer School envelope into its pages at random. Then he put the book, with the protruding envelope, back on top of the pile and shoved the file drawer closed with his foot.

Back at his desk, he snapped on the switch while he completed his tidying up. The monitor was working, and it was remarkably sensitive—he could even hear, faintly, what must be footsteps passing in the corridor outside Billy's room. The room itself was quiet except for soft thumps and scrapes—Williams fixing the cot for himself, probably—and the steady breathing of the sleeper. Meyer switched it off, stuck the library notice in a corner of his desk blotter, and carried the letter from Macauley out of the room with him.

Cars in the state hospital's parking lot had to be kept locked, just in case a locked-ward patient got that far. Meyer needed both hands free, then, so he filed Macauley's letter in his jacket pocket—and that was when he discovered the postcard he'd promised to mail for Billy. There was a mailbox at the corner of his street. Cannon threw the card onto the car seat as soon as he got in. That way, he couldn't possibly forget it.

He didn't, not really. He did drive right by the mailbox, but when he'd pulled into the Reservation's little parking space and opened the car door, the light went on, revealing the postcard. Oh, well, he could just run down to the corner . . . But he did nothing like that, because the card had fallen with its message side up: the light caught what was written there and Cannon stood still, just barely managing not to gnash his teeth. *B-R6*, Billy had printed clearly—and then, instead of his customary *Billy*, he had added a note, for the very first time. *Got you there, Truesdale!* Billy's big, careless scrawl boasted.

The signal, or anyway one of them? If it was, it had been Meyer Cannon's very last chance to see Billy's past rolling in, in time to take some precautions. Even if he'd read it at the last moment, right there in Billy's room— Meyer shut the car door gently and put the card in his pocket. Instead of wasting time repining, he would go see Miss Crabtree—it was still early enough so he could maybe go to her house after dinner—and find out how much and what kind of regained memory Truesdale, whoever he was, indicated.

Trudging around the side of the house toward its front door, Meyer was busy with contingency plans. But he did notice absently the strange car parked near the far end of the row, in what was usually Marcia Dyer's space. Silvestri, Meyer realized as he came close enough to see the Dodge's Buxford license tag. Marcia had simply pulled in beside him, thus bucking the whole line down by one car-width. It didn't matter, because there was plenty of room. In fact, life at the Reservation was distinguished by the kind of civility possible whenever there's enough to go around of whatever people yearn for. It made a nice place to go home to for a hardworking shrink tired of elemental passions. Policemen too, Meyer thought: very likely, Silvestri was also just longing to wallow in courteous velleities.

14
ALLIED COMMAND HQ

"Telephone, Lieutenant."

Guy excused himself to the DiFelices, the young newly-weds from upstairs, and followed Devora Cannon. She was quite a bit younger than Meyer—she really couldn't be more than twenty-five, Guy had calculated—and she must be just about the perfect example of the matter-of-fact sexiness for which the Israeli sabra had become famous, thanks to the appetites of American magazine writers. Guy was wondering idly how it would feel to be in an army with a corps of Devoras, row upon row of them in those tiny uniform skirts, when he was restored to reality, not to say also propriety, by arriving at Meyer Cannon's study.

Obviously, it had once been a sun porch; three of its walls were glass shutters with tilted louvers. Where Meyer's old-fashioned rolltop desk stood now, a cane-seated rocker had doubtless once offered rest among the ferns and rubber plants while you watched the world stroll by down at the end of the long, terraced lawn. Guy's hostess smiled and departed, after again addressing him as "Lieutenant." He wished he knew some way to say "Call me Guy" without sounding like Derek Voorhees; besides, it meant he was losing ground, since she'd begun by calling him "Mr. Silvestri"—which was particularly fetching with her purred r's. That was the only divergence in her speech from purest Mayfair, probably taught her by some leftover from the days of the British Mandate. Israel had been an independent country for all of Devora's life, but nothing sticks like the British culture, Guy thought. He picked up the phone and discovered where she'd got that "lieutenant" from.

Vesey said, "I didn't like to interrupt dinner, but you wanted—"

"Yes. It's all right. Did you find it?" He was being too abrupt, Guy realized. Especially since it had cost Vesey to go poking about in Susan King's room: clearly, he'd volunteered for it as a form of penance. "It must have been a rough job," Silvestri added.

"Well, the book was right where you said it would be, anyway." Vesey hesitated, then apparently couldn't help asking: "How did you know, Guy?"

"It's a long story. Beginning with the fact that I've got five sisters, and they all kept diaries." But not quite like Susan King's, he knew, thankfully. "Did she know the man's name?"

"No, it don't look like it. She had other names for people —like, her dad was Dracula." Vesey paused, to let Silvestri recover from the shock he himself had obviously felt. "So it don't do much good even when she mentions her mama's—boyfriend. And that's not often. Once, I think, she says Lochinvar— he's a lover in a poem, I remember."

"Yes." But all Guy could remember about Lochinvar was that he came out of the west, and he doubted that Susan had weighed every aspect of her literary allusions. "It doesn't matter." That was really what Vera Dozier had said this morning: she thought Callie King had been having an affair, but Vera didn't know with whom and she didn't care because *Callie had something coming to her, Lieutenant. Anybody in town would think so, too ...* And that might even have included Callie King's daughter.

"The girl is typing up that questioning of Coakley and

Johnson. It should be ready by the time you head home, easy."

Guy said,"Okay, good," listening to the footsteps outside the shuttered wall. They were very distinct—he hoped Meyer Cannon wasn't in the habit of discussing anything very confidential in this room. "About the shots," he said, lowering his voice.

"We got one of the bullets, Guy. It was getting too dark, so I figured we could wait on the other one. A .32." The Chief waited, but there was no comment. "Voorhees has a .22 target pistol. Registered and all. Though of course anybody can always pick up a Saturday-night special."

Meyer Cannon came into the room, holding what looked like a letter. Guy nodded, indicating with a gesture *I'll be through in a minute*, while he listened to Vesey saying that Voorhees had been playing golf when somebody fired two shots at Silvestri. "The golf course is ten miles away. I know two of the men who were with him, and the other one's a complete stranger—to him, too. So I don't see—"

"No. Forget it. Why don't you just—follow the other line."

"Somebody come in?"

"Yes."

"Okay, I'll get cracking then."

"Thanks. I'll talk to you later." Guy hung up and turned to Cannon. "I'm sorry. Did you want—"

Meyer had not been waiting to use the phone. He came over to the desk and put Billy's postcard down into the circle of lamplight and began talking.

Guy listened, and then reported his own finds—after he'd announced that it was chilly in here and gone to close the louvers. The unregistered revolver used to kill the three members of the King family and wound Billy was part of the loot from a burglary of a sporting-goods store in Trowbridge last spring. No, he answered Cannon's startled question, that did not mean Julius King had been a part-time burglar: stolen handguns were commonly sold by certain—er—specialists ... Silvestri went on to the matter of the Volvo, which had begun to lose its brake fluid while it was still standing in the King driveway that morning. Two of the police officers who'd been at the scene remembered seeing the spot on the driveway, though it could hardly be proved now that it was brake fluid. And finally, Susan King—

Cannon broke in. "Was Susan going to run away from home, Guy?"

"Yes. She had a rather elaborate plan, as a matter of fact. For the end of the school semester—she had the requirements to pick up her high-school diploma after the first semester, and by that time, she'd be eighteen."

"Was she going to take Billy with her?"

"Oh, yes. He was part of the reason for the planning."

"Then—did he know it?"

"I don't know," Guy said unhappily. That it was important was written all over Meyer's face. "She could've told him, but it would have to have been the last day or so before she died." The last entry in Susan's diary had been nearly a week before her death, so it was possible. Another possibility struck him then: "I think Miss Crabtree may know that, Meyer."

Cannon was eyeing the postcard on the desk. "What this is," he said grimly, "is a piece of the past, a fragment coming to the surface like shrapnel. If I'd read this right away, I could've dug it out and had a neat, sterile wound with very little loss of blood. Instead I missed the chance—and now we've got infection, fever . . ." He saw Guy's puzzled look and went on to explain what had happened in Billy's room tonight, and what might be expected to happen next. Still eyeing the postcard sadly, he called Miss Crabtree and arranged for them to be received right after dinner. And then, cheered somewhat by the prospect of action, he proposed that they go get dinner over with.

That struck Silvestri as rather a cavalier way to treat a pretty wife and what smelled like a very good dinner; but at least it beat gloominess. So he followed the man who had everything out of the room toward where everything was waiting.

It was a delicious dinner—except that there was trifle for dessert: *damn* the British. But Guy spent some of the time contemplating Meyer Cannon, who, by his own admission, had very little time before he must make a move ("Depends on when Billy comes out of it, and *how* he comes out. But with luck, it could be only a couple of days") in an area it was obviously perilous to move in. It scared Guy badly, this double tension: in Human Relations Division, you ran into intricacies, but there wasn't that feeling of Time ticking away just behind your left ear while you tried to unravel them. In other kinds of police work, you got plenty of experience with rapid decision-making; but what was involved was danger without much intricacy. Only on the Bomb Squad, Guy decided, could you find types like Meyer—those heroes with magic hands and iron nerves, who could pull out one wire at a time while the bomb ticked . . .

Silvestri switched his attention to his fellow guests, who were rather easier to understand. The young man they called Roley was the easiest of all—a professional charmer (or rather, a semipro, since it seemed he also taught history) and a permanent boy. He was engaging, but Guy noticed that neither of the married women, Devora Cannon and Alice DiFelice, seemed to take him seriously. It was harder to determine how the unmarried Marcia Dyer took Roley, though, because she seemed to be afraid to risk any response except in minimal degree. Miss Dyer, Guy decided, seemed haunted by a conviction that she would not only have to pay for any pleasure, but she would also be overcharged.

Guy was talking with Dom DiFelice, who, like Guy, had "married out" of the Italian community (but Dom had done it younger, which was harder: by the time Silvestri produced the outlander Kate, his mother was so afraid he wouldn't get married at all that she'd succumbed easily), when Meyer Cannon announced that they had to run. Guy hastily swallowed coffee that deserved sipping: there was no use rebelling against the charismatic Cannon, who had everybody sorry for him instead of furious with him.

As if he felt the weight of his ally's disapproval, Cannon paused to explain that Billy had had some trouble that afternoon, and Miss Crabtree might be able to help.

"Of course. We understand." Miss Dyer's careful gaze slid around to the visitor, who was obviously the cause of Meyer's bad manners.

Alice DiFelice said it was past time poor Billy stopped getting swatted by the fates, and there was a general murmur of sympathy. Only that wasn't enough, it seemed, for Roley—who asked anxiously, "How bad is it, Meyer?"

Marcia said, "Oh Roley, you know he can't—"

"It's a setback," Cannon admitted. "But he'll be all right, I think." He smiled down at Billy's math teacher. "I meant to thank you, Marcia. You really got that math package out in record time." Miss Dyer murmured that it was nothing, really. "I feel particularly bad," Cannon went on, "because all the school people cooperated so promptly, and now I won't be able to use it for a while anyway. Maddening, isn't it—it was delivered this afternoon, and it's just sitting there in my office."

Roley paled. "You mean Billy is—real sick? I thought he was playing chess and all."

"He was. But now—"

Silvestri identified the source of the sharply indrawn breath and looked at Marcia Dyer. Cannon went on, his voice gentle, trying to reduce the dismay he'd caused the history teacher. It would be handy to have the stuff on hand, anyway, he said, because it would be precisely the thing for as soon as Billy felt better. After a setback, he'd need his morale raised promptly . . .

Guy thought he'd probably never seen a look of horror as intense as Miss Dyer's. He turned his eyes away quickly, before her frozen-faced concentration broke enough to make her aware she was being watched. But when he was saying his good-byes to his hostess, he noticed that Marcia Dyer's lips were still compressed tightly.

That was the first of two reasons why Silvestri changed his plans. The second was waiting for him, outside.

The night air of May was sweet and cool, revivifying for a man who'd long since passed beyond simple weariness and now, with a good dinner under his belt, was unfortunately ready for rest. Wistfully, Guy imagined himself lying down, right now, under that big beech tree in the middle of the lawn . . . Then his attention joined his idle gaze, and he came awake in a hurry. But not noticeably: he still ambled along beside Cannon, who was talking about nothing important—fortunately—as he led the way to the parked cars.

Guy had better take his own car, they decided. "You can get on the throughway a couple of blocks behind Miss C.'s house." Meyer stopped behind the dark shape of the parked Dodge. "I'm right next to the exit. So why don't you back out, and then when you see me pull out, just come on up and follow me."

"Okay." Guy heard Cannon's footsteps going away as he unlocked his car door. But it was already too dark to see much.

Meyer started up his car, backed it out, and waited. In his rear-view mirror he saw Silvestri's lights on, but they didn't seem to be moving. Cannon tapped his horn lightly and waited some more: that Dodge didn't look as though it had led an easy life, so maybe Guy was having trouble starting . . . He waited quite a while before he glanced at the mirror again—and saw that Silvestri's headlights were out now. A single spot of light bobbed near the edge of the lot, almost in the rimming bushes. But not coming this way, as it would if that was Guy holding it . . .

Cannon felt his mouth go suddenly dry, confirming what he had long suspected—any courage he owned was likely to be moral and psychological. He rolled down his window and listened, but he'd known at once there was no harmless explanation: there was no motor running, no sound at all, and, so far as Cannon was concerned, no room for the slow processes of logic. Dom and Roley were right there in the house, he told himself, and besides, he himself was no 97-pound weakling. But on the other hand, even a big man could be jumped in the dark, and he'd have to get out in the dark to call Roley and Dom.

Meyer allowed himself one last futile wish for a weapon. But there was nothing useful in the car and all the tire-changing tools were in the trunk, which lighted up when you opened it. Since light was the last thing he wanted, he held down the button to keep the interior light from flashing on when he opened the door and slid out. He also left his motor idling—a very loud sound in the silence, he discovered as he crouched in the car's shadow. Moving quickly and on the balls of his feet, he began to make for the side of the house, where there was not only shadow but also a strip of grass—certainly better than the crunchy gravel and even the paved walk.

Cannon got almost to the corner of the building, thanks to skills learned as the younger brother of the naughty Amos. He was still creeping carefully—and, he believed, soundlessly—along the grass strip when light blazed at him, pinning him. Instinct caused him to cover his face, but it was conditioning that kept him standing stock-still, absurdly afraid to step on the newly bedded petunias he knew were right behind him.

"It's okay, Meyer," Silvestri called softly.

Cannon peered around his prison-circle of light. "Get that off me." He saw the dim figure move then at the opposite side of the DeFelices' convertible and realized that Silvestri had not been foolish enough to be behind the flashlight. Which meant, in addition to a demonstration that these things should be left to specialists, that Guy, too, had felt threatened. Meyer recognized that to be comforted by that meant lack of charity, but—

The flashlight moved, showing Cannon the way, and he crunched across to the Dodge, homing on the beam, to find Guy grinning at him. Danger meant nothing to him, Meyer thought, with irritation and envy. He himself gambled with other people's lives, but Guy did it with his own . . .

"We should've had some signals set up," Silvestri said.

"My God, you weren't about to shoot me, were you?"

"I never shoot people I know. And there isn't anybody around I don't know. I looked, and he's gone. Along with my distributor cap, I guess."

Meyer glanced nervously at the shrubbery in front of the Dodge. "Are you sure? I thought I saw something over there."

"Yup, me. There was a chance they'd just thrown it in the bushes, so I was checking it out. Negative."

"But why would—? If the car won't start at all— It can't, I gather?"

"No way. Not without another distributor cap."

"Well, then, what's the point? If somebody wants you to have an accident, it doesn't make sense to— Oh."

"That's right. The idea is, I don't get to go anywhere." Silvestri grinned. "Not even to have an accident."

"I don't see why you think it's so damn funny."

"I'm sorry." After the shots fired at him this afternoon, presumably to urge him to leave town, this new move to force him to stay around, and the implication that people in Long Valley just couldn't get together on what to do about Silvestri, *was* funny. But Meyer didn't know about this afternoon, so he wasn't equipped to enjoy the joke.

Or to understand the necessary change in strategy, Guy realized. It was time for some intensive conferring among the allies . . . He leaned over and opened the passenger door of the Dodge. "Get in, Meyer." Cannon looked at him quickly and then obeyed without argument: there were, as Guy had observed before, distinct advantages to bright and perceptive allies. He shut the door and went around and climbed into the Dodge himself. Then he rolled up all the windows and began to talk, keeping his voice down and giving Meyer a little time to absorb the initial shock before he outlined specific tactics.

15

JOINT SORTIE

Miss Crabtree was adorable, from the tremulous gray-haired doughnut on top of her head to her narrow, faithfully polished old-lady oxfords. Looking at her as she explained the origin in her own childhood of the tag "Got you there, Truesdale!" Guy felt horribly guilty. Toward the hardworking Sergeant Alonso, who would have loved this so and had been unfairly deprived of it by his mean-spirited, grabby superior. And toward Kate, because it was like jaunting off to see the Grand Canyon and leaving the wife of your bosom, who should share all sweets, home minding the store.

"Poor Papa didn't make much allowance for our tender years," said the old lady who had once been little May, wearing a long dress with a blue sash—and maybe a big blue bow in her hair to match. "I expect he meant to. But sooner or later, he'd be up to every permissible trick. And when he won, he'd call out, 'Got you there, Truesdale!' quite shamelessly crowing." That was where it had become a part of May Crabtree, who brought it with her after that—all the way to Long Valley High School, where her students adopted it too.

Silvestri excused himself as soon as he could, getting himself out of the presence of Miss Crabtree's withered-apple face lost in tenderness for Papa who played croquet and word games so ardently, and into the marble chill of the front hall, where the telephone was. Struggling for patience while the operator inquired whether Mrs. Silvestri would accept a collect call, he wondered what this sudden terrible hunger was all about. True, it had been a long day, and most days—however long and trying—ended with Kate and this one wasn't going to, which inspired a certain understandable wistfulness. But really, it was out of all proportion . . . It was a good thing he'd found the strength of character to decline Miss Crabtree's brandy: add a little alcohol to this mood—and it had been Courvoisier in that decanter, he was willing to bet—and Silvestri would sink without so much as a final glub-glub.

Kate finally succeeded in persuading the operator that she didn't mind the expense, and Guy said "Hi" and then told her quickly, to get it over with, that he wouldn't be home tonight. Not even late. "I'm sorry, but I just have no choice. If it was only catching crooks, I could leave it to somebody else. But Cannon has these special needs, so it has to be done both ways, the law's and his."

"I know. Don't fret about what can't be helped, Guy."

"But I do fret. Particularly now. How do you feel?"

"Dragged out, just like last time at the beginning, remember? But otherwise, fine."

Except that last time, she hadn't had an active Tony to chase all day. "Well, at least you can get to bed early. Maybe even rediscover that eight-hours'-sleep feeling in the morning." Pining for the good-old-days, he sounded, even to himself, like an old-timer.

"Maybe I can," she said. "Unless you're keeping Ed Alonso out tonight, too. Because if you are, Barbara's going to spill over."

She was talking to a man who had recently telephoned Alonso and handed him enough logistics and liaison assignments to keep an entire U.S. Army command busy—Guy had the grace to blush before he said lightly, "Barbara doesn't handle these things with your experienced grace."

"I'll teach her my secret. First you make a doll, then you take about a dozen pins and—"

"Ouch."

"What hurts?" Kate asked eagerly. "Is it your big toe? The left one?"

"That's right."

"Ha."

He couldn't say *I love you, Kate,* not there in Miss Crabtree's front hall, with the patient rumble of Meyer Cannon's voice coming from the parlor. "I'd give anything," he said sadly, "for a western wind tonight. And a small rain." Then his face felt hot as the sweet silvery voice from the parlor reached him— the voice of Miss Crabtree, who taught English literature, he remembered belatedly. She might know the old anonymous quatrain: "O western wind when wilt thou blow,/That the small rain down may rain?/Christ, that my love were in my arms/And I in my bed again!"

His wife, that erstwhile English major, was observing that the rain it raineth every day. But Guy heard, in addition to the love and laughter in her voice, a note of concern. It roused him from his dreamy self-pity to concern for her: one thing he would *not* have was Kate thinking anything was bugging him, so he changed the subject briskly. "What did I miss at bath-time tonight? Any more vocabulary?"

Tony had gone in more for action than words, she reported.

"Smart kid," said the father of Tony, who had doubtless realized that a Mommy, especially a pregnant one, couldn't field a small wet body as expertly as the usual Chamberlain of the Bath.

"The phone rang just when I'd got him trapped in the towel, so he— Oh, yes, I forgot—you missed Herk. He's in Boston for some do. *His* vocabulary is still growing, too. I told him," she said without reproach, "you'd be home, but late. Do you want to call him? He left a number."

Guy said he was sorry to miss Herkimer, and something at the back of his mind told him he really meant it. "I did want to ask him something, but I guess I haven't got time. Anyway, it was kind of a foolish question."

"Can't I do it for you? I know how to ask foolish questions. Like—"

"Ah, don't. The trouble is, I don't remember," Guy said absently. Then suddenly he did: "Yes I do. Listen, ask him if he can think of a play with a scene"—the tableau rose before him, Claud Dozier narrating—"a big scene involving a wife pleading with her husband—" He broke off as memory tickled again. "I have a feeling they'd be in old-fashioned costumes."

"Pleading with her husband to do what?"

"No, to *not* do something. He's setting off for work and she's begging him not to go. Not to stay home, but to not-go—if you see what I mean. Don't go to—' " He stopped, his mind flailing like an aroused sleeper trying to track down a mosquito.

"Don't go to the Forum, Caesar? Or words to that effect. I could look it up, but I put the Shakespeare out of Tony's reach, so it would take me—"

"*Julius Caesar,* by golly. Except I think it was the Senate where they got him."

"Ah so? I'll look it up. But anyway, his wife's name was Calpurnia. And they'd be wearing *very* old-fashioned costumes."

"It was the Ides of March, and she had a premonition he'd get clobbered."

"Apparently you were paying attention in high school," Kate said. "The Red Sox must've been resting that day."

He refused the gambit. He had to, he'd promised Alonso he'd tell her himself. "Kate, listen, I don't want you jumping to conclusions." He knew she was already doing just that. "I assure you, they'd be wrong. But—well, Jones is going to be keeping an eye on the house tonight." He waited, afraid.

"I thought," she said slowly, "this was a big psychological-type case. That's how it was advertised. Not as cops and robbers."

"Nobody's going to do any shooting, Kate." Not anymore, anyway. He could prove it, in fact: he'd been an easy target in the woods behind the King house. And just now outside Cannon's place, when he was bumping around with a flashlight, any fool could've picked him off if that was the idea . . . But it would be ill-advised to offer those in evidence, so he said, "I'm only taking out insurance. Even Alonso thinks it isn't really necessary." Which was true, but Alonso had also thought the precaution desirable, in case keeping the lieutenant in Long Valley tonight was meant to serve somebody's purpose in Buxford. It paid to look in both directions for enemy forces gathering: *the lesson of the Weimar Republic,* the erudite sergeant had pointed out.

"I see." Kate was almost audibly making up her mind not to fuss. "Well, maybe I should invite Jones in. Though in that case, I wish you'd sent Merchant. He plays cribbage."

It was not quite successful, but it was a brave try. "Leave him out there," Guy said, instead of saying *I love you.* "He'll scare the crows away better out front. And you go to bed. Please."

"Well, one of us should." But Kate always gave up gracefully when she gave up. "Good night, darling."

For no apparent reason, Guy tidied his hair after he hung up. As though someone had ruffled it.

Or maybe because there was something about Miss Crabtree that was always holding class. Certainly Silvestri, half-drunk on fatigue, sat in her parlor like a student at an eight o'clock lecture—rousing himself enough to take notes on what he knew he'd need for the exam, but mostly dreamily waiting to come awake. Note: Susan King apparently did know Caesar's wife was not above reproach—only, she'd called her mother not Calpurnia but Madame Bovary. See also, "Dracula," in her diary . . .

Meyer Cannon said thoughtfully, "You don't get mad at Madame Bovary."

"No," Guy put in. "But you do run away from home, I guess."

Miss Crabtree eyed him with disapproval. "Susan was not one of those disturbed adolescents, Lieutenant. She wasn't running away from home, she was *leaving* it. After due consideration and with proper preparation. She was legally entitled to do that, you know, at eighteen. And it was only a matter of months before she'd be—" But not even Miss Crabtree could hold a class in the face of that. All she could do, it seemed, was turn her head, to preserve appearances.

Cannon said sharply, "Take it easy, Guy."

"How? Death hurts."

Miss Crabtree wasn't there then, she'd gone to answer her phone. The call turned out to be for Cannon. Presumably the ruthless Lieutenant Silvestri took advantage of Meyer's absence to harass the poor old lady, because his next note was about Callie King's *amour*. That was what Miss Crabtree called it when she admitted that "in the current loose fashion," it was freely mentioned by Susan. "With compassion, quite clearly. But they naturally wouldn't discuss Mrs. King's illicit *amour* in my presence." Susan herself had believed, apparently, that her mother was afraid of her father. "But her own efforts were directed to not repeating her mother's errors. Which I thought salubrious. The exact nature of those errors seemed to me irrelevant."

Nobody else was going to ask, so Guy did then, though with assurances that he was not scandal-mongering and in as graceful language as he could manage: did Miss Crabtree know who Mrs. King's lover was?

The old face went abruptly from the pink of embarrassment to a frightening pallor. "Did he— Was he responsible for Susan's death?"

Guy understood. She didn't know, but if that was who had killed Susan, this doughty old warrior would set about finding him . . . It was tempting, because she commanded resources the police didn't. But Guy managed to say "No," and then was hugely grateful that Meyer was returning. The old lady was so very pale, surely she needed some doctoring...

Meyer Cannon noticed, even before he'd crossed the big room, that Silvestri was up to that unconscious hand-flexing again. What could be upsetting him now? "Your office called, Guy. Devora gave them the message you left—that you'd be at the Franklin Motel as soon as you'd done a few errands in town." He gave the detective a heavily significant look. "She says it was a Sergeant Miller speaking. Or some such name—she couldn't quite catch it." Then he saw Miss Crabtree and promptly forgot about the phony inquiry Guy had told Devora to expect—correctly, it seemed. But that was only war games; Miss C.'s pallor was part of a real, and deadlier, war. Meyer rushed into action.

The next note was all but written in blood—Guy's. He awoke from idle contemplation of the game laid out on Miss Crabtree's chessboard, on a nearby table, to discover that Meyer's investigations had somehow led to a question about whether Susan King had a steady boyfriend. Miss Crabtree said no, Susan didn't. And then added—after hesitating, apparently reluctant to break a confidence even now—that nobody knew it but "Susan had a crush, as they call it, on Lenny Pritchard. He is employed at the gas station near her house, I believe. It caused her great anguish," Miss Crabtree said sadly, "that he didn't seem to notice her."

This was too much, Guy thought. It wasn't fair: he'd managed to cope with his anger over parents who abdicated their responsibilities and authorities who blundered at theirs. But this tiny, ridiculous, never-to-be-straightened-out mix-up just hurt too much.

Cannon went on. Even, now that his patient was enough recovered, to mild reproach. "Why didn't you tell me Susan was going to r—to leave home, Miss C.? Surely keeping her confidence at Billy's expense—"

Guy intervened hastily. "The point was how much *Billy* knew, wasn't it, Meyer?" Miss Crabtree's look of gratitude confirmed his guess. "He didn't know about his mother's lover, did he?"

"Oh no, Lieutenant. Certainly not."

Note: It wasn't Susan and Billy, then, who had talked *in the current loose fashion.* The "they" who didn't dare gossip in Miss C.'s stuffy presence were Susan and somebody else.

Guy got Meyer out of there by reminding him that they still had one more stop to make before Silvestri could be taken out to the motel. And, he added shamelessly, his office was already hunting for him, right?

"Miss C. didn't know Susan meant to take Billy along," Cannon remarked as he climbed into the car. "She really didn't, don't you agree?"

"Yes. Nobody would've discussed that with her." Guy checked the back seat of the car, which had been standing unlocked outside Miss Crabtree's house, and got in beside Cannon. But he didn't share his speculations about the reason for Miss C.'s ignorance. Like, leaving home would be legal for eighteen-year-old Susan but taking Billy along might not be, because he was still a minor—as somebody knowledgeable about the legalities had perhaps cautioned Susan. For somebody besides May Crabtree had been helping with Susan's plans. Somebody who was cautious not out of principle, like Miss C., but because it was smart to stay on the right side of the law.

"How far was the old lady in on Susan's plans, do you think?" Meyer asked. "She certainly had very profound feelings for the girl."

"Well, she was obviously an essential part of the practical preparations for the new life, et cetera."

"Really? I know Miss C. has money, but she's big on self-reliance. I can't see her just subsidizing—"

"There are a lot of strongminded old ladies in Buxford," Guy interrupted. "The kind with old-fashioned ideas, and money to pay for having them carried out. And I suspect she's very well connected in that set, in Buxford and Boston as well as out here." Susan had made the dress Miss Crabtree was wearing tonight, he told an amazed Meyer, and quite a few similarly out-of-date fashions in different sizes. "I'd imagine Miss C. could easily work up enough of a clientele for Susan to pay her rent." It might not be a very high rent, either: another thing typical of those dowagers was ownership of real estate in good neighborhoods . . . Guy thought of the other side of Susan's dressmaking trade, catering to quite a different kind of customer. It might have been interesting to see who would've won, the swingers or the *grandes dames,* once Susan King was set up on her own. But Silvestri's own guess was that both Susan and Billy would have been at least part-time students in a local college within a year—even if Miss Crabtree had to become a Best-Dressed Woman to subsidize it.

That brought him back to Billy—who was aware of Susan's plans, according to Dr. Cannon, but not according to Miss Crabtree. Since both were telling the truth, Guy thought, the conflict must be a function of time: obviously Susan had not told Billy until very shortly before her death. But why? She'd kept it secret from him up to then, and there was a good six months to go, so why would Susan suddenly tell him last November? Guy asked the question aloud, and got another item for his hypothetical notebook.

"The typing class—the one at the high school, I mean. Susan wanted him to sign up for it, for next semester." Meyer was exhilarated, though he admitted it was mostly vanity. The typing class he'd sent Billy to had really started the memory process going, Meyer thought now. "I can see the signs I couldn't read at the time. Like, Billy thought he was doing it for Simons, and so I did too. But I should've spotted something when he obviously set out to win the prize. *That* wasn't necessary for Will. It was for Susan, and that's why Billy didn't take any pleasure when he did come out on top of the class. It should've tipped me, because he likes winning. As witness the Truesdale bit with—"

"Oh, he's wrong about that, Meyer, did you know? Miss Crabtree may not think of it, but she can get out of his trap. If she moves her queen to Bishop-Three now."

"My God. It's a good thing one of us is a chess whiz, isn't it?" Cannon brushed off the beginnings of modest murmurs from Silvestri. "That reminds me, about your other game—there is no Sergeant Miller, is there? Devora thought he sounded suspiciously young."

There wasn't, Guy said, and anyway he'd called his office even before he called his wife . . . By that time, he was looking out of the car window at the hospital grounds—where the efforts of the sergeant not named Miller should already be bearing fruit. All of a sudden Guy was awake again. He was no longer taking notes in class, because it was time for lab work. And there was nothing that felt quite as good as getting your second wind, when you needed it really badly.

"We're very well patrolled at night," Meyer remarked. "That's when the legislators believe the lunatics will try to escape." Probably for fear of a cut in guard funds, nobody had suggested to the legislative committee that more of the so-called lunatics were sedated at night, Dr. Cannon pointed out. He conducted Guy to his office and left him there while he himself went over to look in on Billy.

The legislators apparently didn't believe doctors needed either space or luxury, Guy decided. Or maybe it was just that Cannon didn't receive delegations in his office. But it was unmistakably his; the cheerful more-or-less-ordered jumble was very like Meyer Cannon. He seemed to live there part of the time: a wool tartan auto robe was folded at one end of the leather sofa, and the top of one of the file cabinets constituted a miniature kitchen where somebody cooked instant coffee and bouillon with the aid of a small electric kettle. There were also two large cans purporting to contain crackers, but one turned out to be half-full of sugar instead.

Guy helped himself to a cracker from the authentic one and then took Billy King's math book from the bottom drawer of the same cabinet and carried it over to the desk. The manila envelope stuck in the book had a brass clasp, but it had been slit open at the top anyway. An enameled-copper letter opener—presumably Israeli handiwork—lay on the desk. Guy opened desk drawers until he found one containing stationery. (And a smiling photo of Devora, maybe stowed out of sight to avoid provoking associations in some patient? The facts of Meyer's professional life were hard, it seemed.) There were no hospital letterheads—apparently that stationery was locked up somewhere, to keep it from resourceful inmates—but Guy found some plain white paper; the fact that it was thin, poor-quality stock was an asset. It would do—and so, come to think of it, would the carbon paper, equally cheap stuff (somebody was thrifty with the taxpayers' money, all right), that he spotted in the drawer.

His look as happily devout as a hobbyist in his workshop, Lieutenant Silvestri laid two sheets of the white paper on the desk and then held the manila envelope from the Mercer School upside down and shook it gently. The tops of the pages inside emerged, and he helped them along, poking them with the letter opener until all four pages were out. Plying the opener, he separated the page covered with purple hectograph script from the others, pushing it until he could pick it up by the corner—which he did casually: it wouldn't matter if he blurred fingerprints, because those already present would be explainable and thus valueless as evidence.

Guy read the purple-printed quiz quickly and then reread the third question. Frowning, he picked up the letter opener and, holding it like a dagger, brought it down sharply half a dozen times on the bottom right-hand corner of the hectograph paper. He inspected the result—a line of tiny, almost invisible round dots like braille writing. Then he carried the page over to the file cabinets, laid it down on top, and investigated the possibilities. The first drawer was locked—patients' records, probably—and the second one contained folders of correspondence. The multiple-murderers study had a folder to itself. Not a very fat one, Guy noted, eyeing it guiltily: Meyer would have nothing to report to that Lambert committee—a fact that had simply slipped out of sight, the way virtuous acts always did, at least when they were other people's. And self-abnegation could virtually count on being invisible . . .

In the back of the drawer, some careful soul had saved for re-use a dozen or so book-mailing envelopes addressed to Dr. Cannon. Guy chose a large one from the Lambert Press, inserted the hectographed math quiz into its padded interior—where it promptly disappeared from view—and put the envelope back among the others. He shut the file drawer and went back to the desk to repeat his identification trick on the remainder of the "math package," stabbing each page twice in the bottom right-hand corner—but this time, he avoided molesting whatever fingerprints they held. Then he took three sheets of the smudgy carbon paper from the desk drawer and laid one, shiny surface down, on each of the pages. He stopped to inspect his fingers, which were a little carbon-blackened even though he'd been careful—more careful than anyone who didn't know about the carbon paper would be. Looking pleased with himself, he got out his handkerchief and wrapped it around his hand before he stacked the pages neatly and added a sheet of Cannon's plain white paper on top, so all the carbons would be hidden. Finally, holding the paper "club sandwich" in his wrapped hand, he coaxed it patiently back into the Mercer School envelope. The results were satisfactory: nobody, he concluded, was going to get those pages out without leaving fingerprints *somewhere* on them.

Silvestri stuck the edge of the Mercer envelope back into Billy's math textbook and checked to make sure the book merged properly with the normal desktop disarray. He decided it might seem a bit conspicuous, so he took some unopened green-striped envelopes from a pile on the other side of the desk and laid them on top of the math book.

That brought the small metal box—some kind of communications equipment, it looked like—to his attention. Wondering where the other end was (for there was no visible secretary's office or even a desk), Guy pushed up the switch. A strange voice, soft but clear, said at once "... only jus' talked more about that there mindwarner, Doc. Still calling my name Will, not Williams." Cannon was saying that he'd be back in less than an hour when Guy clicked off. He knew how this kind of monitor worked: somebody—somebody who didn't know how modest the Silvestri ménage was—had tried to sell him one for the baby's room.

He called Vesey quickly, because Meyer might already be on his way up here and there was no point in letting him know too many of the details of this operation. It would only make him self-conscious when the time came. And besides, Cannon was even more of a civilian than most civilians, Silvestri thought wryly: they preferred to think criminals confessed because of guilty conscience and/or desire to be rehabilitated. They knew better, of course, but it was like people who relished a good steak yet didn't want to hear about slaughterhouses.

Vesey was complaining when Cannon came in, "You don't know how long I've been waiting to get that lousy little twirp."

"I do know, Chief," Guy said. "But it wouldn't pay to blow the whole thing just for that, would it? Besides," he added grimly, "we both want the other fellow a lot more. And this is the only way we're going to get him *and* the story."

Vesey said it was nice of Silvestri not to point out that that was the least Chief Vesey owed Billy King. Satisfied that misguided enthusiasm wouldn't cause the Long Valley police to break cover and mess up his scheme, Guy hung up and turned to Cannon.

Meyer looked discouraged, he decided. "How's Billy?"

"Well, he woke up and talked a little, Williams says."

"I thought that was good. But you don't seem to think so."

"It could be worse," Cannon said. "But he's still with Prince Trad, and that's a step backward."

"From remembering the Truesdale line? I see. But could it be temporary? All over in the morning?"

Cannon smiled and said anything was possible. "Williams has a while to go yet on his shift. Then I'll take over, but I don't think we'll see much change tonight."

Guy looked at the couch with its waiting folded cover. "I hope you're not going to be sleeping here?"

"Oh. That was nice of her, wasn't it? No, we put a cot in Billy's room. I'll just get in it when Williams gets out." He stretched and smothered a yawn apparently inspired by the mere prospect of sleep. "Are you all set now?" He eyed the desk. "Looks quite normal."

"Good. You won't change anything, will you, Meyer? I mean, if you want to do some work—"

Cannon said if he had some time he'd spend it catching up on his journal reading, and he didn't need anything on the desk for that. But it would be nice, he said wistfully, if he could just go home and tuck Devora in first.

"She's perfectly safe," Guy told him. It was a considerable understatement, in view of the number of Vesey's people busy around the Reservation at the moment—among other things, taking a sample of the grasses Silvestri had seen under one of the cars while he was flashing his light around in the parking lot ... "I'm sorry, Meyer, but that would make you available there instead of here. Which we just can't afford." In a little while, it would be necessary to have nobody at all around at the Reservation, to leave a clear field for the confab Silvestri hoped to inspire there. The presence in the house of the sharp-eyed—and come to think of it, in the light of that parking-lot adventure—rather intrepid Dr. Cannon might inhibit the meeting Guy was counting on. "Nobody's going to bother Devora," Guy said flatly. She would follow instructions, he was convinced, whether she actually succeeded in getting to sleep or not. After his brief chat with the pretty little girl who, he'd had to keep reminding himself, had been an officer in a real army, Silvestri had changed his opinion of military training for women.

"Okay, I'm convinced," Cannon said. "In fact, ever since that business in the parking lot tonight, I've been convinced this sort of thing is best left to the experts." He didn't notice Silvestri's startled look, because he was leading the way out of the office.

Cannon didn't notice, either, that the guard at the entrance to the administration building addressed Silvestri as "Lieutenant." Guy noticed, but he let it go in the interests of détente: the man shouldn't have known who Silvestri was, but he couldn't afford any intramural squabbles among the mixed bag of law-enforcement types represented here tonight.

16

SILVESTRI'S OUTPOST

Silvestri should have been visible for miles as he checked in at the office of the Franklin Motel—a concrete box with picture windows on two sides and enough wattage to light up a city—but by way of insurance, he stood directly in front of Meyer Cannon's headlights when the doctor backed out of the parking space in front of Room 14. The detective went on standing there until the red dots of the vanishing car's brake lights were out on the road. Then he stayed where he was for an extra minute, listening to the mutter of a radio somewhere and looking up at the sky. But not at the dark hulk of the familiar Chevy parked in front of Number 8. Finally Lieutenant Silvestri yawned, stopped scratching his chest with the tagged room key, and used it to unlock the door.

He flicked the light switch just inside the door and crossed to the TV, bending over it to study the dial as he turned it on. Only then did he lower the venetian blind over the big front window and draw the draperies across it. By that time, a voice from the TV was mellifluously deploring inflation. And, even though Silvestri was actually sitting on one of the beds and yawning again, enough time had gone by so it would seem normal for the bathroom light to go on.

Rubin came out blinking. "You took your sweet time, Lieutenant."

"Sorry. But anyway, we've got a little wait now." Silvestri unzipped the airline bag he'd brought from Cannon's house and lifted out a thermos of coffee. "Here. By way of apology."

"Oh, wow, thanks. I need it."

Silvestri shook his head suddenly and pointed. They both fell silent while, on the TV screen, a panel of experts stopped arguing to watch a series of charts pass in review. Guy looked at Rubin and pointed his thumb down, and Rubin got up and switched to another channel. There, a patrol car was racing through the night, its siren wailing. Both men grinned. And then Guy went on, as though nothing had interrupted, "Also sandwiches. Mrs. Cannon knows how an army travels."

Rubin was looking into the plastic bag of provisions. "No army I know of travels *this* good. You know the last time I ate?"

Silvestri said he'd love to hear, but he'd borrowed some clean underwear and even a clean shirt, and since he was probably expected to take a shower now, he was going to oblige. Just in case, though—

"Yessir." Rubin turned on the small lamp over the desk and switched off the room lights. He squinted along the line of sight from the door, then turned the armchair around and sat in it, facing the TV screen.

Silvestri surveyed the tableau like a stage director. "Too low. Here." He handed over the two telephone books from the night table. Rubin was settling onto them when Guy padded past to the shower.

The eager beavers in the squad car on the TV had gone by the time he came out, dressed in his borrowed underwear and shirt. A kiss now occupying the TV screen imposed silence while Silvestri pulled on his trousers and Rubin munched Oreo crackers, dunking them so they wouldn't crunch. Finally the lovers came out of the clinch, and as the girl breathed, *we can't do this, it's—wrong*, Rubin breathed, "I hope you didn't steam it up in there. Who knows how long—" He stopped because the girl on the screen was saying *Who knows?*

When they finished laughing, Guy said, "You can't stay in the bathroom anyway. They may want to use the window—and it'd figure I'd leave it open."

"All right, but why would they? The door is ridiculous. It's not worth climbing in a window."

"They aren't pros." Guy stood up. "Let's go."

Politely, Rubin wiped the thermos cup's rim on his sleeve and set it down next to the thermos. He glanced at the dark corner of the room beyond the window, where it would be even darker when the door was opened, and looked inquiringly at the lieutenant. Who nodded, but raised a hand to say *Hold it*: on the screen, the girl was tearfully trying to prevent her father from riding out after the hero, which promised some suitable noise upcoming. In the meantime, Silvestri crossed to the bathroom, unlocked the window and opened it a little, and turned off the light. When he came out, the girl's father was just mounting his horse.

Let's go! called the leader of the waiting posse. Rubin slid smoothly out of the armchair, taking the phone books with him and picking up a luggage stand from the foot of one of the beds as he went by. He set it down beside the bed instead, at the side near the window, and then disappeared from view.

The noise of the horses' hoofs was beginning to diminish when Silvestri parted the draperies and pulled up the blind. He opened the front window and stood breathing deeply of the night air while revealing to the world the blue blur of the TV and a fellow in what surely looked like a pajama jacket, ready for bed. Then he adjusted the window to his liking and lowered the blind. He strolled to the armchair, moved the desk lamp so it was in easy reach, and pushed the button that turned it off. Then he settled back in the chair and poured some coffee, in the light from the TV.

It took quite a while. The thermos was empty and the Western over, and then so was the news, too. Guy began to wonder whether Meyer's shirt, which drooped on him, did look enough like a pajama top after all. Or maybe nobody in Long Valley was efficient, on either side . . . A new movie, the TV said, was about to appear. But first there was a rush of commercials, strung out nose to tail and butting each other along. The fourth was on view when Guy heard the snick of the lock on the door of Number 14. It was a good thing, he thought— carefully relaxing his muscles, which had stiffened themselves without his will—because one more commercial and even Rubin, a good man, might have found it impossible to stay awake.

The door closed, infinitely slowly. *Two of them,* Guy noted. Then a flashlight came on, shielded and pointed at the floor. But it was still too risky, Guy decided: the asleep-at-the-TV bit would have to be ditched, because a movable light might accidentally pick up Rubin . . . With his hand on the lamp button, Guy said, without turning, "Come in, Twirl" and the light came on. It was small and weak, but it should put the flashlight out of business.

It seemed to—the shiny spot he'd seen reflected in the polished wood frame of the TV set disappeared. But it would still be a good idea to keep all attention on himself, so he announced, "I've been waiting for you."

"Don't turn around." Then the young voice added, "Or this thing will go off." Which made it doubtful that he really had a gun, Guy thought.

"Okay." Movie music swelled. "But can't I turn off the TV? I might not hear what you say, and I don't want any accidents."

"Sit still," the sharp voice said. And then, in a different tone, "Okay." Guy stirred, and the voice, panicky now, called, "Not you, fuzz." A hand moved into the blue light and snapped off the television.

"All right," Guy said peaceably, watching the silhouette that had flitted past become a short-haired, probably-blond boy who was crossing to the bathroom door. There was a scrabbling sound in the bathroom, and the young voice behind Silvestri shouted, "Come on, come *on*" with obvious nervousness. Finally the short-haired boy appeared, pulling a girl—lumpy in dark sweatshirt and jeans but with long wheat-colored hair that shone in the lamplight. "This is Trixie, I presume," Silvestri said, nodding politely as she was yanked by. "Is anyone else coming?"

The growl from behind him was incoherent, but unmistakably furious.

The girl pulled loose from her escort, halted, and sent a scornful look over Guy's head. "Don't be a clod, Twirl—he knows who we are. He was probably waiting for us."

The blond boy showed up in the mirror the TV screen had become. He was not quite blocking the troll-like image of Twirl, who, it had to be assumed, held a gun on Silvestri. "She's right," the boy said. "He told us he was waiting for us, didn't he?" His speech was soft and precise, and went with his clothes —which were not only quite clean but hadn't even been made to look tattered.

Trixie apparently remembered Guy's presence then. "You got it right," she told Guy. "I'm Trixie and that's Twirl and—"

"Thomas Mallinson," Silvestri finished. The Registry clerk who'd remembered seeing Susan with "a boy" would certainly have said "a hippie" about anyone who looked like Twirl.

Trixie's face flashed real surprise before she managed to grab at her sliding-away cool. "That's right. Wow. The fuzz's kiddie-computer's really been working. Right, Big Brother?"

Given her youth and inexperience, it wasn't bad. And it was certainly a braver try than Thomas Mallinson managed: from his reflection in the TV screen, he was reacting rather like a pigmy confronted with a camera for the first time. Both of them, Guy noted, were easily awed by a magic-show. He decided to concentrate on the girl. "I didn't need a computer. I just asked Miss Crabtree who Susan's best friend was." He pitched his voice low enough so she had to listen carefully.

Trixie leaned toward him, her face troubled. "It's because I *am* Susan's best friend that I wanted to—"

In the back of Guy's mind, reason protested—*Dammit, I was just getting some diplomacy going*—even while he saw Thomas Mallinson making the move that would get a war started. Rubin must have seen it sooner, for the White County telephone directory was already hurtling through the air. Silvestri was still spectator enough to see it hit Thomas's wrist just as his hand came out of his pocket. The object he dropped didn't fall as heavily as you'd expect. But when Rubin went to war, so did the lieutenant: Guy pulled the girl down and held her in front of him while he braced his feet and shoved hard, backwards. The armchair, with Guy and Trixie lending it weight, hit the invisible Twirl somewhere in the midsection, by the gasping sound of him. He went over backward, with the chair, Guy, and Trixie—in that order—on top of him, and with an astonishing amount of noise.

Taking Trixie with him, Guy scrambled up. Then he thrust her back into the chair, which was still lying on top of Twirl. The noise must have been mostly of human origin, he decided— the desk lamp was lying on its side, but it was unbroken. Guy noted that, then got on with his job. Which was to take out Mallinson while Rubin dealt with Twirl, who theoretically had a gun.

But the efficient Rubin, apparently fearing that his support troops would be tied up with Trixie, had already supported himself: Thomas Mallinson's fair head was sticking up absurdly from the luggage stand he wore around his neck like a sort of mobile pillory. He was holding its wooden frame with both hands, trying to wrestle it off; but the woven plastic strips through which his head had been thrust were both sturdy and flexible. If he'd parted the two relevant ones, he could have taken the whole thing off past his ears like a sweater—but he was clearly beyond logical thought. What his bright-pink face wanted, furiously and intently, was to get to Trixie. To frustrate that would be good enough, so Guy grabbed one of the dangling legs of the luggage stand and gave it a half-twist to bring the wooden bar at one end against Thomas's Adam's-apple. "If you move, I'll break your neck," Guy growled, a few inches from the boy's ear. He twitched the luggage rack gently, for emphasis, and all resistance stopped.

But by that time, the rescue of Trixie was clearly impossible anyhow. She'd managed to get out of the chair's embrace without help, and then to topple it off the prone figure of Twirl. But now, her eyes wide and full of dread, she stood as if hypnotized by the stubby revolver in Rubin's hand.

"Police officer," Rubin said briskly. He backed up toward the aisle between the beds, bringing the gun nearer to Guy—who thus noticed that the safety catch was still on and twitched Thomas's head around by a degree or two so he wouldn't notice, too.

"Surprise, surprise," Twirl mocked. With the light in his eyes, he couldn't possibly see what Guy had seen. Twirl either knew he had no reason to fear the gun, or he was braver than he looked.

Rubin said firmly, "Get up."

"Why? I'm comfortable here."

"For God's sake, take it easy this time, Rubin." Guy's tone made it clear that the trigger-happy Rubin was a constant worry to his lieutenant. He thought about adding *You don't want to be suspended again,* but then he remembered that art consists of knowing when to stop creating.

Besides, he had made his point: the luggage stand vibrated with the sudden tension of the boy it imprisoned. And, across the room, Trixie said frantically, "Twirl, please. Don't play games with them. Not now."

"He's the one playing games," the light voice from the floor pointed out. "I have no gun. Because I have no permit to carry one, and I'm a very law-abiding citizen. And Lieutenant Silvestri won't let Rubin here shoot an unarmed man. Because the lieutenant is the fair-haired boy of the Buxford force, famous for integrity and the smarts, and he's not about to blow that."

Guy spoke quickly, lest Rubin burst out laughing. "Get up. You're interfering with an officer in the performance of his duty.

"Oh, am I? Okay. Nobody told me that, you see." Twirl got to his feet in one lithe movement, his curled-brim Stetson in one hand. Rubin followed him with the gun, and Twirl noticed. "Come on Rubin, knock it off," he said, bending to dust his embroidered denim pants.

He was exactly like the TV portraits, Guy decided—only even more incredible without the intervening camera. And with the addition of the hat, which was a dusty lavender, if you could believe it. It completed the total effective invisibility of Twirl—who could only be described as a long-haired, bearded, drooping-moustached male. If you went in for complete, not to say impressionistic, description, you could add that he was probably young, and he seemed fond of dressing in costumes. But if Twirl had any scars, they were hidden—as was the shape of his ears and even the color of his eyes.

"What did it, Rubin?" Silvestri asked. Because Rubin would still be hidden in the corner if he hadn't seen something.

"The other one has a piece, Lieutenant. He dropped it."

"Okay, wait a minute." Guy caught the end of the venetian blind cord and pulled it through the frame of the luggage rack until it was taut, then tied it in a knot. "You'll be all right if you don't try to move, Tommy," he said pleasantly. He was making for the light switch when the phone rang. "I'll get it." Guy took the only way there was to cross behind Rubin: solemnly—though Trixie's startled face, the mouth an O, almost broke him up—he walked across the two beds. To preserve his composure, he turned his back when he picked up the phone. "Yes?"

"Mr. Silvester, this is the office. I'm sorry, but we've

had several complaints. About noise in your room, I mean."

"You have? Good."

It got by: the owner of the nervous voice didn't have time to listen. He rushed on, getting this chore over with. "We always try to be understanding, sir. But there *are* people here who have to get up for an early start in the morning."

"I see."

"And that's what we're in business for, to give them a good night's rest. Now you can do what you like in your room, but when Number Sixteen says it sounds like you're breaking up the furniture—"

"No. That's a mistake," Guy said authoritatively.

The voice hesitated, having no taste for bucking authority. And besides, they were insured . . . "Well, I'll take your word for it, but I want to remind you you're responsible for any damages to—"

"Correct. That won't be necessary, though."

"Well." But there was more, and the voice suddenly remembered it. "I hope we won't have any unpleasantness, Mr. Silvester. But if I continue to receive complaints, I'll just have to call the police."

"No. Don't do that."

"Well, I certainly don't want to, but—"

"I'll take care of it," Guy said. "That'll be okay—let me know if you run into any trouble, but I'm sure it'll be all right." He hung up without a goodbye and turned to face the others. "Okay, Rubin. That was Jake Woodward. They've got us on their 'scope, so you can put your weapon up."

"Yessir." Rubin tucked his gun away. "That Woodward's a good man."

Guy frowned: Rubin, it seemed, had not learned about the dangers of excess in art. He crossed the room to switch on the lights.

"Well, common sense prevails at last." Twirl was shaking out his limbs elaborately, as though he'd just been released from a boa constrictor's hug. But the attempt to rally his troops was not succeeding. Trixie made a small inarticulate sound that yet managed to transmit disbelief and contempt. She went by Twirl without a look, on her way to help Rubin free Tommy—who was himself too busy to be rallied.

Guy hid a smile and bent to examine the carpet for whatever it was that had looked like a gun. He kicked it before he saw it, and Tommy Mallinson called, "Hey." And then, unnecessarily, because Guy had picked it up and was turning it over in his hands, "That's my *comb*."

"So it is." It was in a black case, with a metal clip on the side. That would have caught the light, the length fit, and the lack of width would have been hidden by the boy's hand, as he drew it, presumably pointing it at the back of Silvestri's head.

Guy held it out for Rubin's inspection, and the detective shook his head wonderingly. Guy studied the comb's owner: Tommy's neck was reddened from the contact with the stretched plastic tapes, but the skin was not broken. "Your hair *is* mussed," he said truthfully. "Here." He held out the comb.

"*Look* at him," Trixie charged furiously. "Just look at his neck, all rubbed raw. And Rubin hurt his wrist with that thing he threw, too."

Guy had looked at the wrist, which didn't show any sign of swelling. "It'll be all right," he told the girl.

"Oh sure, that's lovely. You beat people up and then you say it'll be all right."

From the corner of his eye, Guy saw Twirl, lounging easily against the desk, waiting to pick up the goodies—the same kind he always picked up. It was too much . . . "That thing Rubin threw was a White County telephone directory, which isn't very thick," Guy said. "It was meant to make him drop his gun. And he's damn lucky Rubin decided against shooting it out of his hand instead," he finished, decisively if somewhat inaccurately.

"But it wasn't a gun, it was a comb. Just a simple everyday *comb*. Or don't you people recognize such peaceful realities?"

"Man, I am tired of single-edged peace," Guy exploded. "When people bust in here, tell you they have a gun on you, and then pull something that looks like another one, I think it was positively quixotic of Rubin to throw a phone book. And if you want to know, I think *I* was too damn gentle, too."

"Gentle! You squeezed my stomach right into my backbone."

"For your information, miss," Rubin said, "the way that backward roll is supposed to be done, the Lieutenant should've kicked you in the gut, not picked you up."

Silvestri told the girl soberly, "I really mean it, I am sorry, Trixie. It's no part of my job or my way of life to hurt you, and in fact I'm sworn to risk my life to keep you from being hurt in some circumstances. But certainly not when you're part of an attack on me."

"I wasn't, I was—" Trixie stopped, apparently uncertain just what it was she had been doing there.

"Trix." The blond boy's voice sounded creaky at first, worrying Guy: had the pressure on his throat been more than was intended? But then the voice recovered strength: "He's right, if you look at it. Be fair—Rubin thought he saw me pull a gun on his buddy, so what would you expect him to do? We did say we had a gun, after all."

"No." Twirl stood away from the desk. "Trix, Tom, now hear this." He was grinning because he knew perfectly well why Silvestri had chosen just that moment to hold a chair for the lady: the lieutenant was sharp, you had to give him that, but he couldn't stall forever. Twirl waited till Silvestri had taken the desk chair for himself and Rubin and Tommy were sitting side by side on the end of the nearer bed. Then he told his followers, "You're letting these cats con you. Like, first thing you know, you'll be thinking they're real dolls just for calling off their gang out there without tossing us in the slammer. But the truth is, they can't do that, no way. Forget about understanding and that crap, and stick to the rules, and—"

Rubin said "Oh, wow" in disbelief.

Twirl ignored him. "Like these jocks say, let's go by the book. So what comes out is, we haven't broken any laws and yet we've been viciously attacked by two law-enforcement officers." He saw Trixie starting to shake her head. "Okay, I'll show you. Silvestri, in a court—and I know you're too smart to lie under oath—wouldn't you have to admit that what I said was 'This thing will go off'? Never that I had a gun?"

"Yes, that's true." Guy tried for a hangdog look, thinking it was too bad the way Twirl's ego kept getting in his way. He seemed unaware right now, for example, that his demonstration of wiliness was turning his troops off.

"Okay, Point Two—when you told me I was interfering with an officer et cetera, didn't I promptly stop?"

"You did."

"Thus obeying an officer, like a good citizen should?"

"Well, but wait a minute," Guy objected, in the interests of verisimilitude. "You make it sound— I mean, you *were* in my room, after all."

Twirl smiled with real pleasure. "Yes, I was. But I didn't break any law—you *invited* me in, don't you remember?" He waited, but Silvestri only hung his head and looked unhappy. "You heard him, Rubin. Are you going to try to deny he said 'Come in, Twirl'?"

"Oh my, a jailhouse lawyer," Rubin said disgustedly. "Lieutenant, do we have to—"

"Yes, I'm afraid we do have to let him go." Guy knew that wasn't what Rubin had meant to ask. "I did say those words. So he's right—we can't arrest him."

"You see?" Triumphant, Twirl told his friends, "If you don't let these people intimidate you—"

Guy had seen Tommy's embarrassed flush and Trixie turning her face away. The time was ripe, so he interrupted smoothly, "We'll have to let him go, Rubin. But of course we can hold the other two."

Tommy looked terrified. "Us? You mean arrest us?"

"Well, you aren't covered by Twirl's technicality. I didn't invite *you* in, did I?"

Rubin turned to the boy beside him. "That's rough, kid. But if you've never been in trouble before, sometimes the judge— If you get the right judge, of course."

Tommy paid no attention. He was doing two things: looking at Trixie and trying not to cry. Trixie sank deeper into the armchair and let her curtaining hair fall forward: she not only wanted to look at nobody, she wanted nobody to see her.

As Alonso's report had indicated, Twirl did not lack acumen. The silence went on just long enough for him to make the necessary calculations: to be seen deserting Trixie and Tommy, and right after Tommy had been admiring Rubin for defending *his* buddy, was impossible—Trixie was already wobbling, and with that, she'd be gone. Twirl raised his head and looked at Silvestri. "Okay. What will it take?"

"The whole story. About Susan King, up to and including the day she died."

"But that was just what we came to—" Trixie began to cry, burying her face and the rest of the sentence.

Guy answered it anyway, in case she was listening. "You could have called me. Or Dr. Cannon. You didn't have to play tricks with my car." Like any politician, Twirl was forced to lead in the direction his constituency wanted to go. Tonight, that had been to a talk with Silvestri, because it would help Billy King. So Twirl had fixed it for them—but in his own terms, with himself in charge, showing up the authority figures for the benefit of the gallery . . . He had style, Guy conceded, watching Twirl remove the lavender hat and curl its brim tenderly. But the fact was, he made a career of sowing distrust . . . "Begin the story," Lieutenant Silvestri, his heart hardened, said to Twirl, "with you peddling the murder gun."

"Hey man, don't come on like that." Twirl had replaced his face as well as his hat: a nice kid, a little wild but still a nice kid, was looking anxiously at the policeman now. "You know better, Lieutenant. You know I wouldn't be trading in that kind of goods."

"That thirty-eight was Mrs. King's," Guy said quietly. It had been so obvious, once you recognized that it was perfectly possible for Callie to be using one drawer of her husband's desk—which was, after all, the only desk downstairs. "And she bought it through you." There'd been an agent in between: it wasn't Callie herself but her lover who'd made the necessary contact with somebody who sold illegal weapons. But that was almost undoubtedly via Twirl, so it was Twirl who had what Guy wanted—the name of the only person still alive who knew exactly what happened that November morning, and thus could give Cannon what he needed to help Billy.

Twirl was feeling the pressure. "Listen, you can go to jail for a thing like that, Lieutenant. And I *know* you know I don't do things you can go to jail for."

Guy was not going to win that point, he knew, and Billy was more important than crime and punishment. "All right, let's say you just happened to introduce a buyer to a seller. And let's say if you think back, you can remember at least one of them. I choose the buyer."

Trixie raised her head. "Leave me out of your trades, please." She turned to Silvestri. "I don't know anything about any guns. But I'll tell you everything else." Silvestri nodded, and she bit her lip. Then she began boldly: "Susan had to get out of that house, she *had* to . . ."

A quarter of an hour later, Guy was feeling like an archaeologist who'd turned over a stone and found a whole buried civilization going about its own affairs under the surface of Long Valley life. Not a democracy, but a little satrapy headed by Twirl, who knew how to cope—with the things the proper, adult authorities told youngsters were none of their business yet. In a sense, Guy had to concede, the reign of Twirl was perfectly legitimate, with leadership won on merit and maintained by producing benefits. True, those benefits were for the special few known to Twirl and accepted at his court, but he did take good care of his own. Susan King had been in that category, according to Lenny Pritchard, because of Trixie. And Guy had just noted himself that Trixie counted heavily: for some reason, probably not the obvious one, Twirl seemed to have a need to avoid her scorn.

If the favors Susan had received were any measure, Trixie's clout must be considerable, Silvestri realized as he struggled to readjust his thinking. For apparently Susan's dressmaking had not been just a kind of extension of babysitting but an all-but-full-blown enterprise, the kind the Small Business Administration might have smiled upon. Except that it was Twirl who'd set Susan up in business and provided her with the necessary contacts—which included some rather specialized "salesmen" who customarily visited merchants regularly and had no trouble persuading them to sell Susan's work. And presumably it was through Twirl, directly or indirectly, that Susan had secured a lucrative assignment to design new costumes for a popular singing group.

The details of Susan King's secret life as an entrepreneur would provide a tasty snack for Merchant, Guy predicted to himself—while he listened to Trixie explaining that the whole idea had been for Susan to have a bank account and a credit rating by the time her birthday freed her from Long Valley. "She had to be able to rent an apartment in a straight neighborhood in Buxford." Which, Guy gathered, represented Respectability. For Susan had planned to be no communard, but the head of a household of two—from which Billy would issue forth daily to a good school. Once he reached sixteen, he could earn money during the summers; but he would be fed and clothed and housed by Susan. "She got this great book from the Agriculture Department," Trixie said. "Like about how to use powdered milk and all that, to get the most food value for your money. It tells how many calories for an adolescent boy, and all. She had a budget figured out . . ."

Shame swelled the lump of tribal mourning gathering in Silvestri's throat as he saw how complete was the replacement of adults in Susan's planned new life. Her thoroughness shouted aloud of the failures she'd witnessed, and meant to correct when *she* took over as Billy's parent.

But he wasn't the only one who knew, apparently: "Susan was so gutsy," Tommy Mallinson said urgently. "They let her down, but she didn't run around hollering about it, she got up and figured a way to do better for her kid brother. You just had to help somebody like that, you dig?"

Guy nodded, wondering whether Susan hadn't also helped Tommy by providing him with a needed example. Twirl said, "Susan was good people" and Guy told himself to give credit where it was due: Twirl was no idealist and would do nothing that cost him too much, but he probably hadn't been immune to the general desire to lend a hand to ardor and courage. He had certainly done his best for Susan, equipping her as if he were one of the secret suppliers of passports to anti-Nazi underground heroes in old movies.

The whole affair had clearly had something of that flavor. If not underground, at least underworld—a scene in which you had no way to call the cops if you were robbed, and business was conducted without either conveniences or formal supervision. Susan King's problem that November morning had been a result of the special requirements of that world, Guy gathered. With difficulty, though—because Twirl interrupted whenever Trixie innocently wandered too close to the edge of some kind of admission.

"The man comes to town once a week," she explained, "and if you owe money, you have to catch him that day. Otherwise, you get—"

"The lieutenant knows how that works," Twirl said smoothly.

Managing to disguise sudden unseemly sympathy for him, Guy said he understood the problem. Which was that Susan had

had her money ready (in cash, of course) and an appointment arranged to fit with her school program—how neatly the study of history and Latin had been wound in and out of the need to meet her commercial obligations!—but then it all fell through at the last minute because she couldn't get out of the house. Incredible, Guy thought: plying her way in what was even more of a jungle than business always was, Susan had also been a child hemmed in by adult edicts. When "her mother started coming on like Florence Nightingale," Trixie said, and it was clear there'd be no going to school tomorrow, Susan was caught in a bind. So she called her best friend. "Mrs. King didn't like it much," but was prevailed upon to allow a short visit to the invalid. Trixie went upstairs to Susan's room and Susan handed over the two hundred dollars and—

"Two hundred dollars!" Rubin glared at Twirl, who shrugged and said, "Commissions, you know." Anyway, he added virtuously, *he* hadn't got any of it.

Guy told Rubin to cool it: for Susan, that had been the only game in town and she'd had to pay what it cost. Which was, he guessed drily, not your unimaginative legitimate agent's ten percent. "You cool it too," he ordered Twirl. "I'm only interested in the timing. I'm not listening to who, or where. So you let the girl talk."

Well, it was complicated, Trixie said, because she couldn't go meet the money-man herself: unlike Susan, she had a first-period class—with Miss Crabtree—at the high school, and then a jump over to the Mercer for the second period. So Trixie called in aid. Somebody who qualified by having wheels and being unlikely to rip her off, but who was, Guy gathered from the look on her face, strictly from the bottom of her list. She seemed to have a supply of serviceable swains (when he'd grabbed her, Guy remembered, she'd been startled, but her body had not stiffened in his grasp, as you might expect of a seventeen-year-old virgin). But Harry Moody didn't rate high. So, called that night and asked to do a favor for la belle Trixie, he'd been anxious to please . . . Guy groaned silently, recalling an Eagle Laundry customer who'd mentioned seeing a girl in Moody's truck at 10:30 or so. Half-suspecting it was only Vesey's troops trying belatedly to make brownie points, Guy had dismissed the report as irrelevant . . .

Harry Moody, doubtless with his hair combed and his shoes shined, turned up at the high school with his handy green truck well in time for Trixie's release from English class at 9:10. Which was lucky, because it was probably earlier, that day: the principal, Mrs. Wilder, came in to whisper to Miss C. once, Trixie said, and went out looking not-happy. So there was some kind of flap on that made Miss C. dismiss the class early and beat it from the room. (Guy remembered Alonso's report: Mrs. Wilder had consulted Miss Crabtree about the appropriate reaction to being stood up by Dr. King.) There were practically no kids in the halls yet when Trixie came out and found Harry waiting, so it could've been before 9:10. But it certainly was not later.

By the time Trixie had lined Harry up the night before, it was too late to call Susan, whose mother was fussy. But even Mrs. King wouldn't mind if Trixie called at around nine in the morning, to ask Susan how she felt. So Trixie made Harry wait while she phoned, from a booth in the school, to tell Susan not to worry.

"It didn't answer, of course." There was no of-course about it, so far as Guy knew: Trixie's phone call was at least ten minutes earlier than the earliest no-answer call on record, Mrs. Wilder's. "I let it ring and ring," the girl went on, "because it was weird—I mean, I knew Susan had to be home, and her mother probably was, too." She'd dialed again, just in case she'd made a mistake. But then she was out of time, and Harry was getting fretful (as were his customers, doubtless—but Trixie seemed unaware of obligations not to her). So she gave him the two hundred dollars and he went off to deliver it, after dropping Trixie at the Mercer for her second-period class. She was just going into class when she ran into Billy King coming in, too.

"You were in the same class?" Silvestri asked.

"Yes. Billy's good at math and I'm terrible," she said matter-of-factly. "So he's ahead and I'm behind, and that left us in the same class."

"With Miss Dyer." She nodded, and Guy asked whether she'd taken the math quiz that day. She had, Trixie said, not that it had done her any good. And yes, she guessed her paper was somewhere at home—her mother kept them to cry over. Sure, if Silvestri wanted a look at it, that could be arranged, Trixie said with careful tolerance, like a would-be sophisticate hearing of a new and particularly disgusting perversion.

But the point about the math class, she went on severely, was that she met Billy. So naturally she asked him if there was anything wrong at home. "He said Susan was sitting up in bed, listening to the radio, when he went by her room. She told him to get in there and win for God and country—he had some kind of big game or something that day. Anyway, she was smiling and she said she felt fine." Trixie stopped and they all looked at the last picture of a smiling Susan conscientiously remembering what was important to the kid brother. "Then, I don't know why," Trixie said wearily, "I asked Billy if anything was said at breakfast. What I meant was, maybe they were going to take Susan to the doctor. But Billy just looked at me and sort of wiggled, and I figured I knew what it was—Susan told me about those nicey-nicey fights they had, her parents. I gathered that was what happened that morning, and I was embarrassing Billy so I cooled it, fast—Susan had a real hangup about keeping him innocent, you know. I told him to forget it and we both went on into class."

No, she had not seen Billy after class. She wouldn't expect to—you left when you finished the quiz, and Billy would finish fast. Whereas Trixie needed every minute, and in fact Miss Dyer had been hanging over her at the end, in a hurry because she had to leave for a third-period class at the high school.

Harry Moody was waiting again when Trixie came out, and that was when she began to get really uptight. Because after Harry delivered Susan's money, he went to the King house with the laundry, and found nobody home. Since he knew Susan was sick, he rang and knocked and even went around to see whether anyone was out back. But then he was already real late and worried about getting in trouble, so he left the clean laundry and took off.

Trixie felt in no shape for school by now. She cut the rest of her classes and drove around Harry's route with him for a while, just biting her nails (and being seen by that customer, Guy noted dryly). After about an hour or so of that, she couldn't stand it anymore: she ordered herself driven to Twirl's pad, where she dumped her problem. Twirl gave her some—

"I could see she was upset, so I soothed her," Twirl broke in.

Guy said politely, "Of course."

"What may interest you, Lieutenant, is that I also tried calling Susan." Twirl anticipated the question. "It was ten-fifty. I looked at my watch, because I had things planned but Trixie was in no shape to be left alone. So I had some arranging to do."

After that, what was said mattered less than what could be deduced, Silvestri thought. Obviously Twirl, sensing trouble, had ordered all hatches battened down; since very large trouble occurred almost at once, his easily awed followers had obeyed him blindly ever since. But Trixie, once she recovered from the immediate effects, had begun to discover that what protects also muffles. Responding to the human desire to erect a monument to her dead, she yearned to rescue Billy from the state hospital—which raised waves that were quieted only through an *ad hoc* coalition of Twirl and Miss Crabtree (equally discomfiting on both sides, Guy now knew).

But Trixie had remained restless. So when it turned out a

Buxford detective was looking into the King case and Dr. Cannon, who was "straight" and therefore a reliable measuring tool, didn't mind—which meant it was good for Billy—Trixie began pressing again. On Twirl, since Miss Crabtree was less pressurable. Until finally, unable to afford so much dissidence so near the throne, Twirl obliged the lady by setting up an opportunity—one he thought he could control, of course—for discourse with Silvestri . . .

The only problem left now was the lieutenant's, and it had to do with means: should he lean on Twirl in private, which either would or wouldn't work but would be fast, or surround him in the presence of his cohorts, which would take longer but was more likely to succeed? Guy decided to go the second route, though keeping confrontation in reserve. He began by saying that everybody had been most cooperative, and the details Trixie had supplied would be of great value to Cannon in working with Billy. But to *clear* Billy, Silvestri needed something else—the man who'd been Callie King's lover was the only one who could provide proof of Billy's innocence. Twirl could name the man. And even if nobody present cared about the law, you'd think they'd at least want to stop the vested interests who were trying to keep Billy out of circulation whether he needed it or not.

"What's Voorhees been doing," Trixie asked bluntly, "ripping off the estate?"

Guy nodded at Rubin, who would know most. "If he can be got, we'll get him," Rubin told the girl. "But he isn't any candy-store bandit, you know. It'll take time, even if it can be done."

"Time is the one thing Billy hasn't got," Silvestri pointed out. "You needle me about computers, but what I'm trying to avoid is a computer case, where everything gets tagged. We could take our time and come out with a nice neat record. But meanwhile Billy goes down the drain, and so does what can be salvaged of Susan's plans. Billy in a mental hospital wasn't—"

"Twirl." Trixie's lips were white-rimmed. "You've got to."

"You're letting him do it to you again, baby—he waves the flag and you stand at attention. You don't see it because this time the flag is Susan."

"Twirl has a point, Trix," Tommy Mallinson said.

"Think, guys, *think*. That's the fuzz talking. And what he wants is to put me out of business."

Trixie said angrily, "So your selfish—"

"Selfish? What happens if there's another Susan around? Where does she go for help? Not to me, baby, if I'm in the fuzz's pocket. Try to think a little bigger than the way your tummy feels after the man feeds you a little rhetoric."

It must be because he was so tired that he felt so wrenched, Guy decided. Twirl was perfectly right, though obviously not above a bit of flag-waving himself. But what he was urging was an end to the harmful psuedo-innocence of an idealism that stretched to cover only the immediate: for his own self-serving reasons, Twirl was now trying to teach these kids to make a society rather than a court, and they needed the lesson badly. Because it simply wasn't enough to succor only the needy, you know. The Establishment, for all its Voorheeses, at least provided ways to care for people as an abstract right . . .

"Twirl's making sense, I have to admit it," Rubin said. "But that just means you got a problem with right on both sides—that's what most problems have, after you grow up. So I guess you have to weigh one against the other, and choose."

"All right," Twirl announced, "let's adjourn the debating society. I don't call for a vote, I decide. And I don't have to figure out who I am. I know I'm not a stoolie. Not even for the new-style, high-class, likable fuzz."

"I respect your loyalty, Twirl, and I understand it—" *almost as well as I understand your need to stay in power,* Guy amended silently—"but maybe we're all wrong to put you on the spot. Because it's not really your spot, is it? So if you won't tell me who the man is, would you be willing to at least ask him what *he* wants?" He checked his audience for reactions. Twirl, of course, looked skeptical: bucking a problem down the line was a device of bureaucracy, which was a stage of social development the feudal lord Twirl hadn't reached yet. "This man was Billy's mother's lover," he went on. "That might make Billy not too fond of *him*, but it doesn't mean he's against Billy. Maybe he'll want to go straight to Doctor Cannon and ask how he can help." Guy saw Twirl shift to his public-speech stance and rushed on, forestalling objection and reaching for another flag to wave. "All I'm asking is to have my argument put before the man himself. He never appointed Twirl to act for him, after all. Why can't he hear both sides, and decide for himself?"

Tommy said slowly into the silence, "What Silvestri's talking about is really just free choice." His look at Twirl was almost openly imploring. "That's only fair, isn't it?"

But Trixie preferred candidates to issues. "Are you married, Silvestri?"

"Yes."

"What's your wife's name?"

He beat down the sense of intrusion: it was a matter of public record, after all. "Kate."

"What does she do?"

That wasn't on the record. But he owed something to Kate, by way of defending her status among women, didn't he? "Right now she's having babies. Because we haven't been married very long."

"Do you have a nice house?"

"Not very." He saw now what this was probably for.

"Why not?"

"Well, I'm not the greatest provider. And Kate's not the greatest housekeeper. So it's a small house, old-fashioned. And messy."

"Do you and Kate ever fight?"

Now he was certain. "Yes, sometimes."

"How?"

"You mean, what happens?" Rubin was looking at him with astonishment, he saw. Silvestri's team knew Kate, of course, but the lieutenant's privacy was always strictly observed. "Well, we yell, mostly. She slams doors. There's a lot of noise." He grinned. "It's a small house, so sooner or later the baby wakes up. And then we're both sorry."

"Does Kate cry? Ever?"

Guy forgot Rubin now. "Sometimes she does." These kids were entitled, he thought. He looked at Trixie gravely. "But never about anything I can help."

She returned his look in silence for a moment. Then she said, "Hey, guys." But she was speaking to Tommy. "I could get lynched for this, I guess. But maybe I better say it—there *are* some things we're too young for."

"Meaning what, exactly?" Twirl asked angrily.

"Meaning, well, that all the messes we know about are basically kids' messes. But Mrs. King's boyfriend is old enough to have made a real grown-up mess. So I think we really shouldn't be trying to decide for him."

Victory, Silvestri saw—though for the wrong reason: Trixie, still playing follow-the-leader, had simply changed leaders. Sighing for the fate of democracy, he set about doing what he had to do to secure his winnings, which involved, chiefly, contriving to be left alone with Twirl while Rubin took the others out to their car—thus signaling the "watchers" outside that it was okay to let them pass through the net.

Guy waited till the door closed. "I thought it was better to say this to you without them," he told Twirl quietly. "But I want you to listen, and listen hard. So you understand the pitch you'll be making is really your own."

"Ah, the rhetoric changes now."

"Not yet. But it can—because if you don't talk this man into getting in touch with Cannon right away, I'll bring him in myself. I can get to him by walking over you, baby. And I want to be sure you know that, so you can act accordingly." Guy paused. "You dig? I'll have him either way, but if he doesn't volunteer, I'll get you, too. If he's willing to do the right thing, and you can talk him into letting go of you so you don't go down with him, that's your business. But—"

"Okay, okay. I get the idea—if you have what you want for Billy King, you're willing to do without my blood, right? That's real self-restraint, Lieutenant. I don't suppose," Twirl asked lightly, "you'd care to say just how you plan to tromp on me? John Vesey's been after my neck for a long time, but I'm still walking around."

Guy smiled. "Ah, but he didn't have you that close to a stolen gun before."

"Bluff. You disappoint me, Silvestri. You know that won't work."

"Maybe not. Try this one, then: there are lots of teeny-tiny statutes that would've made your life miserable if they hadn't been ignored. One of the reasons they were ignored was that the local businessmen thought you were cute. But will they still think so when it gets around how you steered us to Voorhees?" He waited. Twirl had dismissed him as bound hand and foot by integrity and now had to manage an image of a Silvestri free to lie, so he needed a little time. "I don't suppose I need to mention Miss Crabtree, too, do I? You must know she's no great admirer of yours. You had your value, so she gave you protection in return. But how fast would she shake you, considering how you must make her itch, when she finds out Billy's progress isn't really the center of your attention?"

"All right. But suppose I do my best and he just won't? I can't make him, but I still don't get credit for trying, the way you've set it up. That isn't fair, Silvestri."

"Isn't it? Well, you could complain about my treating you unfairly, but you'd have to become a citizen first, wouldn't you? As long as you go on playing outside the rules, fair doesn't count. Only power does."

"Okay, I dig." He looked toward the door. "Now I better get going, right? Lots of fast talking to do." Twirl glanced at the phone. "What do I do, call you?"

"I'll know if he moves. And he can't help Billy if he doesn't, so I'm not interested in talk."

"Terrific. And to think Trix is probably sure this minute that you're trusting me to do a far, far better thing." He tipped his lavender hat and ambled out to join his waiting minions.

When Rubin came back in, Silvestri, barefoot and trouser-less, was talking to Cannon on the phone. That figured, Rubin thought: Billy was already in trouble, so anything they'd learned that might help couldn't wait. He sat down and took his own shoes off, just in case they were going to sleep.

". . . that Billy was warned. So it makes his going home— You'd think he might have gone during recess, though; he could've made it there and back, but I suppose the basketball game— And anyway, Meyer, wouldn't he be afraid that if there wasn't anything actually wrong, his mother would yell at him for leaving school early?" Guy listened, and then shook his head. "It's pathetic, isn't it? I mean, with all that blabbing to the press, they didn't say the one thing that— Trixie would probably have realized how much they were hanging on Billy's leaving school, and she might have rebelled earlier. But the fact that it was a juvenile case kept it from getting really full treat-ment. Though not from plenty of selective talk. Billy caught every possible disadvantage of that, didn't he . . ."

Cannon's voice crackled interrogatively.

"No, he couldn't have, Meyer, she wasn't around by then —she'd taken off in the laundry truck again." Silvestri caught sight of Rubin stretching out on one of the beds then, and it seemed to inspire the lieutenant to wind up his conversation. "Look, you talk to Trixie tomorrow, Meyer. But not tonight, even if she calls you, okay? We have to have clear access to you for our man." Cannon asked something again. "I don't know— it's getting close to midnight, now, isn't it. Well, Twirl may take his time at first, until he's sure I'm dealing straight. But it can't be long before he gets started talking. When Twirl is through with him, he should call you right away. After that, all you have to do is tell him what we agreed—to go up to your office and you'll meet him there. Then you can just go home if you want, Meyer. We'll take it from there."

Silvestri said something was fine, and he'd see Cannon. Then he hung up the phone, took one step, and dived, flat out like a swimmer's racing start, onto the unoccupied bed.

Rubin grinned. "Hey, Lieutenant, you want to know why we couldn't find Tommy Mallinson? He's got this new step-father, so the name on everything is—" He stopped because he had looked again. The lieutenant was unmistakably asleep, the thin dark face sealed off and oddly young-looking. His arms, in Meyer Cannon's too-large shirt, were embracing the Franklin Motel's pillow, and it was obvious that he would hear nothing except the expected ring of the telephone.

17

THE WOUNDED & THE DEAD

It wasn't his fault, Meyer Cannon told himself with the querulousness of extreme fatigue. When he went to relieve Williams, he found Hughes waiting with a message: Williams had decided to stay through the night, and was now asleep on the cot in Billy's room. So what was Meyer supposed to do, wake Williams up and start arguing about what was already a fact? Meyer had done what any sensible man would do: he'd gone back to his office and stretched out on the couch there, where he could be reached if Billy woke. Certainly no sensible man would bother to call Silvestri—who was probably trying to catch some sleep too, at the motel—about such a small alteration in the plan.

After that, everything just kept slipping out of the lines of the pattern, somehow. And Cannon, roused by Poley's telephone call from what couldn't have been much more than an hour's sleep, wasn't in real good shape to take a tuck here and let out a seam there. Something like that was needed, because everything went much quicker than they'd thought: Roley must have phoned not from the Reservation but from somewhere on the way, since he was already being escorted down the corridor —by a white-clad orderly Meyer didn't recognize—when Cannon, still bleary-eyed, was only starting to get himself together. And sure he remembered that Roley was supposed to be left alone in the office for a few minutes. But how was Meyer supposed to manage that when everything was backwards and Roley had joined *him* there?

Then there was the unhinging fact, right at the start, that Roley wasn't alone—which certainly wasn't according to the plan. An aggrieved *Hey* was forming in the back of Cannon's mind even while he stood in the office door telling them to "Come in, come in . . ." and trying to think how to let Silvestri know about this development.

There were half a dozen people around (some of them in borrowed white uniforms) who knew just how to let Silvestri know. When they did, the word that formed in the back of his mind was *Oops*. And Guy had a sense of grievance, too: he'd been to some trouble with the math quiz because he assumed she would send Poley for it; the history teacher's fingerprints on it would have been evidence, but hers proved nothing. After only two hours' sleep, it took Guy a while to move on from fretful contemplation of his wasted fingerprint-drill to what mattered about this divergence from his scenario—which was that if Marcia Dyer hadn't sent Poley for the quiz, maybe it was because she couldn't.

But if Silvestri had had a moment to contemplate Miss Dyer's presence on the scene, his arrival was a surprise to her. "Doctor Cannon," she complained, "Roley didn't know the lieutenant was—"

"He's the price, Marcia." Poley's pale face could just about support a strained smile. "Did you think I'd get off scot-free?"

One glance at Meyer Cannon told Silvestri he was virtually on his own now, for Meyer made no alliances that couldn't be set aside for the needs of the sick. James Poley was here because he'd had his arm twisted by Twirl, who'd been squeezed by Lieutenant Silvestri, but that would mean nothing to Dr. Cannon unless he found it useful in treating the sufferer.

What counted was that Poley was frightened and tormented, no matter how he'd got that way.

Marcia Dyer was visibly neither frightened nor tormented. In fact, she was remarkably composed: in the middle of the night, she was wearing a silk suit and smart tan leather pumps, a costume much more businesslike than the dress she'd worn to Devora Cannon's dinner party. Of course, she'd presumably been to bed and then got up and dressed again, probably summoned by Poley. But if a friend in distress wakes you, surely you don't turn out as if ready for attendance at a national convention of mathematics teachers?

Sure you did, Guy decided, if you needed to carry that tan purse. It was virtually briefcase-size—which was necessary because Cannon would remember that none of the contents of the math package had been folded. But the lady couldn't carry such a handbag unless it "passed" because of the matching pumps and the elegantly tailored suit. That was how come the outsized handbag was now carelessly disposed on a corner of Meyer Cannon's desk, with what was under it effectively hidden from sight. A handy arrangement either way, Guy concluded: if she got the chance, the correct math quiz could be slid quickly from her purse to be exchanged for the one she thought was in the envelope on Cannon's desk. But if that couldn't quite be managed, the whole envelope, which was tan, too, could be lifted with the purse and carried off when Miss Dyer left. Cannon might wonder what had become of the math package, but it would take him a while to be certain he hadn't just put it somewhere else. Like on his desk at home, where he would find it later today?

One way or another, she had to make the altered math test disappear, because there was no way to explain it as a careless error: it probably didn't belong to another class, she'd custom-tailored it—before labeling it, in her own hand, a copy of the quiz Billy took that November morning. So she was utterly vulnerable unless it was removed. As Guy had seen, but maybe he'd seen the rest of the picture wrong. He'd been thinking of her as a kind of extreme case of the little woman behind the ambitious politician or the candidate for a Nobel Prize. Thus it would be because of her obsessive desire to protect James Poley—maybe even without his knowledge—that she had tried to delay the return of Billy's memory.

But such a woman should have collapsed in tears when it all went wrong, shouldn't she? Looking at the shape of the relationship on view now, though, Guy couldn't imagine any collapsing-in-tears in the recent background: Poley was not only not here to rescue the little woman from the consequences of her all-for-love act, he didn't even seem to know about it. What was on Poley's mind, quite obviously, was Billy King. Poley had been agitated during the dinner party when Billy's illness was mentioned, and it may well have been that anxiety, at least as much as the fact of the law baying close, that Twirl had manipulated. For Poley had rushed to Dr. Cannon like a pilot flying the serum to somebody stricken with a rare disease. And certainly he seemed to be convinced that every minute must count. Because he said quickly, almost airily, that he had tried to kill Julius King and that was why—

Marcia Dyer interrupted swiftly. "He didn't really want to, did he, Meyer? That's why he blew it. Lieutenant, Doctor Cannon can tell you—"

Poley brushed aside his defense attorney. "Oh, come on, it isn't so hard to believe. I mean, in films they make it look easy to tamper with a car. But if you're not a mechanic and you crawl under and see all that spaghetti, it's a lot harder than you think to figure out which one's for the brake fluid. Especially at three ayem and with a flashlight practically held in your teeth—" He shook his head. "I knew I hadn't done it right."

"He didn't even do enough to matter," Marcia told the jury. "Doctor King did get his car stopped, after all. So it wasn't out of control. It's possible something else could've just gone wrong, and—"

Silvestri blocked that attempt: the brake fluid line had indeed been cut, enough anyway so a substantial amount of the fluid had leaked out. By morning, the detective said flatly, "there was a visible spot of it in the driveway." He reached into the airline bag at his feet, brought out a glass-stoppered reagent bottle, and set it on the desk. Meyer Cannon threw him a doubtful look, which didn't help with Guy's problem—which was that this maneuver had been designed for James Poley, but Miss Dyer seemed more likely to be able to recall that half a year's snows and rains had washed the King driveway before Silvestri appeared on the scene.

Nevertheless, it was still worth a try: "The stain showed up in photographs of the front yard," Silvestri explained. "So we took a sample of the gravel for analysis." It worked in part, he decided—for when Poley groaned and put his head in his hands, Miss Dyer did not remark that putting gravel into a laboratory bottle hardly proved the lab had actually found anything. She just stared, without expression, at the chips of gravel behind the glass.

"I called Callie in the morning," Poley said. "I knew I had to tell her I'd messed up."

Miss Dyer's silence was bothering Silvestri: he still couldn't be sure whether she was only surrendering a trick because she believed she had to lose it anyway—or was it that the rescue of Poley hadn't been what her game was about after all? If a detective could get led astray by unconscious sexism in the first place, he could make it worse by suddenly overcorrecting . . . Guy roused from his worries to ask Poley, "Then Mrs. King wasn't with you while you worked on the Volvo?"

"No, of course not. She was making sure her husband wouldn't come out and find me in the front yard. The way she managed that was—something I didn't go into." Poley's mouth twisted. "Actually, the whole operation didn't get discussed much at that point. Callie called me the night before to say this was it—Susan definitely wouldn't be riding with King in the morning. But she was in a hurry. So she just gave me the Lady Macbeth bit, in a whisper, and hung up before I could say my lines."

Guy looked at him with pity. Callie King had been working from the script of quite another Shakespearean play at eight o'clock the next morning, and obligation to her fellow-conspirator didn't seem to be any part of that role. Because if she'd succeeded in keeping Caesar from setting off for the Senate, where would that have left Roley?

"I couldn't call her before eight fifteen because I was on 'kindergarten detail.' " Poley stopped to explain the teachers' slang for the despised chore of supervising the kids from their arrival at school until classes began at 8:40. Nobody was likely to take your turn at that for you; but if you left early, some kind soul might cover for you. So when he got Callie on the phone and she said her husband had just gone and Roley had better come right away— "and she *meant* right away: I could hear that, loud and clear"—he ducked out and counted on luck. "I had Marcia's Beetle, because I'd promised to take it in for a checkup for her—the garage is nearer the Mercer School, and I had the first period free." He flushed, recognizing the blatant ungallantry of having used the car instead to call on his mistress. "I really couldn't help it. I mean, I couldn't call a cab to take me out to the King place, not in a town this size." He'd even had to be careful with the VW: just in case of passersby, he'd parked down near the brook and come up to the house from the back. "I knew Billy rode his bike to school that way, but I figured he must've already left."

"Oh? Then it was pretty late when you got to the house."

"Well, I couldn't shave much off the kindergarten detail. About all I saved was the travel time, I guess—it must've been close to eight forty. When I came in, Callie was just hanging up the phone . . ."

8:36, P. arrives, Guy was noting. For surely Mrs. King hadn't needed more than a minute to tell Mrs. Price at 8:35 that Susan wouldn't be in school.

He'd gone in the front door, Poley said, without ringing the bell because the door was closed but not latched—either somebody had closed it carelessly or Callie had left it that way for him. "Callie was standing by that little phone table. It's in a kind of hallway between the kitchen and—oh, you know?"

"Yes. How was Mrs. King dressed?"

"A sweater—pink, I think—and a skirt. But she was wearing those green mules: she liked them, and they did make her legs look great. She still hadn't put her hair up, though. It was hanging down with a big ribbon in it, like a kid." Abruptly, Poley looked embarrassed. "She was absolutely ridiculous, if you want to know the truth. Not only ghastly, but absurd— she'd never looked like that before, not either of the ways I was used to seeing her. Like, when she was dressed up and being Mrs. King, she looked like some actress—I can't remember her name, but I've seen her on the late-late show, some film from a thousand years ago."

"Ann Harding," Miss Dyer said quietly.

"That's right, that's who. But then there was a way Callie could look that made you just . . ." His voice trailed off in search of words.

He would get no help from Miss Dyer this time. Guy watched her, with a sympathy he couldn't help feeling, as the blind Roley went on describing what was obviously how Callie King had looked to her lover, with "that incredible mass of really silky hair spread out"—presumably on a pillow. "She could look beautiful in a way you just can't imagine. Like a boys'-book lady, the kind you read before you start substituting those Wonder Woman heroines in boots and torn tunics. What is it, Doctor Cannon, some sort of transition between women as your mother and as sex objects?" He saw Cannon's look and hung his head. "All right, I know I'm stalling. But it's *hard*. I don't really want to remember how— Okay." Poley took his gaze from the doctor like a toddler bravely letting go of a parental hand at the nursery-school door. "Well, the truth is, maybe it isn't fair to say it—because I knew all along how old she was—but with that silly bow in her hair, she was so *old*. Before that morning, she didn't look old to me; she looked timeless, if you know what I mean. But that was the first time she seemed to be trying to look young, so maybe that made the difference."

The scales had fallen from James Poley's eyes for sure, he was saying, that morning. "Of course she looked about as soft and tempting as a Mafia messenger, too—when I finally realized what it was she was laying on me. Not that Callie wasted time on endearments, not then: she let me have it right in the chops. Told me she'd panicked before King left and—oh, you know about her trying to stop him? Well, I didn't know. It was news to me that she'd tried to sell me out."

"Was that what she was doing?" Cannon asked. "She did let King get in the car and drive away, after all. What did she think would happen, do you suppose?"

"Well, either it would work, or she could be damn sure he'd figure the Volvo was gimmicked. Why not, after she'd carried on like that? If King survived—which was likely, considering the lousy job I did—he'd come home with blood in his eye. Anyway, she obviously expected him to walk in any minute. Because she was pushing hard, like she had to get me sold in a hurry." Poley sighed. "I was in a hurry, too—to get out of there. I mean, I hope you understand I wasn't trying to preserve any Us by that time: I didn't want Callie, I just wanted out. But of course, she was ahead of me there. Where was I going to run, she asked—she was grinning like a Halloween mask. And did I really think Julius King wouldn't squash me like a bug?" Poley managed a smile at the doctor. "If Callie maybe hit me like a sickness originally, the cure was sure quick. It only took a minute, once it dawned on me that she had plans for me."

But she had contingency plans, too, Guy thought: was the bow in her hair that made her look absolutely ridiculous to

Poley intended for King, who *had* known her when she was young? And who would come in raging and might need to be beguiled, just in case something went wrong with her plan (her long-term plan?) to force her lover to kill her husband.

Dr. Cannon was interested in when Callie's plans had dawned on Poley.

"Well, I know I sound slow. But keep in mind I'd had like two hours' sleep, and besides the atmosphere was so thick with hysteria I could hardly breathe, much less think. Visual aid is always a help, though, and she had a doozey: the idea that I'd have to kill King for her, to save myself, came to me in a flash when she showed me the gun. I felt like the top of my head was going to come off."

Guy decided it wouldn't do to let Meyer start exploring Poley's symptoms. "The gun you're talking about," he said quickly, "was the unregistered .38 revolver later found in the house?"

"Okay, I bought the gun, is that what you want, Lieutenant?" Marcia Dyer's warning hiss went unheard—by Poley, anyway. "If that's what you want, there it is. Take it, it's yours. Take me, too, I don't give a shit. I bought the gun"—suddenly his voice shifted to a rapid patter—"from a man I never saw before. I met him in a bar, but I don't remember which one. We got to talking and he happened to mention that he had a .38 he wanted to sell. And that's all I remember."

"Did Callie tell you what she wanted it for?" Silvestri asked smoothly.

"Oh God, I suppose so." Having delivered his rote speech, a relaxed Roley had promptly fallen into Guy's trap. But he didn't notice it even now. "I must have made some effort at sanity, so I suppose I did ask her. But I don't remember. I *really* don't," he added, helpfully distinguishing this one from his earlier, Twirl-coached memory failures. "I can't understand it myself, so I know how it must sound to you. But Callie was— Look, it was back when things were different between us. She was pathetic, and beautiful, and she said she was afraid. If a gun would make her feel safe, well, what the hell? Only I couldn't just go out and get a gun permit, because you can imagine the talk: what did I need to defend myself from at the Reservation? Or think of the gags about how Mr. Poley *really* controlled his class . . . So I had to get a piece from—someone less fussy. But it was an absurdly easy thing to do for Callie, so I did it." His voice rose. "For God's sake, didn't you ever do a dumb thing because of a woman? I would've shot Julius King for her, I guess, if she'd asked me to back then. I don't know why she didn't. Maybe her timing was just lousy."

"Or she didn't know how deep her talons were in him," Marcia Dyer said. "Maybe monsters can suffer from low self-esteem, too."

A more practical explanation was that that would have lost Callie King her children. She needed a better way to make her husband vanish, Guy was thinking. Like an auto accident. Or a fight about a faked auto accident that hadn't come off? After which Mrs. King, having seen to it that neither of the two men survived, could wring her hands on the witness stand while she told how she'd tried to stop them?

"Listen, Lieutenant, I don't suppose it makes any difference." Poley wriggled a little closer to Cannon on the couch, as if it were cold out and the doctor gave off warmth. "But that morning, I honest-to-God didn't even think of shooting King. Once I got the message, all I thought about was splitting. If her husband wanted to run me out of town, that was just dandy, and I'd beat him to it if possible. I mean, it was one thing to do the deed for the beautiful princess, but when she turned into a dragon— I swear to you, the minute she picked up the gun and began waving it around—"

"Picked it up from where?"

"The bookcase, in the living room. It was lying on top of the top shelf of books. And when she picked it up, I saw the safety was off." The specific memory started shudders. "A loaded gun in the hands of a madwoman. God."

"You were no good to her dead, you know."

"Sure I know that, now. But what am I, some kind of supercool thriller hero? All I could think was, *My God, she can kill me.* Or worse—it's a heavy weapon, and it kind of drooped in her hand. If she'd squeezed a shot off then, I might not be dead but it would be hard to be glad." He closed his eyes against the image, and suddenly Guy saw how handsome Roley really was. Poor Callie, he thought, whether monster or tragic queen. He glanced at Marcia Dyer, who might also be monstrous but had never been anybody's queen. She was sitting on the corner of Cannon's desk now, and the leg revealed by her pose was certainly shapely; but the effect was as sexless as a store-window manikin. Which might not matter—Guy noted, struggling conscientiously against male chauvinism—except that he didn't think sexless was how Marcia wanted to be seen.

Poley's voice was tired, but he had apparently recovered some of his characteristic light audacity. "Everybody's an athlete if there's enough danger, isn't that so, Doctor? I dived for her knees—just the kind of flying tackle I practiced when I was a kid dreaming of making the team. I didn't make the team, but this time I was awfully damn motivated—Callie went down just like she was supposed to. I rolled away and got up, but she still had the gun. She was on the floor, and her face looked— horrible. And all of a sudden the gun was coming up. I was looking right into the muzzle and—Well, I yanked her arm. That was all I could do, just twist her arm.

"The thing went off, and I can't begin to— maybe the lieutenant can tell you how much noise a .38 makes in a normal-size room. That crazy sound just filled my head until the top really did come off, it felt like. I honest-to-God don't remember after that. I know it happened again, while I was still trying to get her to drop that damn gun. And then I got it loose, or else she let it go, and I was standing there looking at Callie with blood all over the front of her and the gun lying there just out of her reach. And more silence than I ever heard in my life."

The silence in Cannon's office was different, full of small stirs. And a sad sigh from Cannon that made Guy want to say *I'm sorry, Meyer, I have to.* Marcia Dyer sat perfectly still, with nothing at all apparently going on behind her blank, blank face.

"That's when I heard the key in the front door," Poley said. "In a spot like that, you don't think, you run. Where I ran to was the pantry—it was right behind me, a dark room without any windows, and in front of me was Callie dead in the brilliant sunlight, so bright it hurt your eyes ... In the dark, there was something big and soft near the door—I found out later it was the laundry bag. I curled up behind it. And that's where I was, in that dark womb and making myself real small, before Julius King had even finished unlocking his front door.

"I tried not to hear anything. I'm sure you can believe that—I didn't want to know what was happening. But I was surprised, you see—I mean, I thought I'd killed Callie, and there she was, talking. At first. She didn't really talk for long, she started groaning, and then it was like she was strangling. And all between King's yelling—he was making so much noise I know it's incredible I can't remember what he said, because I certainly heard him. But all I can remember is him calling her a lot of names, most of them pretty raw. I guess I should've rushed out to her rescue, but—" He stopped as though there'd been an interruption. But nobody obliged him, not even Cannon.

But finally the doctor said, "Why should you? You agreed with King, didn't you?"

"You know, you're right?" In the pain-filled handsome face, the sudden smile was oddly happy. "I actually realized it myself later. She'd been saying something, and then all of a sudden King let out this huge roar. *'Forgive* you? The hell I'll forgive you.'" And right that minute, I knew—or I think now I knew, Doctor—that I felt the same way he did."

So did Miss Dyer, Guy observed in the tenth of a second before she regained control. Her hands were clasped now, but the whitened knuckles showed how much effort it was taking.

"Except—I can't hate Callie, not really," Poley added suddenly.

Cannon said "No," and Guy, who was still watching Marcia Dyer, knew what he meant. Poley's rage—and probably King's, too—had been hot with the knowledge of betrayal but still inside-rage: Callie King had been a woman you could love with all your heart, even if only briefly, and so maybe neither her husband nor her lover could really hate her. Which could be why Marcia Dyer hated her so, with all the cold fury of the permanent outsider . . .

"It's crazy, but—I really think it was only after that I realized Callie might die after all." The voice had lost its lightness now. But the tone of honest puzzlement—in its way, curiously innocent—was unmistakable as Poley went on to tell how he had wriggled forward, cautious as a soldier under fire, until he could see out of the pantry door without being seen. "King had the gun. Callie was lying there moving her legs sort of slow and heavy, like trying to walk through water, and she was trying to say something. But he'd stopped listening. He yelled, 'Come on, you bastard, can't you see your baby doll wants you?'" Poley wet his lips. "Well, if I had any kind of fellow-feeling for him up to then, Doctor, I lost it fast when I heard what he said after that: 'And I'm going to see that you join her.' Wow. I pulled my head in like a turtle. I wasn't going anywhere, not after that—I was too scared to move. Except for practically *crawling* into that laundry bag."

That was probably when that loud button, with its flaunting slogan, had fallen off. Handsome, swinging Mr. Poley, hip enough to be trusted (at least somewhat) by Twirl, yet detached enough to keep his sex life out of the reach of the high-school girls—the popular young history teacher who simultaneously joined the students' follies and mocked them—was easily the most plausible wearer of that button. Maybe one of the girls, just off the school bus that morning, had given it to him by way of a daring semi-advance?

Guy returned his attention to the handsome, beaten face and the voice that had gone on no side excursions. He had seen the whole thing, Poley said: "That silence, with Callie making a sort of little sigh. And then the sound of the front door. King froze—I couldn't see his face because he was just a silhouette in all that sunlight, but I saw him turn toward where you come in from the hall, you know? He got down on one knee and aimed the gun. Callie—" he stopped, swallowed, and then managed to go on— "she was thrashing around, kind of trying to crawl toward the front hall. She didn't really cover any ground, but she made King mad—he said something about her 'protecting' somebody. Then he steadied the gun, taking aim like a picture in a manual. I could see his finger around the trigger while he was saying, 'Come on, lover-boy.' In a *whisper*, believe it or not."

No disbelief was possible: even hearing about that whisper seemed to fill the air of the room with threat.

"Maybe it was the whisper—mind-blowing, after all that noise—but I had the weirdest reaction. Like—well, look: it was me he wanted, I was 'lover-boy,' right? But I wasn't over there where he was looking . . . So—I swear to you it's really true—all of a sudden it was all I could do to keep myself from jumping up and saying *No, I'm over here,* like some kind of insane teacher correcting a mistake. I know it's incredible. But if I hadn't had that laundry bag to hold onto, I just couldn't have stopped myself." He blew out his breath, resting as if after a climb. He waited, summoning memory or courage or both. "Well, you know—who it was came into the room. Or, she started to: King fired the exact minute she showed in that arch from the front hall. If you're about to ask me did he see her, Lieutenant, yes, I think he did—because I did. I had time to register that it was Susan. But of course *I* knew whoever was coming in couldn't be me, so maybe— I think it was the sound of the front door that really convinced him, though. I don't know why she—"

"She thought the noise came from outside," Silvestri said. It should have been 8:53 when Susan came downstairs: "Fear Me Not, Baby" was played at 8:48, which meant she still had her ear plug in at that point—plus however many seconds it took for her to recognize the song and decide to phone in. From the rough experiments Vesey had made this afternoon, the shots downstairs should have come through to Susan something like firecracker pops, far off—not enough to make her investigate. But once she unplugged herself from the radio, she would hear yells and cries and then maybe begin to wonder about those firecrackers. "The sounds she heard weren't the kind she associated with things happening inside the house," Guy explained dryly. Mr. and Mrs. King's quarrels had been quieter, even if vicious—as Trixie, asking impertinent questions of Lieutenant Silvestri, had known. "We think Susan went downstairs—barefoot, so nobody heard her—and opened the door to look outside." Maybe she thought it was Emilie Dozier up to some mischief. "As she was closing the door, she probably heard something from the living room," Guy went on, thinking about the whisper. He hadn't known about that before. It explained why, when Susan went to see, she didn't call out first: *Mom? What's going on?* Any careless, natural question preceding her into the room might have saved her life. But if what she heard was whispering, she was probably curious—or alarmed?—and thus came in quietly . . .

Poley's face was flushed with shame. "The point—the real point, isn't it?—is that we all forgot about Susan, didn't we? Even though all us dandy parents and parent-figures knew she was home that day."

Silvestri looked at Cannon, who shook his head *No.* So Guy didn't say that Callie King had apparently not forgotten Susan: according to Poley himself, she'd been trying to crawl toward the front door—though she could no longer produce even the moans that maybe also had been meant to remind her husband about Susan, asleep upstairs. The evidence indicated that Mrs. King had put her children above her own desire for freedom from King's tyranny all along, and there was no evidence that it was only herself she was trying to save when she thrashed around on the floor, dying. Okay, so Meyer put the living first, and he apparently didn't think it was good for Roley to have his feeling for Callie stirred up again now. But the fact was, Guy could read Callie King's last thirty minutes of life either way, and he knew which way he chose. *Me and Dozier,* he thought, and was suddenly glad Dozier hadn't had to hear this story.

"I guess King couldn't help it," King's wife's lover said. "Even if he did see Susan when I did, well, I didn't have my finger around a trigger."

Or a revolver already aimed—at what he thought would be a six-foot man. Susan King was only five feet tall, Silvestri had noted when he read her driver-permit application. If you allowed for amateurs always shooting high, and for the fact that Julius King was shooting upward anyway, Susan's being hit in the neck probably meant that he'd been aiming for the man's belly or groin. By all accounts, King was a harsh and vengeful man. And accustomed to acting on his own conclusions, and certainly tense and furious at that moment. So the machinery operating his trigger finger would work faster than any reporting from his senses to *Hold it, something's wrong . . .*

". . . it didn't feel real from that point on, that's all," Roley was saying. He remembered hearing Susan fall, and that then he'd put his head down and concentrated on not being sick. All he knew was that his cheek had been resting on the laundry bag when he heard the other shot. "I just don't know how much time went by in between."

Not much, the way Silvestri figured it. Maybe a minute.

"I don't know how long it took me to come out of there, either. When I finally looked out, King wasn't in sight and Callie wasn't moving. The silence just went on and on—"

Another minute, at most.

"I guess I came out crawling, because I was at floor level when I saw Callie's face. She was dead then, all right—if I'd known how dead dead people look, I wouldn't have thought I'd killed her before."

He'd glanced over at King, lying near the door that led to his study, and then looked away quickly: "Callie seemed peaceful compared to the mess King had made of his head."

"Where was the gun?" Silvestri asked. Cannon looked unhappy but made no attempt to stop him, apparently realizing that this police-type question had to be answered for Billy's sake. "Did you see it?"

"Yes, sure. It was on the hearth, just about in the middle."

"Are you sure?" That would be quite a bit father from King's hand than should be possible. But, though Poley's fingerprints must be part of the indecipherable smudge of them left on the .38 by the earlier scuffle over it, he couldn't have handled it that late in the game without leaving prints at least as clear as Billy's. "Are you sure you didn't move it?" Guy asked.

Even that blatant witness-coaching didn't change Poley's story. "No, I *know* I never touched it, Lieutenant. If you've got my fingerprints on it or something—well, I just can't explain that. Because I swear I never went anywhere near King. Why would I? I was *afraid* of him. The only reason I looked for him at all was to be sure it was safe. It was Susan I— Look, Lieutenant, maybe I'd still be hiding in that damn pantry if I hadn't thought Susan just might be still alive. Because I'd thought Callie was dead when she wasn't, before. So maybe—

"But when I got to Susan, I knew she couldn't be. Nobody that white could be alive. I mean, you don't know what 'white' means if you haven't seen it."

Guy told himself grimly that he was sure learning what compulsion meant. Everyone in the room was silently begging *Stop, stop,* though it was plain that nothing would stop Roley now. And then Roley said, "The blood was coming out of her neck, but it was on the other side, away from me . . ." and Guy saw Meyer Cannon's face and knew the worst horror yet. There was no way to avoid it: corroboration that Susan King had not, in fact, been dead was written all over Cannon; anyone but the obsessed Roley could read it. Meyer knew it from Roley's own words, Guy knew it from the medical examiner's estimate of how long it would have taken Susan to die. The only one who didn't know was Roley, who kept on telling exactly how Susan had looked—and then saying he couldn't stand it . . . Meyer was shaking his head, but sadly this time instead of *No*, and Guy realized it was a message for him—Meyer trying to make him feel better. Because apparently it wouldn't have made any difference if Roley had been wiser that November morning: Susan was as good as gone by the time he got to her.

Poley went on—with Meyer listening, because he had to: he had to know exactly what Billy had seen when he came home. "There was so much blood," Poley said again. His head was between his hands and his gaze was directed at the floor; he seemed indifferent to the questioners now, neither fearing Silvestri nor asking compassion from Cannon. Not anymore. "The problem was literally how to get out without stepping in it. To get past her to the door. I just wanted to get away by then. It felt like I'd been there forever."

Five minutes, Silvestri figured: he'd decided 8:58 was probably when Callie King's lover left.

"I can't stand it," Callie King's lover said shrilly, "but that's what I was really doing—problem-solving. Trying to get out. I can't— Look, put me in jail, or the electric chair. Do whatever you want, but I'm not going to remember any more."

"All right, Roley," Cannon said gently. "It's all right."

Guy watched envy cross Marcia Dyer's face, while her hands twitched in her lap. But she stayed where she was, letting Meyer do the comforting she so clearly yearned to do.

Work was Silvestri's comfort: he forced himself to think

about that gun, which shouldn't have been on the hearth at all. But there was no doubt that Poley had told the truth when he said it was, and that was probably where Billy saw it when he came home. Guy summoned up to his mind every remembered detail of that corner of the room, with the bookcase and the fireplace forming a right angle. As a matter of fact, he'd stood there himself, first by the bookcase and then by the fireplace. He remembered standing on the hearth, looking up at the mantelpiece ornaments. Then he'd bent to examine the rather handsome brass holder with tongs and poker and the other fire-tending tools hanging from it. But there'd been nothing to see—otherwise, he wouldn't have just walked away . . .

He hadn't just walked away, Guy remembered abruptly. He'd slipped. And then looked down, recording the fact that the waxed bricks of the hearth were slippery.

Well, it would have to be tested. But it was possible: the chalked outline of King's arm was near enough to the corner of that brass stand so if the gun falling from his hand had hit the stand and bounced onto the hearth—and then slid along the waxed bricks toward the center . . . Why didn't Poley hear the clang, though? He wouldn't, Guy realized then. The sound of the shot that had killed King would still be echoing. And Poley would be cowering in the pantry, hiding from a killer.

". . . thanks, Doctor, I understand. I suppose if you gave me something now, I could claim I was drugged, right? Okay. But when I finish—?"

"I know you need rest," Cannon said.

"Okay, that's fair enough." Poley took a deep breath. "Well, I ran. Out the front door, then around the house to the back. If it's any help to you, Lieutenant, I thought I heard the phone ringing. Just as I got to the edge of the woods."

Silvestri shrugged. Trixie, probably—if it was a little later than Guy had calculated when Poley left the house, and a little earlier when Trixie left her English class.

Running, Poley had stepped in a puddle and then into the

brook at some point, it seemed. "Actually, I didn't remember I'd been in the brook till Marcia made up that story for Roberts, when she borrowed his galoshes for me. Right then, when she was telling me to remember to say that's what happened, I realized it really had."

Josh Roberts, the Mercer School custodian—and practically the only person on the original list who hadn't been questioned, Guy thought wryly. Robert's statement of the time Billy King got to school that morning was solid, and nobody had asked him about anything else. "What time was that?" Guy turned to Marcia Dyer. "After your first class, I gather."

"My first class was at the high school, and it ended at nine ten." She might have been testifying in a courtroom. "The second period at the Mercer starts at nine thirty. I got a ride over there with Mrs. Price, the school secretary—she ought to be able to tell you what time we left."

He didn't remember looking for Marcia, Poley said; she was just there. She replaced his wet shoes with Josh's galoshes, and Josh gave him a slug of whiskey "out of a plastic bottle from cleaning fluid." He stopped suddenly. "My God, I hope I'm not getting him in trouble. Is this being recorded?" He looked around the room vaguely, as if to spot microphones.

"It's not being recorded." Guy wondered whether he was imagining an almost imperceptible relaxation of tension in Miss Dyer then. But that could happen even if she was only worrying about her contract. As for Roberts, the only way he'd get in trouble was if one day, after maybe too many bracing slugs, he reached for the wrong cleaning-fluid bottle.

"Marcia kept talking about how I'd wandered into the brook where it crosses behind the Mercer's playground. She said if I was going to take a walk on a freezing day, at least I should watch where I was going. I remember her voice was so loud and bright, it was like polished brass in my head. And Josh was grinning and saying I'd maybe overdone the hair-of-the-dog treatment that morning. I guess Marcia told him I'd been drinking—" He looked at her. "Maybe I shouldn't say that?"

She came as close to a real smile as Guy had seen yet. "Never mind. It's all right, Roley."

"Well, everything was so mixed up. Like, I'd been in the brook but not that *part* of it, you see." He drew a hand across his forehead. "And when Marcia asked me about the car, I couldn't remember driving it back. But I did."

Guy had a hunch that what she'd asked Roley about the car was where he'd parked it at the Kings'. What Guy thought Miss Dyer had been worrying about had in fact happened: Emilie Dozier, larking naughtily in the woods with her Pongo that morning, had seen a red car—though of course it was impossible to know at what time.

But it couldn't have been nine o'clock and it could have been a little after eleven, according to Emilie's mother. And Emilie herself said she saw *a green truck and a red car.* Not exactly formal testimony, but Guy was willing to bet she'd seen the laundry truck and the VW, in that order. And he'd perhaps actually begun to bet on it, as soon as he realized how miscast Marcia Dyer was as a self-sacrificing little woman—and that a time schedule too intricate for anyone to plan had maybe just happened anyway ... But he was still puzzled. For, even if his new guess was right, what had Miss Dyer done that morning that would warrant the risks she'd taken since?

"When Marcia left me outside my classroom," Roley was saying apologetically, "I just couldn't go in. Not right away." But eventually he did, and the class was tickled with the story of his wandering into the brook. That necessity to explain his odd footgear led into a lecture on history-via-fashion. "I started talking about how Franklin Roosevelt was President when Josh's galoshes were born, and then I sketched a pair of Cavalier boots on the board, and—well, off we went. It turned out great, the kids were really digging it, so I gave them an extra five minutes after the bell. And I don't know how to say this without sounding like a monster, but I'd forgotten, by the end of that class. I mean, I know it's hard to believe. But it's true—I knew it when I saw Billy King coming in with the other kids, for the next class. It all came over me then, especially the fact that I'd forgotten—I ran out of the room and I just made it to the john before I threw up. Sort of. I mean, nothing came up but Josh's whiskey.

"I got some aspirins and an Alka-Seltzer from the teachers' room before I went back to the classroom. The kids were milling around—arguing about some kind of basketball contest they'd had during recess—so it took a while to get them settled. Then, luckily, they had reports to read. So I just sat there with my hand over my eyes, listening, till the period was over. I really did think Billy was there the whole time. But I certainly didn't look at him—you can just bet on that."

The ordeal ended for Roley after that class—when Marcia Dyer, whose own third-period class at the high school ran only to eleven o'clock, came back to the Mercer to pick him up. She was free for the fourth period (Roley wasn't, but all he had was study hall, which Mrs. Armour took for him), and that was followed by lunch hour, so she was able to take Roley home and get him to bed with a couple of sleeping pills. Then when Marcia had to go back to school at 1:10, she passed him on to Devora Cannon. "I told her he was sick," Marcia said hastily. "He really was." She seemed actively concerned lest Cannon be angry.

Under the ministrations of Devora, Roley went back to sleep and didn't wake up, in any useful sense, until the next day. "That's when I found out Billy was in the hospital because he'd tried to kill himself. I could damn well understand why he would. And of course I felt awful about it, but what good could I do him by opening my mouth?"

"Well, you might have protected him from a murder charge," Silvestri said dryly.

"What murder charge? Did anybody charge him with any-thing? He just went from one hospital to the other, and then Meyer took him over. So there was no question Billy was getting good care, and he obviously needed it. I stuck around, didn't I?" Poley asked plaintively. "In case Billy ever needed it, I'd be ready to tell the truth. But as far as I knew, it wasn't—"

"Secrecy," Cannon said to Guy. "What I wanted was just across the hall at home, all the time. But I couldn't very well ask, could I?"

"I'm not so sure you'd have got answers anyway, Meyer."

"That's not true!" Poley's exhaustion gave way to outright rage. His only claim to self-respect was being snatched from him. He fought with everything he had left—including a reserve of adrenaline, it seemed, because it took both Cannon and Silvestri to get him to stop flailing. Even the cool Miss Dyer had been minded to join the fray at some point, apparently: when the brouhaha was almost over, Guy saw her standing quite near, holding her big purse as if to swing it.

Cannon saw her too. "Sit down, Marcia. He's not hurt." He waited until she'd retreated sullenly to the desk chair and settled herself with her purse on her lap. Then he spread author-ity around evenly: "This is a mental hospital, Roley, and we do have restraints. Any more of that sort of thing, and I'll have to call an orderly." Roley sank back, subdued by the mere hint of straitjackets, and then it was Silvestri's turn. "Guy, I know the frustrations you've been meeting but provocative remarks don't help, do they? It's necessary to remember—"

"I do remember, Meyer. I remember who's the real injured innocent. Not Poley, the professional innocent, but Susan King." Guy's harsh voice stopped abruptly, leaving them all to remember Susan, in whatever detail they could manage. His own picture was complete and painful: fair and tiny and brave and absurd, she padded across her room in her bare feet, on her way to identify "Fear Me Not, Baby" before anybody else did. And thus win money, which she was always worrying about.

Babysitting and Miss Crabtree's sponsorship of a line of Dowager Delight frocks came in handy, but Susan needed enough money to supply a growing boy with proteins and jeans. And the lucrative boutique business she could get through Twirl's associates cost her payoff money, regularly and in cash. "The word one of her friends used was 'gutsy,' " Guy said. "She was that, certainly. But she didn't have a chance against the weak and the scared, did she?"

"Stop it, Guy. Nobody intended Susan any harm."

They'd done her so much harm, though, even before Julius King made the mistake that killed her. She should have been just a soft, gentle little girl with big brown eyes—the one who'd confided to Miss Crabtree her yearning for Lenny Pritchard. Instead, she'd had to be shrewd and ingenious and deceitful, with no room for anything but the attempt to give her little brother the chance at innocence she herself had lost. "And Billy?" Silvestri asked aloud. "Did nobody intend Billy any harm?"

An outraged exclamation came from Poley. But Cannon only looked at Marcia Dyer, his bright dark eyes speculating.

"Well, Miss Dyer?" Guy crossed to the desk and brushed the layer of striped envelopes off the paper-covered math book. It was lying just as he'd left it, apparently—except that there was nothing sticking out of it now. "What about the math quiz Doctor Cannon wanted, to nudge Billy's memory with?" Still watching the woman in the desk chair, Silvestri said, "I'm afraid it wouldn't have done much for Billy's morale, Roley. Because some of the questions had been changed, to make it too hard for him. Not *much* too hard, just enough to make him feel like he'd probably known that once and now couldn't remember. So he'd lose what little self-confidence had been restored to him. I'd say that was about as harmful to Billy as you could get. Right, Doctor?"

Roley began, "Marcia, why would you want—"

"I don't know what he's talking about," Marcia Dyer said.

"You told us yourself, Meyer, he's frustrated. And frustrated fuzz means just one thing—they pick a victim and start hunting him down."

"If you're a victim, Miss Dyer, I promise I won't hunt you down. In fact, I'll even apologize if I'm wrong. We can tell about that in a minute, if you'll let us have a look at the contents of your handbag." Without turning his head, Guy explained, "When Poley started cutting up, she grabbed the envelope and stuck it in her purse. So she could replace the phony math quiz with the real one, when she got a chance. Meanwhile, even if you missed the envelope, Meyer, she figured you wouldn't remember where you left it anyhow."

"But I do remember, Marcia." Cannon's voice was sad. "I left it in that textbook on the desk. And there's nothing in the book now."

"Really. Well, there are several possibilities, Meyer. For one thing, you could simply be wrong—"

Unexpectedly, Roley said, "You could, Meyer. Maybe you just forgot."

"—or you could be lying, to help out your friend the Lieutenant."

Roley's gasp, half-outraged, half-frightened, was like a child who'd seen somebody slap Santa Claus. Meyer Cannon reached over and patted the child's knee, to show him Santa wasn't angry.

"It wouldn't work even if you could bring it off, Miss Dyer," Silvestri said patiently. He watched the narrow shoulders in the silk suit move in a shrug: if she knew her position was desperate, she certainly wasn't showing it. "You'd have found out as soon as you opened the envelope—you can add the correct math quiz, but you can't substitute it. Because there is no hectographed page in the envelope now. Meyer can tell you that."

"That's right, Marcia. Silvestri took the quiz out and put it away somewhere—I wasn't around then, but he did show me the envelope before we put it on the desk, and there wasn't any purple-ink page in it." The doctor looked at her with concern. "You know I'm not lying, Marcia."

No, but you're talking too damn much, Guy thought uneasily. It wasn't easy to fight a war with an ally who kept rushing over to tend the enemy's wounds. It could turn out to be a piece of luck that Meyer wasn't around when he'd marked that hectographed page for identification and hidden it away.

"Marcia," Cannon said quietly. "Is that envelope in your purse?"

"Of course not. But since you don't seem to believe me, you can look for yourself." Her hands steady, she opened the purse's clasp.

Guy leaned across the desk, hoping for a glimpse of purple ink: she must have brought along a copy of the actual math quiz. That would be his best argument, since she was apparently going to "find" the envelope and then accuse him of planting it. But she was also not going to give anybody much chance, if she could help it, to see what else was in there. She stood the big handbag on her lap and opened the flap at the top. Guy bent over quickly, to make the most of his opportunity.

So he was completely off balance when her hand came out from behind that tan manila envelope in the purse—holding a gun. The safety catch clicked off, muffling the startled sounds from the couch, and the gun pointed steadily at Silvestri's middle, half a yard away. "Both hands on the desk, Lieutenant," Miss Dyer said firmly. She dug her feet into the carpet and shoved the wheeled desk chair backward, fetching up not much farther away—but too far for the quick swipe Guy might try.

But he wouldn't, he decided. He'd almost, but he thought not quite, had time for it a second ago; but not now—she was still much to close for him to risk a showdown with a .32 caliber automatic. He put both hands on the desk and when she said "Lean on them," he did that too. After that he did nothing, except watch for any sign of divided attention. But if she couldn't be distracted, she had him.

She clearly wasn't distracted by Roley's shocked *Marcia!* "Sit still," she told him, without looking at him. "I'll tell you what to do in a minute."

"Yes, I was wondering about that," Cannon said.

"Don't try anything, Meyer. I won't hesitate to shoot the cop."

"Don't worry—I don't gamble with my friends' lives. But just what is it you think you can make happen, Marcia?"

"That depends. Mostly on how fast your friend hands over the math quiz." Her look bored into Silvestri. "Well, Lieutenant?"

He didn't know what Meyer had in mind; but he'd got the message: *don't gamble.* And he couldn't see any but wait-and-see possibilities right now anyway. So he only said, "No way, Miss Dyer."

"Guy, for heaven's sake, it's only a piece of paper." Cannon sounded almost amused. "Does it really matter that much? It isn't as though she actually did any harm, you know. Probably she didn't even realize—"

"She realized," Guy said grimly, seeing both Meyer's pretense at innocence and his actual innocence—of Marcia Dyer's ignorance. For Billy's doctor had never briefed her on head wounds, as he had Silvestri and Herk, one night in Buxford.

"After all, why would she want to hurt Billy?" Cannon might not see what Silvestri did, but he was bright. And accustomed to working in the dark. "She had no reason to hate Billy, or even dislike him. Tell him, Marcia."

"I had no reason to dislike Billy," she said blandly. But an uneasiness was lurking in her eyes: Meyer had stirred up something.

"No," Silvestri's voice was soft. "Only to fear him." They were both ignoring the others now. "What is it Billy would remember, Miss Dyer?"

Poley's voice was high and frantic. "It was about me. She tried to stop Billy from getting his memory back because of me. Because I was there that morning."

"But Billy couldn't remember anything that happened when he himself wasn't there," Dr. Cannon pointed out. "We don't know what he saw when he came home, but he—"

"Miss Dyer can tell you that," Guy interrupted quickly, before the doctor could get too instructive about what Billy could and couldn't remember. "Why don't you at least do that much for Billy?" he asked her. "Tell Meyer what Billy saw."

"How would she know?" Poley cried.

"Because she was there. Weren't you, Miss Dyer? You went to the house on your way back from the high school to pick up Roley at the Mercer. You were lucky—if I've got it figured right, the state trooper just missed seeing you."

Cannon was seeing something now: "The little girl, Emilie. That's when she spotted the red car in the woods, wasn't it? Not when Roley parked it there, but later."

"Right. And as a matter of fact, we can show that the same car was there today. When you took those shots at me, Miss Dyer. With the gun you're holding now." Guy saw her smile tightly as sounds of surprise came from both the occupants of the couch, and he knew it had been a mistake to reveal any information gap between himself and Meyer. So long as she could hope for any divide-and-conquer possibilities, she wouldn't give up . . . He had to recoup, so he threw the nearest thing that would damage her self-confidence. "By the way, where did you get the gun, Miss Dyer? Don't tell me Roley went out and did a dumb thing for you, too?"

"No." That had hurt her. She couldn't keep it from showing in her eyes, but her voice didn't give anything away. "What difference does it make, Lieutenant? I haven't killed anybody."

She was as off balance now as she was ever going to be, Guy decided. "But Billy thought you had, didn't he?" He heard Poley cry out and rode over the sound, quickly, so Meyer would get the message and shut up. "Billy saw you there, Miss Dyer. That's why he couldn't be allowed to recover his memory— because when he did, he'd name you as the murderer." He took a deep breath, and then went on, vamping till Meyer (he hoped) was ready. "It would've suited you better if Billy had died of his head wound. But you were still safe as long as he didn't recover his memory."

"Marcia," Roley broke in. "Oh Marcia, why did you— How could you shoot Billy?"

Meyer Cannon, that unreliable ally, came through in the crunch. "She'd think she had to, I guess, Roley. Because if Billy said Miss Dyer had killed his parents and Susan, why wouldn't everybody believe him—especially since he obviously believed it himself? If he told the police he came home and found— Was she in the house when he came home, Guy?"

"No, she got there about five minutes later, we figure." She would come in quietly, not because she was particularly scared, but because Miss Dyer was always cautious. But Billy, alone in the dark room full of blood and death, would hear it as furtive footsteps. Why wouldn't he assume a killer on the loose and, determined not to let the killer get him too, pick up the gun that was visible on the hearth? "Nobody else could have come in the way you did, Miss Dyer. Not knocking or calling out—because you were sure there was nobody there who could hear you—but not startled or frightened either, because Roley had told you what to expect. He must have: he was hysterical by the time he got to the Mercer School that morning. That's why, the first chance you had, you dashed over to the King house to make sure he hadn't left anything lying around. You had to clean up after Roley while Billy—you thought—was still at school."

"But there was still King's abandoned car," Cannon pointed out.

"She didn't know about that—Roley would've left all that out of the story, at that point anyway. And she didn't know

Billy was feeling uncomfortable at school, so she had no idea he'd go home early. She saw him in her math class, but—"

"He wasn't likely to tell her he felt lousy," Cannon said. "Miss Crabtree, yes. But not Miss Dyer."

Silvestri was rapidly upgrading his estimate of Meyer Cannon's firepower in this little war: that salvo had clearly done the enemy some damage. He proceeded to help. "Funny, isn't it? You'd think it would be his math teacher he'd be closest to." She had marvelous control, but it couldn't extend to reflexes like those visible in the pupils of her eyes. "Well, that explains why seeing Billy's bike outside the house didn't alert her—she didn't know he rode it to school." It made her angry to have that pointed out, he saw. It couldn't matter all that much—it must be just knowing she'd made a mistake, however minor, that bothered her. "And it helps with two other points. One was the front door—apparently unless it was closed carefully, the lock didn't catch. And the way Billy had just sort of flung down his bike said he was probably careless, so it seemed odd that the door was properly locked when the officer got there."

"I closed it properly when I left," Poley said quickly. "I know I did," he added while his thin, frightened voice said he really didn't know anything anymore because Marcia, who had always been so sturdy, was turning out to be—something else, and horrible . . .

"Sure you did. Then Billy came home and opened it with his key. But he closed it carelessly, didn't he, Miss Dyer? That's why you could walk right in—as you'd expected, because Roley was usually careless too. You're the one who closed the door properly, Miss Dyer. Just as you're the one who picked up the laundry package from where Billy had dumped it, right inside the door." Silvestri shook his head. "A bad boner, Miss Dyer. Because, to carry the package over to that bench on the other side of the hall, you'd have to catch sight of Susan's body lying in the entrance to the living room—and only somebody to whom that was no surprise could have gone on to finish laying the package down nice and tidy. But nobody else already knew Susan King was dead at that hour in the morning. Except Roley, and he was in plain sight at the Mercer School at the time. So you see," Lieutenant Silvestri said with the dispassionate regret of a man who really disliked seeing a fine structure messed up, "you might as well have left your calling card."

"Well, *nobody* could have behaved completely logically in those circumstances," Cannon defended the silent woman. "Even knowing in advance what she'd find in that house, she had to be *somewhat* disturbed. And then when Billy—"

If they weren't on the same side, it might be interesting to leave Meyer stranded there, Guy thought wickedly; he was willing to bet his intrepid ally had no idea what came next. "Well, of course she was startled to find Billy there, Doctor." That was putting it mildly, considering that, if Silvestri's guess was right, Marcia Dyer had found herself looking into the muzzle of a .38 revolver. Maybe she wasn't in much danger of actually being hit—not with the weapon wobbling in the hand of a frightened, half-hysterical boy who couldn't even see her clearly—but it was not a spot even Silvestri, himself currently being menaced by a very steadily held .32, could really envy. She must have been petrified . . .

But she wasn't now: Guy could see she knew they were coming up on her inning. Truth and reliable guesses had scored against her thus far, wounding her; but now he was down to pure flimflam, and he'd make no direct hits with that. "Well, let's just say," he said smoothly—eyeing Marcia Dyer's automatic and hoping Meyer knew now was the time to commit the reinforcements if he had any—"she knew what she had to do. I don't suppose anybody would ever find it easy to shoot a youngster, and a teacher certainly—"

"No!" Roley cried. "Please. Please, don't—"

"People do do incredible things," Dr. Cannon said, "out of a desire to protect themselves. That's why there are so many forms of murder."

Thanks. The hint was ammunition flung to an infantryman running low. Recognizing that truth alone weakened this enemy, Meyer was reminding him that he had some more truths in stock. Like, what Marcia Dyer, who had not shot Billy, had done to protect herself ... "What were you thinking, Miss Dyer," Lieutenant Silvestri asked, the strength of conviction in his voice now, "when you looked at the boy lying there, with the blood pouring down from that head wound, streaking all over his face?"

"No, stop it. *Stop* it!" Roley was clearly near tears.

Silvestri went on relentlessly. "One of the Long Valley police officers couldn't take it, you know—he ran outside and was sick. But Miss Dyer is made of sterner stuff." He stopped there, so she wouldn't miss the sound of Roley weeping helplessly. She might even be unable to resist snatching a look ...

She was too clever for that: her eyes never left Silvestri. But they sparked with fury. And she was finally forced out of her silence. "That's enough," she said flatly. "You've had your fun, Lieutenant. But I didn't try to kill the boy, and you damn well know it." She looked at Silvestri's slight smile, and then realized what had caused it: she'd broken her silence for Roley's sake, so he could hear her denial; but he hadn't been able to hear it because Dr. Cannon had chosen that very moment to counsel and console Roley. The low murmur of his words were still going on, and still occupying Roley's full attention. She snapped "Meyer!" and then stopped, visibly struggling to control her anger—she had seen that it didn't do to slap Santa Claus. "Could you be quiet a minute, please," she continued politely. "I want—"

"Yes of course," Cannon said. "Guy, you must try to understand—it was a terribly tense situation at that moment in the King house." His bland, professional voice rode on; Marcia Dyer could have done nothing to stop him that would not alienate Roley. "Anything startling that happened would— Like the telephone ringing, maybe? That's certainly a possibility.

Some people just cannot take sudden loud noises, you know. They simply go to pieces."

"Thank you, Doctor," Marcia Dyer said with effort. "But I didn't go to pieces, and I didn't shoot Billy King. Our policeman friend here knows that. And Roley, I want you to listen while he tells you what happened. Lieutenant?"

Silvestri stared at her blankly, but holding her attention— while he got ready, bending his knees slightly and digging in his toes, for the sudden loud noise Meyer was going to come up with. Though keeping in mind, Guy hoped, that even a man who'd been warned still couldn't move faster than a bullet . . . "If I say you couldn't have shot Billy, Miss Dyer"—he saw her nod: she knew her fingerprints weren't on the gun that had wounded Billy King, so she'd known Silvestri was bluffing. But she was a teacher, and she understood the importance of presenting facts effectively; so she wanted Roley to hear it from Silvestri. He took advantage of that to ask her now, "Why should Roley—or anyone else—believe me, with you holding a gun on me?"

"Silvestri, don't push me too far." Her voice tightened with rage, and her face looked suddenly pinched.

"Guy, be careful," Meyer Cannon warned. "She's—"

"I know," Guy interrupted. "She's dangerous. Because out of all those unhappy people, with all their rages and schemes, she's the only one who really had a consistent murderous intent, isn't she?" He heard Roley whimper like a frightened child. Well, Marcia Dyer was something to be frightened of. Meyer was right, there was more than one form of murder. And hers had been especially vicious because—well, what had she really had to fear from Billy King? Maybe he didn't exactly adore his math teacher, but he must certainly have stopped pointing that .38 at her once he recognized her.

But nobody had ever taught Billy how to handle weapons. So when he turned the gun away from what was no longer an unknown menace but Miss Dyer, it was pointed at himself . . .

"Was it for Roley's sake?" Guy asked the woman who had actually seen the accidental shot, the wounded boy falling—and then just gone about her business, doing nothing whatever to help him. Not even, say, an anonymous phone call to the police, just in case Billy wasn't dead. Because she wanted him dead . . . "But *Roley* didn't want Billy dead," Guy said, keeping his tone as much puzzled as accusing.

Roley said "Oh my God" and something that vanished into a strangled noise.

"And Roley certainly didn't want any part of what you tried to do to Billy with the math quiz," Guy went on, watching the woman closely. He didn't think she would shoot because she could calculate at least as well as he could, so she should know it would just cost her too much: no charge that could be made against her now amounted to anything compared to what shooting Silvestri would leave her open to. But of course if she stopped calculating . . . "Roley may take marriage vows lightly, but he takes teaching very seriously, doesn't he? To use it for murdering a child's mind—"

"Roley, control yourself!" Cannon said sharply.

They were getting to her, Guy saw—her eyes had almost flicked sideways that time. And it was taking everything she had just to stay on guard against him: she had to let him talk because that was all she could manage. "It was a double betrayal, wasn't it? Because there was Meyer, too. He was trusting you—why wouldn't he?" Suddenly it was Silvestri who stopped calculating: the thought of what she had done to the lovable, painfully honest Cannon all at once seemed to free Guy of the ugly duty to be guileful. Or even the human need to try to understand her—to see that Billy King, holding a gun on her, had maybe been so frightening that she'd lost her reason. But that wouldn't work: there was Meyer, who clearly felt no animosity toward anything alive and wanted nothing except to heal—and she had tried to turn his very selflessness and devotion into deadly weapons. Meyer Cannon was the kind of man civilizations dream of, Guy thought. And all of a sudden he didn't only want to get a confession out of Marcia Dyer, he wanted to hunt her down.

The experienced, sensitive Dr. Cannon recognized at once that something had changed. "Guy," he said urgently. "You mustn't—"

Miss Dyer sensed it too, though she mistook its direction: "Shut up, Meyer." She planted her elegantly shod feet firmly and raised the level of the gun just a little, as if to make the menace to Silvestri clearer. "If you say one more word—just one more word, Meyer—I'll shoot him. I mean it."

She meant it, all right, Guy thought: she might be desperate, but she was holding the automatic perfectly steady. However, its slight elevation was welcome, increasing his chances of getting under the bullet's trajectory. The odds were still not encouraging, he admitted, listening absently to Roley's half-coherent outburst. But by using the momentum of his leaning weight, it might be possible to get in one quick upward blow as she fired. Now that Meyer had been silenced, there were no more softening-up chances—the *Go* signal should come any minute. Guy relaxed his muscles and waited, alert for the reflex moment, when the sudden loud noise came, that would be his only chance.

He would have done better, though, to pay attention to Roley—who caused all the plans to go agley simply by not having any himself. His hysteria of grief and remorse had barely been held in check by Cannon's few soothing words and comforting presence; but those were not enough to help with the new shocks of guilt, one after the other. *I never wanted, I never knew,* Roley had been wailing as he was forced to realize what had been done—and, according to the detective, for Roley's own sake!—to Callie's little boy. Roley could hardly believe in the strange, cold, dangerous Marcia, once someone who was always there and always reliable, to be needed or used or ignored. And yet, how could he help believing in the menace of anyone who had betrayed Dr. Cannon and now, even more incredibly, had even threatened Meyer?

Roley cried, "Marcia"— a question and a protest. It hung on the air in sudden silence, a plea to her to look at him (but she didn't), and to somebody to explain (but they didn't). He *had* to make somebody understand that Roley knew he was bad but he had never wanted, had never meant, to make such terrible things happen. "Oh *please*," Roley said, heartbroken, into the silence. "Please, *somebody* . . ."

Nobody would have seriously expected Meyer to remain silent then. "It will be all right, Roley. It'll stop hurting soon." He reached out to touch the terrified child who would need more help than that, but certainly needed that.

Only Roley wasn't there. For the double vision, of Marcia as both strength and menace, had operated instantly—as Roley saw that, once again, what he didn't want and didn't mean seemed about to happen. It was too much: this time, he had to stop it. "No! No! It's me!" he shouted, and flung himself across the room—to get to Marcia, to explain that she mustn't hurt Dr. Cannon because it was Roley who'd made him speak the one more word. All the hope Roley had left was concentrated in this single effort to be not-responsible for pain, not this time.

Guy lunged because he had to, with his hands outstretched and his eyes on the gun—so he saw when it suddenly moved, sideways and down. He registered that fatal *down* and knew he couldn't possibly make it now. But there was noplace to go, nowhere to hide in the hard smooth surface of the desk along which he was already extended, his torso flattening itself as if under strafing from the air. He was still sliding forward, still trying to understand how he'd lost even the slim chance he'd been counting on, when the gun went off and his reaching hands touched cloth.

With the last of his forward momentum, he pushed against the cloth and it fell away from him. Then, deafened and choking, he rolled to one side, knocking the math book to the floor. He saw Roley then, fallen forward onto the woman in the chair. So it was safe to stand up. Guy found his footing, in a drift of striped envelopes fallen from the desk, and went on trying to see where the gun was now. He had to find it, though for some reason he was having trouble seeing anything at all.

Rubin's voice said, "I got the weapon, Lieutenant."

Guy blinked at the expanse of white coat that was blocking his vision. "What about Poley? Did she—"

"No, she didn't shoot him." Meyer Cannon spoke from somewhere inside a knot of people gathered behind the desk. "Get his coat off, Officer, will you? I'll be right there."

So it was Roley who'd blown it for him—by darting across the room to cast himself, Guy gathered, on Marcia Dyer's bosom. And sure she hadn't shot Roley, what she'd done was lower the gun so she wouldn't. Thus the helpful Roley—Guy saw, putting it together in his ringing head—had *both* blocked Silvestri's access to the woman and brought the trajectory down far enough so he couldn't get under it. *All because Roley, no hero for Callie King, had decided to rescue Meyer.*

"Easy does it, Lieutenant." Rubin had the coat nearly off. Turning his body to help with the operation, Guy suddenly smelled burned cloth—and then, in rapid sequence, caught sight of Rubin's scared face and recognized the significance of what Meyer had said. It was the *doctor* who was coming, because— The incredible idea burst whole into Guy's resisting mind: it had happened, the thing that happened only to other officers. Amazed, he thought, almost simultaneously, *My God, I'm hit* and *Where?* and *Kate . . .*

"It doesn't hurt," he said aloud, in surprise. Rubin looked up quickly and his face paled to the sickly white of the underbelly of a fish. Guy seemed to see fear jumping from Rubin like an electric spark—and then it charged his own body as the explanation caught up: he was hit in the spine. That's why Rubin got scared when I said it didn't hurt, he thought. A quick flame of pain shot down from the back of his head, all the way down his legs and out at his heels. A phony, Guy recognized: amputees complain that their missing limbs hurt. A terrible vision filled his sight, of the woman great with child and himself helpless, looking up from a wheelchair ... Hands turned him, pulling his shirt out at the back. He felt the air suddenly cool on his spine, but he knew better than to trust that either.

"Nothing," Meyer said with satisfaction. "A little sunburn, maybe." A strange voice above a white coat said, "Let's get that shirt cut off," and Dr. Cannon asked mildly, "Why? It's a perfectly good shirt, just singed a little."

I'm sorry, Guy was telling Kate in his head, *I'm afraid I told you wrong.* Wishing he could stop laughing, he went on apologizing to her—he hadn't lied, he really didn't think there was going to be any danger—and pointing out that at least it wasn't his *own* shirt that had got singed ... Then he stopped laughing so he could concentrate on not trembling at the narrow escape of his suddenly precious body, so intricately engineered, fragile, and chock-full of bones and blood vessels all right there in easy reach beneath the skin so useless as armor. He was so *long,* he remembered Kate saying—as though it were a clever achievement he deserved to be commended for—while her hands reached up to stroke his long back ...

His face hot with embarrassment, as if everybody around had been reading his thoughts, Lieutenant Silvestri got abruptly very busy unbuttoning his cuffs. By the time Rubin pulled the shirt over his head, Guy was ready to reenter the scene around him. It had changed: several of the white coats milling around in it were now gone. James Poley was lying on the couch and Meyer was standing beside it, holding an empty syringe. And Marcia Dyer, somewhat rumpled and without her big tan handbag, was in the doorway—with a state trooper holding her arm.

"It won't take a minute, Roley," Cannon said.

"Thanks, Doc. I'm—I'm so sorry."

"Just lie still. You'll be asleep before you know it."

"Yes. Thank you." The handsome, weary face was already

relaxed: the war was all over for Roley, who'd worn out his only two weapons, wit and psychologizing. "I'm sorry, Doc," he said again. "I tried to—stop her."

"You did fine, Roley. You saved Silvestri's life."

Rubin, standing beside Guy, almost literally sputtered with rage. But nobody noticed him—they were all watching Roley, who said, "Oh, good" in a weak polite voice. And then, in an even weaker voice, "Marcia, I never meant . . ." His eyes closed. Marcia Dyer didn't seem to move, but the trooper noticeably tightened his grip on her arm.

Of course Roley hadn't meant, Guy was thinking. Roley probably hadn't even been scared—why should he be, when it was always other people who got hurt? But then Guy caught sight of Miss Dyer and promptly stopped feeling sorry for himself: cleaning up the messes made by the pretty, indulged types like James W. Poley didn't cost anything like as much as loving them. A singed shirt and a little sunburn didn't look very important beside what Marcia Dyer had already paid, and would go on paying.

"Well, let's have a look at the wounded," Cannon said briskly.

"*You're* mighty lighthearted," his patient observed. "Patching people gives you some kind of high?"

"It takes me back to my youth. In my intern days, I was a deft man with a dressing, I'll have you know." Cannon knitted his no-longer-youthful brow. "There should be some burn ointment in the first-aid kit. I know I have one around, but—"

"Right-hand file cabinet, Rubin," Guy said. "The bottom drawer." He stretched his arms tentatively, discovering an uncomfortable tautness along his backbone. "And the evidence—the math quiz—is in the second drawer. In a Lambert Press book envelope." His duty done, he let himself wonder whether anything besides nostalgia remained of Meyer's intern skills.

He bent over obediently so Cannon could stroke goo along

the bumps of his spine. In a few seconds Cannon wiped his fingers on Guy's shoulder blade and turned to Rubin. "You his buddy from the motel?" Rubin had been studying the track of the bullet in the Lieutenant's coat. He looked up and said, rather stiffly, that he was Detective Rubin of the Buxford Police. Meyer nodded, not noticeably impressed. "Okay, you can take him back and put him to bed." He eyed Rubin's illicit white doctor-jacket and observed that Silvestri shouldn't get chilled, because he'd had a shock. "Better get him a jacket. A sterile one," he added sternly, as though Rubin would otherwise go hunting for the germiest jacket around. Pleased, Guy saw that he was a Patient, and thus still counted. He sent Rubin off with a nod and settled back to try out life as a medically certi-fied sufferer from shock.

The trooper holding Marcia Dyer drew her out of the door-way to let Rubin by, and the movement seemed to stir her to speech. "Is he asleep?" Her voice sounded rusty.

There was only one "he" she could mean. Cannon bent to look at Roley. "I think so." Then he straightened, and in-spected her with a professional eye. "How do you feel, Marcia?"

Her smile was also a little rusty. "He isn't worth it."

"Nobody is," Cannon told her seriously. He glanced at Silvestri. "Does she have to be kept standing there?"

She'd had a shock, too, Guy supposed dourly. He told himself he was probably only showing sibling rivalry for the love of Daddy Cannon, and, with his irritation thus quelled, began to deal with the problem of Miss Dyer. Yes, he was assured, somebody had read her her rights. But not much else had been done, he gathered, because everybody'd been waiting to find out whether Lieutenant Silvestri was going to be the victim or the arresting officer. The woman was certainly arrest-worthy on a considerable array of charges and in more than one jurisdiction: everything she'd done tonight, beginning with interfering with Lieutenant Silvestri in the performance of his duty and ranging on up to Assault with a Deadly Weapon, had happened on state property; but what she'd said, before witnesses, made her at least a material witness in Long Valley's own case . . .

And maybe another case, too? It occurred to Guy then that the deadly weapon she'd assaulted him with might lead to a way to sprinkle salt, after all, on the tail of the elusive Twirl. He asked abruptly, "Miss Dyer, where did you get the gun?" She wasn't required to answer questions now, and she'd dodged that one before, so it wasn't promising. But it was worth a try.

"I have a license for it, Lieutenant," she said calmly. And then she added, wryly, "My father gave it to me. When I was setting off for Long Valley last year. He thought I'd need it to protect myself from the locals, I guess."

Guy couldn't bring himself to follow her gaze to the sleeping local whom nobody, it appeared, had equipped her to protect herself from. "Why don't we all sit down," he told the trooper wearily. Leaning against the desk, he rubbed a hand across his sandpaper chin and managed to refrain from rubbing his eyes—which felt as though they might have the same texture by now. The hell with it, he thought: stick to the law and leave the summarizing for Meyer. He at least seems to know who the victims are.

Rubin returned with the sterile white coat. Guy was about to insert his unsterile arms into it—thinking irritably that it was about time, it felt awful damn cold in here—when a small voice spoke from somewhere around his feet. "Will?" it said clearly, though with an obvious overtone of mechanical reproduction. "Is anybody—"

A man's voice answered quickly, "I'm here, Billy."

Guy dove toward the monitor as Cannon came from the other side, to join in scrabbling among the clutter of fallen objects on the floor beside the desk. It took Guy a minute to realize they were working at cross-purposes, like two suburbanites shoveling snow into each other's yards. And then the boy's voice said "Oh. *Williams*" on a note of faint surprise—and all of a sudden Guy had the whole field to himself. He picked up the box and set it on the desk. Then he nearly knocked it over again as Billy said with awful clarity, "Williams, she— She won't come back."

"I know, Billy." Williams sounded farther away, and a red light on the monitor began flickering rapidly. The aide must be trying to call Meyer, Guy realized. He wished he had some way to tell Williams that Cannon was coming, and on the double.

Billy sounded as if he were right there among the listening people in the office. "I lost—my—" He gave up, and began to cry, hard and noisily.

"Doctor Cannon, stat!" Williams' voice was soft but urgent. There was a pause before they could hear him again, closer: "Now, Billy. Now, now, Billy-boy. Hush now, baby, you hush now, Billy . . ."

Above the crooning, the boy's wail suddenly shaped itself into a word. "*Susan!*" He screamed it. Something fell and bounced, again and again, with a thin plastic clatter that kept repeating itself, never seeming to get any farther away or any closer to ending. They would go on forever, those exactly-alike loops of sound—and inside each loop, another caught instant of that terrible weeping. Guy heard *Pore little kid, you pore little kid* and ached for Williams, the man left on guard at the out-post, frightened and hoping help would come, that somebody would please *do* something.

Somebody did something, Guy realized then. The plastic rattle finally stopped and Billy's cries, still piercing, were at least a little muffled, as if Williams was holding the boy in his arms.

Cannon's running footsteps started a long way away and came up close very rapidly. "You did fine, Williams." He sounded out of breath but matter-of-fact. "Now let's—"

Billy shrieked "Cannon!"

"Yes, Billy. This is Doctor Cannon." The calm reply laid

what Guy thought was an odd emphasis on the word "doctor": surely this was no time to worry about formal titles? Then he heard, "I'm here, Billy. I came to help you get well"—and Guy wondered why he'd never noticed what a beautiful voice Meyer had. He reached for the switch as Billy cried, "Doctor Cannon, she won't—come back. Susan won't— Never. Never—"

With his eyes smarting almost as actively as the long burn down his back, Lieutenant Silvestri snapped off the monitor. In the room, there was a small sound of protest from Rubin, and a sigh from the trooper—who must be as shaken as the rest of them, Guy thought. He jerked his head at Rubin, and the Buxford detective moved over and took Marcia Dyer's other arm, just in case. She murmured something that might have been objection, but Guy was too busy hating her to make sure. If he could have ordered her put in chains right then and there, it wouldn't have seemed to him at all harsh. What *could* be enough punishment for willfully prolonging a child's suffering? For any reason at all—even, he thought bitterly, glancing at the sleeping Roley, a pauperate love. There should be some way to prevent people from growing their twisted plants in society's garden . . .

Sure, said the mocking voice of sanity. Let's all get together and declare it a felony to blight anybody else's life, at least on purpose. And then what? What follows conviction? For Roley, contrite and trying to make amends, a suspended sentence—in the custody of Miss Crabtree, maybe? But you still wouldn't have a sentence for Marcia Dyer.

Silvestri looked at her then, carefully composed, holding herself stiff in the two men's grasp, and the smart-aleck and the avenger in him both got suddenly very quiet. Because there *was* a sentence, and for Miss Dyer, who hated herself for making even the smallest mistake, it would be a heavy one. For, sooner or later, somebody would tell her what Guy had been so afraid Cannon would let slip—that everything she had done, to everyone, in order to protect herself had been totally unnecessary.

Because Billy King, even if he recovered completely, couldn't possibly recall encountering Miss Dyer in the house that November morning, much less mistake her for the murderer of his parents and sister: that whole time had been permanently wiped out of his memory. When Marcia found that out—

"Lieutenant, you got to put this on." Rubin was holding out the white jacket. "The doc said you shouldn't get chilled, remember?"

—maybe Doctor Cannon would be somewhere around, to see her as a victim . . . Amazed, Guy discovered he actually did feel sorry for her. Meyer must be some kind of emotional imperialist—he took you over, and you were under his flag from then on. Or maybe, Lieutenant Silvestri concluded, he really *was* in shock.

Carefully, he put on the jacket borrowed from Cannon's job. And then, weary and smarting, got on with his own.

EPILOGUE
(Late June, Buxford)

"The key to the whole thing had to be the plant stand," Guy said, squinting against the afternoon sun. "It was one of those heavy wrought-iron things, you know the kind? With splayed-out feet to give it stability, and sort of branches at different levels with rings to set flower pots in. We'll never know for sure what happened, of course. But it just figures—that Billy tripped over it, or maybe knocked his elbow on one of those rings."

"Okay so far," Herk said. "But was he really trying to shoot the teacher? Somehow that just doesn't seem to fit."

"Well no, he probably wasn't, not at that point." Silvestri thought a moment and then it came to him, a way to tell it in his hearer's terms. "Think of it like directing an actor, right? Okay, Billy comes in, all but stumbles over his sister's body, kneels beside her, et cetera." It wasn't so easy, though, to think of the scene impersonally. "From that angle, down on the floor, the minute he raises his eyes practically the first thing in his line of sight would be the revolver lying on the hearth. He'd see that maybe even before he saw the bodies of his parents."

"Would he go for the gun, though? Would it be in character? I mean, he doesn't sound like a very belligerent kid."

"Yes, he would," Guy said firmly, banishing a swift

memory of his sister Angie fallen to the gray concrete of the school playground, her nose bleeding. Her little brother, not a very belligerent kid and normally smart enough to stick to his weight class if he did have to fight, had nevertheless instantly lunged for the big boy who'd shoved Angie. Fortunately, there'd been no weapon in Guy's line of sight then; but it had taken the combined efforts of two teachers and the cop from the corner to keep him off Peter Somebody, whom he earnestly intended to kill. (And who was innocent, Guy still remembered with another kind of fury: dear old Angie, it turned out afterward, had actually shoved Peter first.) "Even if you don't buy the psychology," he told Herk now, "there's the logic—why would Billy have been in that part of the room if not to get to the front window? It had to be because he'd heard something outside."

"She wouldn't have tried to be quiet," Herk observed. "She had no reason to."

"Right. And there was a gravel driveway out there. So Billy heard her. But too late—by the time he pulled the curtain aside and looked out, she was probably in the house."

"He wheels around"—Herk's eyes were seeing an actor on a set—"with the gun in his hand. Does he hear her coming in?"

"I think so. As you said, she wasn't trying to be quiet. And that thin paper on the laundry package would certainly crackle when she picked it up, out in the hall."

"Okay then, he knows where the enemy is. He waits, aiming the gun at the doorway, where she has to come in—or does he try to rush her, and that's where he trips?"

"It could be. But it makes more sense, especially judging from how scared Miss Dyer was, that she had time to see Billy standing there in the shadows with a revolver aimed at her. The way I figure it," Guy went on, "there were two separate moves involved. First, when Billy saw that it was Miss Dyer—I don't think he really could've assumed she was the killer, though something he said or did gave her that impression. But it's more likely that she was so firmly in his mind as a teacher that when he saw her he'd realize she *couldn't* be a menace. So he'd—"

"He'd lower the gun, instinctively."

"Or turn it aside. Probably not all the way around, of course; I'd guess the weapon was pointed away from both of them—probably at the window—when Billy made a sudden move. Maybe backing away: he'd sort of scared himself, it seems likely. Or having the real-life Miss Dyer show up in that unreal scene shook him up. But that was the second move—and if he tripped then, or hit his elbow, the effect would be to bring his arm around the rest of the way. So that the cocked thirty-eight he was holding would be pointed at himself . . ." Guy shook his head. "Anything that jolted him even a little bit would've caused it to fire. But the plant stand was the only thing near him that could have jolted him without getting knocked over itself. So it was probably the actual cause of Billy's head wound."

"It does make sense that way," Herk said slowly.

Silvestri sighed, eyeing his sweet peas, which needed tending. He would have preferred to do that, or any other chore in his garden, without talking at all—unless you counted Tony, whose conversation was restfully limited to the present tense.

But Herk was entitled to talk about the past. And now he wanted to know why the trip to the state hospital yesterday— since everything was settled weeks ago. "Oh, that was Meyer. He drafted me for—well, for drama therapy, by golly." Guy grinned at Herkimer, but then sobered quickly as he described the fantasy that had been troubling Billy. "About how he had this killer ray inside him that he couldn't control." Guy kept his voice down, lest his son overhear and maybe catch the infection.

"I thought Billy got over that Trad business."

"Well, this is different—maybe more serious, because it was mostly unconscious. But Meyer actually used the Trad fantasy to fight it." Guy looked self-conscious. "It seems Simons has a Merlin-type character, a kind of oracle—"

"Yup. A well-known device, handy to get things said to the reader that the characters can't know."

"I see. Well, I was the handy device. The 'head cop,' was what Meyer told Billy. The idea was to get rid of the killer-ray idea, plus any bad-seed notion he might be harboring. Because Billy wasn't the Kings' child, so there was no need. But Meyer couldn't be sure whether Susan ever told Billy, so—"

"She knew, then?"

"Well, her diary didn't say so explicitly. But she did figure out why her mother didn't divorce King. Susan had contacts," Guy said a little grimly, "who were minor experts on the juvenile laws. So once she got to wondering, she wouldn't have any trouble getting the facts that explained the bind Callie was in. Like, that anytime she sued for divorce, all King had to do was demand custody of the children and—"

"They weren't his either, though. So would he get them?"

"No. But there hadn't been any official adoption, you see. So they would probably have to be put in a juvenile home while the hassles went on. And that's something no mother—or anybody else, either—would want to see happen: those places are a disgrace. So Callie was effectively blackmailed by the fact that they'd got the children illegally in the first place."

"Well, but King was a professional educator, Guy. Surely he'd have known it if those homes are so bad, so why would he want—"

"Maybe he wouldn't have. Maybe if Callie had actually tried, he'd have backed down." Guy's glance roved toward his small son, who was solemnly digging a hole at the far end of the yard. "*I* think he would have. But she presumably knew him better than anybody, didn't she? And she was afraid to take a chance, so—"

"That's why Madame Bovary," Herk interrupted. "Susan saw her mother as a victim of social forces."

"Well, certainly to the extent that in her diary, her mother is clearly off the hook. It was like Miss Crabtree said—Susan wasn't mad at Callie, she even liked her. But her strongest feeling was a determination not to let herself and Billy get caught in the trap, too." His absent gaze rested on Tony. "Anyway, the odds were that she hadn't told Billy. But it was possible, and odds aren't good enough when it's human beings. So Meyer decided on a frontal assault on the problem, with an official figure—me—coming in to tell Billy formally that he and Susan were adopted."

"How did he react?"

"Very calmly. You can't tell anything from that, of course. But he didn't ask any questions, and I got the impression he just wanted to sort of breathe in and out, keeping his elbows close to his sides. Like he knows he's too frail to venture into any unknowns for a while."

Herk said curiously, "Here we've all been—well, sort of in a war for this kid. And still we've never seen him. Or I haven't anyway. What does he look like?"

"It was a war, all right. With casualties—some people's lives will never be the same again." Silvestri shook off the pangs of pity and the threatening victor-guilt: if you had to be in a war, it was still better to win. "I know what you mean, though. I had a feeling myself that Billy King might not be quite real. He is, though: a small boy for his age, dark and quick—" He stopped, thinking about Susan and Billy, both small and slender, with big dark eyes and deft hands. Billy had Italian eyes, Guy could almost swear it. You'd think somebody would have been struck by the oddity of such markedly Nordic parents having such dark-eyed children ... "He was quiet," Guy went on, "but I imagine any kid would be, in those circumstances. Before we came in, though, he was talking—I heard him telling Williams about a book Meyer gave him. Stevenson's *Black Arrow*. You ever read it?" Herk shook his head. "Well, I did, and I remember what it's about—a boy who thinks a baddie is his real father, so he tries to be loyal to him. But in the end he finds out he isn't really Sir What's-his-name's son."

"Oh, wow. That Cannon doesn't miss a trick, does he?"

Guy didn't answer. He was frowning at his son. "Tony? What did you do with your shirt?"

Herkimer, who had an opinion on everything, said it was warm enough out, so why pick on the poor kid? He stopped when the poor kid trotted up and handed over a small striped polo shirt. Tony announced, "I hot, Daddy," and, apparently not expecting to be picked on, turned and went back to his excavations.

Herk stared after him. "What the hell's the matter with him?"

Guy followed his glance to Tony's naked back, decorated with pink dots down the spine. Tony's father blushed. And then, looking grateful, suddenly leaped to help his not-that-pregnant wife carry a not-that-heavy tray to the table between them.

Kate had clearly heard. And she obviously thought something—perhaps the overdone chivalry?—was amusing. But she told Herk solemnly, "Nothing's the matter with Tony; he just wants to be like Daddy. They take showers together, and he was eaten with envy." Demurely, she handed Guy his glass, ignoring his discomfort. "Of course Guy isn't actually that pink anymore. But calamine lotion was the best I could do. And Tony isn't fussy about nuances."

His host's face, Herkimer noted, was at least calamine-lotion pink, give or take a nuance. But he decided to be merciful—Guy's ridiculous privacy hangup seemed to be being dealt with adequately—so he steered the talk away from the suffering victor and back to the victory. Like, how had Silvestri known Billy and Susan weren't really the Kings' children?

Guy looked grateful for the rescue. "Several ways. To begin with, I found that both youngsters had brown eyes, but I knew the parents had light eyes—blue or green. I don't know much about genetics, but I *was* paying attention in high school"—he shot Kate an obscure glance—"when we learned about Mendel and the primroses. So I got curious. Then, once I started looking around—well, in the house I found pictures of the children but none taken when they were real little babies, although most parents photograph new babies practically incessantly." He stopped, remembering the photo of Julius King with what was for him and his Callie a new baby. The exclamation point she'd added when she wrote *Daddy!* under the picture should have said it all, actually. But that wasn't something Guy wanted to recall, so he went on quickly. "In her bedroom," he said, not particularly wanting to remember that either, "there was no sign of any variety of contraceptive."

"Why only her bedroom? You know everybody doesn't—"

"I looked in her purse," Silvestri interrupted his wife firmly. But he gave her a look conceding *a hit, a palpable hit.* "Since it was likely that Mrs. King—um—"

"Had a greater need abroad than at home," Herk helped him. Poor Guy: women just didn't fight fair. Granted, he *was* kind of stuffy in these matters. But if Kate was going to torment him like that, his buddy would rally round.

"Thank you. And then, I checked with the medical examiner, and King hadn't had a vasectomy. But it was really something less technical, Herk," Silvestri said soberly. "I just didn't see your idea that she'd stayed with Julius King because she loved being pushed around. So it figured there was another reason. Like, that she was afraid of a divorce. And not only afraid for herself."

"All that clever detecting," Kate said. "My."

Both men looked at her, and Herk winced as she turned those amazing gray eyes on her husband. Full power, and she'd even added a sweet smile. Wow. "Why didn't you ask me, darling? I could've told you they weren't her own children."

Ah, well, he was a friend of both sides of the family, Herk reminded himself. Obligingly, he asked Kate how she knew.

"It was easy. I read Shakespeare's *Julius Caesar.*"

"Well, so have I. Of course." Obliging Herk had now given way to the drama critic, who was bridling.

"Have you? Well then, you should have known too, Herk. Calpurnia was barren. It says so in the play." Raising her voice over Guy's impolite guffaw, Mrs. Silvestri asked politely whether anyone had seen the pretzels.

.

F
Re
c.1

Rennert

Operation Calpurnia

DISCARD